EMPEROR
THE GATES OF ROME

Conn Iggulden is one of the most successful authors of historical fiction writing today. His two number one best-selling series, on Julius Caesar and on the Mongol Khans of Central Asia, describe the founding of the greatest empires of their day. Conn Iggulden lives in Hertfordshire with his wife and their children.

www.conniggulden.com

EMPEROR
THE GATES OF ROME

CONN IGGULDEN

HARPER

HARPER

An imprint of HarperCollins*Publishers*
77-85 Fulham Palace Road
Hammersmith, London W6 8JB

www.harpercollins.co.uk

This paperback edition 2011

2

First published in Great Britain by HarperCollins*Publishers* 2003

A catalogue record for this book is available from the British Library

ISBN 978 0 00 794663 1

This novel is entirely a work of fiction.
The names, characters and incidents portrayed in it,
while in some cases based on historical figures, are
the work of the author's imagination.

Typeset in Minion with Trajan Display by Palimpsest Book Production Limited,
Falkirk, Stirlingshire

Printed and bound in Great Britain by
Clays Ltd, St Ives plc

MIX
Paper from
responsible sources
FSC® C007454

To my son Cameron and to my brother Hal,
the other member of the Black Cat Club

ACKNOWLEDGEMENTS

Without the help and support of a number of people, this book would never have been started or finished. I would like to thank Victoria, who has been a constant source of help and encouragement. Also, the editors at HarperCollins, who steered it through the process without too much pain. Any mistakes that remain are, unfortunately, my own.

Also, Richard, who helped to cook the raven and made Marcus possible. Finally, my wife Ella, who had more faith than I did and made the way seem easy.

CHAPTER ONE

The track in the woods was a wide causeway to the two boys strolling down it. Both were so dirty with thick, black mud as to be almost unrecognisable as human. The taller of the two had blue eyes that seemed unnaturally bright against the cracking, itching mud that plastered him.

'We're going to be killed for this, Marcus,' he said, grinning. In his hand, a sling spun lazily, held taut with the weight of a smooth river pebble.

'Your fault, Gaius, for pushing me in. I told you the river bed wasn't dry all the way.'

As he spoke, the shorter boy laughed and shoved his friend into the bushes that lined the path. He whooped and ran as Gaius scrambled out and set off in pursuit, sling whirring in a disc.

'Battle!' he shouted in his high, unbroken voice.

The beating they would get at home for ruining their tunics was far away and both boys knew every trick to get out of trouble – all that mattered was charging through the woodland paths at high speed, scaring birds. Both boys were barefoot, already with calluses developing, despite not having seen more than eight summers.

'This time, I'll catch him,' Gaius panted to himself as he ran. It was a mystery to him how Marcus, who had the same number of legs and arms, could yet somehow make them move faster than he could. In fact, as he was shorter, his stride should have been a little less, surely?

The leaves whipped by him, stinging his bare arms. He could hear Marcus taunting him up ahead, close. Gaius showed his teeth as his lungs began to hurt.

Without warning, he broke into a clearing at full pelt and skidded to a sudden, shocked stop. Marcus was lying on the ground, trying to sit up and holding his head in his right hand. Three men – no, older boys – were standing there, carrying walking staffs.

Gaius groaned as he took in his surroundings. The chase had carried the two boys off his father's small estate and into their neighbours' part of the woods. He should have recognised the track that marked the boundary, but he'd been too caught up in catching Marcus for once.

'What do we have here? A couple of little mudfish, crawled up out of the river!'

It was Suetonius who spoke, the eldest son of the neighbouring estate. He was fourteen and killing time before he went into the army. He had the sort of trained muscles the two younger boys hadn't begun to develop. He had a mop of blond hair over a face speckled with white-headed eruptions that covered his cheeks and forehead, with a sprinkling of angry-looking red ones disappearing under his *praetexta* tunic. He also had a long straight stick, friends to impress and an afternoon to while away.

Gaius was frightened, knowing he was out of his depth. He and Marcus were trespassing – the best they could expect was a few blows, the worst was a beating with broken bones. He glanced at Marcus and saw him try to stagger to his feet. He'd obviously been belted with something as he ran into the older boys.

'Let us go, Tonius, we're expected back.'

'*Speaking* mudfish! We'll make our fortune, boys! Grab hold of them, I have a roll of twine for tying up pigs that will do just as well for mudfish.'

2

Gaius didn't consider running, with Marcus unable to get away. This wasn't a game – the cruelty of the boys could be managed if they were treated carefully, talked to like scorpions, ready to strike without warning.

The two other boys approached with their staffs held ready. They were both strangers to Gaius. One dragged Marcus to his feet and the other, a hefty, stupid-looking boy, rammed his stick into Gaius' stomach. He doubled up in agony, unable to speak. He could hear the boy laughing as he cramped and groaned, trying to curl into the pain.

'There's a branch that will do. Tie their legs together and string them up to swing. We can see who's the best shot with javelins and stones.'

'Your father knows my father,' Gaius spat out, as the pain in his stomach lessened.

'True – doesn't like him though. My father is a proper patrician, not like yours. Your whole family could be his servants if he wanted. I'd make that mad mother of yours scrub the tiles.'

At least he was talking. The thug with the horsehair twine was intent on tying knots at Gaius' feet, ready to hoist him into the air. What could he say to bargain? His father had no real power in the city. His mother's family had produced a couple of consuls – that was it. Uncle Marius was a powerful man, so his mother said.

'We are *nobilitas* – my Uncle Marius is not a man to cross . . .'

There was a sudden high-pitched yelp as the string over the branch went tight and Marcus was swung into the air upside down.

'Tie the end to that stump. This fish next,' Tonius said, laughing gleefully.

Gaius noted that the two friends followed his orders without question. It would be pointless trying to appeal to one of them.

'Let us down, you spot-covered pus-bag!' Marcus shouted as his face darkened with the rush of blood.

Gaius groaned. Now they would be killed, he was sure.

'You idiot, Marcus. Don't mention his spots; you can see he must be sensitive about them.'

Suetonius raised an eyebrow and his mouth opened in astonishment. The heavy-set boy paused as he threw the twine over the same branch as Marcus.

'Oh, you have made a mistake, little fish. Finish stringing that one up, Decius, I'm going to make him bleed a little.'

Suddenly, the world tilted sickeningly and Gaius could hear the twine creak and a low whistle in his ears as his head filled with blood. He rotated slowly and came round to see Marcus in a similar predicament. His nose was a little bloody from being knocked down the first time.

'I think you've stopped my nosebleed, Tonius. Thanks.' Marcus' voice trembled slightly and Gaius smiled at his bravery.

When he'd first come to live with them, the little boy had been naturally nervous and a little small for his age. Gaius had shown him around the estate and they'd ended up in the hay barn, right at the top of the stacked sheaves. They had looked down at the loose pile far below and Gaius had seen Marcus' hands tremble.

'I'll go first and show you how it's done,' Gaius had said cheerfully, launching himself feet first and whooping.

Below, he'd looked up at the edge for a few seconds, waiting to see Marcus appear. Just as he'd thought it would never happen, a small figure shot into the air, leaping high. Gaius had scrambled out of the way as Marcus crashed into the hay, winded and gasping.

'I thought you were too scared to do it,' Gaius said to the prone figure, blinking in the dust.

'I was,' Marcus had replied quietly, 'but I won't *be* afraid. I just won't.'

The hard voice of Suetonius broke into Gaius' spinning thoughts: 'Gentlemen, meat must be tenderised with mallets. Take your stations and begin the technique, like so.'

He swung his stick at Gaius' head, catching him over the ear.

The world went white, then black and when he next opened his eyes everything was spinning as the string twisted. For a while, he could feel the blows as Suetonius called out, 'One-two-three, one-two-three . . .'

He thought he could hear Marcus crying and then he passed out to the accompaniment of jeers and laughter.

He woke and went back under a couple of times in the daylight, but it was dusk when he was finally able to stay conscious. His right eye was a heavy mass of blood and his face felt swollen and caked in stickiness. They were still upside down and swinging gently as the evening breeze came in from the hills.

'Wake up, Marcus – Marcus!'

His friend didn't stir. He looked terrible, like some sort of demon. The crust of crumbling river mud had been broken away and there was now only a grey dust, streaked with red and purple. His jaw was swollen, and a lump stood out on his temple. His left hand was fat and had a blueish tinge in the failing light. Gaius tried to move his own hands, held by the twine. Though painfully stiff, they both worked and he set about wriggling them free. His young frame was supple and the burst of fresh pain was ignored in the wave of worry he felt for his friend. He had to be all right, he had to be. First though, Gaius had to get down.

One hand came free and he reached down to the ground, scrabbling in the dust and dead leaves with his fingertips. Nothing. The other hand came free and he widened his area of search, making his body swing in a slow circle. Yes, a small stone with a sharp edge. Now for the difficult part.

'Marcus! Can you hear me? I'm going to get us down, don't you worry. Then I'm going to kill Suetonius and his fat friends.'

Marcus swung gently in silence, his mouth open and slack. Gaius took a deep breath and readied himself for the pain.

Under normal circumstances, reaching up to cut through a piece of heavy twine with only a sharp stone would have been difficult, but with his abdomen a mass of bruises, it felt like an impossible task.

Go.

He heaved himself up, crying out with the pain from his stomach. He jackknifed up to the branch and gripped it with both hands, lungs heaving with the effort. He felt weak and his vision blurred. He thought he would vomit and could do no more than just hold on for a few moments. Then, inch by inch, he released the hand with the stone and leaned back, giving himself enough room to reach the twine and saw at it, trying not to catch his skin where it had bitten into the flesh.

The stone was depressingly blunt and he couldn't hold on for long. Gaius tried to let go before his hands slipped so he could control the fall back, but it was too hard.

'Still got the stone,' he muttered to himself. 'Try again, before Suetonius comes back.'

Another thought struck him. His father could have returned from Rome. He was due back any day now. It was growing dark and he would be worried. Already, he could be out looking for the two boys, coming nearer to this spot, calling their names. He must not find them like this. It would be too humiliating.

'Marcus? We'll tell everyone we fell. I don't want my father to know about this.'

Marcus creaked round in a circle, oblivious.

Five times more, Gaius spasmed up and sawed at the twine before it parted. He hit the ground almost flat and sobbed as his torn and tortured muscles twitched and jumped.

He tried to ease Marcus to the ground, but the weight was too much for him and the thump made him wince.

As Marcus landed, he opened his eyes at the fresh pain.

'My hand,' he whispered, his voice cracking.

'Broken, I'd say. Don't move it. We have to get out of here in case Suetonius comes back or my father tries to find us. It's nearly dark. Can you stand?'

'I can, I think, though my legs feel weak. That Tonius is a bastard,' Marcus muttered. He did not try to open his swollen jaw, but spoke through fat and broken lips.

Gaius nodded grimly. 'True – we have a score to settle there, I think.'

Marcus smiled and winced at the sting of opening cuts. 'Not until we've healed a bit though, eh? I'm not up to taking him on at the moment.'

Propping each other up, the two boys staggered home in the darkness, walking a mile over the cornfields, past the slave quarters for the field workers and up to the main buildings. As expected, the oil lamps were still lit, lining the walls of the main house.

'Tubruk will be waiting for us; he never sleeps,' Gaius muttered as they passed under the pillars of the outer gate.

A voice from the shadows made them both jump.

'A good thing too. I would have hated to miss this spectacle. You are lucky your father is not here, he'd have taken the skin off your backs for returning to the villa looking like this. What was it this time?'

Tubruk stepped into the yellow light of the lamps and leaned forward. He was a powerfully built ex-gladiator, who'd bought the position of overseer to the small estate outside Rome and never looked back. Gaius' father said he was one in a thousand for organising talent. The slaves worked well under him, some from fear and some from liking. He sniffed at the two young boys.

'Fall in the river, did we? Smells like it.'

They nodded happily at this explanation.

'Mind you, you didn't pick up those stick marks from a river bottom, did you? Suetonius, was it? I should have kicked his

7

backside for him years ago, when he was young enough for it to make a difference. Well?'

'No, Tubruk, we had an argument and fought each other. No one else was involved and even if there had been, we would want to handle it ourselves, you see?'

Tubruk grinned at this from such a small boy. He was forty-five years of age, with hair that had gone grey in his thirties. He had been a legionary in Africa in the Third Cyrenaica legion, and had fought nearly a hundred battles as a gladiator, collecting a mass of scars on his body. He put out his great spade of a hand and rubbed his square fingers through Gaius' hair.

'I do see, little wolf. You are your father's son. You cannot handle everything yet though, you are just a little lad and Suetonius – or whoever – is shaping into a fine young warrior so I hear. Mind yourselves, his father is too powerful to be an enemy in the Senate.'

Gaius drew himself up to his full height and spoke as formally as he knew how, trying to assert his position.

'It is luck then, that this Suetonius is in *no* way attached to ourselves,' he replied.

Tubruk nodded as if he had accepted the point, trying not to grin.

Gaius continued more confidently: 'Send Lucius to me to look at our wounds. My nose is broken and almost certainly Marcus' hand is the same.'

Tubruk watched them totter into the main house and resumed his post in the darkness, guarding the gate on first watch, as he did each night. It would be full summer soon and the days would be almost too hot to bear. It was good to be alive with the sky so clear and honest work ahead.

The following morning was an agony of protest from muscles, cuts and joints; the two days after that were worse. Marcus had succumbed to a fever that the physician said entered his head through the broken bone of his hand, which swelled to astonishing proportions as it was strapped and splinted. For days he was hot and had to be kept in darkness, while Gaius fretted on the steps outside.

Almost exactly one week after the attack in the woods, Marcus was lying asleep, still weak, but recovering. Gaius could still feel pain as he stretched his muscles and his face was a pretty collection of yellow and purple patches, shiny and tight in places as they healed. It was time, though: time to find Suetonius.

As he walked through the woods of the family estate, his mind was full of thoughts of fear and pain. What if Suetonius didn't show up? There was no reason to suppose that he made regular trips into the woods. What if the older boy was with his friends again? They would kill him, no doubt about it. Gaius had brought a bow with him this time, and practised drawing it as he walked. It was a man's bow and too large for him, but he found he could plant the end in the ground and pull an arrow back enough to frighten Suetonius, if the boy refused to back down.

'Suetonius, you are a pus-filled bag of dung. If I catch you on my father's land, I will put an arrow through your head.'

He spoke aloud as he went along. It was a beautiful day to walk in the woods and he might have enjoyed it if it wasn't for his serious purpose in being there. This time, too, he had his brown hair oiled tight against his head and clean, simple clothes that allowed him easy movements and an unrestricted draw.

He was still on his side of the estate border, so Gaius was surprised when he heard footsteps up ahead and saw Suetonius and a giggling girl appear suddenly on the wide track. The older boy didn't notice him for a moment, so intent was he on grappling with the girl.

'You're trespassing,' Gaius snapped, pleased to hear his voice come out steady, even if it was high. 'You're on my father's estate.'

9

Suetonius jumped and swore in shock. As he saw Gaius plant one end of the bow in the path and understood the threat, he began to laugh.

'A little wolf now! A creature of many forms, it seems. Didn't you get enough of a beating last time, little wolf?'

The girl seemed very pretty to Gaius, but he wished she would go away and lose herself. He had not imagined a female present for this encounter and felt a new level of danger from Suetonius.

Suetonius put a melodramatic arm around the girl.

'Careful, my dear. He is a dangerous fighter. He is especially dangerous when upside down, then he is unstoppable!' He laughed at his own joke and the girl joined in.

'Is he that one you mentioned, Tonius? Look at his angry little face!'

'If I see you here again, I'll put an arrow through you,' Gaius said quickly, the words tumbling over themselves. He pulled the shaft back a few inches. 'Leave now or I will strike you down.'

Suetonius had stopped smiling as he weighed up his chances.

'All right then, *parvus lupus,* I'll give you what you seem to want.'

Without warning, he rushed at him and Gaius released the arrow too quickly. It struck the tunic of the older boy, but fell away without piercing. Suetonius yelled in triumph and stepped forward with his hands outstretched and his eyes cruel. Gaius whipped the bow up in panic, hitting the older boy on the nose. Blood spurted and Tonius roared in rage and pain, his eyes filling with tears. As Gaius raised the bow again, Tonius seized it with one hand and Gaius' throat with the other, carrying him back six or seven paces with the sheer fury of his charge.

'Any other threats?' he growled as his grip tightened. Blood poured from his nose and stained his praetexta tunic. He wrenched the bow away from Gaius' grasp and set about him with it, raining blows, but all the time keeping hold of his throat.

'He's going to kill me and pretend it was an accident,' Gaius thought desperately. 'I can see it in his eyes. I can't breathe.'

He pummelled at the larger boy with his own fists, but his reach was not enough to do any real damage. His vision lost colour, becoming like a dream; his ears ceased to hear sound. He lost consciousness as Tonius threw him down onto the wet leaves.

Tubruk found Gaius on the path about an hour later and woke him by pouring water onto his bruised and battered head. Once again, his face was a crusted mess. His barely scabbed eye had filled with blood, so that his vision was dark on that side. His nose had been rebroken and everything else was a bruise.

'Tubruk?' he murmured, dazed. 'I fell out of a tree.'

The big man's laugh echoed in the closeness of the dense woods.

'You know, lad, no one doubts your courage. It's your ability to fight I'm not too sure about. It's time you were properly trained before you get yourself killed. When your father is back from the city, I'll raise it with him.'

'You won't tell him about . . . me falling from the tree? I hit a lot of branches on the way down.' Gaius could taste blood in his mouth, leaking back from the broken nose.

'Did you manage to hit the tree at all? Even once?' Tubruk asked, looking at the scuffed leaves and reading the answers for himself.

'The tree has a nose like mine, I'd say.' Gaius tried to smile, but vomited into the bushes instead.

'Hmmm. Is this the end of it, do you think? I can't let you carry on and see you crippled or dead. When your father is away in the city, he expects you to begin to learn your responsibilities as his heir and a patrician, not an urchin involved in pointless brawls.' Tubruk paused to pick up a battered bow from the under-growth. The string had snapped and he tutted.

'I should tan your backside for stealing this bow as well.'

Gaius nodded miserably.

'No more fights, understand?' Tubruk pulled him to his feet and wiped away some of the mud from the track.

'No more fights. Thank you for coming to get me,' Gaius replied.

The boy tottered and almost fell as he spoke and the old gladiator sighed. With a quick heave, he lifted the boy up to his shoulders and carried him down to the main house, shouting, 'Duck!' when they came to low branches.

Except for the splinted hand, Marcus was back to his usual self by the following week. He was shorter than Gaius by about two inches, brown-haired and strong-limbed. His arms were a little out of proportion, which he claimed would make him a great swordsman when he was older because of the extra reach. He could juggle four apples and would have tried with knives if the kitchen slaves hadn't told Aurelia, Gaius' mother. She had screamed at him until he promised never to try it. The memory still made him pause whenever he picked up a blade to eat.

When Tubruk had brought the barely conscious Gaius back to the villa, Marcus was out of bed, having crept down to the vast kitchen complex. He'd been in the middle of dipping his fingers into the fat-smeared iron pans when he heard the voices and trotted past the rows of heavy brick ovens to Lucius' sickroom.

As always when they hurt themselves, Lucius, a physician slave, tended to the wounds. He looked after the estate slaves as well as the family, binding swellings, applying maggot poultices to infections, pulling teeth with his pliers and sewing up cuts. He was a quiet, patient man who always breathed through his nose as he concentrated. The soft whistle of air from the elderly physician's lungs had come to mean peace and safety to the boys. Gaius knew

12

that Lucius would be freed when his father died, as a reward for his silent care of Aurelia.

Marcus sat and munched on bread and black fat as Lucius set the broken nose yet again.

'Suetonius beat you again then?' he asked.

Gaius nodded, unable to speak or to see through watering eyes.

'You should have waited for me, we could have taken him together.'

Gaius couldn't even nod. Lucius finished probing the nasal cartilage and made a sharp pull, to set the loose piece in line. Fresh blood poured over the day's clotted mixture.

'By the bloody temples, Lucius, careful! You almost had my nose right off then!'

Lucius smiled and began to cut fresh linen into strips to bind around the head.

In the respite, Gaius turned to his friend. 'You have a broken, splinted hand and bruised or cracked ribs. You cannot fight.'

Marcus looked at him thoughtfully. 'Perhaps. Will you try again? He'll kill you if you do, you know.'

Gaius gazed at him calmly over the bandages as Lucius packed up his materials and rose to leave.

'Thanks, Lucius. He won't kill me because I'll beat him. I simply need to adjust my strategy, that's all.'

'He's going to kill you,' repeated Marcus, biting into a dried apple, stolen from the winter stores.

A week later to the day, Marcus rose at dawn and began his exercises, which he believed would stimulate the reflexes needed to be a great swordsman. His room was a simple cell of white stone, containing only his bed and a trunk with his personal possessions. Gaius had the adjoining room and, on his way to the toilet, Marcus kicked the door to wake him up. He entered the small room and

13

chose one of the four stone-rimmed holes that led to a sewer of constantly running water, a miracle of engineering that meant there was little or no smell, with the night soil washing out into the river that ran through the valley. He removed the capstone and pulled up his night shift.

Gaius had not stirred when he returned, and he opened the door to chide him for his laziness. The room was empty and Marcus felt a surge of disappointment.

'You should have taken me with you, my friend. You didn't have to make it so obvious that you didn't need me.'

He dressed quickly and set out after Gaius as the sun cleared the valley rim, lighting the estates even as the field slaves bent to work in the first session.

What mist there was burned off rapidly, even in the cooler woods. Marcus found Gaius on the border of the two estates. He was unarmed.

As Marcus came up behind him, Gaius turned, a look of horror on his face. When he saw it was his friend he relaxed and smiled.

'Glad you came, Marcus. I didn't know what time he'd arrive, so I've been here a while. I thought you were him for a moment.'

'I'd have waited with you, you know. I'm your friend, remember. Also, I owe him a beating as well.'

'Your hand is broken, Marcus. Anyway, I owe him two beatings to your one.'

'True, but I could have jumped on him from a tree, or tripped him as he ran in.'

'Tricks don't win battles. I will beat him with my strength.'

For a moment, Marcus was silenced. There was something cold and unforgiving in the usually sunny boy he faced.

The sun rose slowly, shadows changed. Marcus sat down, at first in a crouch and then with his legs sprawled out in front of him. He would not speak first. Gaius had made it a contest of seriousness. He could not stand for hours, as Gaius seemed

14

willing to do. The shadows moved. Marcus marked their positions with sticks and estimated that they had waited three hours when Suetonius appeared silently, walking along the path. He smiled a slow smile when he saw them and paused.

'I am beginning to like you, little wolf. I think I will kill you today, or perhaps break your leg. What do you think would be fair?'

Gaius smiled and stood as tall and as straight as he could. 'I would kill me. If you don't, I will keep fighting you until I am big and strong enough to kill you. And then I will have your woman, after I have given her to my friend.'

Marcus looked in horror as he heard what Gaius was saying. Maybe they should just run. Suetonius squinted at the boys and pulled a short, vicious little blade from his belt.

'Little wolf, mudfish – you are too stupid to get angry at, but you yap like puppies. I will make you quiet again.'

He ran at them. Just before he reached the pair, the ground gave way with a crack and he disappeared from sight in a rush of air and an explosion of dust and leaves.

'Built you a wolf trap, Suetonius,' Gaius shouted cheerfully.

The fourteen-year-old jumped for the sides and Gaius and Marcus spent a hilarious few minutes stamping on his fingers as he tried to gain a purchase in the dry earth. He screamed abuse at them and they slapped each other on the back and jeered at him.

'I thought of dropping a big rock in on you, like they do with wolves in the north,' Gaius said quietly when Suetonius had been reduced to sullen anger. 'But you didn't kill me, so I won't kill you. I might not even tell anyone how we dropped Suetonius into a wolf trap. Good luck in getting out.'

Suddenly, he let rip with a war whoop, quickly followed by Marcus, their cries and ecstatic yells disappearing into the woods as they pelted away, on top of the world.

15

As they pounded along the paths, Marcus called over his shoulder, 'I thought you said you'd beat him with your strength!'

'I did. I was up all night digging that hole.'

The sun shone through the trees and they felt as if they could run all day.

Left alone, Suetonius scrabbled up the sides, caught an edge and heaved himself over and out. For a while, he sat there and contemplated his muddy praetexta and breeches. He frowned for most of the way home, but, as he cleared the trees and came out into the sunshine, he began to laugh.

CHAPTER TWO

Gaius and Marcus walked behind Tubruk as he paced out a new field for ploughing. Every five paces, he would stretch out a hand and Gaius would pass him a peg from a heavy basket. Tubruk himself carried twine wrapped in a great ball around a wooden spindle. Ever patient, he would tie the twine around a peg and then hand it to Marcus to hold while he hammered it into the hard ground. Occasionally, Tubruk would sight back along the lengthening line at the landmarks he had noted and grunt in satisfaction before carrying on.

It was dull work and both boys wanted to escape down to the Campus Martius, the huge field just outside the city where they could ride and join in the sports.

'Hold it steady,' Tubruk snapped at Marcus as the boy's attention wandered.

'How much longer, Tubruk?' Gaius asked.

'As long as it takes to finish the job properly. The fields must be marked out for the ploughman, then the posts hammered in to set the boundary. Your father wants to increase the estate revenues and these fields have good soil for figs, which we can sell in the city markets.'

Gaius looked around him at the green and golden hills that made up his father's land.

'Is this a rich estate then?'

Tubruk chuckled. 'It serves to feed and clothe you, but we don't have enough land to plant much barley or wheat for bread. Our crops have to be small and that means we have to concentrate on the things the city wants to buy. The flower gardens produce seeds that are crushed to make face oils for high-born city ladies and your father has purchased a dozen hives to house new swarms of bees. You boys will have honey at every meal in a few months and that brings in a good price as well.'

'Can we help with the hives when the bees come?' Marcus spoke up, showing a sudden interest.

'Perhaps, though they take careful handling. Old Tadius used to keep bees before he became a slave. I hope to use him to collect the honey. Bees don't like to have their winter stores stolen away from them and it needs a practised hand. Hold that peg steady now – that's a stade, six hundred and twenty-five feet. We'll turn a corner here.'

'Will you need us for much longer, Tubruk? We were hoping to take ponies into the city and see if we can listen to the Senate debate.'

Tubruk snorted. 'You were going to ride into the Campus, you mean, and race your ponies against the other boys. Hmm? There's only this last side to mark out today. I can have the men set the posts tomorrow. Another hour or two should see us finished.'

The two boys looked at each other glumly. Tubruk put down his spindle and mallet and stretched his back with a sigh. He tapped Gaius on the shoulder gently.

'This is your land we're working on, remember. It belonged to your father's father and when you have children, it will belong to them. Look at this.'

Tubruk crouched down on one knee and broke the hard ground with the peg and mallet, tapping until the churned, black soil was visible. He pressed his hand into the earth and gripped a handful of the dark substance, holding it up for their inspection.

Gaius and Marcus looked bemused as he crumbled the dirt between his fingers.

'There have been Romans standing where we are standing for hundreds of years. This dirt is more than just earth. It is *us*, the dust of the men and women who have gone before us. You came from this and you will go back to it. Others will walk over you and never know you were once there and as alive as they themselves.'

'The family tomb is on the road to the city,' Gaius muttered, nervous in the face of Tubruk's sudden intensity.

The old gladiator shrugged. 'In recent years, but our people have been here for longer than there was ever a city there. We have bled and died in these fields in long-forgotten wars. We will again perhaps, in wars in years to come. Put your hand into the ground.'

Reaching out to the reluctant boy, he took Gaius' hand and pushed it into the broken soil, closing the fingers over as he withdrew it.

'You hold history, boy. Land that has seen things we cannot. You hold your family and Rome in your hand. It will grow crops for us and feed us and make money for us so that we can enjoy luxuries. Without it, we are nothing. Land is everything and wherever you travel in the world, only this soil will be truly yours. Only this simple black muck you hold will be home to you.'

Marcus watched the exchange, his expression serious. 'Will it be home to me as well?'

For a moment, Tubruk did not answer, instead holding Gaius' gaze as the boy gripped the soil tightly in his hand. Then he turned to Marcus and smiled.

'Of course, lad. Are you not Roman? Is not the city as much yours as anyone's?' The smile faded and he returned his gaze to Gaius. 'But this estate is Gaius' own and one day he will be master of it and look down on shaded fig groves and buzzing hives and remember when he was just a little lad and all he wanted was to show new tricks on his pony to the other boys of the Campus Martius.'

He did not see the sadness that came onto Marcus' face for a moment.

Gaius opened his hand and placed the earth back in the broken spot Tubruk had made, pressing it down thoughtfully.

'Let us finish the marking then,' he said and Tubruk nodded as he rose to his feet.

The sun was going down as the two boys crossed one of the Tiber bridges that led to the Campus Martius. Tubruk had insisted they wash and change into clean tunics before setting out, but even at the late hour the vast space was still full of the young of Rome, gathered in groups, throwing discuses and javelins, kicking balls to each other and riding ponies and horses with shouted encouragement. It was a noisy place and the boys loved to watch the wrestling tournaments and chariot practices.

Young as they were, they were both confident in the high saddles that gripped them at the groin and buttocks, holding them secure through manoeuvres. Their legs hung long over the ribs of the steeds, gripping tight in the turns for added stability.

Gaius looked around for Suetonius and was pleased not to see him in the crowds. They hadn't met again after trapping him in the wolf pit, and that was how Gaius wanted to leave it – with the battle won and over. Further skirmishes could only mean trouble.

He and Marcus rode up to a group of children near their own age and hailed them, dismounting with a leg flung over the pony's side. No one they knew was there, but the group parted as they approached and the mood was friendly, their attention on a man with a discus gripped in his right hand.

20

'That's Tani. He's the champion of his legion,' one boy muttered aloud to Gaius.

As they watched, Tani launched himself, spinning on the spot and releasing the disc at the setting sun. There were whistles of appreciation as it flew and one or two of the boys clapped.

Tani turned to them. 'Take care. It'll be coming back this way in a moment.'

Gaius could see another man run to the fallen disc and pick it up before spinning it into flight once more. This time, the discus was released at a wide angle and the crowd scattered as it soared towards them. One boy was slower than the rest and when the discus hit and skipped, it caught him in the side with a thump, even as he tried to dodge. He fell winded, and groaned as Tani ran up to his side.

'Good stop, lad. Are you all right?'

The boy nodded, clambering to his feet, but still holding his side in pain. Tani patted him on the shoulder, stooping smoothly to pick up the fallen discus. He returned to his spot to throw again.

'Anyone racing horses today?' Marcus asked.

A few turned and weighed him up, casting gazes at the sturdy little pony Tubruk had chosen for him.

'Not so far. We came to watch the wrestling, but it finished an hour ago.' The speaker indicated a trampled space nearby where a square had been marked out on the grassy ground. A few men and women stood in clusters nearby, talking and eating.

'I can wrestle,' Gaius broke in quickly, his face lighting up. 'We could have our own competition.'

The group murmured interest. 'Pairs?'

'All at once – last one standing is the winner?' Gaius replied. 'We need a prize, though. How about we all put in what money we have and last one standing takes the collection?'

The boys in the crowd discussed this and many began to search in their tunics for coins, giving them to the largest, who walked with confidence as the pile of coins grew in his hands.

'I'm Petronius. There's about twenty *quadrantes* here. How much have you got?'

'Any coins, Marcus? I have a couple of bronze bits.' Gaius added them to the boy's handful and Marcus added three more.

Petronius smiled as he counted again. 'A fair collection. Now, as I'm taking part, I'll need someone to hold it for me until I win.' He grinned at the two newcomers.

'I'll hold it for you, Petronius,' a girl said, accepting the coins into her smaller hands.

'My sister, Lavia,' he explained.

She winked at Gaius and Marcus, a smaller but still stocky version of her brother.

Chatting cheerfully, the group made their way over to the marked square and only a few remained on the outside to watch. Gaius counted seven other boys in addition to Petronius, who began limbering up confidently.

'What rules?' Gaius said as he stretched his own legs and back.

Petronius gathered the group together with a gesture. 'No punching. If you land on your back you are out. All right?'

The boys agreed grimly, the mood becoming hostile as they eyed each other.

Lavia spoke from the side: 'I'll call start. All ready?'

The contestants nodded. Gaius noted that a few other people were wandering over, always ready to view or bet on a contest in whatever form. The air smelled cleanly of grass and he felt full of life. He scuffed his feet and remembered what Tubruk had said about the soil. Roman earth, fed with the blood and bones of his ancestors. It felt strong under his feet and he set himself. The moment seemed to hold, and nearby he could see Tani the discus champion spin and release again, his discus flying high and straight over the Campus Martius. The sun was reddening as it sank, giving a warm cast to the tense boys in the square.

'Begin!' Lavia shouted.

Gaius dropped to one knee, spoiling a lunge that went over his head. He shoved up then, with all the strength of his thighs, taking another boy off his feet and leaving him flat on the dusty grass. As Gaius rose, he was hammered from the side, but spun as he fell so that his unknown attacker hit the ground first, with Gaius' weight knocking the wind from him.

Marcus was locked in a grip with Petronius, their hands tight on each other's armpits and shoulders. Another struggling combatant was shoved blindly into Petronius and the pair fell roughly, but Gaius' moment of inattention was punished by an arm circling his neck from behind and tightening on his windpipe. He kicked out backwards and raked his sandals down someone's shin, hacking back with an elbow at the same time. He felt the grip loosen but then they were both sent sprawling by a knot of fighting boys. Gaius hit the ground hard and scrambled to get to the side of the square, even as a foot clouted into his cheek, splitting the skin.

Anger swelled for a moment, but he saw his attacker hadn't even registered him and he retired to the edge of the square, cheering on Marcus, who had regained his feet. Petronius was down and out, knocked cold, and only Marcus and two others were still in the competition. The crowd that had gathered to watch were yelling encouragement and making side bets. Marcus grabbed one of the pair by the crotch and neck and tried to lift him into the air for throwing. The boy struggled wildly as his feet came off the ground and Marcus staggered with him just as the last gripped him around his own chest and knocked him over backwards in a heaving pile of limbs.

The stranger came to his feet with a whoop and took a circuit of the square with his hands held high. Gaius could hear Marcus laughing and breathed deeply in the summer air as his friend stood up, brushing off the dust.

In the middle distance, beyond the vast Campus, Gaius could see the city, built on seven ancient hills centuries before. All around him were the shouts and cries of his people and underneath his feet, his land.

In hot darkness, lit only by a crescent moon that signalled the month coming to a close, the two boys made their way in silence over the fields and paths of the estate. The air was filled with the smell of fruit and flowers and crickets creaked in the bushes. They walked without speaking until they reached the place where they had stood with Tubruk earlier in the day, at the corner of the peg-marked line of a new field.

With the moon giving so little light, Gaius had to feel along the twine until he came to the broken spot at the corner and then he stood and drew a slim knife from his belt, taken from the kitchens. Concentrating, he drew the sharp blade across the ball of his thumb. It sank in deeper than he had intended and blood poured out over his hand. He passed the blade to Marcus and held the thumb high, slightly worried by the injury and hoping to slow the bleeding.

Marcus drew the knife along his own thumb, once, then twice, creating a scratch from which he squeezed a few swelling beads of blood.

'I've practically cut my thumb off here!' Gaius said irritably.

Marcus tried to look serious, but failed. He held out his hand and they pressed them together so that the blood mingled in the darkness. Then Gaius pushed his bleeding thumb into the broken ground, wincing. Marcus watched him for a long moment before copying the action.

'Now you are a part of this estate as well and we are brothers,' Gaius said.

Marcus nodded and in silence they began the walk back to the sprawling white buildings of the estate. Invisibly in the darkness, Marcus' eyes brimmed and he wiped his hand over them quickly, leaving a smear of blood on his skin.

Gaius stood on the top of the estate gates, shading his eyes against the bright sun as he looked towards Rome. Tubruk had said his father would be returning from the city and he wanted to be the first to see him on the road. He spat on his hand and ran it through his dark hair to smooth it down.

He enjoyed being up away from the chores and cares of his life. The slaves below rarely looked up as they passed from one part of the estate buildings to another and it was a peculiar feeling to watch and yet be unobserved: a moment of privacy and quiet. Somewhere, his mother would be looking for him to carry a basket for her to collect fruit, or Tubruk would be looking for someone to wax and oil the leather harness of the horses and oxen, or a thousand other little tasks. Somehow, the thought of all those things he was not doing raised his spirits. They couldn't find him and he was in his own little place, watching the road to Rome.

He saw the dust trail and stood up on the gatepost. He wasn't sure. The rider was still far away, but there weren't too many estates that could be reached from their road and the chances were good.

After another few minutes he was able to see the man on the horse clearly and let out a whoop, scrambling to the ground in a rush of arms and legs. The gate itself was heavy, but Gaius threw his weight against it and it creaked open enough for him to squeeze through and run off down the road to meet his father.

His child's sandals slapped against the hard ground and he pumped his arms enthusiastically as he raced towards the approaching figure. His father had been gone for a full month and Gaius wanted to show him how much he had grown in the time. Everyone said so.

'Tata!' he called and his father heard and reined in as the boy ran up to him. He looked tired and dusty, but Gaius saw the beginnings of a smile crease against the blue eyes.

'Is this a beggar, or a small bandit, I see on the road?' his father said, reaching out an arm to lift his son to the saddle.

Gaius laughed as he was swung into the air and gripped his father's back as the horse began a slower walk up to the estate walls.

'You are taller than when I saw you last,' his father said, his voice light.

'A little. Tubruk says I am growing like corn.'

His father nodded in response and there was a friendly silence between them that lasted until they reached the gates. Gaius slid off the horse's back and heaved the gate wide enough for his father to enter the estate.

'Will you be home for long this time?'

His father dismounted and ruffled his hair, ruining the spit-smoothness he'd worked at.

'A few days, perhaps a week. I wish it was more, but there is always work to be done for the Republic.' He handed the reins to his son. 'Take old Mercury here to the stables and rub him down properly. I'll see you again after I have inspected the staff and spoken to your mother.'

Gaius' open expression tightened at the mention of Aurelia and his father noticed. He sighed and put his hand on his son's shoulder, making him meet his gaze.

'I want to spend more time away from the city, lad, but what I do is important to me. Do you understand the word "Republic"?'

Gaius nodded and his father looked sceptical.

'I doubt it. Few enough of my fellow senators seem to. We live an idea, a system of government that allows everyone to have a voice, even the common man. Do you realise how rare that is?

Every other little country I have known has a king or a chief running it. He gives land to his friends and takes money from those who fall out with him. It is like having a child loose with a sword.

'In Rome, we have the rule of law. It is not yet perfect or even as fair as I would like, but it tries to be and that is what I devote my life to. It is worth my life – and yours too when the time comes.'

'I miss you, though,' Gaius replied, knowing it was selfish.

His father's gaze hardened slightly, then he reached out to ruffle Gaius' hair once more.

'And I miss you too. Your knees are filthy and that tunic is more suitable for a street child, but I miss you too. Go and clean yourself up – but only after you have rubbed Mercury down.'

He watched his son trudge away, leading the horse, and smiled ruefully. He *was* a little taller, Tubruk was right.

In the stables, Gaius rubbed the flanks of his father's horse, smoothing away sweat and dust and thinking over his father's words. The idea of a republic sounded very fine, but being a king was clearly more exciting.

Whenever Gaius' father Julius had been away for a long absence, Aurelia insisted on a formal meal in the long *triclinium*. The two boys would sit on children's stools next to the long couches, on which Aurelia and her husband would recline barefoot, with the food served on low tables by the household slaves.

Gaius and Marcus hated the meals. They were forbidden to chatter and sat in painful silence through each course, allowing the table servants only a quick rub of their fingers between dipping them into the food. Although their appetites were large, Gaius and Marcus had learned not to offend Aurelia by eating too quickly and so were forced to chew and swallow as slowly as the adults while the evening shadows lengthened.

Bathed and dressed in clean clothes, Gaius felt hot and

uncomfortable with his parents. His father had put aside the informality of their meeting on the road and now talked with his wife as if the two boys did not exist. Gaius watched his mother closely when he could, looking for the trembling that would signal one of her fits. At first, they had terrified him and left him sobbing, but after years an emotional callousness had grown, and occasionally he even hoped for the trembling so that he and Marcus would be sent from the table.

He tried to listen and be interested in the conversation, but it was all about developments in the laws and city ordinances. His father never seemed to come home with exciting stories of executions or famous street villains.

'You have too much faith in the people, Julius,' Aurelia was saying. 'They need looking after as a child needs a father. Some have wit and intelligence, I agree, but most have to be protected . . .' She trailed off and silence fell.

Julius looked up and Gaius saw a sadness come into his face, making him look away, embarrassed, as if he had witnessed an intimacy.

'Relia?'

Gaius heard his father's voice and looked back at his mother, who lay like a statue, her eyes focused on some distant scene. Her hand trembled and suddenly her face twisted like a child's. The tremor that began in her hand spread to her whole body and she twisted in spasm, one arm sweeping bowls from the low table. Her voice erupted violently from her throat, a torrent of screeching sound that made the boys wince backwards.

Julius rose smoothly from his seat and took his wife in his arms.

'Leave us,' he commanded and Gaius and Marcus went out with the slaves, leaving behind them the man holding the twisting figure.

* * *

28

The following morning, Gaius was woken by Tubruk shaking his shoulder.

'Get up, lad. Your mother wants to see you.'

Gaius groaned, almost to himself, but Tubruk heard.

'She is always quiet after a . . . bad night.'

Gaius paused as he pulled clothes on. He looked up at the old gladiator.

'Sometimes, I hate her.'

Tubruk sighed gently.

'I wish you could have known her as she was before the sickness began. She used to sing to herself all the time and the house was always happy. You have to think that your mother is still there, but can't get out to you. She does love you, you know.'

Gaius nodded and smoothed his hair down carelessly.

'Has my father gone back to the city?' he asked, knowing the answer. His father hated to feel helpless.

'He left at dawn,' Tubruk replied.

Without another word, Gaius followed him through the cool corridors to his mother's rooms.

She sat upright in bed, her face freshly washed and her long hair braided behind her. Her skin was pale, but she smiled as Gaius entered and he was able to smile back.

'Come closer, Gaius. I am sorry if I scared you last night.'

He came into her arms and let her hold him, feeling nothing. How could he tell her he wasn't scared any more? He had seen it too many times, each worse than the last. Some part of him knew that she would get worse and worse, that she was already leaving him. But he could not think of that – better to keep it inside, to smile and hug her and walk away untouched.

'What are you going to do today?' she asked as she released him.

'Chores with Marcus,' he replied.

She nodded and seemed to forget him. He waited for a few

seconds and when there was no further response turned and walked from the room.

When the tiny space in her thoughts faded and she focused again on the room, it was empty.

Marcus met him at the gates, carrying a bird net. He looked into his friend's eyes and made his tone light and cheerful.

'I feel lucky today. We'll catch a hawk – two hawks. We'll train them and they'll sit on our shoulders, attacking on our command. Suetonius will run when he sees us.'

Gaius chuckled and cleared his mind of thoughts of his mother. He missed his father already, but the day was going to be a long one and there was always something to do in the woods. He doubted Marcus' idea of hawk-catching would work, but he would go along with it until the day was over and all the paths had been walked.

The green gloom almost made them miss the raven that sat on a low branch, not far from the sunlit fields. Marcus froze as he saw it first and pressed a hand against Gaius' chest.

'Look at the size of it!' he whispered, unwrapping his bird net.

They crouched down and crept forward, watched with interest by the bird. Even for a raven it was large and it spread heavy black wings as they approached, before almost hopping to the next tree with one lazy flap.

'You circle around,' Marcus whispered, his voice excited. He backed this up with circling motions of his fingers and Gaius grinned at him, slipping into the undergrowth to one side. He crept around in a large circle, trying to keep the tree in sight while checking the path for dry twigs or rustling leaves.

When Gaius emerged on the far side, he saw the raven had changed tree again, this time to a long trunk that had fallen years before. The gentle slope of the trunk was easy to climb and Marcus had already begun to inch up it towards the bird, at the same time trying to keep the net free for throwing.

Gaius padded closer to the base of the tree. 'Why doesn't it fly away?' he thought, looking up at the raven. It cocked its large head to one side and opened its wings again. Both boys froze until the bird seemed to relax, then Marcus levered himself upwards again, legs dangling on each side of the thick trunk.

Marcus was only feet from the bird when he thought it would fly off again. It hopped about on the trunk and branches, seemingly unafraid. He unfolded the net, a web of rough twine usually used for holding onions in the estate kitchens. In Marcus' hands, it had instantly become the fearsome instrument of a bird-catcher.

Holding his breath, he threw it and the raven took off with a scream of indignation. It flapped its wings once again and landed in the slender branches of a young sapling near Gaius, who ran at it without thinking.

As Marcus scrambled down, Gaius shoved at the sapling and felt the whole thing give with a sudden crack, pinning the bird in the leaves and branches on the ground. With Gaius pressing it all down, Marcus was able to reach in and hold the heavy bird, gripped tightly in his two hands. He raised it triumphantly and then hung on desperately as the raven struggled to escape.

'Help me! He's strong,' Marcus shouted and Gaius added his own hands to the struggling bundle. Suddenly an agonising pain shot through him. The beak was long and curved like a spear of black wood. It jabbed at his hand, catching and gripping the piece of soft flesh between thumb and first finger.

Gaius yelped. 'Get it off. It's got my hand, Marcus.' The pain was excruciating and they panicked together, with Marcus fighting to hold his grip while Gaius tried to lever the vicious beak off his skin.

'I can't get it off, Marcus.'

'You'll have to pull it,' Marcus replied grimly, his face red with the effort of holding the enraged bird.

'I can't, it's like a knife. Let it go.'

'I'm *not* letting it go. This raven is ours. We caught it in the wild, like hunters.'

Gaius groaned with pain.

'It caught us, more like.' His fingers waved in agony and the raven let go without warning, trying to snap at one of them. Gaius gasped in relief and backed off hurriedly, holding his hands against his groin and doubling over.

'He's a fighter, anyway,' Marcus said with a grin, shifting his grip so the searching head couldn't find his own flesh. 'We'll take him home and train him. Ravens are intelligent, I've heard. He'll learn tricks and come with us when we go to the Campus Martius.'

'He needs a name. Something war-like,' Gaius replied, in between sucking his torn skin.

'What's the name of that god who goes round as a raven or carries one?'

'I don't know, one of the Greek ones, I think. Zeus?'

'That's an owl, I think. Someone has an owl.'

'I don't remember one with a raven, but Zeus is a good name for him.'

They smiled at each other and the raven went quiet, looking around him with apparent calmness.

'Zeus it is then.'

They walked back over the fields to the estate with the bird held firmly in Marcus' grasp.

'We'll have to find somewhere to hide him,' he said. 'Your mother doesn't like us catching animals. You remember when she found out about the fox?'

Gaius winced, looking at the ground. 'There's an empty chicken coop next to the stables. We could put him in there. What do ravens eat?'

'Meat, I think. They scavenge battlefields, unless that's crows.

We can get a few scraps from the kitchens and see what he takes, anyway. That won't be a problem.'

'We'll have to tie twine to his legs for the training, otherwise he'll fly off,' Gaius said, thoughtfully.

Tubruk was talking to three carpenters who were to repair part of the estate roof. He spotted the boys as they walked into the estate yard and motioned them over to him. They looked at each other, wondering if they could run, but Tubruk wouldn't let them get more than a few paces, for all his apparent inattention as he had turned back to the workers.

'I'm not giving Zeus up,' Marcus whispered harshly.

Gaius could only nod as they approached the group of men.

'I'll come along in a few minutes,' Tubruk instructed as the men walked to their tasks. 'Take the tiles off the section until I get there.'

He turned to the boys. 'What's this? A raven. Must be a sick one if you caught it.'

'We trapped him in the woods. Followed him and brought him down,' Marcus said, his voice defiant.

Tubruk smiled as if he understood and reached out to stroke the bird's long beak. Its energy seemed to have gone and it panted almost like a dog, revealing a slender tongue between the hard blades.

'Poor thing,' Tubruk muttered. 'Looks terrified. What are you going to do with him?'

'His name's Zeus. We're going to train him as a pet, like a hawk.'

Tubruk shook his head once, slowly. 'You can't train a wild bird, boys. A hawk is raised from a chick by an expert and even they stay wild. The best trainer can lose one every now and then if it flies too far from him. Zeus is fully grown. If you keep him, he'll die.'

'We can use one of the old chicken coops,' Gaius insisted. 'There's nothing in there now. We'll feed him and fly him on a string.'

Tubruk snorted. 'Do you know what a wild bird does if you keep him locked up? He can't stand walls around him. Especially a tiny space like one of the chicken coops. It will break his spirit and, day by day, he will pull his own feathers out in misery. He won't eat, he'll just hurt himself until he dies. Zeus here will choose death over captivity. The kindest thing you can do for him is to let him go. I don't think you could have caught him unless he was sick, so he might be dying anyway, but at least let him spend his last days in the woods and the air, where he belongs.'

'But . . .' Marcus fell silent, looking at the raven.

'Come on,' Tubruk said. 'Let's go out into the fields and watch him fly.'

Glumly, the boys looked at each other and followed him back out of the gates. Together, they stood gazing down the hill.

'Set him free, boy,' Tubruk said and something in his voice made them both look at him.

Marcus raised and opened his hands and Zeus heaved himself into the air, spreading large black wings and fighting for height. He screamed frustration at them until he was just a dot in the sky over the woods. Then they saw him descend and disappear.

Tubruk reached out and held the necks of the two boys in his rough hands.

'A noble act. Now there are a number of chores to do and I couldn't find you earlier, so they've piled up waiting for your attention. Inside.'

He steered the boys through the gate into the courtyard, taking a last look over the fields towards the woods before he followed them.

CHAPTER THREE

That summer saw the start of the boys' formal education. From the beginning, they were both treated equally, with Marcus also receiving the training necessary to run a complex estate, albeit a minor one. In addition to continuing the formal Latin that had been drummed into them since birth, they were taught about famous battles and tactics as well as how to manage men and handle money and debts. When Suetonius left to be an officer in an African legion the following year, both Gaius and Marcus had begun to learn Greek rhetoric and the skills of debate that they would need if, as young senators later on, they ever chose to prosecute or defend a citizen on a matter of law.

Although the three hundred members of the Senate met only twice each lunar month, Gaius' father Julius remained in Rome for longer and longer periods, as the Republic struggled to deal with new colonies and the swiftly growing wealth and power. For months, the only adults Gaius and Marcus would see were Aurelia and the tutors, who arrived at the main house at dawn and left with the sun sinking behind them and denarii jingling in their pockets. Tubruk was always there too, a friendly presence who stood no nonsense from the boys. Before Suetonius had left, the old gladiator had walked the five miles to the main house of the neighbouring estate and waited eleven hours, from dawn to dusk, to be admitted to see the eldest son of the house. He didn't tell

Gaius what had transpired, but had returned with a smile and ruffled Gaius' hair with his big hand before going down to the stables to see to the new mares as they came into season.

Of all the tutors, Gaius and Marcus enjoyed the hours with Vepax the best. He was a young Greek, tall and thin in his toga. He always arrived at the estate on foot and carefully counted the coins he earned before walking back to the city. They met with him for two hours each week in a small room Gaius' father had set aside for the lessons. It was a bare place, with a stone-flagged floor and unadorned walls. With the other tutors, droning through the verses of Homer and Latin grammar, the two boys often fidgeted on the wooden benches, or drifted in concentration until the tutor noticed and brought them back with sharp smacks from the cane. Most were strict and it was difficult to get away with much with only the two of them to take up the master's attention. One time, Marcus had used his stylus to draw a picture of a pig with a tutor's beard and face. He had been caught trying to show it to Gaius and had to hold out his hand for the stick, suffering miserably through three sharp blows.

Vepax didn't carry a cane. All he ever had with him was a heavy cloth bag full of clay tablets and figures, some blue and some red to show different sides. By the appointed hour, he would have cleared the benches to one side of the room and set out his figures to represent some famous battle of the past. After a year of this, their first task was to recognise the structure and name the generals involved. They knew Vepax would not limit himself to Roman battles; sometimes the tiny horse and legionary figures were representing Parthia or ancient Greece or Carthage. Knowing Vepax was Greek himself, the boys had pushed the young man to show them the battles of Alexander, thrilled by the legends and what he had achieved at such a young age. At first, Vepax had been reluctant, not wanting to be seen to favour his own history, but he had allowed himself to be persuaded and showed them every major battle where records and maps survived. For the Greek wars, Vepax never opened a book, placing and moving each piece from memory.

He told the boys the names of the generals and the key players in each conflict as well as the history and politics when they had a direct bearing on the day. He made the little clay pieces come alive for Marcus and Gaius, and every time it came to the end of the two hours they would look longingly at them as he packed them away in his bags, slowly and carefully.

One day, as they arrived, they found most of the little room covered in the clay characters. A huge battle had been set out and Gaius counted the blue characters quickly, then the red, multiplying it in his head as he had been taught by the arithmetic tutor.

'Tell me what you see,' Vepax said quietly to Gaius.

'Two forces, one of more than fifty thousand, the other nearly forty. The red is . . . the red is Roman, judging by the heavy infantry placed to the front in legion squares. They are supported by cavalry on the right and left wings, but they are matched by the blue cavalry facing them. There are slingers and spearmen on the blue side, but I can't see any archers, so missile attacks will be over a very short range. They seem roughly matched. It should be a long and difficult battle.'

Vepax nodded. 'The red side is indeed Roman, well-disciplined veterans of many battles. What if I told you the blues were a mixed group, made up of Gauls, Spaniards, Numidians and Carthaginians? Would that make a difference to the outcome?'

Marcus' eyes gleamed with interest. 'It would mean we were looking at Hannibal's forces. But where are his famous elephants? Didn't you have elephants in your bag?' Marcus looked hopefully over at the limp cloth sack.

'It is Hannibal the Romans were facing, but by this battle, his elephants had died. He managed to find more later and they were terrifying at the charge, but here he had to make do without them.

He is outnumbered by two legions. His force is mixed where the Roman one is unified. What other factors might affect the outcome?'

'The land,' Gaius cried. 'Is he on a hill? His cavalry could smash . . .'

Vepax waved a hand gently.

'The battle took place on a plain. The weather was cool and clear. Hannibal should have lost. Would you like to see how he won?'

Gaius stared at the massed pieces. Everything was against the blue forces. He looked up.

'Can we move the pieces as you explain?'

Vepax smiled. 'Of course. Today I will need both of you to make the battle move as it did once before. Take the Roman side, Gaius. Marcus and I will take Hannibal's force.'

Smiling, the three faced each other over the ranks of figures.

'The battle of Cannae, one hundred and twenty-six years ago. Every man who fought in the battle is dust, every sword rusted away, but the lessons are still there to be learned.'

Vepax must have brought every clay soldier and horse he had to form this battle, Gaius realised. Even with each piece representing a five hundred, they took up most of the available room.

'Gaius, you are Aemilius Paulus and Terentius Varro, experienced Roman commanders. Line by line you will advance straight at the enemy, allowing no deviation and no slackness in discipline. Your infantry is superb and should do well against the ranks of foreign swordsmen.'

Thoughtfully, Gaius began moving his infantry forward, group by group.

'Support with your cavalry, Gaius. They must not be left behind or you could be flanked.'

Nodding, Gaius brought the small clay horses up to engage the heavy cavalry Hannibal commanded.

'Marcus. Our infantry *must* hold. We will advance to meet them, and our cavalry will engage theirs on the wings, holding them.'

Heads bowed, all three moved figures in silence until the armies had shifted together, face to face. Gaius and Marcus imagined the snorts of the horses and the war cries splitting the air.

'And now, men die,' Vepax murmured. 'Our infantry begin to buckle in the centre as they meet the best-trained enemy they have ever faced.' His hands flew out and switched figure after figure to new positions, urging the boys along as they went.

On the floor in front of them, the Roman legions pushed back Hannibal's centre, which buckled before them, close to rout.

'They cannot hold,' Gaius whispered, as he saw the great crescent bow that grew deeper as the legions forced themselves forward. He paused and looked over the whole field. The cavalry were stationary, held in bloody conflict with the enemy. His mouth dropped as Marcus and Vepax continued to move pieces and suddenly the plan was clear to him.

'I would not go further in,' he said and Vepax's head came up with a quizzical expression.

'So soon, Gaius? You have seen a danger that neither Paulus nor Varro saw until it was too late. Move your men forward, the battle must be played out.' He was clearly enjoying himself, but Gaius felt a touch of irritation at having to follow through moves that would lead to the destruction of his armies.

The legions marched through the Carthaginian forces and the enemy let them in, falling back quickly and without haste, losing as few men as possible to the advancing line. Hannibal's forces were moving from the back of the field to the sides, swelling the trap, and, after what Vepax said was only a couple of hours, the entire Roman force was submerged in the enemy on three sides, which slowly closed behind them until they were caught in a box of Hannibal's making. The Roman cavalry were still held by equally skilled forces and the final scene needed little explanation to reveal the horror of it.

'Most of the Romans could not fight, trapped as they were in the middle of their own close formations. Hannibal's men killed all day long, tightening the trap until there was no one left alive. It was annihilation on a scale rarely seen before or since. Most battles leave many alive, at least those who run away, but these Romans were surrounded on all sides and had nowhere to flee to.'

The silence stretched for long moments as the two boys fixed the details in their minds and imaginations.

'Our time is up today, boys. Next week I will show you what the Romans learned from this defeat and others at the hands of Hannibal. Although they were unimaginative here, they brought in a new commander, known for his innovation and daring. He met Hannibal at the battle of Zama fourteen years later and the outcome was very different.'

'What was his name?' Marcus asked excitedly.

'He had more than one. His given name was Publius Scipio, but because of the battles he won against Carthage he was known as Scipio Africanus.'

As Gaius approached his tenth birthday, he was growing into an athletic, well-coordinated lad. He could handle any of the horses, even the difficult ones that required a brutal hand. They seemed to calm at his touch and respond to him. Only one refused to let him remain in the saddle and Gaius had been thrown eleven times when Tubruk sold the beast before the struggle killed one or the other of them.

To some extent, Tubruk controlled the purse of the estate while Gaius' father was away. He could decide where the profits from grain and livestock would be best spent, using his judgement. It was a great trust and a rare one. It wasn't up to Tubruk, however, to engage specialist fighters to teach the boys the art of war. That was the decision of the father – as was every other aspect of their upbringing. Under Roman law, Gaius' father could even have had the boys strangled or sold into slavery if they displeased him. His power in his household was absolute and his goodwill was not to be risked.

Julius returned home for his son's birthday feast. Tubruk attended him as he bathed away the dust of the journey in the mineral pool. Despite being ten years older than Tubruk, the years sat well on his sun-dark frame as he eased through the water. Steam rose in wisps as a sudden rush of fresh hot water erupted from a pipe into the placid waters of the bath. Tubruk noted the signs of health to himself and was pleased. In silence, he waited for Julius to finish the slow immersion and rest on the submerged marble steps near the inflow pipe, where the water was shallow and warmest.

Julius lay back against the coldness of the pool ledges and raised an eyebrow at Tubruk. 'Report,' he said and closed his eyes.

Tubruk stood stiffly and recited the profits and losses of the previous month. He kept his eyes fixed on the far wall and spoke fluently of minute problems and successes without once referring to notes. At last, he came to the end and waited in silence. After a moment, the blue eyes of the only man who'd ever employed him without owning him opened once again and fixed him with a look that had not been melted by the heat of the pool.

'How is my wife?'

Tubruk kept his face impassive. Was there a point in telling this man that Aurelia had worsened still further? She had been beautiful once, before childbirth had left her close to death for months. Ever since Gaius had come into the world, she had seemed unsteady on her feet, and no longer filled the house with laughter and flowers that she would pick herself out in the far fields.

'Lucius attends her well, but she is no better . . . I have had to keep the boys away some days, when the mood has come on her.'

Julius' face hardened and a heat-fattened vein in his neck started twitching with the load of angry blood.

'Can the doctors do nothing? They take my aureus pieces without a qualm, but she worsens every time I see her!'

Tubruk pressed his lips together in an expression of regret. Some things must simply be borne, he knew. The whip falls and hurts and you must quietly wait for it to fall no more.

Sometimes she would tear her clothes into rags and sit huddled in a corner until hunger drove her out of her private rooms. Other days, she would be almost the woman he had met and loved when he first came to the estate, but given to long periods of distraction. She would be discussing a crop and suddenly, as if another voice had spoken, she would tilt her head to listen, and you might as well have left the room for all she remembered you.

Another rush of hot water disturbed the slow-dripping silence and Julius sighed like escaping steam.

'They say the Greeks have much learning in the area of medicine. Hire one of those and dismiss the fools who do her so little good. If any of them claim that only their skills have kept her from being even worse, have him flogged and dumped on the road back to the city. Try a midwife. Women sometimes understand themselves better than we do – they have so many ailments that men do not.'

The blue eyes closed again and it was like a door shutting on an oven. Without the personality, the submerged frame could have been any other Roman. He held himself like a soldier and thin white lines marked the scars of old actions. He was not a man to be crossed and Tubruk knew he had a ferocious reputation in the Senate. He kept his interests small, but guarded those interests fiercely. As a result, the powermongers were not troubled by him and were too lazy to challenge the areas where he was strong. It kept the estate wealthy and they would be able to employ the most expensive foreign doctors that Tubruk could find. Wasted money, he was sure, but what was money for if not to use it when you saw the need?

'I want to start a vineyard on the southern reaches. The soil there is perfect for a good red.'

They talked over the business of the estate and, again, Tubruk took no notes, nor felt the need after years of reporting and discussing. Two hours after he had entered, Julius smiled at last.

'You have done well. We prosper and stay strong.'

Tubruk nodded and smiled back. In all the talk, not once had Julius asked after his own health or happiness. They both knew that serious problems would be mentioned and small problems dealt with alone. It was a relationship of trust, not between equals, but between an employer and one whose competence he respected. Tubruk was no longer a slave, but he was a freedman and could never have the total confidence of those born free.

'There is another matter, a more personal one,' Julius continued. 'It is time to train my son in warfare. I have been distracted from my duty as a father to some extent, but there is no greater exercise to a man's talents than the upbringing of his son. I want to be proud of him and I worry that my absences, which are likely to get worse, will be the breaking of the boy.'

Tubruk nodded, pleased at the words. 'There are many experts in the city, trainers of boys and the young men of wealthy families.'

'No. I know of them and some have been recommended to me. I have even inspected the products of this training, visiting city villas to see the young generation. I was not impressed, Tubruk. I saw young men infected with this new philosophical learning, where too much emphasis is placed on improving the mind and not enough on the body and the heart. What good is the ability to play with logic if your fainting soul shrinks away from hardship? No, the fashions in Rome will produce only weaklings, with few exceptions, as I see it. I want Gaius trained by people on whom I can depend – you, Tubruk. I'd trust no other with such a serious task.'

Tubruk rubbed his chin, looking troubled.

'I cannot teach the skills I learned as a soldier and gladiator, sir. I know what I know, but I don't know how to pass it on.'

Julius frowned in annoyance, but didn't press it. Tubruk never spoke lightly.

'Then spend time making him fit and hard as stone. Have him run and ride for hours each day, over and over until he is fit to represent me. We will find others to teach him how to kill and command men in battle.'

'What about the other lad, sir?'

'Marcus? What about him?'

'Will we train him as well?'

Julius frowned further and he stared off into the past for a few seconds.

'Yes. I promised his father when he died. His mother was never fit to have the boy, it was her running away that practically killed the old man. She was always too young for him. The last I heard of her, she was little better than a party whore in one of the inner districts, so he stays in my house. He and Gaius are still friends, I take it?'

'Like twin stalks of corn. They're always in trouble.'

'No more. They will learn discipline from now on.'

'I will see to it that they do.'

Gaius and Marcus listened outside the door. Gaius' eyes were bright with excitement at what he'd heard. He grinned as he turned to Marcus and dropped the smile as he saw his friend's pale face and set mouth.

'What's wrong, Marc?'

'He said my mother's a whore,' came the hissing reply. Marcus' eyes glinted dangerously and Gaius choked back his first joking reply.

'He said he'd heard it – just a rumour. I'm sure she isn't.'

'They told me she was dead, like my father. She ran away and left me.' Marcus stood and his eyes filled with tears. 'I hope she *is* a whore. I hope she's a slave and dying of lung-rot.' He spun round and ran away, arms and legs flailing in loose misery.

Gaius sighed and rejected the idea of going after him. Marcus would probably go down to the stables and sit in the straw and the shadows for a few hours. If he was followed too soon, there would be angry words and maybe blows. If he was left, it would all have gone with time, the change of mood coming without warning, as his quick thoughts settled elsewhere.

It was his nature and there was no changing it. Gaius pressed his head again to the crack between the door and the frame that allowed him to hear the two men talk of his future.

'. . . unchained for the first time, so they say. It should be a mighty spectacle. All of Rome will be there. Not all the gladiators will be indentured slaves – some are *freedmen* who have been lured back with gold coins. Renius will be there, so the gossips say.'

'Renius – he must be ancient by now! He was fighting when I was a young man myself,' Julius muttered in disbelief.

'Perhaps he needs the money. Some of the men live too richly for their purses, if you understand me. Fame would allow him large debts, but everything has to be paid back in the end.'

'Perhaps he could be hired to teach Gaius – he used to take pupils, I remember. It has been so long, though. I can't believe he'll be fighting again. You will get four tickets then, my interest is definitely aroused. The boys will enjoy a trip into the city proper.'

'Good – though let us wait until after the lions have finished with ancient Renius before we offer him employment. He should be cheap if he is bleeding a little,' Tubruk said wryly.

'Cheaper still if he's dead. I'd hate to see him go out. He was unstoppable when I was young. I saw him fight in exhibitions against four or five men. One time they even blindfolded him against two. He cut them down in two blows.'

'I saw him prepare for those matches. The cloth he used allowed in enough light to see the outlines of shapes. That was all the edge he needed. After all, his opponents thought he was blind.'

'Take a big purse for hiring trainers. The circus will be the place to find them, but I will want your eye for the sound of limb and honour.'

'I am, as always, your man, sir. I will send a message tonight to collect the tickets on the estate purse. If there is nothing else?'

'Only my thanks. I know how skilfully you keep this place afloat. While my senatorial colleagues fret at how their wealth is eroded, I can be calm and smile at their discomfort.' He stood and shook hands in the wrist grip that all legionaries learned.

Tubruk was pleased to note the strength still in the hand. The old bull had a few years in him yet.

Gaius scrambled away from the door and ran down to see Marcus in the stables. Before he had gone more than a little way, he paused and leaned against a cool, white wall. What if he was still angry? No, surely the prospect of circus tickets – with unchained lions no less! – surely this would be enough to burn away his sorrow. With renewed enthusiasm and the sun on his back, he charged down the slopes to the outbuildings of teak and lime plaster that housed the estate's supply of workhorses and oxen. Somewhere, he heard his mother's voice calling his name, but he ignored it, as he would a bird's shrill scream. It was a sound that washed over him and left him untouched.

The two boys found the body of the raven close to where they had first seen it, near the edge of the woods on the estate. It lay in the damp leaves, stiff and dark, and it was Marcus who saw it first, his depression and anger lifting with the find.

'Zeus,' he whispered. 'Tubruk said he was sick.' He crouched by the track and reached out a hand to stroke the still glossy feathers. Gaius crouched with him. The chill of the woods seemed to get through to both of them at the same time and Gaius shivered slightly.

'Ravens are bad omens, remember,' he murmured.

'Not Zeus. He was just looking for a place to die.'

On an impulse, Marcus picked up the body again, holding it in his hands as he had before. The contrast saddened both of them. All the fight was gone and now the head lay limply, as if held only by skin. The beak hung open and the eyes were shrivelled, hollow pits. Marcus continued to stroke the feathers with his thumb.

'We should cremate him – give him an honourable funeral,' said Gaius. 'I could run back to the kitchens and fetch an oil lamp. We could build a pyre for him and pour some of the oil over it. It would be a good send-off for him.'

Marcus nodded and placed Zeus carefully on the ground.

'He was a fighter. He deserves something more than just being left to rot. There's a lot of dry wood around here. I'll stay to make the pyre.'

'I'll be as quick as I can,' Gaius replied, turning to run. 'Think of some prayers or something.'

He sprinted back to the estate buildings and Marcus was left alone with the bird. He felt a strange solemnity come upon him, as if he was performing a religious rite. Slowly and carefully, he gathered dry sticks and built them into a square, starting with thicker branches that were long dead and building on layers of twigs and dry leaves. It seemed right not to rush.

The woods were quiet as Gaius returned. He too was walking slowly, shielding the small flame of an oily wick where it protruded from an old kitchen lamp. He found Marcus sitting on the dry path, with the black body of Zeus lying on a neat pile of dead wood.

'I'll have to keep the flame going while I pour the oil, so it could flare up quickly. We'd better say the prayers now.'

As the evening darkened, the flickering yellow light of the lamp seemed to grow in strength, lighting their faces as they stood by the small corpse.

'Jupiter, head of all the gods, let this one fly again in the under-world. He was a fighter and he died free,' Marcus said, his voice steady and low.

Gaius readied the oil for pouring. He held the wick clear, avoiding the little flame and poured on the oil, drenching the bird and the wood in its slipperiness. Then he touched the flame to the pyre.

For long seconds, nothing happened except for a faint sizzling, but then an answering flame spread and blazed with a sickly light. The boys stood and Gaius placed the lamp on the path. They watched with interest as the feathers caught and burned with a terrible stink. The flames flickered over the body and fat smoked and sputtered in the fire. They waited patiently.

'We could gather the ashes at the end and bury them, or spread them around in the woods or the stream,' Gaius whispered.

Marcus nodded in silence.

To help the fire, Gaius poured on the rest of the oil from the lamp, extinguishing its small light. Flames grew again and most of the feathers had been burned away, except for those around the head and beak, which seemed obstinate.

Finally, the last of the oil burned to nothing and the fire sank to glowing embers.

'I think we've cooked him,' whispered Gaius. 'The fire wasn't hot enough.'

Marcus took a long stick and poked at the body, now covered

in wood ash but still recognisably the raven. The stick knocked the smoking thing right out of the ashes and Marcus spent a few moments trying to roll it back in without success.

'This is hopeless. Where's the dignity in this?' he said angrily.

'Look, we can't do any more. Let's just cover him in leaves.'

The two boys set about gathering armfuls and soon the scorched raven was hidden from view. They were silent as they walked back to the estate, but the reverent mood was gone.

CHAPTER FOUR

The circus was arranged by Cornelius Sulla, a rising young man in the ranks of Roman society. The king of Mauretania had entertained the young senator while he commanded the Second Alaudae legion in Africa. To please him, King Bocchus sent a hundred lions and twenty of his best spearmen to the capital. With these as a core, Sulla had put together a programme for five days of trials and excitement.

It was to be the largest circus ever arranged in Rome and Cornelius Sulla had his reputation and status assured by the achievement. There were even calls raised in Senate for there to be a more permanent structure to hold the games. The wooden benches bolted and pegged together for great events were unsatisfactory and really too small for the sort of crowds that wanted to see lions from the dark, unknown continent. Plans for a vast circular amphitheatre capable of holding water and staging sea battles were put forward, but the cost was huge and they were vetoed by the people's tribunes as a matter of course.

Gaius and Marcus trotted behind the two older men. Since Gaius' mother had become unwell, the boys were rarely allowed into the city proper any more, as she fretted and rocked in misery at the thought of what could happen to her son in the vicious streets. The noise of the crowd was like a blow and their eyes were bright with interest.

Most of the Senate would travel to the games in carriages, pulled or carried by slaves and horses. Gaius' father scorned this and chose to walk through the crowds. That said, the imposing figure of Tubruk beside him, fully armed as he was, kept the plebeians from shoving too rudely.

The mud of the narrow streets had been churned into a stinking broth by the huge throng and after only a short time their legs were spattered almost to the knees by filth, their sandals covered. Every shop heaved with people as they passed and there was always a crowd ahead and a mob behind pushing them on. Occasionally, Gaius' father would take side streets when the roads were blocked completely by shopkeepers' carts carrying their wares around the city. These were packed with the poor, and beggars sat in doorways, blind and maimed, with their hands outstretched. The brick buildings loomed over them, five and six storeys high, and, once, Tubruk put a hand out to hold Marcus back as a bucket of slops was poured out of an open window into the street below.

Gaius' father looked grim, but walked on without stopping, his sense of direction bringing them through the dark maze back onto the main streets to the circus. The noise of the city intensified as they grew close, with the shouted cries of hot-food sellers competing with the hammering of coppersmiths and bawling, screaming children who hung, snot-nosed, on their mothers' hips.

On every street corner, jugglers and conjurors, clowns and snake charmers performed for thrown coins. That day, the pickings were slim, despite the huge crowds. Why waste your money on things you could see every day when the amphitheatre was open?

'Stay close to us,' Tubruk said, bringing the boys' attention back from the colours, smells and noise. He laughed at their wide-mouthed expressions. 'I remember the first time I saw a circus – the Vespia, where I was to fight my first battle, untrained and slow, just a slave with a sword.'

'You won, though,' Julius replied, smiling as they walked.

'My stomach was playing me up, so I was in a terrible mood.'
Both men laughed.

'I'd hate to face a lion,' Tubruk continued. 'I've seen a couple on the loose in Africa. They move like horses at the charge when they want to, but with fangs and claws like iron nails.'

'They have a hundred of the beasts and two shows a day for five days, so we should see ten of them against a selection of fighters. I am looking forward to seeing these black spearmen in action. It will be interesting to see if they can match our javelin throwers for accuracy.'

They walked under the entrance arch and paused at a series of wooden tubs filled with water. For a small coin, they had the mud and smell scrubbed from their legs and sandals. It was good to be clean again. With the help of an attendant, they found the seats reserved for them by one of the estate slaves, who'd travelled in the previous evening to await their arrival. Once they were seated, the slave stood to walk the miles back to the estate. Tubruk passed him another coin to buy food for the journey and the man smiled cheerfully, pleased to be away from the backbreaking labour of the fields for once.

All around them sat the members of the patrician families and their slaves. Although there were only three hundred representatives in the Senate, there must have been close to a thousand others. Rome's lawmakers had taken the day off for the first battles of the five-day run. The sand was raked smooth in the vast pit; the wooden stands filled with thirty thousand of the classes of Rome. The morning heat built and built into a wall of discomfort, largely ignored by the people.

'Where are the fighters, Father?' Gaius asked, searching for signs of lions or cages.

'They are in that barn building over there. You see where the gates are? There.'

He opened a folded programme, purchased from a slave as they went in.

'The organiser of the games will welcome us and probably thank Cornelius Sulla. We will all cheer for Sulla's cleverness in making such a spectacle possible. Then there are four gladiatorial combats, to first blood only. One will follow that is to the death. Renius will give a demonstration of some sort and then the lions will roam "the landscapes of their Africa", whatever that means. Should be an impressive show.'

'Have you ever seen a lion?'

'Once, in the zoo. I have never fought one, though. Tubruk says they are fearsome in battle.'

The amphitheatre fell quiet as the gates opened and a man walked out dressed in a toga so white it almost glowed.

'He looks like a god,' Marcus whispered.

Tubruk leaned over to the boy. 'Don't forget they bleach the cloth with human urine. There's a lesson in there somewhere.'

Marcus looked at Tubruk in surprise for a moment, wondering if a joke had been made of some kind. Then he forgot about it as he tried to hear the voice of the man who had strode to the centre of the sand. He had a trained voice, and the bowl of the amphitheatre acted as a perfect reflector. Nonetheless, part of his announcement was lost as people shuffled or whispered to their friends and were shushed.

'. . . welcome that is due . . . African beasts . . . Cornelius Sulla!'

The last was said in crescendo and the audience cheered dutifully, more enthusiastically than Julius or Tubruk had been expecting. Gaius heard the words of the old gladiator as he leaned in close to his father.

'He may be a man to watch, this one.'

'Or to watch out for,' his father replied with a meaningful look.

Gaius strained to see the man who rose from his seat and bowed. He too wore a simple toga, with an embroidered hem of gold. He was sitting close enough for Gaius to see this really was a man who looked like a god. He had a strong, handsome face

53

and golden skin. He waved and sat down, smiling at the pleasure of the crowds.

Everyone settled back for the main excitement, conversations springing up all around. Politics and finance were discussed. Cases being argued in law were raked and chewed over by the patricians. They were still the ultimate power in Rome and therefore the world. True, the people's tribunes, with their right to veto agreements, had taken some of the edge off their authority, but they still had the power of life and death over most of the citizens of Rome.

The first pair of fighters entered wearing tunics of blue and black. Neither was heavily armoured, as this was a display of speed and skill rather than savagery. Men did die in these contests, but it was rare. After a salute to the organiser and sponsor of the games, they began to move, short swords held rigid and shields moving in hypnotic rhythms.

'Who will win, Tubruk?' Gaius' father suddenly snapped.

'The smaller, in the blue. His footwork is excellent.'

Julius summoned one of the runners for the circus betting groups and gave over a gold aureus coin, receiving a tiny blue plaque in return. Less than a minute later, the smaller man side-stepped an over-extended lunge and drew his knife lightly over the other's stomach as he stepped through. Blood spilled as over the lip of a cup and the audience erupted with cheers and curses. Julius had earned two aurei for the one he'd wagered and he pocketed the profit cheerfully. For each match that followed, he would ask Tubruk who would win as they began to feint and move. The odds sank after the start, of course, but Tubruk's eye was infallible that day. By the fourth match, all nearby spectators were craning to catch what Tubruk said and then shouting for the betting slaves to take their money.

Tubruk was enjoying himself.

'This next one is to the death. The odds favour the Corinthian fighter, Alexandros. He has never been stopped, but his opponent, from the south of Italy, is also fearful and has never been beaten to first blood. I cannot choose between them at this point.'

'Let me know as soon as you can. I have ten aurei ready for the wager – all our winnings and my original stakes. Your eye is perfect today.'

Julius summoned the betting slave and told him to stand close. No one else in the area wanted to bet, as they all felt the luck of the moment and were content to wait for the signal from Tubruk. They watched him, some with held breath, poised for the first signal.

Gaius and Marcus looked at the crowd.

'They are a greedy lot, these Romans,' Gaius whispered and they grinned at each other.

The gates opened again and Alexandros and Enzo entered. The Roman, Enzo, wore a standard set of mail covering his right arm from hand to neck and a brass helmet above the darker iron scales. He carried a red shield in his left. His only other garments were a loincloth and wrappings of linen around his feet and ankles. He had a powerful physique and carried few scars, although one puckered line marked his left forearm from wrist to elbow. He bowed to Cornelius Sulla and saluted the crowd first, before the foreigner.

Alexandros moved well, balanced and assured as he came to the middle of the amphitheatre. He was identically dressed, although his shield was stained blue.

'They are not easy to tell apart,' Gaius said. 'In the armour, they could be brothers.'

His father snorted. 'Except for the blood in them. The Greek is not the same as the Italian. He has different and false gods. He believes things that no decent Roman would ever stand for.' He spoke without turning his head, intent on the men below.

'But will you bet on such a man?' Gaius continued.

'I will if Tubruk thinks he will win,' came the response, accompanied by a smile.

The contest would begin with the sounding of a ram's horn. It was held in copper jaws in the first row of seats and a short bearded man was waiting for his own signal to set his lips to it. The two gladiators stepped close to each other and the horn sound wailed out across the sand.

Before Gaius could tell whether the sound had stopped, the crowd was roaring and the two men were hammering blows at each other. In the first few seconds, strike after strike landed, some cutting, some sliding from steel made suddenly slippery with bright blood.

'Tubruk?' came his father's voice.

Their area of the stands was torn between watching the fantastic display of savagery and getting in on the bet.

Tubruk frowned, his chin on his bunched fist.

'Not yet. I cannot tell. They are too even.'

The two men broke apart for a moment, unable to keep up the pace of the first minute. Both were bleeding and both were spattered with dust sticking to their sweat.

Alexandros rammed his blue shield up under the other's guard, breaking his rhythm and balance. His sword arm came up and over, looking for a high wound. The Italian scrambled back without dignity to escape the blow and his shield fell in the dust as he did so. The crowd hooted and jeered, embarrassed by their man. He rose again and attacked, perhaps stung by the comments of his countrymen.

'Tubruk?' Julius laid his hand on the man's arm. The fight could be over in seconds and if there was an obvious advantage to one of the fighters, the betting would cease.

'Not yet. Not . . . yet . . .' Tubruk was a study in concentration.

On the sand, the area around the fighters was speckled darkly where their blood had dripped. Both paced to the left and then the right, then rushed in and cut and sliced, ducked and blocked, punched and tried to trip the other. Alexandros caught the Italian's sword on his shield. It was partially destroyed in the force of the blow and the blade was trapped by the softer metal of the blue rectangle. Like the other, it too was wrenched to the sand and both men faced each other sideways on, moving like crabs so that their arm-mail would protect them. The swords were nicked and blunted and the exertions in the raging Roman heat were beginning to tell on their strength.

'Put it all on the Greek, quickly,' Tubruk spoke.

The betting slave looked for approval to the owner behind him. Odds were whispered and the bets went on, with much of the crowd taking a slice.

'Five to one against on Alexandros – could have been a lot better if we'd gone earlier,' Julius muttered, as he watched the two fighters below.

Tubruk said nothing.

One of the gladiators lunged and recovered too fast for the other. The sword whipped back and into his side, causing a gout of blood to rush. The riposte was viciously fast and sliced through a major leg muscle. A leg buckled and as the man went down, his opponent hacked into his neck, over and over, until he was thumping at a corpse. He lay in the mixing blood, as it was sucked away by the dry sand and his chest heaved with the pain and exertion.

'Who won?' Gaius asked frantically. Without the shields it wasn't clear, and a murmur went around the seats as the question was repeated over and over. Who had won?

'I think the Greek is dead,' the betting slave said.

His master thought it was the Roman, but until the victor rose and removed his helmet, no one could be sure.

'What happens if they both die?' Marcus asked.

'All bets are off,' replied the owner and financier of the betting slave. Presumably he had a lot of money riding on the outcome as well. Certainly he looked as tense as anyone there.

For maybe a minute, the surviving gladiator lay exhausted, his blood spilling. The crowd grew louder, calling on him to rise and take off the helmet. Slowly, in obvious pain, he grasped his sword and pushed himself up on it. Standing, he swayed slightly and reached down to take a handful of sand. He rubbed the sand into his wound, watching as it fell away in soft red clumps. His fingers too were bloody as he raised them to remove the helmet.

Alexandros the Greek stood and smiled, his face pale with loss of blood. The crowd threw abuse at the swaying figure. Coins glittered in the sun as they were thrown, not to reward, but to hurt. With curses, money was exchanged all around the amphi-theatre and the gladiator was ignored as he sank to his knees again and had to be helped out by slaves.

Tubruk watched him go, his face unreadable.

'Is he a man to see about training?' Julius asked, ebullient as his winnings were counted into a pouch.

'No – he won't last out the week, I should think. Anyway, there was little schooling in his technique, just good speed and reflexes.'

'For a Greek,' said Marcus, trying to join in.

'Yes, good reflexes for a Greek,' Tubruk replied, his mind far away.

While the sand was being raked clean, the crowd continued with their business, although Gaius and Marcus could see one or two spectators re-enacting the gladiators' blows with shouts and mock cries of pain. As they waited, the boys saw Julius tap Tubruk on his arm, bringing to his attention a pair of men approaching through the rows. Both seemed slightly out of place at the circus, with their togas of rough wool and their skins unadorned by metal jewellery.

Julius stood with Tubruk and the boys copied them. Gaius' father put out his hand and greeted the first to reach them, who bowed his head slightly on contact.

'Greetings, my friends. Please take a seat. This is my son and another boy in my care. I'm sure they can spend a few minutes buying food?'

Tubruk handed a coin to both of them and the message was clear. Reluctantly, they moved off between the rows and joined a queue at a food stall. They watched as the four men bent their heads close and talked, their voices lost in the crowd.

After a few minutes, as Marcus was buying oranges, Gaius saw the two newcomers thank his father and take his hand again. Then each moved over to Tubruk, who put coins in their hands as they left.

Marcus had bought an orange for each of them and when they'd returned to their seats he handed them out.

'Who were those men, Father?' Gaius asked, intrigued.

'Clients of mine. I have a few bound to me in the city,' Julius replied, skinning his orange neatly.

'But what do they do? I have never seen them before.'

Julius turned to his son, registering the interest. He smiled.

'They are *useful* men. They vote for candidates I support, or guard me in dangerous areas. They carry messages for me, or . . . a thousand other small things. In return, they get six denarii a day, each man.'

Marcus whistled. 'That must add up to a fortune.'

Julius transferred his attention to Marcus, who dropped his gaze and fiddled with the skin of his orange.

'Money well spent. In this city, it is good to have men I can call on quickly, for any sudden task. Rich members of the Senate may have hundreds of clients. It is part of our system.'

'Can you trust these clients of yours?' Gaius broke in.

Julius grunted. 'Not with anything worth more than six denarii a day.'

* * *

59

Renius entered without announcement. One moment, the crowd were chatting amongst themselves with the dirty sand ring empty, and the next a small door opened and a man walked out of it. At first, he wasn't noticed, then people pointed and began to stand.

'Why are they cheering so loudly?' Marcus asked, squinting at the lone figure standing in the burning sun.

'Because he has come back one more time. Now you will be able to say you saw Renius fight when you have children of your own,' Tubruk replied, smiling.

Everyone around them seemed lit up by the spectacle. A chant began and swelled: 'Ren-i-us . . . Ren-i-us.' The noise drowned out all the shuffling of feet and rustling clothing. The only sound in the world was his name.

He raised his sword in salute. Even from a distance, it was clear that age had not yet taken a good twisting grip on him.

'Looks good for sixty. Belly's not flat, though. Look at that wide belt,' Tubruk muttered almost to himself. 'You've let yourself go a little, you silly old fool.'

As the old man received the plaudits of the crowd, a single file of fighting slaves entered the sandy ring. Each wore a cloth around his loins that allowed free movement and carried a short *gladius*. No shields or armour could be seen. The Roman crowd fell quiet as the men formed a diamond with Renius at the centre. There was a moment of stillness and then the animal enclosure opened.

Even before the cage was dragged out onto the sand, the short, hacking roars could be heard. The crowd whispered in anticipation. There were three lions pacing the cage as it was dragged out by sweating slaves. Through the bars they were obscene shapes; huge humped shoulders, head and jaws tapering back to hindquarters almost as an afterthought. They were created to crush out life with massive jaws. They swiped with their paws in unfocused rage as the cage was jarred and finally came to rest.

Slaves lifted hammers aloft to knock out the wooden pegs that held the front section of the cage. The crowd licked dry lips. The hammers fell, and the iron lattice dropped onto the sand, an echo clearly heard in the silence. One by one, the great cats moved out of the cage, revealing a speed and sureness of step that was frightening.

The largest roared defiance at the group of men that faced it across the sand. When they made no move, it began to pace up and down outside the cage, watching them all the while. Its companions roared and circled and it settled back onto its haunches.

Without a signal, without a warning, it ran at the men, who shrank back visibly. This was death coming for them.

Renius could be heard barking out commands. The front of the diamond, three brave men, met the charge, swords ready. At the last moment, the lion took off in a rushing leap and smashed two of the slaves from their feet, striking with a paw on each chest. Neither moved, as their chests were shards and daggers of bone. The third man swung and hit the heavy mane, doing little damage. The jaws closed on his arm in a snap like the strike of a snake. He screamed and carried on screaming as he staggered away, one wrist holding the pumping red remains of the other. A sword scraped along the lion's ribs and another cut a hamstring so that the rear quarters went suddenly limp. This served only to enrage the beast and it snapped at itself in red confusion. Renius growled a command and the others stepped back to allow him the kill.

As he landed the fatal blow, the other two lions attacked. One caught the head of the wounded man who had wandered away. A quick crack of the jaws and it was over. That lion settled down with the corpse, ignoring the other slaves as it bit into the soft abdomen and began to feed. It was quickly killed, speared on three blades in the mouth and chest.

Renius met the charge of the last to his left. His protecting slave was tumbled by the strike and over him came the snapping rage that was the male cat. Its paws were striking and great dark claws stood out like spear points, straining to pierce and tear. Renius balanced himself and struck into the chest. A wound opened with a rush of sticky dark blood, but the blade skittered off the breastbone and Renius was struck by a shoulder, only luck letting the jaws snap where he had been. He rolled and came up well, still with sword in hand. As the beast checked and turned back on him, he was ready and sent his blade into the armpit and the bursting heart. The strength went out of it in the instant, as if the steel had lanced a boil. It lay and bled into the sand, still aware and panting, but become pitiful. A soft moan came from deep within the bloody chest as Renius approached, drawing a dagger from his belt. Reddish saliva dribbled onto the sand as the torn lungs strained to fill with air.

Renius spoke softly to the beast, but the words could not be heard in the stands. He lay a hand on the mane and patted it absently, as he would a favourite hound. Then he slipped the blade into the throat and it was over.

The crowd seemed to draw breath for the first time in hours and then laughed at the release of tension. Four men were dead on the sand, but Renius, the old killer, still stood, looking exhausted. They began to chant his name, but he bowed quickly and left the ring, striding to the shadowed door and into darkness.

'Get in quickly, Tubruk. You know my highest price. A year, mind – a full year of service.'

Tubruk disappeared into the crowds and the boys were left to make polite conversation with Julius. However, without Tubruk to act as a catalyst, the conversation died quickly. Julius loved his son, but had never enjoyed talking to the young. They prattled and knew nothing of decorum and self-restraint.

'He will be a hard teacher, if his reputation is accurate. He was once without equal in the empire, but Tubruk tells the stories better than I.'

62

The boys nodded eagerly and determined to press Tubruk for the details as soon as they had the opportunity.

The seasons had turned towards autumn on the estate before the boys saw Renius again, dismounting from a gelding in the stone yard of the stables. It was a mark of his status that he could ride like an officer or a member of the Senate. Both of them were in the hay barn adjoining, and had been jumping off the high bales onto the loose straw. Covered in hay and dust, they were not fit to be seen and peered out at the visitor from a corner. He glanced around as Tubruk came to meet him, taking the reins.

'You will be received as soon as you are refreshed from your journey.'

'I have ridden less than five miles. I am neither dirty nor sweating like an animal. Take me in now, or I'll find the way myself,' snapped the old soldier, frowning.

'I see you have lost none of your charm and lightness of manner since you worked with me.'

Renius didn't smile and for a second the boys expected a blow, or a violent retort.

'I see you have not yet learned manners to your elders. I expect better.'

'*Every*one is younger than you. Yes, I can see how you would be set in your ways.'

Renius seemed to freeze for a second, slowly blinking. 'Do you wish me to draw my sword?'

Tubruk was still, and Marcus and Gaius noticed for the first time that he too wore his old gladius in a scabbard.

'I wish you only to remember that I am in charge of the running of the estate and that I am a free man, like yourself. Our agreement benefits us both; there are no favours being done here.'

Renius smiled then. 'You are correct. Lead on then to the master

63

of the house. I would like to meet the man who has such interesting types working for him.'

As they left, Gaius and Marcus looked at each other, eyes aglow with excitement.

'He will be a hard taskmaster, but will quickly become impressed at the talent he has on his hands . . .' Marcus whispered.

'He will realise that we will be his last great work, before he drops dead,' Gaius continued, caught up in the idea.

'I will be the greatest swordsman in the land, aided by the fact that I have stretched my arms every night since I was a baby,' Marcus went on.

'The fighting monkey, they will call you!' Gaius declared in awe.

Marcus threw hay at his face and they grabbed each other with mock ferocity, rolling around for a second until Gaius ended up on top, sitting heavily on his friend's chest.

'I will be the slightly better swordsman, too modest to embarrass you in front of the ladies.'

He struck a proud pose and Marcus shoved him off into the straw again. They sat panting and lost in dreams for a moment.

At length, Marcus spoke: 'In truth, you will run this estate, like your father. I have nothing and you know my mother is a whore . . . no, don't say anything. We both heard your father say it. I have no inheritance save my name and that is stained. I can only see a bright future in the army, where at least my birth is noble enough to allow me high position. Having Renius as my trainer will help us both, but me most of all.'

'You will always be my friend, you know. Nothing can come between us.' Gaius spoke clearly, looking him in the eye.

'We will find our paths together.'

They both nodded and gripped hands for a second in the pact. As they let go, Tubruk's familiar bulk appeared as he stuck his head into the hayloft.

'Get yourselves cleaned up. Once Renius has finished with your father, he'll want some sort of inspection.'

They stood slowly, nervousness obvious in their movements.

'Is he cruel?' Gaius asked.

Tubruk didn't smile.

'Yes, he is cruel. He is the hardest man I have ever known. He wins battles because the other men feel pain and are frightened of death and dismemberment. He is more like a sword than a man and he will make you both as hard as himself. You will probably never thank him – you will hate him, but what he gives you will save your lives more than once.'

Gaius looked at him questioningly. 'Did you know him before?'

Tubruk laughed, a short bark with no humour. 'I should say so. He trained me for the ring, when I was a slave.'

His eyes flashed in the sun as he turned and he was gone.

Renius stood with his feet shoulder-width apart and his hands clasped behind his back. He frowned at the seated Julius.

'No. If anyone interferes, I will leave on that hour. You want your son and the whore's whelp to be made into soldiers. I know how to do that. I have been doing it, one way or another, all my life. Sometimes they only learn as the enemy charges, sometimes they never learn, and I have left a few of those in shallow foreign graves.'

'Tubruk will want to discuss their progress with you. His judgement is usually first-rate. He was, after all, trained by you,' Julius said, still trying to regain the initiative he felt he had lost.

This man was an overwhelming force. From the moment he entered the room, he had dominated the conversation. Instead of setting out the manner of his son's teaching, as he had intended, Julius found himself on the defensive, answering questions about his estate and training facilities. He knew better now what he did *not* have than what he did.

'They are very young, and . . .'

'Any older would be too late. Oh, you can take a man of twenty and make him a competent soldier, fit and hard. A child, though, can be fashioned into a thing of metal, unbreakable. Some would say you have already left it too late, that proper training should commence at five years. I am of the opinion that ten is the optimum to ensure the proper development of muscle and lung capacity. Earlier can break their spirits; later and their spirits are too firmly in the wrong courses.'

'I agree, to some ext—'

'Are you the real father of the whore's boy?' Renius spoke curtly, but quietly, as if inquiring after the weather.

'What? Gods, no! I –'

'Good. That would have been a complication. I accept the year contract then. My word is given. Get the boys out into the stable yard for inspection in five minutes. They saw me arrive so they should be ready. I will report to you quarterly in this room. If you cannot make the appointment, be so good as to let me know. Good day.'

He turned on his heel and strode out. Behind him, Julius blew air out of puffed cheeks in a mixture of amazement and contentment.

'Could be just what I wanted,' he said, and smiled for the first time that morning.

CHAPTER FIVE

The first thing they were told was that they would get a good night's sleep. For eight hours, from before midnight to dawn, they were left alone. At all other times they were being taught, or toughened, or cramming food into their mouths in hasty, snatched breaks of only minutes.

Marcus had had the excitement knocked out of him on that first day, when Renius took his chin in his leathery hand and peered at him.

'Weak-spirited, like his mother was.'

He'd said no more at the time, but Marcus burned with the humiliating thought that the old soldier he wanted so much to like him might have seen his mother in the city. From the first moment, his desire to please Renius became a source of shame to him. He knew he had to excel at the training, but not in such a way that the old bastard would approve.

Renius was easy to hate. From the first, he called Gaius by his name, while only referring to Marcus as the boy, or the 'whore's boy'. Gaius could see it was deliberate, some attempt to use their hatred as a tool to improve them. Yet he could not help but feel annoyance as his friend was humbled over and over again.

A stream ran through the estate, carrying cold water down to the sea. One month after his arrival, they had been taken down to the water before noon. Renius had simply motioned to a dark pool.

'Get in,' he said.

They'd looked at each other and shrugged.

The cold was numbing from the first moments.

'Stay there until I come back for you,' was the command called over his shoulder as Renius walked back up to the house, where he ate a light lunch and bathed, before sleeping through the hot afternoon.

Marcus felt the cold much more than his friend. After only a couple of hours, he was blue around the face and unable to speak for shivering. As the afternoon wore on, his legs went numb and the muscles of his face and neck ached from shivering. They talked with difficulty, anything to take their minds off the cold. The shadows moved and the talk died. Gaius was nowhere near as uncomfortable as his friend. His limbs had gone numb long before, but breathing was still easy, whereas Marcus was sipping small breaths.

The afternoon cooled unnoticed outside the eternal chill of the shaded section of fast-flowing water. Marcus rested with his head leaning to one side or the other, with an eye half-submerged and slowly blinking, seeing nothing. His mind could drift until his nose was covered, when he would splutter and raise himself straight again. Then he would dip once more, as the pain worsened. They had not spoken for a long time. It had become a private battle, but not against each other. They would stay until they were called for, until Renius came back and ordered them to climb out.

As the day fled, they both knew that they could not climb out. Even if Renius appeared at that moment and congratulated them, he would have to drag them out himself, getting wet and muddy in the process if the gods were watching at all.

Marcus slipped in and out of waking, coming back with a sudden start and realising he had somehow drifted away from the cold and the darkness. He wondered then if he would die in the river.

In one of those dreaming dozes, he felt warmth and heard the welcoming crackle of a good log fire. An old man prodded the burning wood with his toe, smiling at the sparks. He turned and seemed to notice the boy watching him, white and lost.

'Come closer to the warm, boy, I'll not hurt ye.'

The old man's face carried the wrinkles and dirt of decades of labour and worry. It was scarred and seamed like a stitched purse. The hands were covered in rope veins that shifted under the skin as the swollen knuckles moved. He was dressed like a travelling man, with patched clothes and a dark-red cloth wrapping his throat.

'What do we have here? A mudfish! Rare for these parts, but good eating on one, they say. You could cut a leg off and feed us both. I'd stop the bleeding, boy, I'm not without tricks.'

Huge eyebrows bristled and raised in interest at the thought. The eyes glittered and the mouth opened to reveal soft gums, wet and puckered. The man patted his pockets and the shadows copied his movements, flapping on dark-yellow walls that were lit only by the flames.

'Hold still, boy, I have a knife with a saw edge for you . . .' A hand like rough stone was pressed over his whole face, suddenly larger than a hand had any right to be.

The old man's breath was warm on his ear, smelling foully of rotting teeth.

He awoke choking and heaving dryly. His stomach was empty and the moon had risen. Gaius was beside him still, his face barely above the black glass water, head nodding in and out of the darkness.

It was enough. If the choice was to fail or to die, then he would fail and not mind the consequences. Tactically, that was the better choice. Sometimes, it is better to retreat and marshal your forces.

69

That was what the old man wanted them to know. He *wanted* them to give up and was probably waiting somewhere nearby, waiting for them to learn this most important of lessons.

Marcus didn't remember the dream, except for the fear of being smothered, which he still felt. His body seemed to have lost its familiar shape and just sat, heavy and waterlogged beneath the surface. He had become some sort of soft-skinned, bottom-dwelling fish. He concentrated and his mouth hung slackly, dribbling back water as cold as himself. He swayed forward and brought up his arm to hold a root. It was the first time a limb had cleared the water in eleven hours. He felt the cold of death on him and had no regrets. True, Gaius was still there, but they would have different strengths. Marcus would not die to please some poxed-up old gladiator.

He slithered out, an inch at a time, mud plastering his face and chest as he dragged himself to the bank. His bloated stomach did seem buoyant in the water, as if filled from within. The sensation as his full weight finally came to bear on the hard ground was one of ecstasy. He lay and began to shudder in spasmodic fits of retching. Yellow bile trickled weakly out of his lips and mixed with the black mud. The night was quiet and he felt as if he'd just crawled out of the grave.

Dawn found him still there and a shadow blocking the pale sun. Renius stood there and frowned, not at Marcus, but at the tiny pale figure of the boy still in the water, eyes closed and lips blue. As Marcus watched him, he saw a sudden spasm of worry cross the iron face.

'Boy!' snapped the voice they had already come to loathe. 'Gaius!'

The figure in the water lolled in the moving current, but there was no response. A muscle in Renius' jaw clenched and the old soldier stepped up to his thighs into the pool, reaching down and scooping up the ten-year-old like a puppy over his shoulder. The eyes opened with the sudden movement, but there was no focus. Marcus rose as the old man strode away with his burden, obviously heading back to the house. He tottered after, muscles protesting.

Behind them, Tubruk stood in the shadows of the opposite bank, still hidden from sight by the foliage as he had been all night. His eyes were narrowed and as cold as the river.

Renius seemed to be fuelled by a constant anger. After months of training, the boys had not seen him smile except in mockery. On bad days, he rubbed his neck as he snapped at them and gave the impression that his temper was cracking every second. He was worst in the midday sun, when his skin would mottle with irritation at the slightest mistake.

'Hold the stone straight in front!' he barked at Marcus and Gaius as they sweated in the heat. The task that afternoon was to stand with arms outstretched in front, with a rock the size of a fist held in their hands. It had been easy at first.

Gaius' shoulders were aching and his arms felt loose. He tried to tense the muscles, but they seemed out of his control. Perspiring, he watched the stone drop by a hand's width and felt a stripe of pain over his stomach as Renius struck with a short whip. His arms trembled and muscles shuddered under the pain. He concentrated on the rock and bit his lip.

'You will not let it fall. You will welcome the pain. You will not let it fall.'

Renius' voice was a harsh chant as he paced around the boys. This was the fourth time they had raised the stones and each time was harder. He barely allowed them a minute to rest their aching arms before the order to raise came again.

'Cease,' Renius said, watching to see they controlled the descent, his whip held ready. Marcus was breathing heavily and Renius curled his lip.

71

'There will come a time when you think you can't stand the pain any more and men's lives will depend on it. You could be holding a rope others are climbing, or walking forty miles in full kit to rescue comrades. Are you listening?'

The boys nodded, trying not to pant with exhaustion, just pleased he was talking instead of ordering the stones up again.

'I have seen men walk themselves to death, falling onto the road with their legs still twitching and trying to lift them. They were buried with honour.

'I have seen men of my legion keep rank and move in forma-tion, holding their guts in with one hand. They were buried with honour.' He paused to consider his words, rubbing the back of his neck as though he had been stung.

'There will be times when you want to simply sit down, when you want to give up. When your body tells you it is done and your spirit is weak.

'These are false. Savages and the beasts of the field break, but we go on.

'Do you think you are finished now? Are your arms hurting you? I tell you that you will raise that rock another dozen times this hour and you will hold it. And another dozen if you let one fall below a hand's width.'

A slave girl was washing dust from a wall at the side of the courtyard. She never looked at the boys, though occasionally she jumped slightly as the old gladiator barked a command. Gaius saw she looked exhausted herself, but he had noticed she was attractive, with long dark hair and a loose slave shift. Her face was delicate, with a pair of dark eyes and a full mouth pressed into a line by the concentration of her work. He thought her name was Alexandria.

As Renius spoke, she bent low to dip the cloth in the bucket and paused to wash the dirt from the material. Her shift gaped as she pressed the cloth into the water and Gaius could see the smooth skin of her neck running down to the soft curves of her breasts. He thought he could see right down to the skin of her stomach and imagined her nipples gently grazing against the rough cloth as she moved.

In that moment, Renius was forgotten, despite the pain in his arms.

The old man stopped speaking and turned on his heel to see what was distracting the boys from their lesson. He growled as he saw the slave and crossed to her with three quick strides, taking her arm in a cruel grip that made her cry out. His voice was a bellow.

'I am teaching these children a lesson that will save their lives and you are flashing your paps at them like a cheap whore!'

The girl cowered from his anger, pulling as far as she could reach from the held wrist.

'I . . .' she stammered, seeming dazed, but Renius swore and took her by the hair. She winced in pain and he swung her to face the boys.

'I don't care if there are a thousand of these behind my back. I am teaching you to concentrate!'

In one brutal move, he flicked her legs away with a sweep of his foot and she fell. Still holding her hair, Renius raised his whip in his other hand and brought it down sharply, in sequence with his words.

'You will *not* dis*tract* these *boys* while I *teach*.'

The girl was crying as Renius let her go. She crawled a couple of paces, then came up to a crouch and ran from the yard, sobbing.

Marcus and Gaius looked dumbfounded at Renius as he turned back to them. His expression was murderous.

'Close your mouths, boys. This was never a game. I will make you good enough and hard enough to serve the Republic after I am gone. I will not allow weakness of any kind. Now raise the stones and hold them until I say to cease.'

Once again, the boys raised their arms, not even daring to exchange glances.

That evening, when the estate was quiet and Renius had departed for the city, Gaius delayed his usual exhausted collapse into sleep to visit the slave quarters. He felt guilty being there and kept an eye out for Tubruk's shadow, though he couldn't quite have explained why.

The household slaves slept under the same roof as the family, in a wing of simple rooms. It was not a world he knew and he felt nervous as he walked along the darkening corridors, wondering whether he should knock at doors, or call her name, if it really was Alexandria.

He found her sitting on a low ledge outside an open door. She seemed lost in thought and he cleared his throat gently as he recognised her. She scrambled to her feet in fright and then held herself still, looking at the floor. She had cleaned the dust of the day from her skin and it was smooth and pale in the evening light. Her hair was tied back with a scrap of cloth and her eyes were wide with darkness.

'Is your name Alexandria?' he said quietly.

She nodded.

'I came to say sorry for today. I was watching you at your chores and Renius thought you were distracting us.'

She stood perfectly still in front of him and kept her gaze on the floor at his feet. The silence stretched for a moment and he blushed, unsure how to continue.

'Look, I am sorry. He was cruel.'

Still, she said nothing. Her thoughts were pained, but this was the son of the house. 'I am a slave,' she longed to say. 'Every day is pain and humiliation. You have nothing to say to me.'

Gaius waited for a few more moments and then walked away, wishing he hadn't come.

Alexandria watched him leave, watched the confident walk and the developing strength that Renius was bringing out. He would be as vicious as that old gladiator when he was older. He was free and Roman. His compassion came from his youth and that was fast being burned away in the training yard. Her face was hot with the anger she had not dared show. It was a small victory not to have talked to him, but she cherished it.

Renius reported their progress at the end of each quarter-year. On the evening before the appointed day, Gaius' father would return from his lodgings in the capital and receive Tubruk's summary of the estate's wealth. He would see the boys and spend a few minutes extra with his son. The following day, he would see Renius at dawn and the boys would sleep in, grateful for the slight break in their routine.

The first report had been frustratingly short.

'They have made a beginning. Both have some spirit,' Renius had stated flatly.

After a long pause, Julius realised that there was to be no further comment.

'They are obedient?' he asked, wondering at the lack of information. For this he'd paid so much gold?

'Of course,' Renius replied, his expression baffled.

'They er . . . they show promise?' Julius battled on, refusing to allow this conversation to go the way of the last one, but again feeling as if he addressed one of his old tutors instead of a man in his employ.

'A beginning has been made. This work is not accomplished quickly.'

'Nothing of value ever is,' Julius replied quietly.

They looked at each other calmly for a moment and both nodded. The interview was at an end. The old warrior shook hands with a brief touch of dry skin in a quick, hard grip and left. Julius remained standing, gazing at the door that closed behind his exit.

Tubruk thought the training methods were dangerous and had mentioned an incident where the boys could have drowned without supervision. Julius grimaced. He knew that to mention the worry to Renius would be to sever their agreement. Preventing the old murderer from going too far would rest with the estate manager.

Sighing, he sat down and thought about the problems he faced in Rome. Cornelius Sulla had continued to rise in power, bringing some towns in the south of the country into the Roman fold and away from their merchant controllers. What was the name of that last? Pompeii, some sort of mountain town. Sulla kept his name in the mind of the vacuous public with such small triumphs. He commanded a group of senators with a web of lies, bribery and flattery. They were all young and brought a shudder to the old soldier as he thought of some of them. If this was what Rome was coming to, in his lifetime!

Instead of taking the business of empire seriously, they seemed to live only for sordid pleasures of the most dubious kinds, worshipping at the temple of Aphrodite and calling themselves the 'New Romans'. There were few things that still caused outrage in the temples of the Capitol, but this new group seemed intent on finding the limits and breaking them, one by one. One of the people's tribunes had been found murdered, one who opposed Sulla whenever possible. This would not have been too remarkable in itself; he had been found in a pool, made red by a swiftly opened vein in his leg, a not uncommon mode of death. The problem was that his children too had been found killed, which looked like a warning to others. There were no clues and no witnesses. It was unlikely the murderer would ever be found, but before another tribune could be elected, Sulla had forced through a resolution that gave a general greater autonomy in the field. He had argued the need himself and was eloquent and passionate in his persuasion. The Senate had voted and his power had grown a little more, while the power of the Republic was nibbled away.

Julius had so far managed to stay neutral, but as he was related by marriage to another of the power players, his wife's brother Marius, he knew eventually that sides would have to be chosen. A wise man could see the changes coming, but it saddened him that the equalities of the Republic were felt as chains by more and more of the hotheads in Senate. Marius too felt that a powerful man could use the law rather than obey it. Already, he had proven this by making a mockery of the system used to elect consuls. Roman law said that a consul could only be elected once by the Senate and must then step down from the position. Marius had recently secured his third election with martial victories against the Cimbri tribes and the Teutones, whom he had smashed with the Primigenia legion. He was still a lion of the emerging Rome, and Julius would have to find the protection of his shadow if Cornelius Sulla continued to grow in power.

Favours would be owed and some of his autonomy would be lost if he threw his colours into the camp of Marius, but it might be the only wise choice. He wished he could consult his wife and listen to her quick mind dissect the problem as she had used to. Always, she could see an angle on a problem, or a point of view that no one else could see. He missed her wry smile and the way she would press her palms against his eyes when he was tired, bringing a wonderful coolness and peace . . .

He moved quietly through the corridors to Aurelia's rooms and paused outside the door, listening to her long slow breaths, barely audible in the silence.

Carefully, he entered the room and crossed over to the sleeping figure, kissing her lightly on the brow. She didn't stir and he sat by the bed, watching her.

Asleep, she seemed the woman he remembered. At any moment,

she could wake and her eyes would fill with intelligence and wit. She would laugh to see him sitting there in the shadows and pull back the covers, inviting him in to the warmth of her.

'Who can I turn to, my love?' he whispered. 'Who should I support and trust to safeguard the city and the Republic? I think your brother Marius cares as little for the idea as Sulla himself.' He rubbed his jaw, feeling the stubble.

'Where does safety lie for my wife and my son? Do I throw in my house to the wolf or the snake?'

Silence answered him and he shook his head slowly. He rose and kissed Aurelia, imagining just for one moment more that, if her eyes opened, someone he knew would be looking out. Then he left quietly, shutting the door softly behind him.

When Tubruk walked his watch that evening, the last of the candles had guttered out and the rooms were dark. Julius still sat in his chair, but his eyes were closed and his chest rose and fell slowly, with a soft whistle of air from his nose. Tubruk nodded to himself, pleased he was getting some rest from worry.

The following morning, Julius ate with the two boys, a small breaking of the fast with bread, fruit and a warm tisane to counter the dawn chill. The depressive thoughts of the day before had been put aside and he sat straight, his gaze clear.

'You look healthy and strong,' he said to the pair of them. 'Renius is turning you into young men.'

They grinned at each other for a second.

'Renius says we will soon be fit enough for battle training. We have shown we can stand heat and cold and have begun to find our strengths and weaknesses. All this is internal, which he says is the foundation for external skill.' Gaius spoke with animation, his hands moving slightly with his words.

Both boys were clearly growing in confidence and Julius felt a

78

pang for a moment that he was not able to see more of their growth. Looking at his son, he wondered if he would come home to a stranger one day.

'You are my son. Renius has trained many, but never a son of mine. You will surprise him, I think.' Julius looked at Gaius' incredulous expression, knowing the boy was not used to praise or admiration.

'I will try to. Marcus will surprise him too, I expect.'

Julius did not look at the other boy at the table, although he felt his eyes. As if he was not present, he answered, wanting the point to be remembered and annoyed at Gaius' attempt to bring his friend into the conversation.

'Marcus is not my son. You carry my name and my reputation with you. You alone.'

Gaius bowed his head, embarrassed and unable to hold his father's strangely compelling gaze. 'Yes, Father,' he muttered and continued to eat.

Sometimes, he wished there were other children, brothers or sisters to play with and to carry the burden of his father's hopes. Of course, he would not give up the estate to them, that was his alone and always had been, but occasionally he felt the pressure as an uncomfortable weight. His mother especially, when she was quiet and placid, would croon to him that he was all the children she had been allowed, one perfect example of life. She often told him that she would have liked daughters to dress and pass on her wisdom to, but the fever that had struck her at his birth had taken that chance away.

Renius came into the warm kitchen. He wore open sandals with a red soldier's tunic and short leggings that ended on his calves, stretched tight over almost obscenely large muscles, the legacy of life as an infantryman in the legions. Despite his age, he seemed to burn with health and vitality. He halted in front of the table, his back straight and his eyes bright and interested.

'With your permission, sir, the sun is rising and the boys must run five miles before it clears the hills.'

Julius nodded and the two boys stood quickly, waiting for his dismissal.

'Go – train hard,' he said, smiling. His son looked eager, the other – there was something else there in those dark eyes and brows. Anger? No, it was gone. The pair raced off and the two men were once again left alone. Julius indicated the table.

'I hear you are intending to begin battle school with them soon.'

'They are not strong enough yet; they may not be this year, but I am not just a fitness instructor to them, after all.'

'Have you given any thought to continuing their training after the year contract is up?' Julius asked, hoping his casual manner masked his interest.

'I will retire to the country next year. Nothing is likely to change that.'

'Then these two will be your last students – your last legacy to Rome,' Julius replied.

Renius froze for a second and Julius let no trace of his emotions betray themselves on his face.

'It is something to think about,' Renius said at last, before turning on his heel and going into the grey dawn light.

Julius grinned wolfishly behind him.

CHAPTER SIX

'As officers, you will ride to the battle, but fighting from horseback is not our chief strength. Although we use cavalry for quick, smashing attacks, it is the footmen of the twenty-eight legions that break the enemy. Every man of the one hundred and fifty thousand legionaries we have in the field at any given moment of any day can walk thirty miles in full armour, carrying a pack that is a third his own weight. He can then fight the enemy, without weakness and without complaint.'

Renius eyed the two boys who stood in the heat of the noon sun, returned from a run and trying to control their breathing. More than three years he had given them, the last he would ever teach. There was so much more for them to learn! He paced around them as he spoke, snapping the words out.

'It is not the luck of the gods that has given the countries of the world into the palms of Rome. It is not the weakness of the foreign tribes that leads them to throw themselves onto our swords in battle. It is our *strength*, greater and deeper than anything they can bring to the field. That is our first tactic. Before our men even reach the battle, they will be unbreakable in their strength and their morale. More, they will have a discipline that the armies of the world can blood themselves against without effect.

'Each man will know that his brothers at his side will have to be killed to leave him. That makes him stronger than the most

81

heroic charge, or the vain screams of savage tribes. We walk to battle. We stand and they die.'

Gaius' breathing slowed and his lungs ceased to clamour for oxygen. In the three years since Renius had first arrived at his father's villa, he had grown in height and strength. Approaching fourteen years of age, he was showing signs of the man he would one day be.

Burned the colour of light oak by the Roman sun, he stood easily, his frame slim and athletic, with powerful shoulders and legs. He could run for hours round the hills and still find reserves for a burst of speed as his father's estate came into view again.

Marcus too had undergone changes, both physically and in his spirit. The innocent happiness of the boy he had been came and went in flashes now. Renius had taught him to guard his emotions and his responses. He had been taught this with the whip and without kindness of any kind for three long years. He too had well-developed shoulders, tapering down into lightning-fast fists that Gaius could not match any more. Inside him, the desire to stand on his own, without help from his line or the patronage of others, was like a slow acid in his stomach.

As Renius watched, both boys became calm and stood to attention, watching him warily. It was not unknown for him to suddenly strike at an exposed stomach, testing, always testing for weakness.

'Gladii, gentlemen – fetch your swords.'

Silently, they turned away and collected the short swords from pegs on the training yard wall. Heavy leather belts were buckled around their waists, with a leather 'frog' attached, a holder for the sword. The scabbard slid snugly into the frog, tightly held by lacing so that it would remain immobile if the blade was suddenly drawn.

Properly attired, they returned to the attention position, waiting for the next order.

'Gaius, you observe. I will use the boy to make a simple point.'

Renius loosened his shoulders with a crack and grinned as Marcus slowly drew the gladius.

'First position, boy. Stand like a soldier, if you can remember how.'

Marcus relaxed into the first position, legs shoulder-width apart, body slightly turned from full frontal, sword held at waist height, ready to strike for the groin, stomach or throat, the three main areas of attack. Groin and neck were favourites as a deep cut there would mean the opponent bled to death in seconds.

Renius shifted his weight and Marcus' point wavered to follow the movement.

'Slashing the air again? If you do that, I'll see it and pattern you. I only need one opening to cut your throat out, one blow. Let me guess which way you're going to shift your weight and I'll cut you in two.' He began to circle Marcus, who remained relaxed, his eyebrows raised over a face blank of expression. Renius continued to talk.

'You want to kill me, don't you, boy? I can *feel* your hatred. I can *feel* it like good wine in my stomach. It cheers me up, boy, can you believe that?'

Marcus attacked in a sudden move, without warning, without signal. It had taken hundreds of hours of drill for him to eliminate all his 'tells', his telegraphing tensions of muscle that gave away his intentions. No matter how fast he was, a good opponent would gut him if he signalled his thoughts before each move.

Renius was not there when the stabbing lunge ended. His gladius pressed up against Marcus' throat.

'Again. You were slow and clumsy as usual. If you weren't faster than Gaius, you'd be the worst I'd ever seen.'

Marcus gaped and, in a split second, the sun-warmed gladius was pressed against his inner thigh, by the big pulsing vein that carried his life.

Renius shook his head in disgust.

'*Never* listen to your opponent. *Gaius* is observing, you are fighting. You concentrate on how I am moving, not the words I speak, which are simply to distract you. Again.'

They circled in the shadows of the yard.

'Your mother was clumsy in bed at first.' Renius' sword snaked out as he spoke and was snapped aside with a bell ring of metal. Marcus stepped in and pressed his blade against the leathery old skin of Renius' throat. His expression was cold and unforgiving.

'Predictable,' Marcus muttered, glaring into the cold blue eyes, nettled nonetheless.

He felt a pressure and looked down to see a dagger held in Renius' left hand, touching him lightly on the stomach. Renius grinned.

'Many men will hate you enough to take you with them. They are the most dangerous of all. They can run right onto your sword and blind you with their thumbs. I've seen that done by a woman to one of my men.'

'Why did she hate him so much?' Marcus asked as he took a pace away, sword still ready to defend.

'The victors will always be hated. It is the price we pay. If they love you, they will do what you want, but when they want to do it. If they fear you, they will do your will, but when you want them to. So, is it better to be loved or feared?'

'Both,' Gaius said, seriously.

Renius smiled. 'You mean adored and respected, which is the impossible trick if you are occupying lands that are only yours by right of strength and blood. Life is never a simple problem from question to answer. There are always many answers.'

The two boys looked baffled and Renius snorted in irritation.

'I will show you what discipline means. I will show you what you have already learned. Put your swords away and stand back to attention.'

The old gladiator looked the pair over with a critical eye.

Without warning, the noon bell sounded and he frowned, his manner changing in an instant. His voice lost the snap of the tutor and, for once, was low and quiet.

'There are food riots in the city, did you know that? Great gangs that destroy property and stream away like rats when someone is brave enough to draw a sword on them. I should be there, not playing games with children. I have taught you for two years longer than my original agreement. You are not ready, but I will not waste any more of my evening years on you. Today is your last lesson.' He stepped over to Gaius, who stared resolutely ahead.

'Your father should have met me here and heard my report. The fact that he is late for the first time in three years tells me what?'

Gaius cleared his dry throat. 'The riots in Rome are worse than you believed.'

'Yes. Your father will not be here to see this last lesson. A pity. If he is dead and I kill you, who will inherit the estate?'

Gaius blinked in confusion. The man's words seemed to jar with his reasonable tone. It was as if he were ordering a new tunic.

'My uncle Marius, although he is with the Primigenia legion – the First-Born. He will not be expecting –'

'A good standard, the Primigenia, did well in Egypt. My bill will be sent to him. Now I will indulge you as the current master of the estate, in your father's absence. When you are ready, you will face me for real, not a practice, not to first blood, but an attack such as you might face if you were walking the streets of Rome today, among the rioters.

'I will fight fairly, and if you kill me you may consider yourself to have graduated from my tutelage.'

'Why kill us after all the time you have –' Marcus spluttered, breaking discipline to speak without permission.

'You have to face death at some point. I cannot continue to train you and there is a last lesson to be learned about fear and anger.'

For a moment, Renius looked unsure of himself, but then his head straightened and the 'snapping turtle', as the slaves called him, was back, his intensity and energy overpowering.

'You are my last pupils. My reputation as I go into retirement hangs on your sorry necks. I will not let you go improperly trained, so that my name is blackened by your deeds. My name is something I have spent my life protecting. It is too late to consider losing it now.'

'We would not embarrass you,' Marcus muttered, almost to himself.

Renius rounded on him. 'Your every stroke embarrasses me. You hack like a butcher attacking a bull carcass in a rage. You cannot control your temper. You fall for the simplest trap as the blood drains from your head! And YOU!' He turned to Gaius, who had begun to grin. 'You cannot keep your thoughts from your groin long enough to make a Roman of you. Nobilitas? My blood runs cold at the thought of boys like you carrying on my heritage, my city, my people.'

Gaius dropped the grin at the reference to the slave girl that Renius had whipped in front of them for distracting the boys. It still shamed him and a slow anger began to grow as the tirade continued.

'Gaius, you may choose which of you will duel first. Your first tactical decision!' Renius turned and strode away onto the fighting square laid out in mosaic on the training ground. He stretched his leg muscles behind them, seemingly oblivious to their dumb-struck gazes.

'He has gone mad,' Marcus whispered. 'He'll kill us both.'

'He is still playing games,' Gaius said grimly. 'Like with the river. I'm going to take him. I think I can do it. I'm certainly not going to refuse the challenge. If this is how I show him that he has taught me well, then so be it. I will thank him in his own blood.'

Marcus looked at his friend and saw his resolution. He knew

86

that, as much as he didn't want either of them to fight Renius, it was he who had the better chance. Neither could win outright, but only Marcus had the speed to take the old man with him into the void.

'Gaius,' he murmured. 'Let me go first.'

Gaius looked him in the eye, as if to gauge his thoughts.

'Not this time. You are my friend. I do not want to see him kill you.'

'Nor I you. Yet I am the fastest of us – I have a better chance.'

Gaius loosened his shoulders and smiled tightly. 'He is only an old man, Marcus. I'll be back in a moment.'

Alone, Gaius took up his position.

Renius watched him through eyes narrowed against the sun. 'Why did you choose to fight first?'

Gaius shrugged. 'All lives end. I chose to. That is enough.'

'Aye, it is. Begin, boy. Let's see if you have learned anything.'

Gently, smoothly, they began to move around each other, gladii held out and flat-bladed, catching the sun.

Renius feinted with a sudden shift of a shoulder. Gaius read the feint and forced the old man back a step, with a lunge. The blades clashed and the battle began. They struck and parried, came together in a twist of heaving muscle and the old warrior threw the young boy backwards, sprawling in the dust.

For once, Renius didn't mock him, his face remaining impassive. Gaius rose slowly, balanced. He could not win with strength.

He took two quick steps forward and brought the blade up in a neat slice, breaking past the defence and cutting deeply into the mahogany skin of Renius' chest.

The old man grunted in surprise as the boy pressed the attack without pause, cut after cut. Each was parried with tiny shifts of weight and movements of the blade. The boy would clearly tire himself in the sun, ready for the butcher's knife.

Sweat poured into Gaius' eyes. He felt desperate, unable to think

87

of new moves that might work against this hard-eyed thing of wood that read and parried him so easily. He flailed and missed and, as he overbalanced, Renius extended his right arm, sinking the blade into the exposed lower abdomen.

Gaius felt his strength go. His legs seemed weak sticks and folded beyond his control under him, rubbery and painless. Blood spattered the dust, but the colours had gone from the courtyard, replaced by the thump of his heartbeat and flashes in his eyes.

Renius looked down and Gaius could see his eyes shine with moisture. Was the old man crying?

'Not . . . good . . . enough,' the old gladiator spat. Renius stepped forward, his eyes full of pain.

The brightness of the sun was blocked by a dark bar of shadow as Marcus slid his sword under the sagging throat skin of the old warrior. One step behind Renius, he could see the old man stiffen in surprise.

'Forgotten me?' It would be the work of a single thought to pull the blade back sharply and end the vicious old man, but Marcus had glanced at the body of his friend and knew the life was pouring out of him. He allowed the rage to build inside him for a moment and the chance for a quick death disappeared as Renius stepped smoothly away and brought up his bloody sword again. His face was stone, but his eyes shone.

Marcus began his attack, in past the guard and out before the old man had a chance to move. If he had been trying for a fatal blow, it would have landed, as the old man held immobile, his face rigid with tension. As it was, the blow was simply a loosener and the life in the old man came back with a rush.

'Can't you even kill me when I hold still for the strike?' Renius snapped as he began to circle again, keeping his right side to Marcus.

'You were always a fool – you have a fool's pride,' Marcus almost

88

growled at him, forced to pay attention to this man as his friend died in the heat, alone.

He attacked again, his thought become deeds, no reflection or decision, simply blows and moves, unstoppable. Red mouths opened on the old body and Marcus could hear the spatter of blood on the dust like spring rain.

Renius had no time to speak again. He defended desperately, his face showing shock for a second before settling into his gladiatorial mask. Marcus moved with extraordinary grace and balance, too fast to counter, a warrior born.

Again and again, the old man only knew he had stopped a blow when he heard the clash of metal as his body moved and reacted without conscious thought. His mind seemed detached from the fight.

His thoughts spoke in a dry voice: 'I am an old fool. This one may be the best I have trained, but I have killed the other – that was a mortal blow.'

His left arm hung, flapping obscene and loose, the shoulder muscle sliced. The pain was like a hammer and he felt sudden exhaustion slam into him, like the years catching up with him at last. The boy had never been this fast before, it was as if the sight of his friend dying had opened doors within him.

Renius felt his strength desert him in one despairing sigh. He had seen so many at this point where the spirit cannot take the flesh further. He warded off the battered blade of the gladius without energy, batting it away for what he knew would be the last time.

'Cease, or I will drop you where you stand,' came a new voice, quiet, but carrying somehow through the courtyard and house.

Marcus didn't pause. He had been trained not to react to taunts and no one was taking this kill from him. He tensed his shoulders to drive in the iron blade.

'This bow will kill you, boy. Put the sword down.'

Renius looked Marcus in the eyes, seeing madness there for a moment. He *knew* the lad would kill him and then the light was gone and control had come back.

Even with the heat of his own blood warming his limbs, the yard seemed cold to the old man as he watched Marcus glide backwards out of range and then turn to look at the newcomer. Renius had rarely been so certain of his own death to come.

There was a bow, with a glinting arrowhead. An old man, older than Renius, held the bow without a shiver of muscle, despite the obvious heft of the draw. He wore a rough brown robe and a smile that stretched over only a few teeth.

'No one has to die here today. I would know. Put the weapon away and let me summon doctors and cool drinks for you.'

Reality came back to Marcus in a rush. The gladius dropped from his hand as he spoke.

'Gaius, my friend, is injured. He may die. He needs help.'

Renius sank onto one knee, unable to stand. His sword fell from nerveless fingers and the red stain widened around him as his head bowed. Marcus walked past him without a downward glance, over to where Gaius lay.

'His appendix has been ruptured, I see,' the old man said over his shoulder.

'Then he is dead. When the appendix swells, it is always fatal. Our doctors cannot remove the swollen thing.'

'I have done it, once before. Summon the slaves of the house to bear this boy inside. Fetch me bandages and heated water.'

'Are you a healer?' Marcus asked, searching the man's eyes for hope.

'I have picked up a few things on my travels. It is not over yet.' Their eyes met.

Marcus looked away, nodding to himself. He trusted the stranger, but could not have said why.

Renius slid onto his back, his chest barely moving. He looked like what he was, a frail old brown stick of a man, made hard but brittle in the Roman sun. As Marcus' gaze fell on him, he tried to rise, shuddering with weakness.

Marcus felt a hand press down on his shoulder, interrupting his rage as it grew again. Tubruk stood beside him, his face black with anger. Marcus could feel the ex-gladiator's hand shake slightly.

'Relax, boy. There'll be no more fighting. I have sent for Lucius and your mother's doctor.'

'You saw?' Marcus stammered.

Tubruk tightened his grip.

'The end of it. I hoped you would kill him,' he said grimly, looking over to where Renius bled. Tubruk's expression was hard as he turned back to the newcomer.

'Who are you, ancient? A poacher? This is a private estate.'

The old man stood slowly and met Tubruk's eyes.

'Just a traveller, a wanderer,' he said.

'Will he die?' Marcus interrupted.

'Not today, I think,' the old man replied. 'It would not be right after I have arrived – am I not a guest of the house now?'

Marcus blinked in confusion, trying to weigh the reasonable sound of the words with the still swirling pain and rage inside him.

'I don't even know your name,' he said.

'I am Cabera,' the old man said, softly. 'Peace now. I will help you.'

CHAPTER SEVEN

Gaius lifted into consciousness, woken by angry voices in the room. His head pounded and he felt weak in every bone. Pain from below his waist heaved in great waves, with answering throbs at pulse points on his body. His mouth was dry and he could not speak or keep his eyes open. The darkness was soft and red and he tried to go back under, not yet willing to join the conscious struggle again.

'I have removed the perforated appendix, and tied off the severed vessels. He has lost a great deal of blood, which will take time to be replenished, but he is young and strong.' A stranger's voice – one of the estate doctors? Gaius didn't know or care. As long as he wasn't going to die, they should just leave him alone to get well.

'My wife's doctor says you are a charlatan.' His father's voice, no give in it.

'He would not operate on such a wound – so you have lost nothing, yes? I have removed the appendix once before, it is not a fatal operation. The only problem is the onset of fever, which he must fight on his own.'

'I was taught that it was always fatal. The appendix swells and bursts. It cannot be removed as you might cut off a finger.' His father sounded tired, Gaius thought.

'Nevertheless, I have done so. I have also bandaged the older

92

man. He too will recover, although he will never fight again, with the damage to his left shoulder. All will live here. You should sleep.'

Gaius heard footsteps cross his room and felt the warm, dry skin of his father's palm on his damp forehead.

'He is my only child; how can I sleep, Cabera? Would you sleep if it was your child?'

'I would sleep like a baby. We have done all that we can. I will continue to watch over him, but you must get your rest.' The other voice seemed kind, but not the rounded tones of the physicians that tended his mother. There was a trace of a strange accent, a mellifluous rhythm as he spoke.

Gaius sank into sleep again as if he held a dark weight on his chest. The voices continued on the edge of hearing, slipping in and out of fever dreams.

'Why have you not closed the wound with stitches? I've seen a lot of battle wounds, but we close them and bind them . . .'

'This is why the Greek dislikes my methods. The wound must have a drain for the pus that will fill it as the fever strengthens. If I closed it tight, the pus would have nowhere to go and poison his flesh. Then he would surely die, as most do. This could save him.'

'If he dies, I will cut your own appendix out myself.'

There was a cackle and a few words in a strange language that echoed in Gaius' dreams.

'You would have a job finding it. Here is the scar from when my father removed mine many years ago – with the drain.'

Gaius' father spoke with finality: 'I will trust your judgement then. You have my thanks and more if he lives.'

Gaius woke as a cool hand touched his forehead. He looked into blue eyes, bright in skin the colour of walnut wood.

'My name is Cabera, Gaius. It is good to meet you at last and

93

at such a moment in your life. I have been travelling for thousands of your miles. It is enough to make me believe in the gods to have arrived here when I was needed. No?'

Gaius couldn't respond. His tongue was thick and solid in his mouth. As if reading his thoughts, the old man reached over and brought a shallow bowl of water to his lips.

'Drink a little. The fever is burning the moisture from your body.'

The few drops slid into his mouth and loosened the gummy saliva that had gathered there. Gaius coughed and his eyes closed again. Cabera looked down at the boy and sighed for a moment. He checked that there was no one around and then placed his bony old hands over the wound, around the thin wood tube that still dribbled sluggish fluid.

A warmth came from his hands that Gaius could feel even in his dreams. He felt tendrils of heat spread up into his chest and settle into his lungs, clearing away fluid.

The heat built until it was almost painful and then Cabera took his hands away and sat still, his breathing suddenly harsh and broken.

Gaius opened his eyes again. He still felt too weak to move, but the feeling of liquid moving inside him had gone. He could breathe again.

'What did you do?' he murmured.

'Helped a little, yes? You needed a little help, even after all my skills as a surgeon.' The old face was deeply lined with exhaustion, but his eyes still shone out from the dark creases. The hand was pressed against his forehead again.

'Who are you?' he whispered.

The old man shrugged. 'I am still working on an answer to that. I have been a beggar and the chief of a village. I think of myself as a seeker after truths, with a new truth for each place I reach.'

94

'Can you help my mother?' Gaius kept his eyes closed, but he could hear the soft sigh that came from the man.

'No, Gaius. Her problem is in her mind, or the soul, perhaps. I can help a little with physical hurt, but nothing more. It is much simpler. I am sorry. Sleep now, lad. Sleep is the real healer, not I.'

Darkness came, as if ordered.

When he woke again, Renius was sitting on the bed, his face unreadable as always. As Gaius opened his eyes, he took in the changed appearance of his teacher. His left shoulder was heavily bound close to the body and there was a pallor under the sun-darkened skin.

'How are you, lad? I can't tell you how good it is to see you getting better. That old tribesman must be a miracle worker.' The voice at least was the same, curt and hard.

'I think he may be, yes. I'm surprised to see you here after almost killing me,' Gaius murmured, feeling his heart pump faster as the memories came fresh. He felt sweat break out on his forehead.

'I did not mean to cut you badly. It was a mistake. I am sorry.' The old man looked into his eyes for forgiveness and found it there waiting for him.

'Don't be sorry. I am alive and you are alive. Even you make mistakes.'

'When I thought I'd killed you . . .' There was pain in the old face.

Gaius struggled to sit up and found, to his surprise, that his strength was growing.

'You did not kill me. I will always be proud to say it was you who trained me. Let there be no more words on this. It is done.'

For a second Gaius was struck by the ridiculousness of a thirteen-year-old boy comforting the old gladiator, but the words came easily as he realised he felt a genuine affection for this

95

man, especially now he could see him as a man and not a perfect warrior, cut from some strange stone.

'Is my father still here?' he asked, hoping he would be.

Renius shook his head. 'He had to return to the city, though he sat by your bed for the first few days, until we were sure you were on the mend. The riots grow worse and Sulla's legion has been recalled to establish order.'

Gaius nodded and held out his clenched hand before him.

'I would like to be there, to see the legion come through the gates.'

Renius smiled at the young man's enthusiasm.

'Not this time, I think, but you will see more of the city when you are well again. Tubruk is outside. Are you strong enough to see him?'

'I feel much better, almost normal. How long has it been?'

'A week. Cabera gave you herbs to keep you asleep. Even so, you've healed incredibly quickly, and I've seen a lot of wounds. That old man calls himself a seer. I think he does have a little magic about him, that one. I'll call Tubruk.'

As Renius rose, Gaius put out his hand. 'Will you be staying on?'

Renius smiled, but shook his head. 'The training is over. I am retiring to my own little villa, to grow old in peace.'

Gaius hesitated for a second. 'Do you . . . have a family?'

'I had one, once, but they are long gone. I will spend my evenings with the other old men, telling lies and drinking good red wine. I will keep an eye on your life, though. Cabera says you are someone special, and I don't believe that old devil is wrong very often.'

'Thank you,' Gaius said, unable to put into words what the gladiator had given him.

Renius nodded and took his hand and wrist in a firm grip. Then he was gone and the room felt suddenly empty.

Tubruk filled the doorway and smiled a slow smile. 'You look better. There is colour in your cheeks.'

Gaius grinned at him, beginning to feel like his old self again. 'I feel stronger. I have been lucky.'

'No such thing. Cabera's responsible. He is an amazing man. He must be eighty, but when your mother's latest doctor complained about how you were treated, Cabera took him outside and gave him a hiding. I haven't laughed so hard in a long time. He has a lot of strength in those skinny arms and a fast right cross as well. You should have seen it.' He chuckled at the memory, then his face became sober.

'Your mother wanted to see you, but we thought it would . . . distress her too much until you were well. I'll bring her in tomorrow.'

'Now would be all right. I am not too tired.'

'No. You are still weak and Cabera says you shouldn't be overworked with visitors.'

Gaius' face showed mock surprise at Tubruk taking advice from anyone.

Tubruk smiled again. 'Well, as I said, he is an amazing man and, after what he managed with you, what he says goes, as far as your care is concerned. I only let Renius in here because he was leaving today.'

'I am glad you did. I would not have liked to leave unfinished business.'

'That's what I thought.'

'I'm surprised you didn't take his head off,' Gaius said cheerfully.

'I thought about it, but accidents happen in training. He just went too far, that's all. For what it's worth, he's proud of both of you. I think the old bastard developed a liking for you, probably for your stubbornness – you're as bad as he is, I think.'

'How is Marcus?' Gaius asked.

'Itching to get in here, of course. You might try to convince him it wasn't his fault. He says he should have forced you to let him fight first, but . . .'

'It was my decision and I don't regret it. I lived, after all.'

Tubruk snorted. 'Don't become overconfident. It makes a man believe in the power of prayer to see you survive a wound like that. If it wasn't for Cabera, you would not have survived it. You do owe him your life. Your father has been trying to get him to accept some sort of reward, but he won't take anything except his keep. I still don't really know why he is here. He seems to believe . . . that we are moved by the gods like we throw dice, and they wanted him to see the glorious city of Rome before he was too old.' The bluff freedman looked perplexed and Gaius thought that it wouldn't help to mention his strange memory of the heat from Cabera's hands. That would keep, no doubt.

'I will get some soup brought in. Would you like some fresh bread with it?'

Gaius' stomach agreed wholeheartedly and Tubruk left, smiling once again.

Renius gained the saddle of his gelding with difficulty. His left arm felt useless, the pain more than the simple ache of healing gashes he had known so many times before.

He was pleased there were no servants or slaves around to see his clumsiness. The great estate house seemed deserted.

At last, he was able to grip the body of the horse with his legs, allowing his muscles to support their weight. Even with evening coming on, he would make it back to the city before complete darkness. He sighed at the thought. What was there, really, for him now? He would sell his town house, although the prices had dropped during the rioting. Perhaps it would be better to wait until the streets were quiet again. With Sulla leading his legion into the city, there would be executions and public floggings, but order would eventually be restored. It had happened before. The Romans did not like war on their doorstep. They thrilled to hear of broken armies of barbarians, but no one enjoyed the brutality of martial law, with a curfew and the scarcity of food that would inevitably . . .

He heard a sound behind him and his thoughts were interrupted.

Marcus stood watching him, his face calm. 'I came to wish you goodbye.'

Almost unconsciously, Renius noticed the developed shoulders and the easy way of standing the boy had. He would make a name for himself in some future the old warrior would not be there to see.

A shiver touched him at the thought. No one lives for ever, not an Alexander, not a Scipio or a Hannibal, not even a Renius.

'I am glad Gaius is healing,' Renius replied, clearly.

'I know. I did not come to be angry at you, but to apologise,' Marcus replied, looking at the sand at his feet.

Renius raised his eyebrows.

Marcus took a deep breath. 'I am sorry I did not kill you, you twisted, evil bastard. If our paths ever cross in later years, I will take your throat out.'

Renius swayed in the saddle, as if the words were blows. He could feel the hatred and it cheered him up immensely. Laughter threatened to overcome him as the little cockerel made its threats, but he realised he could give a last gift to his pupil, if he chose his words carefully.

'Such hatred will kill you, boy. And then you won't be there to protect Gaius.'

'I will always be there for him.'

'No. Not until you can keep your temper. You will die in some brawl in a stinking bar room, unless you can find calm in yourself.

99

You would have killed me, yes; at my age, my stamina melts faster than I care to admit. But if we had met when I was young, I would have cut through you faster than corn falls to the knife. Remember that the next time you meet a young man with a reputation to make.' Renius grinned then and it was like seeing the teeth of a shark, lips sliding back over a cruel expression.

'He may get the chance sooner than you think,' Cabera said, coming out of the shadows.

'What? You were listening, you old devil?' Renius said, still smiling, although his expression eased at the sight of the healer, whom he had come to respect.

'Look to the city. You will not be going anywhere tonight, I think,' Cabera continued, his expression serious.

Both Marcus and Renius turned to look out over the hills. Although Rome was hidden by the rise of the land, an orange glow grew brighter as they watched in horror.

'Jupiter's balls – they've set the city on fire!' Renius spat. His beloved city.

For a moment, he thought of spurring the horse away, knowing his place should be in the streets. Men knew his face, he could help restore order. A cool hand touched his ankle and he looked down into the face of old Cabera.

'I see the future occasionally. If you go there now, you will be dead by dawn. This is truth.'

Renius shifted his weight and the gelding clopped its hooves on the sand, feeling his emotions.

'And if I stay?' he snapped.

Cabera shrugged. 'You may die here too. The slaves will be coming to loot this place. We don't have long now.'

Marcus gaped at the words. There were close to five hundred slaves on the estate. If they all went wild, there would be butchery. Without another word, he ran back into the buildings, shouting for Tubruk to raise the alarm.

'Would you like a hand dismounting from that fine gelding?' asked Cabera, his eyes wide and innocent.

Renius grimaced, suddenly able to muster his usual anger despite the cheerful old man.

'The gods don't tell us what is going to happen,' he said.

Cabera smiled wistfully. 'I used to believe that. When I was young and arrogant I used to think I could somehow read people, see their true selves and guess at what they would do. It was years before I was humble enough to know it could not be me. It isn't like glancing through a clear window. I just look at you and towards the city and I feel death. Why not? Many men have talents that could almost be magic to those without them. Think of it like that if it makes you more comfortable. Come on. You will be needed here tonight.'

Renius snorted. 'I suppose you have made a lot of money with this talent of yours?'

'Once or twice I have, but money does not stay with me. It steals out into the hands of wine merchants and loose women and gamblers. All I have is my experiences, but they are worth more than coin.'

After a few moments of thought, Renius accepted the helping hand and was not surprised to find it steady and strong, not after seeing those skinny shoulders pull the heavy bow in the training yard.

'You will have to hold my scabbard for me, old man. I will be all right when my sword is out.' He began to lead the horse back into the stables, stroking its nose and murmuring that they would ride later, when all the excitement was over. He paused for a moment.

'You can see the future?'

Cabera grinned and hopped from one foot to the other, amused.

'You want to know if you will live or die here, yes?' he chattered. 'That is what everyone asks.'

Renius found his usual sourness coming back in force.

'No. I don't think I do want to know that. Keep it to yourself, magician.' He led the horse away without looking back, his shoulders showing his irritation.

When he had gone, Cabera's face filled with grief. He liked the man and was pleased to find that a sort of decency still resided in his heart, despite the fame and money he had won in his life.

'Perhaps I should have let you go and wither with the other old men, my friend,' he muttered to himself. 'You might even have found happiness somewhere. Yet if you had left, the boys would have been surely killed, so this is a sin I can live with, I think.' His eyes were bleak as he turned to the great gates of the estate outer wall and began to push them closed. He wondered if he too would die in this foreign land, unknown in his own. He wondered if his father's spirit was close by and watching and decided that it probably wasn't. His father at least had the sense not to sit in the cave and wait for the bear to come home.

Galloping hoof-beats sounded in the distance. Cabera held the main gate open as he watched the approaching figure. Was it the first of the attackers, or a messenger from Rome? He cursed his vision that allowed him such fragmentary glimpses into the future, and never anything that involved himself. Here he was holding the door for the rider, so he had had no warning. The clearest visions were those in which he wasn't involved at all, which was probably meant to be a lesson from the gods – one rather wasted on him, on the whole. He had found that he could not live life as an observer.

A tail of dark dust followed the figure, barely showing in the gloom of the gathering twilight.

'Hold the gate!' a voice commanded.

Cabera raised an eyebrow. What did the man think he was doing?

Gaius' father Julius came thundering through the opening. His face was red and his rich clothes were stained with soot.

'Rome is on fire,' he said as he jumped to the ground. 'But they will not get my home.' In that moment, he recognised Cabera and patted his shoulder in greeting.

'How is my son?'

'Doing well. I am . . .' Cabera tailed off, as the vigorous older version of Gaius strode away to organise the defences. Tubruk's name echoed around the internal corridors of the estate.

Cabera looked puzzled for a moment. The visions had changed a little – the man was a force of nature and might just be enough to tip the balance in their favour.

His mind went blank again as he heard the shouts rise in the fields. Muttering in frustration, Cabera climbed the steps up to the estate wall, to use his eyes where his internal vision had failed.

Darkness filled every horizon, but Cabera could see pinpoint pricks of light moving in the fields, meeting and multiplying like fireflies. Each would be a lamp or a torch held by angry slaves, their blood warmed by the heat of the sky over the capital. They were already marching towards the great estate.

CHAPTER EIGHT

All the house servants and slaves stayed loyal. Lucius the estate doctor unwrapped his bandages and materials, spreading vicious-looking metal tools on a piece of cloth on one of the wide kitchen tables. He collared two of the kitchen boys as they were grabbing cleavers to help in the battle.

'You two stay with me. You'll get your fill of cutting and blood right here.' They were reluctant, but Lucius was more of an old family friend and his word had always been law to them before. The lawlessness that was rife in Rome had not yet spread to the estate.

Outside, Renius had everyone in the yard. Grimly, he counted them. Twenty-nine men and seventeen women.

'How many of you have been in the army?' his voice rapped.

Six or seven hands rose.

'You men have priority for swords. The rest of you go and find anything that will cut or crush. Run!'

The last word shocked the frightened men and women out of their lethargy and they scattered. Those who had already found weapons remained, their faces dark and full of fear.

Renius walked up to one of them, a short, fat cook with an enormous cleaver resting on his shoulder. 'What's your name?' he said.

'Caecilius,' came the reply. 'I'll tell my children I fought with you when this is over.'

'That you will. We don't have to break a full assault. The attackers are out for easy targets to rape and rob. I mean to make this estate a little too hard to crack for them to bother with. How's your nerve?'

'Good, sir. I'm used to killing pigs and calves, so I won't faint at a drop or two of blood.'

'This is a little different. These pigs have swords and clubs. Don't hesitate. Throat and groin. Find something to block a blow – some sort of shield.'

'Yes, sir, directly.'

The man attempted to salute and Renius forced himself to smile, biting back his temper at the sloppy manners. He watched the fat figure run away into the buildings and wiped the first beads of sweat from his brow. Strange that such men as that should understand loyalty where so many others threw it aside at the first hint of freedom. He shrugged. Some men would always be animals and others would be . . . men.

Marcus walked out into the yard, his sword out of its scabbard. He was smiling.

'Would you like me to stand near you, Renius? Cover your left side for you?'

'If I wanted help, puppy, I'd ask you. Until that time, take yourself to the gate and keep a lookout. Call me when you can see numbers.'

Marcus snapped off a salute, much crisper than that of the cook, yet held a little too long. Renius could sense his insolence and considered breaking the boy's mouth for him. No, right now, he needed that stupid confidence of youth. He'd learn soon enough what killing was like.

As the men returned, he sent them to positions along the walls. They were far too few, but he believed what he had said to Caecilius. The outbuildings would be burned, no doubt; the granaries would probably go and the animals would be slaughtered, but the main

105

complex would not be worth the deaths it would take. An army could take it in minutes, he knew – but these were slaves, drunk on stolen wine and freedom that would vanish again with the morning sun. One strong man with a good sword arm and a ruthless temperament could handle a mob.

There was no sign yet of Julius or Cabera. No doubt the former was putting on his breastplate and greaves, the full uniform. But where had the old healer got to? That bow of his would be a useful asset in the first few minutes of bloodshed.

The noise of the men on the walls was like a flock of geese, cackling in excited nervousness.

'Silence!' Renius snapped. 'The next man to speak will get back down here and face me.'

In the sudden absence of chatter, they could again hear the screams and yells of the slaves in the fields.

'We need to listen to what is going on outside. Keep silent and stretch a few muscles. Keep a distance from the next man along, so you can swing without cutting his head off.'

The men shuffled apart from the little knots that had formed out of a need for contact. The fear was in all their eyes. Renius cursed to himself. Ten good men from his old legion and he could hold this place until dawn. These were children with sticks and knives. He took a deep breath as he tried to find words to encourage them. Even the iron legions had needed speeches to fire their blood and they were confident of their skills.

'There is nowhere to run to. If the mob breaks past you, everyone in this house will die. That is your responsibility. You must not leave your position – we are stretched thinly enough as it is. The wall is four feet wide – one long pace. Learn it – if you take more than one step back, you will fall.'

He watched as the men shuffled around on the wall, checking the width for themselves. His face hardened.

'I will keep fighters in the courtyard to deal with any that get

106

over the wall. Do not look down, even if you see your friends being killed before you.'

Cabera came out of the buildings, his bow restrung in his hand.

'This is how you inspire them? Your empire is built on this sort of speech?' he muttered.

Renius frowned at him. 'I have never lost a battle. Not with my legion, not in the arena. I have never had a man run or break under my command. If you run, you will pass me, and I will not run.'

'I won't run,' Marcus said clearly, into the silence.

Renius met his eyes, seeing a touch of the madness he had witnessed before.

'Nor will I, Renius,' said another.

The others all nodded and murmured that they would sooner die, but still the faces of a few were puckered in terror.

'Your children, your brothers, your fathers will ask you if you did. Be sure you can look them all in the eye.'

Heads nodded and shoulders lifted a little straighter.

'Better,' Cabera muttered again.

Julius moved easily through the open door onto the courtyard. His breastplate and leggings were oiled and smooth. His short scabbard swung as he walked. His face was a brutal mask, as an obvious rage burned inside. The men on the wall turned away from him, looking out over the fields.

'I will take the heads of every man from my estate not within these walls,' he growled.

Cabera shook his head quickly, not wanting to disagree with the man while those on the wall were listening.

'Sir,' he whispered. 'They all have friends outside. Good men and women who are trapped, or unable to fight through to you. Such a threat hurts their morale.'

'It pleases me. Every man outside these walls will be killed and I will pile their heads inside the gates! This is my home and Rome

107

is my city. We will cut out the filth that burn the houses and scatter them on the wind! Do you hear me, little man?' His internal fury built into incandescent rage. Renius and Cabera stared at him as he climbed up the corner steps and walked the length of the wall, shouting orders and noting sloppiness.

'For a man in politics, he has an unusual approach to a problem,' Cabera said quietly.

'Rome is full of men like him. That, my friend, is why we have an empire, not empty speeches.' Renius smiled his shark smile and walked over to where the women waited in a quietly murmuring group.

'What can we do?' asked a slave girl. He recognised her as the one he had whipped so many months ago, for distracting the boys in their training. Her name was Alexandria, it came back to him. While the others shrank from his gaze, as befitted the rank of slaves of the house, she held his eyes and waited for his answer.

'Fetch some knives. If anyone gets past the wall, you must fall on them and keep stabbing until they are dead.'

A gasp came from a couple of the older women, and one looked a little sick.

'Do you want to be raped and killed? Gods, woman, I am not asking you to stand on the wall, just to protect our backs. There are too few men to bring some down to protect you as well!' He had no patience with their softness. Good for bed, but when you had to depend on one . . . Gods!

Alexandria nodded. 'Knives. The spare wood axe is in the stable, unless someone has it. Go and search for some, Susanna. Quickly now.'

A matronly type, still looking pale, trotted off on the errand.

'Can we carry water, arrows? Fire? Is there anything else we can do?'

'Nothing,' Renius snapped, losing patience. 'Just make sure you kill anyone that lands in the yard. Put a knife in their throat before they can regain their feet. It's a ten-foot fall, there'll be a moment of weakness when you must strike.'

'We won't let you down, sir,' Alexandria replied.

He held her gaze for a second longer, noting the flash of hate that broke through the calm demeanour. He seemed to have more enemies in this place than outside the walls!

'See you don't,' he said curtly and turned on his heel.

The cook had returned with a large metal plate strapped to his chest. His enthusiasm was embarrassing, but Renius clapped him on the shoulder as he went to join the others.

Tubruk was standing with Cabera, holding a strung bow in his large hands.

'Old Lucius is a fine shot with a bow, but he's in the kitchens setting up for the wounded,' he said, his face grim.

'Get him out here. He can climb down later, when he's done the job,' Renius replied, without looking at him. He was scanning the walls, noting the positions, looking for failing nerves. They couldn't hold against a proper attack, so he prayed to his household god that the slaves outside couldn't mount one.

'Will the slaves have bows?' he asked Tubruk.

'One or two small ones for hares, perhaps. There's not a decent bow on the estate except for this – and Cabera's.'

'Good. Otherwise, they could pick us all off. We'll have to light the torches in the yard soon, to give them light to kill by. It will silhouette the men, but they can't fight in the dark, not this lot.'

'They may surprise you, Renius. Your name has a lot of power still. Remember the crowds at the games? Every man here will have a story for all the generations of his family to come, if he survives.'

Renius snorted. 'You'd better get to the wall, there's a space on the far side.'

Tubruk shook his head. 'The others have accepted you as leader, I know. Even Julius will listen to you once his temper calms down. I will stay by Marcus, to protect him. With your permission?'

Renius stared at him. Would nothing work properly? Fat cooks, girls with knives, arrogant children? And now his orders were to be ignored just before a fight? His right fist lifted in a smashing uppercut that seemed to lift Tubruk up and backwards. He hit the dust unmoving and Renius ignored him, turning to Cabera.

'When he awakes, tell him the boy can look after himself. I know. Tell him to take his place or I will kill him.'

Cabera smiled, his eyes wide, but the old man's face was like winter. In the distance, there was a sudden clamour of metal beating on metal. Sound rose in a wave and chants filled the black night. The torches were lit just as the first few slaves reached the estate wall. Behind them were hundreds from Rome, burning everything in their path.

CHAPTER NINE

It very nearly ended before it had begun. As Renius had thought, the wild-looking slaves that streamed up to the estate walls had little idea of how to overcome armed defenders and milled around, shouting and screaming. Although it was a perfect opportunity for bowmen, Renius had shaken his head at Cabera and Lucius, who watched with arrows ready and cold eyes. There was still a chance the slaves would look for easier targets, and a few arrows might fan their rage into white-hot desperation.

'Open the gates!' someone shouted from the mass of torch-bearers. In the flickering light, it could have been a festival if it were not for the brutal expressions of the attackers. Renius watched them, weighing options. More and more came from the rear. Clearly there were already more than a small estate could support. Rogue slaves from Rome swelled the ranks with nothing to lose, bringing hate and violence where reason might have won the day. Those at the front were pushed forward and Renius raised his arm, ready to have his two lonely archers send the first shafts into the crowd. They could hardly miss at this range.

A man stepped forward. He was heavily muscled and sported a thick black beard that made him look like a barbarian. Probably, only days previously, he had been meekly carrying rocks in a quarry, or training horses for some indulgent master. Now his chest was splashed with someone else's blood and his face was a sneer of hate, his eyes glimmering in the flames of his torch.

'You on the walls. You are slaves like us. Kill those who call themselves your betters. Kill them all and we will welcome you as friends.'

Renius dropped his arm and Cabera put a feathered shaft through the man's throat.

In the moment of silence, Renius roared at the crowd of slaves: 'That is what you will get from me. I am Renius and you will not pass here. Go home and wait for justice!'

'Justice like that?' came a scream of rage. Another man ran to the walls and jumped for the high ledge. The moment had arrived and suddenly the crowd howled and came forward in a rush.

Few had swords. Most were armed, like the defenders, with whatever they could find. Some had no weapons except their frenzied rage and Renius dispatched the first of these with a slick blow to his neck, ignoring the quivering fingers that scrabbled at his breastplate. All along the line, screams rose above the crash of metal on metal and metal into flesh. Renius could see Cabera drop his bow and raise a wicked-looking short knife, with which he stabbed and leapt away, letting the bodies fall back on their fellows. The old man stamped on fingers that gained easier and easier holds on the wall as the bodies of the dead served as props for new attackers.

Renius grew slightly light-headed and knew his shoulder had torn again, feeling the sudden warmth from the bandages accompanied by a blistering pain. He set his teeth against it and slammed his gladius into a man's stomach, almost losing the weapon in the slimy grip of his guts as he toppled backwards. Another took his place and another and Renius could not see an end to them. He took a blow from a length of timber that left him dazed for a second. He staggered back, reeling, trying to find the energy to lift the sword to meet the next one. His muscles ached and the exhaustion he had felt fighting Marcus came back to hit him once again.

'I am too old for this,' he muttered, spitting blood over his chin.

There was a movement to his left and he swung to meet it, too slowly. It was Marcus, grinning at him. He was covered in blood and looked like a demon from the ancient myths.

'I am a little worried about the speed of my low guard. I wonder if you could observe it for me? Let me know where the trouble is?'

As he spoke, he shoulder-barged a man as he tried to straighten. The man fell badly, toppling backwards onto his head with a yell.

'I told you not to leave your position,' Renius gasped, trying not to show his weakness.

'You were going to be killed. That honour is mine – not to be given away lightly to motherless scum like these, I think!' He nodded over to the other side of the gate, where the man Caecilius, known to most simply as Cook, was grinning hugely, cutting around him with abandon.

'Come pigs, come cattle. I will cut you to pieces.' Underneath the fat there must have been muscle, for he waved the enormous cleaver as if it were made of light wood.

'Cook is holding them without me. In fact, he is having the time of his life,' Marcus went on cheerfully.

Three men breasted the wall at once, leaping from the pile of bodies that was now half as high as the top. The first swung a sword at Marcus, who slid his own into the man's chest from the side, letting the wild lunge carry the man onto the cobbles of the yard below. The second he dispatched with a reverse cut that caught the man at eye-level, cutting into meat and bone. He died instantly.

The third whooped with pleasure as he closed on Renius. He knew the old man for who he was and in his mind was already telling the story to friends as Renius brought his sword up under his guard, ripping into his chest.

Renius let the man fall, and the sword slid clear. His left arm was hurting again, but this time it was a deep ache. His chest pulsed with pain and he groaned.

'Are you hurt?' Marcus asked, without taking his eyes off the wall.

'No. Get back to your post,' Renius snapped, his face suddenly grey.

Marcus looked at him for a long moment. 'I think I'll stay a while longer,' he said softly. More men surged over the wall and his sword danced, licking from one throat to the next unstoppably.

Gaius' father barely noticed those who fell beneath his sword. He fought as he had been trained: thrust, guard, reverse. The bodies piled most thickly at the foot of the gate and a little voice was telling him they should have broken by now. They were only slaves. They did not have to pass this wall. Why didn't they break? He would have the wall raised to the height of three men when this was over.

It seemed as if they threw themselves onto his sword, which wetted itself in their blood, drenching the wall and gates with the gushing fluids, drenching him. His shoulders ached, his arm was leaden. Only his legs were still strong beneath him. They must break soon and look for easier targets, surely? Thrust, guard and reverse. He was locked in the legionary's rhythm of death, but more and more were climbing the piles of flesh to get into the estate. His sword had lost its edge on bone and blades and his first cut only scraped a man leaping at him. A dagger punctured the hard muscle of his stomach and he grunted in agony, whipping his sword through the man's jaw and dropping him.

Alexandria stood in the yard, in a pool of darkness. The other women were crying softly to themselves. One was praying. She could see Renius was exhausted and was disappointed when the boy Marcus stepped in to save him. She wondered why he had done it and widened her eyes at the contrast between them. On the one side, the grizzled warrior, veteran of a thousand conflicts, slow and in pain. On the other, Marcus was a smooth-moving murderer, smiling as he brought death to the slaves that met his

114

sword. It did not matter if they had swords or clubs. He made them look clumsy and then took away their strength in a slice or a blow. One man clearly didn't realise he was dying. His blood poured from his chest, but he still kept hacking away with a broken spear shaft, his face manic.

Curious, Alexandria strained to see the man's face, and she caught the stricken moment when he felt the pain and saw the darkness coming.

All her life she had heard stories of men's strength and glory and they seemed to hang over this butchery like golden ghosts, not quite fitting the reality. She looked for moments of comradeship, of bravery in the face of death, but, down in the shadows, she could not see it.

The cook was enjoying the fight, that was obvious. He had begun to sing some vulgar song about a market day and pretty maids, thumping out the chorus with more volume than tune, as he buried his cleaver in skulls and necks. Men fell from his blade and his song grew more raucous as they dropped.

On her left, one of the defenders fell into the yard from the walkway. He made no attempt to protect himself from the impact and his head smashed on the hard stone with a wet sound. Alexandria shuddered and grabbed the shoulder of another woman in the darkness. Whoever it was, was sobbing quietly to herself, but there was no time for that.

'Quickly – they'll be coming through the gap!' she hissed, pulling the other along with her, not trusting herself to do the job alone.

As they moved, there was another crunching thud from a different section of the wall. Screams of triumph sounded. A man scrambled down, hanging for a moment, before letting go and falling the last couple of feet.

He spun, a wild, bloody nightmare, and as his eyes lit up at the lack of defenders, Alexandria rammed her blade up into his heart. Life escaped him with a sigh and another man hit the cobbles nearby. The snap of his ankle was audible even over the baying from outside the walls. The matronly Susanna, usually so careful over the exact setting of the master's table at banquets, slipped a skinning knife across his throat and walked away from him as he shuddered and spasmed behind her.

Alexandria looked up at the bright ring of torches above. At least they had light! How awful it was to die in the dark.

'More torches here!' she yelled, hoping that someone would answer.

Hands grabbed her from behind and her head was wrenched to one side. She tensed for the agony that would come, but the weight on her shoulders fell away suddenly and she turned to see Susanna, her knife hand freshly covered in red wetness.

'Keep your spirits up, love. The night's not over yet.' Susanna smiled and the moment of panic passed for Alexandria. She checked the yard with the others and barely winced when another defender fell, this time screaming as he hit the yard. Three men came through the gap he had left this time, with two more visible as they struggled up over the slippery bodies.

All the women drew their knives and the torchlight caught the blades, even down in the yard's blackness. Before the men's eyes could adjust to the gloom, the women were on them, gripping and stabbing.

Gaius came awake with a start. His mother Aurelia sat by the bed, holding a damp cloth. Its touch had awakened him and, as he looked at her, she pressed it to his forehead, crooning gently to herself. In the distance, he could hear screams and the clear sounds of battle. How had he remained asleep? Cabera had given him a warm drink as the evening darkened. There must have been something in it.

'What is going on, Mother? I can hear fighting!'

116

Aurelia smiled at him sadly.

'Shhh, my darling. You must not excite yourself. Your life is slipping away and I have come to make your last hours peaceful.'

Gaius blanched a little. No, he felt weak, but sound.

'I am not dying. I am getting better. Now, what is happening in the yard? I should get out there!'

'Shhh, shhh. I know they said you were getting better, but I also know they lie to me. Now be still and I will cool your brow for you.'

Gaius looked at her in disbelief. All his life, this shambling idiot had been coming to the fore, dragging away the lively, quick-witted woman he missed. He winced in anticipation of the screaming fit that would follow a wrong word from him.

'I want to feel the night air on my skin, Mother. One last time. Please leave so that I may dress.'

'Of course, my darling. I'll go back to my rooms now that I have said goodbye to you, my perfect son.' She giggled for a moment and sighed as if she carried a great weight.

'Your father is out there getting himself killed instead of looking after me. He has never looked after me properly. We have not made love in years now.'

Gaius didn't know what to say. He sat up and closed his eyes against the weakness. He couldn't even hold his hand in a fist, but he had to know what was going on. Gods, why wasn't there someone around? Were they all out there? Tubruk?

'Please leave, Mother. I must dress. I want to sit outside in my last moments.'

'I understand, my love. Goodbye.' Her eyes filled with tears as she kissed his forehead and then the little room was empty again.

For a moment, he was tempted simply to fall back on the pillows. His head felt thick and heavy and he guessed the drug Cabera had given him would have kept him under till morning if his mother hadn't had one of her ideas. Slowly, he swung his

117

legs out and pressed his feet against the floor. Weak. Clothes. One thing at a time.

Tubruk knew they couldn't hold much longer. He ran himself ragged trying to cover a gap where two other men had once stood beside him. Again and again, he spun barely in time to meet the attack of those who were creeping up on him as he killed those in front. His breath came in wheezing gasps and, for all his skill, he knew death was close.

Why would they not break? Damn all the gods to hell, they must break! He cursed himself for not arranging for some sort of fallback position, but there really was none. The walls were the only defence the estate had and these trembled on the brink of being completely overwhelmed.

He slipped in blood and went down badly, the air rushing out of him. A dagger punched into his side and a dirty bare foot tried to crush his face, pressing his head down. He bit it and distantly heard someone scream. He made it to one knee too late to stop two scrambling figures dropping down into the yard. He hoped the women could handle them. Gingerly he felt his side and winced at the trickle of blood, watching it for air bubbles. There were none and he could still breathe; though the air tasted like hot tin and blood.

For a few moments, no one came at him and he was able to look around the walls. Of the original twenty-nine, there were fewer than fifteen left. They had worked miracles up on the wall, but it wasn't going to be enough.

Julius fought on, despairing as his strength flowed from his wounds. He pulled the dagger out of his flesh with a groan and instantly lost it in the chest of the next man to face him. His breath was burning his throat and he looked into the yard, seeing his son come out. He smiled and the pride felt as if it would burst his chest. Another blade entered him, shoved down into the gap

118

between his breastplate and his neck, deep into his lung. He spat blood and buried his gladius into the attacker without seeing or knowing his face. His arms dropped away and the sword fell from his grasp, clattering on the stones of the courtyard below. He could only watch as the rest came on.

Tubruk saw Julius collapse under a mass of bodies that spilled past him over the narrow walkway and down into the dark. He cried out his grief and rage, knowing he couldn't reach him in time. Renius was still on his feet, but only Marcus' care kept the old warrior from death, and even that blinding whirl of blades was faltering as Marcus bled from wounds, his life dribbling away in a score of gashes.

Gaius climbed up beside Tubruk, his face white from the effort of dragging himself up the steps to the wall. His gladius was out and he swung it as he reached the top, cutting into a man levering himself up over the dark bodies. Tubruk slid his blade into the man's ribs as Gaius swayed, but still the slave wouldn't die. He flailed with a dagger and cut Gaius across the face. Gaius hammered another blow at his neck and then the life was gone. More faces appeared, shouting and cursing as they struggled onto the slippery stones.

'Your father, Gaius.'

'I know.' Gaius' sword arm came up without a quiver to block a spear, relic of some old battle. He stepped inside its reach and took out the man's throat in a spray of bloody wetness. Tubruk charged two more, making one drop over the edge, but falling to his knees in the sticky mess of the floor as he did so. Gaius cut the next down as he reversed his blade to plunge it into Tubruk. Then he staggered back a pace, his face white under the blood, his knees buckling. They waited together for the next one up to the edge.

The night suddenly became brighter as the feed barns were set alight and still no new attacker came to end it for him.

'One more,' Tubruk swore through bloody lips. 'I can take one more with me. You should go down, you're not fit to fight.'

Gaius ignored him, his mouth a grim line. They waited, but no

119

one came. Tubruk edged closer to the outer wall and looked over, at the mangled limbs and broken carcasses that were piled beneath the ledge, sprawled in slippery gore and glassy expressions. There was no one there waiting for him with a dagger, no one at all.

The light from the burning barns silhouetted leaping figures as they capered around in the darkness. Tubruk began to chuckle to himself, wincing as his lips split again.

'They've found the wine store,' he said and the laughter could not be stopped, despite the wrenching pain it brought.

'They are leaving!' Marcus growled, amazed. He hawked and spat blood at the floor, wondering vaguely if it was his own. He turned and grinned at Renius, seeing how he sat slumped, propped against two carcasses. The old warrior just looked at him, and for a moment Marcus began to remember his acid dislike.

'I . . .' He paused and took two quick steps to the old man. He was dying, that was obvious. Marcus pressed a hand made black with blood and dirt onto Renius' chest, feeling the heart flutter and miss. 'Cabera! Over here, quickly,' he shouted.

Renius closed his eyes against the noise and the pain.

Alexandria panted as if she was in labour. She was exhausted and covered in blood, which she had never imagined would be as sticky and foul as it actually was. They never mentioned this in the stories either. The stuff was slippery for a few moments, then gummed up your hands, making every surface tacky to the touch. She waited for the next one to drop into the yard, walking around almost drunkenly, her knife held in a stiff arm by her side.

She stumbled over a body and realised it was Susanna. She would never cut a goose again, or put fresh rushes down in the kitchens, or feed scraps to stray puppies on her shopping trips in Rome. This last thought brought clear-water tears that ran through the mud and stink. Alexandria kept walking, kept the patrol going, but no new enemies appeared, landing in the yard like crows. No one came, but still she staggered on, unable to stop. Two hours to dawn and she could still hear screaming in the fields.

'Stay on the walls! No man leaves his post until dawn,' Tubruk bellowed around the yard. 'They could still be back.'

He didn't think they would, though. The wine store held the best part of a thousand wax-sealed amphorae. Even if the slaves smashed a few, there should still be enough to keep them happy until sun-up.

After that final command was given, he wanted to climb down himself to cross quickly to where Julius lay among the dead, but someone had to hold the place.

'Go to your father, lad.'

Gaius nodded once and descended, bracing himself against the wall for support. The pain was agonising. He could feel that the operation incision had ripped open, and touching the area left his fingers red and glistening. As he dragged himself back up the stone steps to the defenders' positions, his wounds tore at his will, but he held on.

'Are you dead, Father?' he whispered as he looked down at the body. There could be no answer.

'Hold your positions, lads. It's over for now,' Tubruk's voice snapped across the yard.

Alexandria heard the news and dropped the knife onto the cobbles. Her wrists were being held by another slave girl from the kitchens, saying something to her. She could not make out the words over the screaming of the wounded, suddenly breaking into what she had thought was silence.

'I have been in silence and darkness for ever,' she thought. 'I have seen hell.'

Who was she again? The lines had blurred somewhere in the evening, as she killed slaves who wanted freedom as much as she did. The weight of it all bore her down to the ground and she began to sob.

Tubruk could not resist any longer. He limped down from his place on the wall and up again to where Julius lay. He and Gaius looked down at the body without words.

Gaius tried to feel the reality of the man's death. He could not. What lay on the floor was a broken thing, torn and gashed, in spreading pools of a liquid that looked more like oil than blood in the torchlight. His father's presence was gone.

He spun round suddenly, his hand coming up to ward something off.

'There was someone next to me. I could feel someone standing there, looking down with me,' he began to babble.

'That would be him, all right. This is a night for ghosts.'

The feeling had gone, though, and Gaius shivered, his mouth set tight against a grief that would drown him.

'Leave me, Tubruk. And thank you.'

Tubruk nodded, his eyes dark shadows as he limped down the steps into the yard. Wearily, he climbed back up to his old place on the wall and looked over each body he'd cut down, trying to remember the details of each death. He could recognise only a few and he soon gave that up and sat against a post, with his sword between his legs, watching the waning flicker of fire from the fields and waiting for the dawn.

Cabera placed his own palms over Renius' heart.

'This is his time, I think. The walls inside him are thin and old. Some are leaking blood where there should be none.'

'You healed Gaius. You can heal him.'

'He is an old man, lad. He was already weak and I . . .' Cabera paused as he felt a hot blade touch his back. Slowly and carefully, he turned his head to look at Marcus. There was nothing to reassure him in the grim expression.

'He lives. Do your work, or I'll kill just one more today.'

At the words, Cabera could feel a shift and different futures came into play, like gambling chips slotting into position with a silent click. His eyes widened, but he said nothing as he began to summon his energies for the healing. What a strange young man who had the power to bend the futures around him! Surely he had come to the right place in history. This was indeed a time of flux and change, without the usual order and safe progression.

He pulled an iron needle from the hem of his robe and threaded it neatly and quickly. He worked with care, sewing the bloody lips of slashed flesh together, remembering what it was to be young, when anything seemed possible. As Marcus watched, Cabera pressed his brown hands against Renius' chest and massaged the heart. He felt it quicken and stifled an exclamation as life came flooding back into the old body. He held his position for a long time, until the etched pain eased from Renius' expression and he looked as if he were merely asleep. As Cabera rose to his feet, swaying with exhaustion, he nodded to himself as if a point had been confirmed.

'The gods are strange players, Marcus. They never tell us all their plans. You were right. He will see a few more dawns and sunsets before the end.'

CHAPTER TEN

The fields were deserted by the time the sun came over the horizon. Those who had broken into the wine store were no doubt lying amongst the corn, still in the deep slumber of drunkenness. Gaius looked out over the wall to see sluggish smoke rising from the blackened ground. Scorched trees stood stark and bare, and the winter grain still smouldered in the skeletal wrecks of the feed barns.

It was a strangely peaceful scene, with even the morning birds silent. The violence and emotions of the night before were somehow distant when you were able to look out across the fields. Gaius rubbed his face for a moment, then turned to walk down the steps into the courtyard.

Brown stains spattered every white wall and surface. Pools of blood congealed in corners and obscene smears showed where the bodies had already been shifted, dragged outside the gates to be taken to pits when carts could be arranged. The defenders were laid out on clean cloths in cool rooms, their limbs arranged for dignity. The others were simply thrown onto a growing pile where arms and legs stuck out at angles. Gaius watched the work, and in the background heard the screams of the wounded as they were stitched or made ready for amputation.

He burned with anger and had nowhere to unleash it. He had been locked away for safety while everyone he loved risked their lives and while his father had given his in defence of his family and the estate. True, he had still been weak from the operation, his scabs barely healed, but to be denied the chance to help his father! There were no words, and when Cabera had come to him to offer sympathy Gaius ignored him until he went away. He sat exhausted and trickled dust through his fingers, remembering Tubruk's words years before and understanding them at last. His land.

A slave approached, one whose name Gaius did not know, but who bore wounds that showed he had been part of the defence.

'The dead are all outside the gates, master. Shall we find carts for them?'

It was the first time any man had addressed him as anything but his own name. Gaius hardened his expression so as not to reveal his surprise. His mind was full of pain and his voice sounded as if from a deep pit.

'Bring lamp oil. I'll burn them where they lie.'

The slave ducked his head in acknowledgement and ran for the oil. Gaius walked outside the gates and looked on the ungainly mass of death. It was a grisly sight, but he could find no sympathy in him. Each one there had chosen this end when they had attacked the estate.

He doused the pile in oil, sloshing it over the flesh and faces, into open mouths and unblinking eyes. Then he lit it and found he couldn't watch the corpses burn after all. The smoke brought back a memory of the raven he and Marcus had caught and he called a slave over to him.

'Fetch barrels from the stores and keep it burning until they are ash,' he said grimly. He went back inside as the heat built and the smell followed him like an accusing finger.

He found Tubruk lying on his side and biting onto a piece of leather as Cabera probed a dagger wound in his stomach in the great kitchen. Gaius watched for a while, but no words were exchanged.

He moved on, finding the cook sitting on a step with a bloody cleaver still in his hand. Gaius knew his father would have had words of encouragement for the man, who looked desolate and lost. He himself could not summon up anything except cold anger and stepped over the figure, who stared off into space as if Gaius wasn't there. Then he stopped. If his father would have done it, then so would he.

'I saw you fight on the wall,' he said to the cook, his voice strong and firm at last.

The man nodded and seemed to gather himself. He struggled to stand.

'I did, master. I killed a great number, but I lost count after a while.'

'Well, I've just burned one hundred and forty-nine bodies, so it must have been many,' Gaius said, trying to smile.

'Yes. No one got past me. I have never known such luck. I was touched by the gods, I think. We all were.'

'Did you see my father die?'

The cook stood and raised an arm as if to put it on the boy's shoulder. At the last moment, he thought better of it and turned the gesture into a wave of regret.

'I did. He took a great many with him and many before. There were piles around him at the end. He was a brave man and a good one.'

Gaius felt his calm waver at the kind thought and his jaw clenched. When he had overcome his surge of sorrow, he spoke graciously: 'He would be proud of you, I know. You were singing when I caught a glimpse of you.'

To his surprise, the man blushed deeply.

'Yes. I enjoyed the fight. I know there was blood and death all around, but everything was simple, you see. Anyone I could see was to be killed. I like things to be clear.'

'I understand,' Gaius said, forcing a bleak smile. 'Rest now. The kitchens are open and soup will be brought around soon.'

'The kitchens! And I am here! I must go, master, or the soup will be fit for nothing.'

Gaius nodded and the man bolted off, leaving his enormous cleaver resting against the step, forgotten. Gaius sighed. He wished his own life was that simple, to be able to take on and cast off roles without regret.

Lost in thought as he was, he didn't notice the man's return until he spoke.

'Your father would be proud of you too, I think. Tubruk says you saved him when he was exhausted at the end, and with you injured as well. I would be proud if my son were as strong.'

Tears came unbidden to Gaius' eyes and he turned away so the other would not see them. This was not the time to be breaking apart, not when the estate was in a shambles and the winter feed all burned. He tried to busy himself with the details, but he felt helpless and alone and the tears came more strongly, as his mind touched again and again on his loss, like a bird pecking at weeping sores.

'Ho there!' came a voice from outside the main gate.

Gaius heard the cheerful tone and composed himself. He was the head of the estate, a son of Rome and his father, and he would not embarrass the old man's memory. He walked the steps to the top of the wall, barely aware of the phantom images that came rushing at him. Those were all from the dark. In the sun the shadows had little reality.

At the top, he looked down on the bronze helmet of a slim officer on a fine gelding that pawed the ground restlessly as it waited. The officer was accompanied by a *contubernium* of ten legionaries. Each man appeared alert and smartly turned out. The officer looked up and nodded to Gaius. He was around forty, tanned and fit-looking.

'We saw your smoke. Came to investigate in case it was more of the slaves on the rampage. I see you've had trouble here. My name is Titus Priscus. I am a centurion with Sulla's legion, who have just blessed the city with their presence. My men are ranging the countryside hereabouts, on clean-up and execution detail. May I speak to the master of the estate?'

'That would be me,' Gaius said. 'Open the gates,' he called below.

Those words achieved what all the marauders of the night before could not and the heavy gates were pulled open, allowing the men entry.

'Looks like you had it rough out here,' Titus said, all trace of cheerfulness gone from his voice and manner. 'I should have known from the pile of bodies, but . . . did you lose many of your own?'

'Some. We held the walls. How is the city?' Gaius was at a loss as to what to say to the man. Was he meant to make polite conversation?

Titus dismounted and gave the reins to one of his men.

'Still there, sir, although hundreds of wooden houses went up and there are a few thousand dead in the streets. Order has been restored for the moment, though I can't say it would be safe to stroll out after dark. At the moment, we're rounding up all the slaves we can find and crucifying one in ten to make an example – Sulla's orders – on all the estates near Rome.'

'Make it one in three if they're on my land. I'll replace them when things have settled. I don't like the thought of letting anyone who fought against me last night go without punishment.'

The centurion looked at him for a second, unsure.

'Begging your pardon, sir, but are you able to give that order? You'll excuse me checking, but, in the circumstances, is there anyone to back you?'

For a second, anger flared in Gaius, but then he remembered what he must look like to the man. There had been no opportunity to clean himself up after Lucius and Cabera had restitched and

128

rebandaged his wounds. He was dirty and bloodstained and unnaturally pale. He didn't know that his blue eyes were also rimmed with red from the oily smoke and crying and that only something in his manner kept a seasoned soldier like Titus from cuffing the boy for his insolence. There was something, though, and Titus couldn't have said exactly what it was. Just a feeling that this young man was not someone to cross lightly.

'I would do the same in your position. I will fetch my estate manager, if the doctor is finished with him.' Gaius turned away without another word.

It would have been politeness to offer the men refreshment, but Gaius was annoyed that he had to summon Tubruk to establish his bona fides. He left them waiting.

Tubruk was at least clean and dressed in good, dark clothing. His wounds and bandages were all concealed under his woollen tunic and *bracae* – leather trousers. He smiled as he saw the legionaries. The world was turning the right way up again.

'Are you the only ones in this area?' he asked without preamble or explanation.

'Er, no, but . . .' Titus began.

'Good.' Tubruk turned to Gaius. 'Sir, I suggest you have these men send out a message that they will be delayed. We need men to get the estate back in order.'

Gaius kept his face as straight as Tubruk's, ignoring Titus' expression.

'Good point, Tubruk. Sulla has sent them to help the outlying estates, after all. There is much work to be done.'

Titus tried again. 'Here, now look . . .'

Tubruk noticed him once more. 'I suggest you take the message yourself. These others look fit enough for a little hard labour. Sulla won't want you to abandon us to our wreckage, I'm sure.'

The two men faced each other and Titus sighed, reaching up to remove his helmet.

'Never let it be said that I shirked a job of work,' he muttered. Turning to one of the legionaries, he jerked his head back to the fields. 'Get back out and join up with the other units. Spread the word that I'll be held up here for a few hours. Any slaves you find – tell them one in three, all right?'

The man nodded cheerfully and took off.

Titus began to unbuckle his breastplate. 'Right, where do you want my lads to start?'

'You handle this, Tubruk. I'll go and check on the others.' Gaius turned away, showing his appreciation with a quick grip of the other's shoulder as he left. What he wanted to do was to go for a long walk in the woods by himself, or sit by the river pool and settle his thoughts. That would come later, though, after he had seen and spoken with every man and woman who had fought for his family the night before. His father would have done the same.

As he passed the stables, he heard a pulsing sob from the darkness within. He paused, unsure whether he should intrude. There was so much grief in the air, as well as inside him. Those who had fallen had friends and relatives who had not expected to begin this day alone. He stood for a moment longer, still smelling the oily stink of the bodies he had fired. Then he went into the cool shadow of the stalls. Whoever it was, their grief was now his responsibility, their burdens were his to share. That was what his father had understood and why the estate had prospered for so long.

His eyes adjusted slowly after the morning glare and he peered into each stall to find the source of the sounds. Only two held horses and they snickered gently to him as he reached and stroked their soft muzzles. His foot scraped against a pebble and the sobbing ceased on the instant, as if someone was holding their breath. Gaius waited, as still as Renius had taught him to stand, until he heard the sigh of released air and knew where the person was.

In the dirty straw, Alexandria sat with her knees tight against her chin and her back to the far stone wall. She looked up as he came into sight and he saw that the dirt on her face was streaked with tears. She was close to his own age, maybe a year older, he recalled. The memory of her being flogged by Renius came into his mind with a stab of guilt.

He sighed. He had no words for her. He crossed the short distance and sat against the wall next to her, taking care to leave space between them as he leaned back so that she would not be threatened. The silence was calm and the smells and feel of the stables had always been a comforting place to Gaius. When he was very young, he too had escaped here to hide from his troubles or from punishment to come. He sat, lost in memory for a while, and it didn't seem awkward between them, though nothing was said. The only sounds were the horses' movements and the occasional sob that still escaped Alexandria.

'Your father was a good man,' she whispered at last.

He wondered how many times he would hear the phrase before the day was over and whether he could stand it. He nodded mutely.

'I'm so sorry,' he said to her, feeling rather than seeing her head come up to look at him. He knew she'd killed, had seen her covered in blood down in the yard as he'd come out the night before. He thought he understood why she was crying and had meant to try and comfort her, but the words unlocked a rush of sorrow in him and his eyes filled with tears. His face twisted in pain as he bowed his head to his chest.

Alexandria looked at him in astonishment, her eyes wide. Before she had time to think, she had reached over to him and they were holding each other in the darkness, a blot of private grief while the world went on in the sun outside. She stroked his hair with one hand and whispered comfort to him as he apologised over and over, to her, his father, to the dead, to those he had burned.

When he was spent, she began to release him, but in the last fragment of time before he was too far she pressed her lips lightly

131

on his, feeling him start slightly. She pulled away, hugging her knees tightly and, unseen in the shadows, her face burned. She felt his eyes on her, but couldn't meet them.

'Why did you . . .?' he muttered, his voice hoarse and swollen from crying.

'I don't know. I just wondered what it would be like.'

'What was it like?' he replied, his voice strengthening with amusement.

'Terrible. Someone will have to teach you to kiss.'

He looked at her, bemused. Moments before, he had been drowning in a sorrow that would not diminish or wane in him. Now he was noticing that beneath the dirt and wisps of straw and smell of blood – beneath her own sadness – there was a rare girl.

'I have the rest of the day to learn,' he said quietly, the words stumbling out past nervous blockages in his throat.

She shook her head. 'I have work to do. I should be back in the kitchen.'

In a smooth movement, she rose from her crouch and left the stall, as if she was going to walk right away without another word. Then she paused and looked at him.

'Thank you for coming to find me,' she said and walked out into the sunlight.

Gaius watched her go. He wondered if she had realised he had never kissed a girl before. He could still feel a light pressure on his lips as if she had marked him. Surely she hadn't meant terrible? He saw again the stiff way she had carried herself as she left the stables. She was like a bird with a broken wing, but she would heal with time and space and friends. He realised he would as well.

Marcus and Tubruk were laughing at something Cabera had said, as Gaius came into the room. At the sight of him, they all fell silent.

'I came . . . to thank you. For doing what you did on the walls,' Gaius began.

Marcus cut him off, stepping closer and grabbing his hand. 'You never need to thank me for anything. I owe more than I could ever pay to your father. I was sorry to hear he fell at the last.'

'We came through. My mother lives, I live. He would do it again if offered the chance, I know. You took some wounds?'

'Towards the end. Nothing serious, though. I was untouchable. Cabera says I will be a great fighter.' Marcus broke into a grin.

'Unless he gets himself killed, of course. That would slow him down a little,' Cabera muttered, busying himself with applying wax to the wood of his bow.

'How is Renius?' Gaius asked.

Both seemed to pause for a second at the question. Marcus looked evasive. There was something odd there, Gaius thought.

'He'll live, but it will be a long time before he's ever fit again,' Marcus said. 'At his age an infection would be the end of him, but Cabera says he'll make it.'

'He will,' Cabera said firmly.

Gaius sighed and sat down. 'What happens now? I'm too young to take my father's place, to represent his interests in Rome. In truth, I would not be happy running only the estate, but I never had time to learn about the rest of his affairs. I don't know who looked after his wealth, or where the deeds to the land are.' He turned to Tubruk. 'I know you are familiar with some of it and I would trust you to control the capital until I am older, but what do I do now? Continue to hire tutors for Marcus and myself? Life seems suddenly vague; without direction, for the first time.'

Cabera stopped polishing at this outburst.

'Everyone feels this at some time. Did you think I planned to be here when I was a young boy? Life has a way of taking twists and turns you did not expect. I would not have it any other way,

133

for all the pain it brings. Too much of the future is already set, it is good that we cannot know every detail or life would become a grey, dull sort of death.'

'You will have to learn fast, that is all,' Marcus continued, his face alight with enthusiasm.

'With Rome as it is? Who will teach me? This is not a time of peace and plenty, where my lack of political skill can be overlooked. My father was always very clear about that. He said Rome was full of wolves.'

Tubruk nodded grimly. 'I will do what I can, but already some will be looking at which estates have been weakened and might be bought cheaply. This is not the time to be defenceless.'

'But I don't know enough to protect us!' Gaius went on. 'The Senate could take everything I own if I don't pay taxes, for example, but how do I pay? Where is the money and where do I take it and how much should I pay? Where are the names of my father's clients? You see?'

'Be calm,' Cabera said, beginning the slow strokes along the wood of his bow again. 'Think instead. Let us begin with what you do have and not what you don't know.'

Gaius took a deep breath and once again wished his father were there to be the rock of certainty in his life.

'I have you, Tubruk. You know the estate, but not the other dealings. None of us know anything about politics or the realities of the Senate.'

He looked again at Cabera and Marcus. 'I have you two and I have Renius on hand, but none of us have even entered the Senate chambers and my father's allies are strangers to us.'

'Concentrate on what we *have*, otherwise you will despair. So far you have named some very capable people. Armies have been started with less. What else?'

'My mother and her brother Marius, but my father always said he was the biggest wolf of them all.'

'We need a big wolf right now, though. Someone who knows the politics. He is your blood, you must go and see him,' Marcus said quietly.

'I don't know if I can trust him,' Gaius said, his expression bleak.

'He will not desert your mother. He must help you to keep control of the estate, if only for her,' Tubruk declared.

Gaius agreed slowly.

'True. He has a place in Rome I could visit. There is no one else to help, so it must be him. He is a stranger to me, though. Since my mother began her sickness, he has rarely been to the estate.'

'That will not matter. He will not turn you away,' Cabera said peacefully, eyeing the shine he had wrought in the bow.

Marcus looked sharply at the old man. 'You seem very sure,' he said.

Cabera shrugged. 'Nothing is sure in this world.'

'Then it is settled. I will send a messenger before me and visit my uncle,' Gaius said, something of his gloom lifting.

'I will come with you,' Marcus said quickly. 'You are still recovering from your wounds and Rome is not a safe place at the moment, you know.'

Gaius smiled properly for the first time that day.

Cabera muttered, as if to himself, 'I came to this land to see Rome, you know. I have lived in high mountain villages and met tribes thought lost to antiquity on my travels. I believed I had seen everything, but all the time people told me I had to visit Rome before I died. I said to them, "This lake is true beauty", and they would reply, "You should see Rome." They say it is a wondrous place, the centre of the world, yet I have never stepped inside its walls.'

Both boys smiled at the old man's transparent subterfuge.

'Of course you will come. I consider you a friend of the house.

135

You will always be welcome anywhere I am, on my honour,' Gaius replied, his tone formal, as if repeating an oath.

Cabera laid the bow aside and stood with his hand outstretched. Gaius took it firmly.

'You too will always be welcome at my home fires,' Cabera said. 'I like the climate around here, and the people. I think my travels will wait for a little while.'

Gaius released the grip, his expression thoughtful.

'I will need good friends around me if I am to survive my first year of politics. My father described it as walking barefoot in a nest of vipers.'

'He seems to have had a colourful turn of phrase, and not a high opinion of his colleagues,' Cabera said, giving out a dry chuckle. 'We will tread lightly and stamp on the occasional head as it becomes necessary.'

All four smiled and felt the strength that comes from such a friendship, despite the difference in age and background.

'I would like to take Alexandria with us,' Gaius added suddenly.

'Oh, yes? The pretty one?' Marcus replied, his face lighting up.

Gaius felt his cheeks grow red and hoped it wasn't obvious. Judging by the expressions of the others, it was.

'You will have to introduce me to this girl,' Cabera said.

'Renius whipped her, you know, for distracting us at practice,' Marcus continued.

Cabera tutted to himself. 'He can be charmless. Beautiful women are a joy in life . . .'

'Look, I . . .' Gaius began.

'Yes, I'm sure you want her simply to hold the horses or something. You Romans have such a way with women, it is a wonder your race has survived.'

Gaius left the room after a while, leaving laughter behind him.

*　*　*

Gaius knocked at the door of the room where Renius lay. He was alone for the moment, although Lucius was nearby and had just been in to check the wounds and stitches. It was dark in the room and at first Gaius thought the old man was asleep.

He turned to leave rather than disturb the rest he must need, but a whispering voice stopped him.

'Gaius? I thought it was you.'

'Renius. I wanted to thank you.' Gaius approached the bed and drew up a chair beside the figure. The eyes were open and clear and Gaius blinked as he took in the features. It must have been the dim light, but Renius looked younger. Surely not, yet there was no denying that some of the deep-seam wrinkles had lessened and a few black hairs could be seen at the temples, almost invisible in the light, but standing out against the white bristles.

'You look . . . well,' Gaius managed.

Renius gave a short, hard chuckle. 'Cabera healed me and it has worked wonders. He was more surprised than anyone, said I must have a destiny or something, to be so affected by him. In truth, I feel strong, although my left arm is still useless. Lucius wanted to take it off, rather than have it flapping around. I . . . may let him, when the rest of me has healed.'

Gaius absorbed this in silence, fighting back painful memories.

'So much has happened in such a short time,' he said. 'I am glad you are still here.'

'I couldn't save your father. I was too far away and finished myself. Cabera said he died instantly, with a blade in his heart. Most likely, he wouldn't even have known it.'

'It's all right. You don't need to tell me. I know he would have wanted to be on that wall. I would have wanted it too, but I was left in my room, and . . .'

'You got out though, didn't you? I'm glad you did, as it turned out. Tubruk says you saved him right at the end, like a . . . reserve force.' The old man smiled and coughed for a while. Gaius waited patiently until the fit was over.

'It was my order to leave you out of it. You were too weak for hours of fighting and your father agreed with me. He wanted you safe. Still, I'm glad you got out for the end of it.'

'So am I. I fought with Renius!' Gaius said, his eyes brimming with tears, though he smiled.

'I always fight with Renius,' muttered the old man. 'It isn't that much to sing about.'

CHAPTER ELEVEN

The dawn light was cold and grey; the skies clear over the estate lands. Horns sounded low and mournful, drowning the cheerful birdsong that seemed so inappropriate for a day marking the passing of a life. The house was stripped of ornament save for a cypress branch over the main gate to warn priests of Jupiter not to enter while the body was still inside.

Three times the horns moaned and finally the people chanted, '*Conclamatum est*' – the sadness has been sounded. The grounds inside the gates were filled with mourners from the city, dressed in rough wool togas, unwashed and unshaven to show their grief.

Gaius stood by the gates with Tubruk and Marcus and watched as his father's body was brought out feet first and laid gently in the open carriage that would take him to the funeral pyre. The crowd waited, heads bowed in prayer or thought as Gaius walked stiffly to the body.

He looked down into the face he had known and loved all his life and tried to remember it when the eyes could open and the strong hand reach out to grip his shoulder or ruffle his hair. Those same hands lay still at his sides, the skin clean and shining with oil. The wounds from the defence of the walls were covered by the folds of his toga, but there was nothing of life there. No rise and fall of breath; the skin looked wrong, too pale. He wondered if it would be cold to the touch, but could not reach out.

'Goodbye, my father,' he whispered and almost faltered as grief swelled in him. The crowd watched and he steadied himself. No shame in front of the old man. Some of them would be friends, unknown to him, but some would be carrion birds, come to judge his weakness for themselves. He felt a spike of anger at this and was able to smother the sadness. He reached out and took his father's hand, bowing his head. The skin felt like cloth, rough and cool under his grip.

'Conclamatum est,' he said aloud and the crowd murmured the words again.

He stood back and watched in silence as his mother approached the man who had been her husband. He could see her shaking under her dirty wool cloak. Her hair had not been tended by slaves and stood out in wild disarray. Her eyes were bloodshot and her hand trembled as she touched his father for the last time. Gaius tensed, and begged inside that she would complete the ritual without disgrace. Standing so close, he alone could hear the words she said as she bent low over the face of his father.

'Why have you left me alone, my love? Who will now make me laugh when I am sad and hold me in the darkness? This is not what we dreamed. You promised me you would always be there when I am tired and angry with the world.'

She began to sob in heaves and Tubruk signalled to the nurse he'd hired for her. As with the doctors, she had brought no physical improvement, but Aurelia seemed to draw comfort from the Roman matron, perhaps simply from female companionship. It was enough for Tubruk to keep her on, and he nodded as she took Aurelia's arm gently and led her away into the darkened house.

Gaius breathed out slowly, suddenly aware of the crowd again. Tears came into his eyes and were ignored as they brimmed and held against his lashes.

Tubruk approached and spoke quietly to him. 'She will be all right,' he said, but they both knew it wasn't true.

One by one, the other mourners came to pay their respects to the body and more than a few spoke to Gaius afterwards, praising his father and pressing him to contact them in the city.

'He was always straight with me, even when profit lay the other way,' said one grey-haired man in a rough toga. 'He owned a fifth part of my shops in the city and lent me the money to buy them. He was one of the rare ones you could trust with anything and he was always fair.'

Gaius gripped his hand strongly. 'Thank you. Tubruk will make arrangements to discuss the future with you.'

The man nodded. 'If he is watching me, I want him to see me being straight with his son. I owe him that and more.'

Others followed and Gaius was proud to see the genuine sadness his father had left behind. There was a world in Rome that the son had never seen, but his father had been a decent man and that mattered to him, that the city was a little poorer because his father would no longer walk the streets.

One man was dressed in a clean toga of good white wool, standing out in the crowd of mourners. He did not pause at the carriage, but came straight to Gaius.

'I am here for Marius the consul. He is away from the city, but wanted to send me to let you know your father will not be forgotten by him.'

Gaius thanked him politely, his mind working furiously, 'Send the message that I will call on Consul Marius when he is next in the city.'

The man nodded. 'Your uncle will receive you warmly, I am sure. He will be at his town house three weeks from today. I will let him know.' The messenger made his way back through the crowd and out of the gates and Gaius watched him go.

Marcus moved to his shoulder, his voice low. 'Already you are not so alone as you were,' he said.

Gaius thought of his mother's words. 'No. He has set my standard and I will meet it. I will not be a lesser man when I lie there and my son greets those who knew me. I swear it.'

Into the dawn silence came the low voices of the *praeficae* women, singing softly the same phrases of loss over and over. It was a mournful sound and the world was filled with it as the horses pulled the carriage with his father out of the gates in slow time, with the people falling in behind, heads bowed.

In only a few minutes the courtyard was empty again and Gaius waited for Tubruk, who had gone inside to check on Aurelia.

'Are you coming?' Gaius asked him as he returned.

Tubruk shook his head. 'I will stay to serve your mother. I don't want her alone at this time.'

Tears came again into Gaius' eyes and he reached out for the older man's arm.

'Close the gates behind me, Tubruk. I don't think I can do it.'

'You must. Your father is gone to the tomb and you must follow, but first the gates must be shut by the new master. It is not my place to take yours. Close up the estate for mourning and go and light the funeral pyre. These are your last tasks before I will call you master. Go now.'

Words would not come from his throat and Gaius turned away, pulling the heavy gates shut behind him. The funeral procession had not gone far with their measured step and he walked after them slowly, his back straight and his heart aching.

The crematorium was outside the city, near the family tomb. For decades, burials within the walls of Rome had been forbidden as the city filled every scrap of available space with buildings. Gaius watched in silence as his father's body was laid on a high pyre that hid him from view in the centre of it. The wood and straw were soaked with perfumed oils and the odour of flowers hung heavily in the air as the praeficae changed their dirge to one of hope and rebirth. Gaius was brought a sputtering torch by the

142

man who had prepared his father's body for the funeral. He had the dark eyes and calm face of a man used to death and grief and Gaius thanked him with distant politeness.

Gaius approached the pyre and felt the gaze of all the mourners on him. He would show them no public weakness, he vowed to himself. Rome and his father watched to see if he would falter, but he would not.

Close, the smell of the perfumes was almost overpowering. Gaius reached out with a silver coin and opened his father's loose mouth, pressing the metal against the dry coolness of the tongue. It would pay the ferryman, Charon, and his father would reach the quiet lands beyond. He closed the mouth gently and stood back, pressing the smoking torch against the oily straw stuffed between the branches at the base of the pyre. A memory of the smell of burning feathers slipped into his mind and was gone before he could identify it.

The fire grew quickly, with popping twigs and a crackle that was loud against the soft songs of the praeficae. Gaius stepped back from the heat as his face reddened and held the torch limply in his hand. It was the end of childhood while he was yet a child. The city called him and he did not feel ready. The Senate called him and he was terrified. But he would not fail his father's memory and would meet the challenges as they came. In three weeks, he would leave the estate and enter Rome as a citizen, a member of the nobilitas.

At last, he wept.

CHAPTER TWELVE

'Rome – the largest city in the world,' Marcus said, shaking his head in wonder as they passed into the vast paved expanse of the forum. Great bronze statues gazed down on the small group as they walked their horses through the bustling pedestrians.

'You don't realise how big everything is until you get up close,' Cabera replied, his usual confidence muted. The pyramids of Egypt seemed larger in his memory, but the people there looked always to the past with their tombs. Here, the great structures were for the living and he felt the optimism of it.

Alexandria too seemed awed, though in part it was at how much everything had changed in the five years since Gaius' father had bought her to work in his kitchens. She wondered if the man who had owned her mother was somewhere still in the city and shuddered as she recalled his face, remembering how he had treated them. Her mother had never been free and died a slave after a fever struck her and several others in the slave pens beneath one of the sale houses. Such plagues were fairly common and the big slave auctions were accustomed to passing over a few bodies each month, accepting a few coins for them from the ash-makers. She remembered, though, and the waxen stillness of her mother still pressed against her arms in dreams. She shuddered again and shook her head as if to clear it.

'I will not die a slave,' she thought to herself, and Cabera turned to look at her, almost as if he had heard the thought. He nodded and winked and she smiled at him. She had liked him from the first. He was another who didn't quite fit, wherever he found himself.

'I will learn useful skills and make things to sell and buy myself free,' she thought, knowing the glory of the forum was affecting her and not caring. Who wouldn't dream in such a place that looked as if it had been built by gods? You could see how to make a hut, just by looking at it, but who could imagine these columns being raised? Everything was bright and untouched by the filth she remembered, narrow dirty streets and ugly men hiring her mother by the hour, with the money going to the owner of the house.

There were no beggars or whores in the forum, only well-dressed, clean men and women, buying, selling, eating, drinking, arguing politics and money. On each side, the eye was filled with gargantuan temples in rich stone; huge columns with their head and feet gilded; great arches erected for military triumphs. Truly, this was the beating heart of empire. Each of them could feel it. There was a confidence here, an arrogance. While most of the world scrubbed in the dirt still, these people had power and astonishing wealth.

The only sign of the recent troubles was the grim presence of legionaries standing to attention at every corner, watching the crowds with cold eyes.

'It is meant to make a man feel small,' Renius muttered.

'But it does not!' Cabera continued, gaping around him. 'It makes me feel proud that man can build this. What a race are we!'

Alexandria nodded silently. It showed that anything could be achieved; even, perhaps, freedom.

Small boys advertised their master's wares from hundreds of tiny shops along the edges; barbers, carpenters, butchers, stonemasons, gold and silver jewellers, potters, mosaic makers, rug weavers, the list was endless, the colours and noises a blur.

'That is the temple of Jupiter, on the Capitoline hill. We will come back and make a sacrifice when we have seen your uncle Marius,' Tubruk said, relaxed and smiling in the morning sun. He was leading the group and raised his arm to halt them.

'Wait. That man's path will cross ours. He is a senior magistrate and must not be hindered.'

The others drew up and halted.

'How do you know who he is?' Marcus asked.

'Do you see the man beside him? He is a lictor, a special attendant. Do you see that bundle on his shoulder? Those are wooden rods for scourging and a small axe for beheading. If the magistrate was bumped by one of our horses, say, he could order a death on the spot. He needs neither witnesses nor laws to apply. Best to avoid them completely, if we can.'

In silence, they all watched the man and his attendant as they crossed the plaza, seemingly unaware of the attention.

'A dangerous place for the ignorant,' Cabera whispered.

'Everywhere is, in my experience,' Renius grunted from the back.

Past the forum, they entered lesser streets that abandoned the straight lines of the main ones. Here, there were fewer names on the intersections. The houses were often four or even five storeys high and Cabera, in particular, gaped at these.

'The view they must have! Are they very expensive, these top houses?'

'Apartments, they are called, and no, they are the cheapest. They have no running water at that height and are in great danger from fire. If one starts on the bottom floor, those at the top rarely get out. You see how the windows are so small? That is to keep out the sun and rain, but it also means you can't jump from them.'

They wound their way through the heavy stepping stones that

146

crossed the sunken roads at intervals. Without these, the fastidious pedestrians would have had to step down into the slippery muck left by horses and donkeys. The wheels of carts had to be set a regulation width apart so that they could cross in the gaps and Cabera nodded to himself as he watched the process.

'This is a well-planned city,' he said. 'I have never seen another like it.'

Tubruk laughed. 'There is no other like it. They say Carthage was of similar beauty, but we destroyed that more than fifty years ago, sowing the land with salt so that it could never again rise in opposition to us.'

'You speak almost as if a city is a living thing,' Cabera replied.

'Is it not? You can feel the life here. I could feel her welcoming me as I came through the gate. This is my home, as no other house can be.'

Gaius too could feel the life around him. Although he had never lived within the walls, it was his home as it was Tubruk's – maybe more so as he was nobilitas, born free and of the greatest people in the world. 'My people built this,' he thought. 'My ancestors put their hands on these stones and walked these streets. My father may have stood at that corner and my mother could have grown up in one of the gardens I can glimpse off the main street.'

His grip on the reins relaxed and Cabera looked at him and smiled, sensing the change of mood.

'We are nearly there,' Tubruk said. 'At least Marius' house is well away from the smell of dung in the streets. I don't miss that, I can assure you.'

They turned off the busy road and walked the horses up a steep hill and a quieter, cleaner street.

'These are the houses of the rich and powerful. They have estates in the country but mansions here, where they entertain and plot for more power and even more wealth,' Tubruk continued, his voice blank enough of emotion to make Gaius glance at him.

The houses were sealed from the public gaze by iron gates, taller than a man. Each was numbered and entered by a small door for those on foot. Tubruk explained that this was only the least part; the buildings went back and back, from private baths to stables to great courtyards, all hidden from the vulgar plebeians.

'They set great store by privacy in Rome,' Tubruk said. 'Perhaps it is part of living in a city. Certainly, if you were just to drop in to a country estate you would be unlikely to cause offence, but here you must make appointments and announce yourself and wait and wait until they are ready to receive you. This is the one. I will tell the gatekeeper we have arrived.'

'I'll leave you here then,' Renius said. 'I must go to my own house and see if it has been damaged in the rioting.'

'Do not forget the curfew. Be inside as the sun sets, my friend. They are still killing everyone left on the streets after dark.'

Renius nodded. 'I'll watch out.'

He turned his horse away and Gaius reached out to put a hand on his good right arm.

'You're not leaving? I thought . . .'

'I must check my house. I need to think alone for a while. I don't feel ready to settle down with the other old men, not any more. I will be back tomorrow dawn to see you and . . . well, tomorrow dawn it is.' He smiled and rode away.

As he trotted down the hill, Gaius noted again the darkness of his hair and the energy that filled the man's frame. He turned and looked at Cabera, who shrugged.

'Gatekeeper!' Tubruk shouted. 'Attend to us.'

After the heat of the Roman streets, the cool stone corridors that led into the house grounds were a welcome relief. The horses and bags had been whisked away and the five visitors were taken into the first building, beckoned on by an elderly slave.

148

They stopped at a door of gold wood and the slave opened it, gesturing inside.

'You will find all you need, Master Gaius. Consul Marius has given you leave to wash and change after your journey. You are not expected to appear before him until sunset, three hours from now, when you will dine. Shall I show your companions the way to the servants' rooms?'

'No. They will stay with me.'

'As you wish, master. Shall I take the girl to the slave quarters?'

Gaius nodded slowly, thinking.

'Treat her with kindness. She is a friend of my house.'

'Of course, sir,' replied the man, motioning to Alexandria.

She flashed a glance at Gaius and the expression was unreadable in her dark eyes.

Without another word, the quiet little man left, his sandals making no noise on the stone floor. The others looked at one another, each taking some form of comfort from the company of friends.

'I think she likes me, that one,' Marcus mused to himself.

Gaius looked at him in surprise and Marcus shrugged. 'Lovely legs, as well.' He went in to their quarters, chuckling, leaving Gaius stupefied behind him.

Cabera whistled softly as he entered the room. The ceiling was forty feet from the mosaic floor, a series of brass rafters that crossed and recrossed the space. The walls were painted in the dark reds and oranges that they had seen so often since entering the city, but the floor was the thing that caught the attention, even before they looked up at the vault of a roof. It was a series of circles, gripping a marble fountain in the middle of the huge room. Each circle contained running figures, racing to catch the one in front and frozen in the attempt. The outer circles were figures from the markets, carrying their wares, then, as the eye followed the circles inwards, different aspects of society could be seen. There were the slaves, the magistrates, the members of the Senate, legionaries, doctors. One circle contained only kings, naked except for their crowns. The innermost ring, forming a belt around the actual fountain, contained pictures of the gods and they alone were still. They stood looking up at all the running hordes that sprinted around but could never leap from one circle to another.

Gaius walked across the rings to the fountain and drank, using a cup that rested on the marble edge. In truth, he was tired and, impressed as he was by the beauty of the room, the most important fact was that no food or couches were included in the splendour. The others followed him through an arch into the next room.

'This is more like it,' Marcus said cheerfully. A polished table was laid with food: meat, bread, eggs, vegetables and fish. Fruit was piled in bowls of gold. Soft couches stood around invitingly, but another door led onwards and Gaius could not resist looking.

The third room had a deep pool in the centre. The water steamed invitingly and bare wooden benches lined the walls, piled high with soft white cloths. Robes hung from stands by the water and four male slaves stood by low tables, ready to give massage if needed.

'Excellent,' Tubruk said. 'Your uncle is a fine host, Gaius. I am for a bath first, before I eat.' As he spoke, he began to pull off his clothes. One of the slaves walked to him and held out an arm for the garments as they were removed. When Tubruk was naked, the slave disappeared with them out of the only door. A few moments later, another entered and took up his place at the tables.

Tubruk lowered himself completely into the water, holding his breath as he slid below the surface and relaxing every muscle in the heat. By the time he surfaced, Gaius and Marcus had scrambled out of their garments, flung them at another slave and plunged into the opposite end, naked and laughing.

A slave held his arm out for Cabera's clothes and the old man frowned at him. Then he sighed and began stripping the robe from his skinny body.

'Always new experiences,' he said as he eased into the water, wincing.

'Shoulders, lad,' Tubruk called to one of the attendants.

The man nodded and knelt at the side of the pool, pressing his thumbs into Tubruk's muscles, unknotting the stresses that had been there since the slave attack on the estate.

'Good,' Tubruk sighed and he began to doze, lulled by the heat.

Marcus was first out onto the massage table, lying on the smooth cloth and steaming in the colder air. The nearest slave detached some instruments from his belt, almost like a set of long brass keys. He poured warm olive oil on liberally and then began to scrape Marcus' wet skin, as if he was skinning a fish, working the dirt of the journey off the surface and wiping a surprising amount of black filth onto a cloth at his waist. Then he rubbed the skin dry and poured a little more oil on for the massage, beginning great sweeping strokes along the spine.

Marcus groaned with satisfaction. 'Gaius, I think I'm going to like it here,' he muttered through slack lips.

Gaius lay in the water and let his mind drift free. Marius might not want to have the two boys around. He had no children of his own and the gods knew it was a difficult time for the Republic. All the fragile freedoms his father had loved were coming under threat with soldiers on every corner. As consul, Marius was one of the two most powerful men in the city, but, with Sulla's legion on the streets, his power became a fiction, his life at Sulla's whim. Yet how could Gaius protect his father's interests without his uncle's help? He had to be introduced to the Senate, sponsored by another. He could not just take his father's old place; they would throw him out and that would be the end of everything. Surely the blood tie to his mother would be worth a little help, but Gaius could not be sure. Marius was the golden general who had dropped in on his sister occasionally when Gaius was small. But the visits had become fewer and fewer as her illness progressed and it had been years since the last visit.

'Gaius?' Marcus' voice interrupted his thoughts. 'Come and have a massage. You're thinking too much again.'

Gaius grinned at his friend and rose from the water. It did not occur to him to be embarrassed at his nakedness. No one was.

'Cabera? Ever had a massage?' he asked as he passed the old man, whose eyes were drooping.

'No, but I'll try anything once,' Cabera replied, wading towards the steps.

'You're in the right city then,' Tubruk chuckled, eyes closed.

Clean and cool in fresh clothes and with the edge taken off their hunger, the four were escorted to Marius at sundown. As a slave, Alexandria did not accompany them, and for a moment Gaius was disappointed. When she was with them, he hardly knew what to say to her, but when she was gone his mind filled with clever pieces of wit that he could never quite remember to say later. He had not brought up the kiss in the stables with her and wondered if she thought of it as often as he did. He cleared his mind of her, knowing he had to be sharp and focused to meet a consul of Rome.

A portly slave stopped them outside the door to the chamber and fussed with their clothing, producing a carved ivory comb to pull Marcus' curls back into place and straightening Tubruk's jacket. As the fleshy fingers approached Cabera, the old man's hands shot out and slapped them away.

'Don't touch!' he snapped waspishly.

The slave's face remained blank and he carried on improving the others. At last he was satisfied, although he permitted himself a frown at Cabera.

'The master and mistress are present this evening. Bow first to the master as you present yourselves and keep your eyes on the floor as you bow. Then bow to Mistress Metella, an inch or two less deep. If your barbarian slave requires it, he can knock his head on the floor a few times as well.'

Cabera opened his mouth to retort, but the slave turned away and pushed the doors open.

Gaius entered first and saw a beautiful room with a garden in the centre, open to the sky. Around the rectangle of the garden was a walkway, with other rooms leading off it. Columns of white stone held the overhang of roof and the walls were painted with scenes from Roman history: the victories of Scipio, the conquest of Greece. Marius and his wife Metella stood to receive their guests and Gaius forced a smile onto his face, suddenly feeling very young and very awkward.

As he approached, he could see the man sizing him up and wondered what conclusions he was drawing. For his own part, Marius was an impressive figure. General of a hundred campaigns, he wore a loose toga that left his right arm and shoulder bare, revealing massive musculature and a dark weave of hair on the chest and forearms. He wore no jewellery or adornment of any kind, as if such things were unnecessary to a man of his stature. He stood straight and radiated strength and will. His face was stern and dark-brown eyes glared out from under heavy brows. Every feature revealed the city of his birth. His arms were clasped behind him and he said nothing as Gaius approached and bowed.

Metella had once been a beauty, but time and worry had clawed at her face, lines of some nameless grief gripping her skin with an old woman's talons. She seemed tense, the cords of sinew on her neck standing out. Her hands quivered slightly as she looked at him. She wore a simple dress of red cloth, complemented with earrings and bracelets of bright gold.

'My sister's son is always welcome in my house,' Marius said, his voice filling the space.

Gaius almost sagged with relief, but held himself firm.

Marcus came up beside him and bowed smoothly. Metella locked eyes with him and the quivering in her hands increased. Gaius caught Marius' sideways glance of worry at her as she stepped forward.

'Such beautiful boys,' she said, holding out her hands. Bemused, they took one each. 'What you have suffered in the uprising! What you have seen!'

She put a hand to Marcus' cheek. 'You will be safe here, do you understand? Our home is your home, for as long as you want.'

Marcus put his hand up to cover hers and whispered, 'Thank you.' He seemed more comfortable with the strange woman than Gaius was. Her intensity reminded him too painfully of his own mother.

'Perhaps you could check on the arrangements for the meal, my dear, while I discuss business with the boys,' Marius boomed cheerfully from behind them.

She nodded and left, with a backward glance at Marcus.

Marius cleared his throat.

'I think my wife likes you,' he said. 'The gods have not blessed us with children of our own and I think you will bring her comfort.'

His gaze passed over them.

'Tubruk – I see you are still the concerned guardian. I heard you fought well in the defence of my sister's house.'

'I did my duty, sir. It was not enough in the end.'

'The son lives, and his mother. Julius would say that was enough,' Marius replied. At this, his eyes returned to Gaius.

'I can see your father's face in yours. I am sorry for his leaving. I cannot say we were truly friends, but we had respect for each other, which is more honest than many friendships.

I could not attend his funeral, but he was in my thoughts and prayers.'

Gaius felt the beginnings of liking for this man. Perhaps that is his talent, warned an inner voice. Perhaps that is why he has been elected so many times. He is a man whom others follow.

'Thank you. He always spoke well of you,' he replied out loud.

Marius laughed, a short bark.

'I doubt it. How is your mother, is she . . . the same?'

'Much the same, sir. The doctors despair.'

Marius nodded, his face betraying nothing. 'You must call me uncle from now on, I think. Yes. Uncle suits me well. And you, who is this?' Once again, his eyes and focus had switched without warning, this time to Cabera, who looked back impassively.

'He is a priest and healer, my adviser. Cabera is his name,' Gaius replied.

'Where are you from, Cabera? Those are not Roman features.'

'The distant east, sir. My home is not known in Rome.'

'Try me. I have travelled far with my legion in my lifetime.' Marius did not blink, his gaze was relentless.

Cabera didn't seem perturbed by it.

'A hill village a thousand miles east of Aegyptus. I left it as a boy and the name is lost to me. I too have travelled far since then.'

The flame gaze snapped away as Marius lost interest. He looked again at the two boys.

'My house is your home from now on. I presume Tubruk will be returning to your estate?'

Gaius nodded.

'Good. I will arrange your entrance to the Senate as soon as I have sorted out a few problems of my own. Do you know Sulla?'

Gaius was painfully aware that he was being assessed. 'He controls Rome at present.'

Marius frowned, but Gaius went on: 'His legion patrols the streets and that gives him a great deal of influence.'

'You are correct. I see living on a farm hasn't kept you completely away from the affairs of the city. Come and sit down. Do you drink wine? No? Then this is as good a time as any to learn.'

As they sat on couches around the food-laden table, Marius bowed his head and began to pray aloud: 'Great Mars. Grant that I make the right decisions in the difficult days to come.' He straightened and grinned at them, motioning for a slave to pour wine.

'Your father could have been a great general, if he had wanted,' Marius said. 'He had the sharpest mind I have ever encountered, but chose to keep his interests small. He did not understand the reality of power – that a strong man can be above the rules and laws of his neighbours.'

'He set great stock by the laws of Rome,' Gaius replied, after a moment's thought.

'Yes. It was his one failing. Do you know how many times I have been elected consul?'

'Three,' Marcus put in.

'Yet the law only allows one term. I shall be elected again and again until I grow tired of the game. I am a dangerous man to refuse, you see. It comes down to that, for all the laws and regulations that are so dear to the old men of the Senate. My legion is loyal to me and me alone. I abolished the land qualification to join, so many of them owe their only livelihood to me. True, some of them are the scrapings of the gutters of Rome, but loyal and strong despite their origins and birth.

'Five thousand men would tear this city apart if I were assassinated, so I walk the streets in safety. *They* know what will happen if I die, do you see?

'If they can't kill me, they have to accommodate me, except that Sulla has finally come into the game, with a legion of his own, loyal only to him. I can't kill him and he can't kill me, so we growl at each other across the Senate floor and wait for a weakness. At present, he has the advantage. His men are in the streets as you say, whereas mine are camped outside the walls. Stalemate. Do you play latrunculi? I have a board here.'

This last question was to Gaius, who blinked and shook his head.

'I will teach you. Sulla is a master, and so am I. It is a good game for generals. The idea is to kill the enemy king, or to remove his power so that he is helpless and must surrender.'

A soldier entered in full, shining uniform. He saluted with a stiff right arm.

'General. The men you requested have arrived. They entered the city from different directions and gathered here.'

'Excellent! You see, Gaius, another move in the game is upon us. Fifty of my men are with me in my home. Unless Sulla has spies on every gate, he will not know they have entered the city. If he guesses my intentions, there will be a century from his legion waiting outside at daybreak, but all life is a gamble, yes?'

He addressed the guard.

'We will leave at dawn. Make sure my slaves look after the men. I will come along in a while.'

The soldier saluted again and left.

'What are you going to do?' Marcus asked, feeling completely out of his depth.

Marius rose and flexed his shoulders. He called a slave over and told him to prepare his uniform, ready for dawn.

'Have you ever seen a Triumph?'

'No. I don't think there has been one for a few years,' Gaius replied.

'It is the right of every general who has captured new lands: to march his legion through the streets of his beloved capital city and receive the love of the crowd and the thanks of the Senate.

'I have captured vast tracts of lush farming land in northern Africa, like Scipio before me. Yet a Triumph has been denied me by Sulla, who has the Senate under his thumb at the moment. He says the city has seen too much upheaval, but that is not the reason. What is his reason?'

'He does not want your men in the city, under any pretext,' Gaius said quickly.

'Good, so what must I do?'

'Bring them in anyway?' Gaius hazarded.

Marius froze. 'No. This *is* my beloved capital city. It has never had a hostile force enter its gates. I will not be the first. That is blind force, which is always chancy. No, I am going to ask! Dawn is in six hours. I suggest you get a little sleep, gentlemen. Just let one of the slaves know when you want to be taken to your rooms. Good night.' He chuckled and strode off, leaving the four of them alone.

'He . . .' Cabera began, but Tubruk held up a warning finger, motioning with his eyes at the slaves who stood by so unobtrusively.

'Life will not be dull here,' he said quietly.

Both Marcus and Gaius nodded and grinned at each other.

'I'd like to see him "ask",' Marcus said.

Tubruk shook his head quickly. 'Too dangerous. There will certainly be bloodshed, and I have not brought you to Rome to see you killed the first day! If I had known Marius planned something of this sort, I would have delayed.'

Gaius put a hand on the man's arm. 'You have been a good protector, Tubruk, but I too want to see this. We will not be refused in this.'

His voice was quiet, but Tubruk stared as if Gaius had shouted. Then he relaxed.

'Your father was never this foolhardy, but if you are set, and Marius agrees, I will come along to watch your back, as I have always done. Cabera?'

'Where else would I go? I still wander the same path as you.'

Tubruk nodded. 'Dawn then. I suggest you rise at least an hour or two before daybreak, for stretching exercises and a light breakfast.' He rose and bowed to Gaius. 'Sir?'

'You may leave, Tubruk,' Gaius said, his face straight.

Tubruk left.

Marcus raised an eyebrow, but Gaius ignored him. They were not in private and could not enjoy the casual relationship of the estate. Kin or not, Marius' house was not a place to relax. Tubruk had reminded them of this in his formal style.

Marcus and Cabera departed soon after, leaving Gaius to his thoughts. He lay back on a couch and stared at the night stars over the open garden.

He felt his eyes fill. His father was gone and he was stuck with strangers. Everything was new and different and overwhelming. Every word had to be considered before it left his mouth, every decision had to be judged. It was exhausting and, not for the first time, he wished he were a child again, without responsibility. He had always been able to turn to others when he made mistakes, but who could he turn to now? He wondered if his father or Tubruk had ever felt as lost as he did. It didn't seem possible that they knew the same fears. Perhaps everyone had them, but hid their worries from others.

When he was calm again, he rose in the darkness and walked silently out of the room, barely admitting his destination to himself. The corridors were silent and seemed deserted, but he had walked only a few paces before a guard stepped towards him and spoke.

'Can I help you, sir?'

Gaius started. Of course Marius would have guards around his house and gardens.

'I brought a slave in with me today. I would like to check on her before I sleep.'

'I understand, sir,' the guard replied, with a small smile. 'I'll show you the way to the slave quarters.'

Gaius gritted his teeth. He knew what the man was thinking, but speaking again would only worsen his suspicions. He followed in silence until they came to a heavy door at the end of the passage. The soldier knocked quietly and they waited for only a few moments before it opened.

A senior female glared at the guard. Her hair was greying and her face quickly set into disapproving lines, clearly a common expression with her.

'What do you want, Thomas? Lucy is asleep and I've told you before . . .'

'It's not for me. This young man is Marius' nephew. He brought a girl in with him today?'

The woman's manner changed as she perceived Gaius, who was shaking his head in painful silence, wondering how public things were going to get.

'Alexandria, wasn't it? Beautiful girl. My name is Carla. I'll show you to her room. Most of the slaves are asleep by now, so tread quietly, if you please.' She beckoned for Gaius to follow and he did so, neck and back stiff with embarrassment. He could feel Thomas' eyes on his back before the door closed gently behind him.

This part of Marius' house was plain but clean. A long corridor was lined with closed doors and there were small candles in holders along the walls at intervals. Only a few were lit, but enough light was shed for Gaius to see where they were going.

Carla's voice was lowered to a harsh whisper as she turned to him.

'Most of the slaves sleep in a few large rooms, but your girl was put in one of her own, that we keep for favoured ones. You said to treat her kindly, is that true?'

Gaius blushed. He had forgotten the interest that Marius' slaves would take in Alexandria and himself. It would be all over the house by the morning that he had visited her in the night.

They turned a final corner and Gaius froze in astonishment. The final door of the corridor was open and, against the low light from within, he could see Alexandria standing there, beautiful in the flickering candlelight. She alone would have caused him to take a quick breath, but there was someone with her, leaning against the wall in the shadows.

Carla darted forward and they both recognised Marcus at the same time. For his part, he seemed just as surprised to see them.

'How did you get in here?' Carla asked, her voice strained.

Marcus blinked.

'I crept about the place. I didn't want to wake everyone up,' he answered.

Gaius looked at Alexandria and his chest tightened with jealousy. She looked annoyed, but the glint in her eyes only heightened her tousled appearance. Her voice was curt.

'As you can both see, I am fine and quite comfortable. Slaves have to be up before dawn, so I would like to go to sleep, unless you want to bring Cabera or Tubruk along as well?'

Marcus and Gaius looked on her with surprised expressions. She really seemed quite angry.

'No? Then good night.' She nodded to them, her mouth firm, and gently closed the door.

Carla stood with her mouth open in astonishment. She wasn't sure how to start apologising.

'What are you doing here, Marcus?' Gaius demanded, keeping his voice low.

'Same thing as you. I thought she might be lonely. I didn't know you were going to make it a social occasion, did I?'

Doors were opening along the corridor and a low female voice called, 'Everything all right, Carla?'

'Yes, dear. Thank you,' Carla hissed back. 'Look. She's gone to bed. I suggest you two follow her example before the whole house turns out to see what's happening.'

Grim-faced, they nodded and walked back down the corridor together, leaving Carla with her hand over her mouth to stop her laughing before they were out of earshot. She nearly made it.

* * *

161

As Alexandria had predicted, the house of Marius came suddenly alive a good two hours before dawn. The kitchen ovens were lit, the windows opened, torches placed along the walls until the sun rose. Slaves bustled around, carrying trays of food and towels for the soldiers. The silence of the dark hours was broken by coarse laughter and shouts. Gaius and Marcus were awake at the first sounds, with Tubruk only a little behind them. Cabera refused to get up.

'Why would I want to? I will just throw on my robe and walk to the gates! Two more hours till dawn sounds good to me.'

'You can wash and have breakfast,' Marcus said, his eyes lively.

'I washed yesterday and I don't eat much before noon. Now go away.'

Marcus retreated and joined the others as they ate a little bread and honey, washed down with a hot, spiced wine that filled their bellies with warmth. They had not spoken of the events of the night before and both could feel a small tension between them and silences in the spaces they would usually have filled with light talk.

Finally, Gaius took a deep breath.

'If she likes you, I will stay out of it,' he said, each word pronounced clearly.

'Very decent of you,' Marcus replied, smiling. He drained his cup of hot wine and walked out of the room, smoothing his hair with one hand.

Tubruk glanced at Gaius' expression and barked out a laugh before following.

Looking fresh and rested, Marius strode back into the garden rooms with the clatter of iron-soled sandals on stone. He seemed even bigger in the general's uniform, an unstoppable figure. Marcus found himself watching the walk for weaknesses, as he had learned to watch any opponent. Did he dip a once-injured shoulder or favour a slightly weaker knee? There was nothing. This was a man who had never been close to death, who had never known despair. Though he had no children, a single weakness. Marcus wondered if it was Marius or his wife who was barren. The gods were known to be capricious, but what a jest to give so much to a man yet leave him unable to pass it on.

Marius wore a chestplate of bronze and a long red cloak over his shoulders. He had a simple legionary's gladius strapped to his waist, though Marcus noted the silver handle that set it apart from common blades. His brown legs were mostly bare under a leather kilt. He moved well, uncommonly well for a man of his age. His eyes glittered with some excitement or anticipation.

'Good to see you all up and about. You'll be marching with my men?' His voice was deep and steady, with no trace of nerves.

Gaius smiled, pleased not to have had to ask.

'We all are, with your permission . . . Uncle.'

Marius nodded his head at the word.

'Of course, but stay well back. This is a dangerous morning's entertainment, no matter how it turns out. One thing – you don't know the city and, if we do become separated, this house may no longer be safe. Seek out Valcinus at the public baths. They will be shut until noon, but he'll let you in if you mention my name. All set?'

Marcus, Gaius and Tubruk looked at each other, dazed at the speed of events. At least two of them were a little excited at the same time. They fell in behind Marius as he strode out to the yard where his men waited patiently.

Cabera joined them at the last minute. His eyes were as sharp as ever, but white stubble showed on his cheeks and chin. Marcus grinned at him and received a scowl as reply. They stood near the back of the group of men and Gaius took in the countenances of the soldiers around him. Brown-skinned and dark-haired to a man, they carried rectangular shields strapped to their left arms. On the brass face of each shield was the simple crest of the house of Marius – three arrows crossing each other. In that moment, Gaius understood what Marius had been explaining. These were Roman soldiers who would fight in defence of their city, but their loyalty was to the crest they carried.

All was silent as they waited for the great gates to swing open. Metella appeared out of the shadows and kissed Marius, who responded with enthusiasm, grasping a buttock. His men regarded this impassively, not sharing his lively mood. Then she turned and kissed Gaius and Marcus. To their surprise, they could see tears shine in her eyes.

'You come back safe to me. I will wait for you all.'

Gaius looked around for Alexandria. He had a vague notion that he could tell her of his noble decision to make way for Marcus. He hoped that she would be touched by his sacrifice and scorn Marcus' affections. Unfortunately, he could not see her anywhere, and then the gates opened and there was no more time.

Gaius and Marcus fell in with Tubruk and Cabera as the soldiers of Marius clattered out onto the dawn streets of Rome.

CHAPTER THIRTEEN

Under normal circumstances, the streets of Rome would have been empty at dawn, with the majority of the people waking in the late morning and continuing business up to midnight. With the curfew in force, the rhythm of the day had changed and the shops were opening as Marius and his men marched out.

The general led the soldiers, his step easy and sure. Shouts of warning went up from passers-by and Gaius could see people duck back into doorways as they spotted the armed men. After the recent riots, no one was in the mood to stand and watch the procession as it wound its way down the hill to the city forum where the Senate had its buildings.

At first, the main roads emptied as the early-rising workers stood well back for the soldiers. Gaius could feel their eyes on them and heard angry mutters. One word was repeated from hard faces: 'Scelus!' – a crime for soldiers to be on the streets. The dawn was damp and cold and he shivered slightly. Marcus too looked grim in the grey light and he nodded as their eyes met, his hand on the hilt of his gladius. The tension was heightened by the clatter and crash as the men moved. Gaius had not realised how noisy fifty soldiers could be, but in the narrow streets the clank of iron-shod sandals echoed back and forth. Windows opened in the high apartments as they passed and someone shouted angrily, but they marched on.

165

'Sulla will cut your eyes out!' one man howled before slamming his door shut.

Marius' men ignored the taunts and the crowd gathering behind them, drawn by the excitement and danger into a swelling mob.

Up ahead, a legionary carrying Sulla's mark on his shield turned at the noise and froze. They marched towards him and Gaius could feel the sudden excitement as every eye fixed on the lone man. He chose discretion over valour and set off at a trot, disappearing around a corner. A man at the front with Marius leaned forward as if to follow, but the general put a hand against his chest.

'Let him go. He'll tell them I'm coming.' His voice carried back through the ranks and Gaius marvelled at his calmness. No one else spoke and they continued, feet crashing down in time.

Cabera looked behind them and blanched as he saw the streets filling with followers. There was nowhere to retreat; a crowd was dogging their footsteps, their eyes bright with excitement, calling and hooting to each other. Cabera reached into his robe and brought forth a small blue stone on a thong, kissing it and mumbling a short prayer. Tubruk looked at the old man and put a hand out to his shoulder, gripping it briefly.

By the time they reached the great expanse of the forum, the crowd had spread to fill parallel roads and spilled out behind and around them. Gaius could feel the nervousness of the men he walked behind and saw their muscles tense as they loosened their swords in the scabbards, ready for action. He swallowed and found his throat dry. His heart beat quickly and he felt light-headed.

As if in mockery of the mood, the sun chose the moment they entered the forum to break from behind the morning mists, lighting the statues and temples on one side with gold. Gaius could see the steps of the Senate building ahead and licked suddenly dry lips as white-robed figures came out from the darkness and stood waiting for them. He counted four of Sulla's legionaries on the steps, hands on swords. Others would be on their way.

166

Hundreds of people were filling the forum from every direction, and jeers and calls could be heard echoing in the nearby streets. They all watched Marius and his men and they left an avenue to the Senate, knowing his destination without having to be told. Gaius clenched his teeth. There were so many people! They showed no sign of fear or awe and pointed, shouted, jostled and shoved each other for a better view. Gaius was beginning to regret having asked to accompany the soldiers.

At the foot of the steps, Marius halted his men and took one pace forward. The crowd pushed in around them, filling every space. The air smelled of sweat and spiced food. Thirty wide steps led up to the doors of the debating chamber. Nine senators stood on them.

Gaius recognised the face of Sulla, standing on the highest step. He stared straight at Marius without expression, his face like a mask. His hands were held behind his back, as if he was about to begin a lecture. His four legionaries had taken up position on the lowest step and Gaius could see that they at least were nervous of what would happen next.

Responsive to some invisible cue, the swelling crowd fell silent, broken here and there by mutters and curses as people struggled for better positions.

'You all know me,' Marius bellowed. His voice carried far in the silence. 'I am Marius, general, consul, citizen. Here, before the Senate, I claim my right to hold a Triumph, recognising the new lands my legion has conquered in Africa.'

The crowd pressed closer and one or two came to blows, sharp yelps breaking the tension of the moment. They pressed against the soldiers and two had to raise their arms and shove figures back into the mass, with more angry shouts in response. Gaius could feel the ugly mood of the crowd. They had gathered as they did when the games were on, to see death and violence and be entertained.

Gaius noticed that the other senators looked to Sulla to respond.

167

As the only other consul, it was his word that carried the authority of the city.

He took two steps down, closer to the soldiers. His face reddened with anger, but his words were quiet.

'This is unlawful. Tell your men to disperse. Come inside and we will discuss this when the full Senate has convened. You know the law, Marius.'

Those in the crowd who could hear him cheered this, while others shouted vulgarities, knowing they were protected from being seen by the churning mass of people.

'I do know the law! I know that a general has the right to demand a Triumph. I make that demand. Do you deny me?' Marius too had taken a step forward and the crowd surged with him, pushing and shoving, spilling onto the Senate steps between the two men.

'*Vappa! Cunnus!*' They screamed abuse at the soldiers who rebuffed them and Marius turned to the front row of his fifty. His eyes were cold and black.

'*Enough.* Make room for your general,' he said, his voice grim.

The front ten men drew their swords and cut down the nearest members of the crowd. In seconds, gashed bodies spat blood over the marble steps. They did not stop, killing with a cold intensity, men and women falling before them. A wail went up as the crowd tried to back away, but those at the rear could not see what was happening and continued to push forward. Every man of the fifty soldiers drew his gladius and cut around him, careless of who fell under the blade.

It must have been only a few seconds from start to finish, but it seemed hours to Gaius and Marcus who could only watch in horror as the ranks of the crowd were sliced down like wheat. The bodies littered the forum and the crowd was suddenly fighting to get away, the message having finally got through. A few more seconds and there was a great ring around Marius and his men, growing wider as citizens and slaves alike ran from the red swords.

Not a word had been said. Blades were wiped on the dead and resheathed. The men returned to their positions and Marius looked up at the senators again.

The stones of the forum were slicked wet with blood. The other men on the steps had gone pale, taking involuntary paces backwards away from the slaughter. Only Sulla had held firm and his lips twisted into a bitter grimace as the stench of fresh blood and opened bowels came to him.

The two men looked at each other for a long moment, as if only they were in the forum. The moment stretched and Marius raised his hand as if to give another command to his waiting men.

'One month from today,' Sulla snapped. 'Hold your Triumph, General, but remember you have made an enemy today. Savour the moments of joy that are due to you.'

Marius inclined his head.

'My thanks, Sulla, for your wisdom.'

He turned his back on the senators and called the turn, walking through the ranks to take up position at the front again. The crowd held back, but anger was on every bitter face.

'Forward,' came the bellow and, once again, the crash of iron on stone was heard as the half-century followed their general out of the plaza.

Gaius shook his head in wonderment at Tubruk and Marcus, saying nothing. Out of the corner of his eye, he saw a century of Sulla's men enter the plaza from a side street, each man running with his sword out and in hand. He tensed and would have shouted a warning, but caught Tubruk's shake of the head.

Behind them, Sulla had raised his hand to halt his men and they stood to attention, watching Marius leave with angry expressions. As Gaius reached the edge of the forum, he saw Sulla make a circle with his right hand in the air.

'A little too close in timing for my liking,' Tubruk whispered.

Marius snorted up ahead, overhearing. He strode forward, his voice carrying back.

'Close formation in the streets, men. This is not over yet.'

The soldiers drew into a tightly packed unit. Marius looked back over his shoulder.

'Watch the side streets. Sulla will not let us get clean away if he can help it. Keep your wits about you and your swords loose.'

Gaius felt dazed, carried along by events beyond his control. This was the safety of his uncle's shadow? He walked along with the others, hemmed in by legionaries.

A short, barking scream sounded from behind and Gaius whirled, almost knocked off his feet by the soldier behind him. One of the men was lying on the cobbles, in the filth of the road. Blood pooled around him and Gaius caught a glimpse of three men stabbing and cutting in a frenzy.

'Don't look,' Tubruk warned, turning Gaius forward with gentle pressure on his shoulder.

'But the man! Shouldn't we stop?' Gaius shouted, astonished.

'If we stop, we'll all die. Sulla has unleashed his dogs.'

Gaius glanced into a side street as they passed and saw a group of men with daggers drawn, running towards them. By their bearing, they were legionaries, but without uniforms. Gaius drew his sword almost at one with all the others. His heart began to pound again and he felt sweat break out on his forehead.

'Hold your nerve! We stop for nothing,' Marius shouted back, his neck and back muscles rigid.

The knife men attacked the back row again as it passed, one of them going down with a gladius in his ribs before the others bore their man down onto the ground. He yelled in fear as his sword was wrenched from his grasp and then the yell was cut suddenly short.

As they marched on, Gaius could hear hoots of triumph from behind. He sneaked a look back and wished he hadn't as the attackers raised a bloody head and howled like animals. The men around him swore viciously and one of them suddenly stopped, raising his sword.

'Come on, Vegus, we're nearly there,' another urged him, but he shook off the hands on his shoulders and spat at the ground.

'He was my friend,' he muttered and broke rank, racing back towards the bloody group. Gaius tried to watch what happened. He could hear the cry as they saw him coming, but then men seemed to pour out of the alleyways and he was torn apart without a sound.

'Steady,' Marius shouted, and Gaius could hear the anger in the voice, the first touch of it he'd seen in the man. 'Steady,' he called again.

Marcus took a dagger from the man on his right and drifted back through the ranks. He was in the last row of three when they passed the dark mouth of an alleyway and four others sprang, their knives held to kill. Marcus ducked and took the weight of an attacker as they crashed together in a violent embrace. He pulled his knife across the throat he saw so close to his own and blinked as the blood spurted out over him. He used the body to block another thrust and then threw it at the remaining attackers. As it landed, the men went down to swift, punching stabs from the three legionaries, who then rejoined the ranks without a word. One of them clapped a hand on Marcus' shoulder and Marcus grinned at him. He ghosted up through the ranks again and arrived at Gaius' side, panting slightly. Gaius clasped the back of his neck for a second.

Then the gates were opening in front of them and they were safe, holding formation until the last man was through into the courtyard.

As the gates closed, Gaius went back to look down the hill they'd walked together. It was deserted, not a face showed. Rome seemed as quiet and orderly as ever.

CHAPTER FOURTEEN

Marius almost glowed with pleasure and energy as he walked amongst his men, clapping his hands to shoulders and laughing. They grinned wryly, like schoolboys being congratulated by a tutor.

'We've done it, boys!' Marius shouted. 'We'll show this city a day to remember a month from today.' They cheered him and he called for wine and refreshments, summoning every slave of his home to treat the men like kings.

'Anything they want!' he bellowed. Wine cups of gold and silver were pressed into the rough hands of every man back in through the gates, Gaius and Marcus included. Dark purple wine sloshed and gurgled as it was poured from clay jugs. Alexandria was with the other slaves and smiled at both Marcus and Gaius. Gaius nodded to her, but Marcus winked as she passed him.

Tubruk sniffed his wine and chuckled. 'The best.'

Marius held his cup high, his expression sombre. Silence fell after a few seconds.

'To those who didn't make it today, who died for us. Tagoe, Luca and Vegus. Good men all.'

'Good men all!' Every voice echoed his in a guttural chorus, and the cups were tipped back and held out for refills from the waiting slaves.

'He knew their names,' Gaius whispered to Tubruk, who brought his head close to reply.

'He knows all their names,' he muttered. 'That is why he is a good general. That is why they love him. He could tell you some of the history of every man here and a good portion of the legion outside Rome as well. Oh, you can call it a trick if you like, a cheap way to impress the men who serve. I know that's what he would say, if you asked him.' He paused to look at the general as he caught a huge and husky soldier in a headlock and walked through the crowd with him. The man bellowed, but didn't struggle. He bore it as it was meant.

'They're his children, I think. You can see how much he loves them. That big man could probably tear Marius' arms off if he wanted. On another day, he'd put a dagger in a man for looking at him with a squint in the noonday sun. But Marius can lead him around by the head and he laughs. I'm not sure you can train a man into that skill – I think it's born into you, or not. You don't even need to have it to be a good general.

'These men would follow Sulla, if they were in his legion. They'd fight for him and hold formation and die for him. But they love Marius, so they can't be bribed or bought and in battle they will not ever run, not to the last man. Not while he's watching, anyway. There used to be a land qualification to be in the legions, but Marius abolished it. Now anyone can make a career fighting for Rome, at least for him. Half these men wouldn't have made it into the army before Marius had his law passed by the Senate. They owe him a great deal.'

The men began to walk out of the entrance square, off to be bathed and massaged by the prettiest female slaves on the grounds. Several beauties had taken arms and were already gasping and exclaiming at stories of battle prowess. When Marius let go of the big legionary's head, he immediately called a girl over, a slim brunette with kohl-dark eyes. The big man took one look and grinned like a wolf, gathering her up into his arms. The echoes of her laughter came back off the brick walls as he trotted into the main buildings.

One young soldier dropped a powerfully muscled arm onto Alexandria's shoulder and said something to her. Marcus came up behind the man quickly.

'Not this girl, friend. She's not from this house.'

The soldier looked at him and took in the boy's bearing and determined expression. He shrugged and called to another slave girl as she passed by. Gaius stood watching the exchange and when Alexandria caught his eye, her face filled with anger. She turned her back on Marcus and strode into the cool interior of the garden rooms.

Marcus turned to his friend. He had noticed her expression and his own was thoughtful.

'Why was she so annoyed?' Gaius said, exasperated. 'I wouldn't have thought she wanted to go with that big ox. You saved her.'

Marcus nodded. 'That may be the problem. Perhaps she didn't want me to. Perhaps she wanted you to save her.'

'Oh.' Gaius' face lit up. 'Really?'

Marius staggered over to Gaius and his friends, still laughing, his hair plastered to his forehead with wine emptied over him. His eyes were shining with pleasure. He took Gaius by both shoulders.

'Well, lad? How was your first taste of Rome?'

Gaius grinned back at him. You couldn't help it. The man's emotions were infectious. When he frowned, dark clouds of fear and anger followed him around and touched all who met him. When he smiled, you wanted to smile. You wanted to be one of his men. Gaius could feel the power of the man and for the first time wondered if he could ever command that kind of loyalty himself.

'It was frightening, but exciting as well,' he replied, unable to stop his lips smiling.

'Good! Some don't feel it, you know. They just add up supply figures and calculate how many men it would take to hold a ravine. They just don't feel the excitement.'

174

He looked over at Marcus, Tubruk and Cabera.

'Get drunk if you like, have a woman if you can find one by now. We'll do no work today and no one can leave until it's dark after that trouble we had. Tomorrow, we'll start planning how to bring five thousand men fifty miles and all the way through Rome. Do you know anything about supply?'

Both Marcus and Gaius shook their heads.

'You'll learn. The best army in the world is lost without food and water, boys. That's the thing to know. Everything else falls into place. My home is your home, remember. I'm going to sit in the fountain and get drunk.' He collected three unopened jugs of wine from the remaining male slaves and walked away – a man with a mission.

Tubruk watched him leave the courtyard with a wry smile.

'Once, in North Africa, on the eve of a battle against a savage tribe, they say Marius walked alone into the enemy camp carrying a jug of wine in each hand. Remember, this was the camp of seven thousand of the most brutal warriors the legion had encountered. He drank all night with the chief of the tribe, despite not understanding a word of each other's language. They toasted life and the future and courage. Then the next morning he staggered back to his own lines.'

'What happened next?' Marcus said.

'They wiped out the tribe to the last man. What would you expect?' Tubruk laughed.

'Why didn't the chief kill him?' Marcus continued.

'I suppose he liked him. Most people do.'

Metella came into the courtyard and held out her hands to Gaius and Marcus, smiling.

'I'm glad you are safely returned to us. I want you both to think of this house as a place of peace and refuge for you.'

She gazed into Marcus' eyes and he looked back calmly. 'Is it true you grew up without a mother?'

Marcus blushed a little, wondering how much Marius had told her. He nodded and Metella gave a little gasp.

'You poor boy. I would have brought you to me earlier if I had known.'

Marcus was wondering if she knew what the legionaries were getting up to with her female slaves. She didn't seem to fit into the bluff world of Marius and his legion. He wondered what his own mother was like, and for the first time considered trying to find her. Marius would probably know, but it was not a question he wished to ask the man. Perhaps Tubruk would tell him before he returned to the estate.

Metella took her hand away from his and reached up to brush his cheek.

'You have had a rough time of it, but that is all over now.'

Slowly, he touched her hand with his and it was as if they had reached some private understanding. Suddenly her eyes glistened with tears and she turned and walked away along the cloisters.

Marcus looked at Gaius and shrugged.

'You have a friend there,' Tubruk said, watching her retreating figure. 'She has taken a liking to you.'

'I'm a bit old to need a mother,' Marcus muttered.

'Possibly, but she's not too old to need a son.'

At noon, there was a commotion at the house gates. Some of the legionaries turned out with swords drawn in case it was a reprisal for the morning's work. Gaius and Marcus rushed to the courtyard with the rest and then stopped and gaped.

Renius was there, draped through the metal poles and singing a drunken dirge. He used the crossbar of the gate to steady himself, but his tunic was soaked with wine and specks of vomit. A guard stepped up to the bars and spoke to him as Gaius and Marcus came up, Tubruk just behind them.

Suddenly, Renius reached up to the man's hair and pulled his head into the metal with a clang. Unconscious, the soldier fell away and the others began to shout in anger.

'Let him in and kill him!' yelled one man, but another said it could be a trap of Sulla's to make them open the gates. This gave them all pause and it was Gaius and Marcus who approached the gates next.

'Can we help you?' Marcus said, raising his eyebrows in polite inquiry.

Renius mumbled angrily, 'I'll stick my sword up you, whore's boy.'

Marcus started to laugh.

'Open the gates,' Gaius called to the other guard. 'It's Renius – he's with me.'

The guard ignored him as if he had not spoken, making it clear that Gaius could not give orders in that house. As Gaius stepped towards the gate, a legionary took a pace to stand in front of him, shaking his head slowly.

Marcus sidled over to the gate and said a few quiet words to the guard there.

The man was in the middle of replying when Marcus butted him savagely, knocking him down into the dust. Ignoring the guard as he flailed and tried to get up, Marcus ran back the big bolts that held the door secure and opened it.

Renius fell into the yard and lay flat, his good arm twitching. Marcus chuckled and began to close the gate when he heard the smooth metallic sound of a knife coming from a sheath. He spun and was just in time to block a thrust from the furious guard with his forearm. With his left hand, he backhanded the man across the mouth and sent him sprawling again. Marcus shut the gate.

Two more of the men ran up to grab him, but a voice called, 'Hold!' and everyone froze for a second. Marius walked into the courtyard, showing no effects from the wine he had been putting away steadily for two hours. As he approached, the two men kept their eyes on Marcus, who looked calmly back at them.

'Gods! What is going on in my house?' Marius came up and put a heavy hand on the shoulder of one of the men facing Marcus.

'Renius is here,' Gaius said. 'He came with us from the estate.'

Marius looked down at the sprawling figure, peacefully asleep on the stones.

'He never got drunk when he was a gladiator. I can see why if this is how it affects him. What happened to you?' The last question was addressed to the guard who had resumed his post. His mouth and nose were bloody and his eyes sparked with indignation, but he knew better than to complain to Marius.

'Caught myself in the face with the gate when I was opening it,' he said slowly.

'Damned careless of you, Fulvio. You should have let my nephew help you with it.'

The message was clear. The man nodded and wiped a little of the blood away with his hand.

'Glad we've cleared that up. Now, you and you' – he pointed a stiff finger at Gaius and Marcus – 'come with me to my study. We need to discuss a couple of things.'

He waited until Gaius and Marcus had walked in front of him before falling in behind. Over his shoulder, he called, 'Get that old man somewhere to sleep it off and keep that damned gate shut.'

Marcus caught the eye of the legionaries nearby and found they were all grinning, whether in malice or genuine amusement, he couldn't say.

Marius opened the door of his study and let the two go through into a room lined with maps on every wall, showing Africa and the empire and Rome herself. He closed the door quietly and then turned to face them. His eyes were cold and Gaius felt a momentary pang of fear as the man focused his dark gaze on him.

'What did you think you were doing?' Marius spat from between clenched teeth.

Gaius opened his mouth to say he was letting Renius in when he thought better of it.

'I'm sorry. I should have waited for you.'

Marius banged his heavy fist on the desk.

'I suppose you realise that if Sulla had had twenty picked men in the street waiting for just such an opportunity, we would most likely be dead by now?'

Gaius blushed miserably.

Marius swivelled to face Marcus. 'And you. Why did you attack Fulvio?'

'Gaius gave the order to open the gates. The man ignored him. I made it happen.'

There was no give in Marcus. He looked up at the older man and met his gaze unflinchingly.

The general raised his eyebrows in disbelief.

'You expected him, a veteran of thirty conflicts, to take orders from a beardless boy of fourteen?'

'I . . . didn't think about it.' For the first time, Marcus looked unsure of himself and the general turned back to Gaius.

'If I back you in this, I will lose some of the respect of the men. They all know you made a mistake and will be waiting to see what I do about it.'

Gaius' heart sank.

'There is a way out of this, but it will cost you both dearly. Fulvio is the boxing champion of his century. He lost a lot of face today when you clipped him, Marcus. I dare say he would be willing to take part in a friendly fight, just to clear the air. Otherwise, he may well put a knife in you when I am not around to step in.'

'He'll kill me,' Marcus said quietly.

'Not in a friendly match. We won't use the iron gloves, because of your tender age, just goatskin ones to protect your hands. Have you been trained at all?'

The boys murmured that they had, thinking of Renius.

Marius turned to Gaius again.

'Of course, win or lose, if your friend shows courage, the men will love him and I can't have my nephew in his shadow, do you understand?'

Gaius nodded, guessing what was coming.

'I'll put you in against one of the others. They're all champions at some skill or other, which is why I chose them for the escort duty to the Senate. You'll both take a beating, but if you handle yourselves well enough the incident will be forgotten and you may even gain a bit of standing with my men. They are the scum of the gutters, most of them; they fear nothing and have respect only for strength. Oh, I can just order them back to duties and do nothing, letting you hide in the shadow of my authority, but that won't do, d'you see?'

Their faces were bleak, and he snorted suddenly.

'Smile, boys. You might as well. There is no other way out of this, so why not spit in old Jupiter's eye while you're at it?'

They looked at each other, and both grinned.

Marius laughed again.

'You'll do. Two hours. I'll tell the men and announce the opponents. That'll give Renius time to sober up a little. I should think he would want to see this. By all the gods, *I* want to see this! Dismissed!'

Gaius and Marcus walked slowly back to their rooms. Their initial levity had faded, leaving a sick churning in both their stomachs at what was to come.

'Hey! Do you realise I put a century boxing champion on his back? I am damn well going to try and win this match. If I can hit him once, I can knock him out. One good strike is all it takes.'

'But this time he'll be expecting it,' Gaius replied morosely. 'I'll probably get that big ape Marius was leading around by the head earlier; that would be just the sort of joke he likes.'

'Big men are slow. You're fast with the cross, but you'll have to stay out of range. All these soldiers are heavy and that means they can hit harder than we can. Keep moving your feet and wear them down.'

'We're going to be murdered,' Gaius replied.

'Yes, I think we probably are.'

Tubruk was calmly accepting when he heard the news back at their rooms.

'I expected something like it. Marius loves contests and is forever staging them between his own men and those of the other legions. This is just his style – a bit of cheering and a deal of blood and everything is forgotten and forgiven.

'Thankfully, you haven't drunk more than a cup or two of wine. Come on, two hours is not long to get you warmed up and ready. You'd better spar for a while in one of the training rooms. Get a slave to direct you to one and I'll find you as soon as I have some gloves. One thing – don't let Marius down. Especially you, Gaius. You're his kin, you have to put on a good show.'

'I understand,' Gaius replied grimly.

'Then get going. I'll have some of the slaves throw ice water on Renius – from a distance so that he doesn't go berserk.'

'What happened with him? Why was he drunk so early in the day?' Gaius asked, curiously.

'I don't know. Concentrate on one thing at a time. You'll have a chance to speak to Renius this evening. Now go!'

* * *

While the rest of Rome slept through the heat of the afternoon, the men from the First-Born legion gathered in the largest training room, lining the walls, laughing, chatting and sipping cool beer and fruit juices. After the fights, Marius had promised them a ten-course feast of good food and wine, and the mood was relaxed and cheerful. Tubruk stood with Marcus and Gaius, loosening the shoulders of one then the other. Cabera sat on a stool, his face inscrutable.

'They are both right-handed,' Tubruk said quietly. 'Fulvio you know; the other, Decidus, is a javelin champion. He has very strong shoulders, though he doesn't look fast. Stay away from them, make them come to you.'

Marcus and Gaius nodded. Both were a little pale under their tanned skin.

'Remember, the idea is to stay upright long enough to show you have nerve. If you go down early, get up. I'll stop it if you're in real trouble, but Marius won't like that, so I will have to be careful.' He put a hand on each of their shoulders.

'Both of you have skill and courage and wind. Renius is watching. Don't let us down.'

Both boys glanced over to where Renius sat, his useless arm strapped to his belt. His hair was still damp and murder glinted from his expression.

Cheering began as Marius entered. He held up his hands for quiet and it came quickly.

'I expect each man to do his best, but know that my money will be on my nephew and his friend. Two bets, twenty-five aurei on each. Do I have any takers?'

For a moment, the silence held. Fifty gold pieces was a huge bet for a private fight, but who could resist? The gathered men emptied their pouches and some left for their rooms to fetch more coins. After a while, the money was there and Marius added his own pouch so that one hundred gold pieces were held in his great hand, enough to buy a smallholding, or a warhorse and full armour and weapons.

'Will you hold the bag for us, Renius?' Marius asked.

'I will,' he replied, his tone solemn and formal. He seemed to have thrown off most of the effects of drink, but Gaius noticed he did not try to rise and waited until the money was brought to him.

Fulvio and Decidus entered the training hall to more cheering from the men. There was now no question where their support lay.

Both men were wearing only a tight-fitting cloth wrapped around their groins and upper thighs, held by a wide belt. Decidus had the sort of shoulders and physique usually seen on the statues of the forum. Gaius watched him closely, but there were no obvious weaknesses. Fulvio did not wave to the crowd. His nose was bound with a strip of cloth tied at the back of his head and his lips were swollen and angry-looking.

Gaius nudged Marcus. 'Looks like you broke his nose with that butt earlier on. He'll be expecting you to hit it again, you realise. Wait for a good opportunity.'

Marcus nodded, engrossed as Gaius had been with his study of the man and his movements.

Marius raised his hands again to be heard over the lively soldiers.

'Marcus and Fulvio will fight the first bout. No time limits, but a round ends when one man has a knee or more on the ground. When one is unable to rise, the bout is over and the other will begin. Come to your marks.'

Fulvio and Marcus came to stand on either side of the general. 'When the horn is blown, you begin. Good luck.'

Marius walked sedately to the sidelines with the men and signalled to one to sound the horn usually used in battle. A hush fell and the blare resonated as a pure note.

Marcus loosened his shoulders, rocked his head from side to

side and stepped forward. He held his hands high as he had been taught by Renius, but Fulvio kept his fists relaxed, his arms only slightly bent. He swayed as Marcus jabbed with his left and the blows went by harmlessly. One fist shot out and thumped into Marcus' chest, over the heart. He gasped in pain and backed away, then set his teeth and came in again. He launched a fast jab followed immediately by a straight right, but, again, Fulvio moved out of the way with a single step and hammered the same spot with his gloved right hand. Marcus felt the air explode out of him with the pain.

The men had begun cheering and only Gaius, Tubruk and Cabera cheered for the younger fighter. Fulvio was smiling and Marcus began to think. The man was fast and difficult to hit. At present, Marcus was doing all the work, winning nothing for his efforts. He growled in rage and surged forward, his right arm cocked. He saw Fulvio steady himself and then pulled up suddenly, letting the blow that should have knocked him out go past his chin. Marcus punched fast and hard at Fulvio's nose and was gratified at the crunch of bones he felt. At that second, a cross caught him on the side of his head and he went down hard on the wooden floor, dazed and winded.

He panted as he came up onto one knee and looked up at Fulvio standing a couple of paces away. Blood streamed from his nose again and he looked murderous.

Marcus got up into a flurry of blows. He tried to stay away and fend off the worst of them, but Fulvio was all over him, thumping fists into his stomach and kidneys from all angles, chopping him to pieces, and when the pain made him hunch, catching Marcus with swift uppercuts to the head, rocking him back. He fell again and lay there, his chest heaving painfully. He tasted blood in his mouth and his left eye was swelling shut under the assault of Fulvio's straight right.

This time he rose and took three quick steps backwards to give him time to compose himself. Fulvio came with him remorselessly, moving his head and body from side to side as he looked for the best place to hit. The man resembled a snake about to bite and Marcus knew the next time he went down he was unlikely to get up. Anger flooded him and he ducked the first punch on sheer reflexes, batting the follow-through away with his arm. He felt Fulvio's forearm slide under his fingers and suddenly gripped the wrist. His right fist came into the man's stomach with all the power of his shoulders behind it and he was rewarded with a slight whoosh of pain.

Still holding the arm, he tried to repeat the punch, but Fulvio brought his left over and clipped him hard on the jaw. The world went black and he fell down, barely feeling the hard, wooden boards underneath him. His legs seemed to have lost all strength and he could only manage to get himself up onto all fours, panting like a beast.

Fulvio waved a glove at him to get up, still unsatisfied. Marcus looked down at the floor and wondered if he should. Blood dribbled from between his lips and he watched it spatter into a small pool.

Ah well, he thought. One more try.

This time Fulvio didn't rush him. He was grinning again and beckoned with his hands for Marcus to come on. Marcus tightened his jaw. He was going to put the man on his back one more time if it killed him. He imagined each of Fulvio's fists held a dagger, so that any contact would mean death. He felt his spirits rise. He knew how to fight with swords and knives, so why was this so different? He let himself sway a little, wanting Fulvio to come in. Most of his knife training had revolved around counter-strikes and he wanted the boxer to throw another punch. Fulvio quickly lost patience and came in fast, fists bobbing.

Marcus watched the fists and when one exploded towards him, he blocked, lifting it with his forearm and counter-punched into

Fulvio's abdomen. Fulvio grunted and the left came over the top again in reflex, but this time Marcus dropped his head and the blow skidded over him, leaving Fulvio open for a split second. Marcus hammered everything into a straight left stopper, wishing it were his right. Fulvio's head rocked back and, when it came level, the right was ready and Marcus smacked it into the boxer's broken nose again. Fulvio took a sudden seat and fresh blood poured from his battered nose.

Before Marcus could feel any pleasure, the man leapt up and poured out a string of blows, seeming to move twice as fast as he had before. Marcus went down after the first two and caught two more as he fell. This time he didn't get up and didn't hear the cheers or the horn as Marius nodded to end the match.

Fulvio raised his hands in triumph and Marius ruefully signalled the first fifty of the hundred gold coins to be given back to the men. They gathered together in a momentary huddle and then, when silence had fallen, one of them offered the bag back to Marius.

'We'll let the win ride for the next one, sir, if you're willing,' he said.

Marius grimaced in mock horror, but nodded and said he would cover the bet. The men cheered again.

Marcus woke up as Tubruk threw a cup of wine in his face.

'Did I win?' he said through smashed lips.

Tubruk chuckled and wiped some of the blood and wine off his face.

'Not even close, but you were still astonishing. You shouldn't have been able to touch him.'

'Touched him properly though,' he mumbled, smiling and wincing as his lips cracked. 'Knocked him on his arse.'

Marcus looked around for somewhere to spit and, finding nothing handy, swallowed a gummy mixture of phlegm and blood.

Every part of him hurt, worse than it had when he'd been tied up by Suetonius years before. He wondered if he'd be as good-looking when he'd healed, but his thoughts were interrupted by Fulvio coming over, taking off his gloves as he walked.

'Good fight. I had three gold pieces on me, myself. You're very fast – in a few years, you could be seriously dangerous.'

Marcus nodded and put out his hand. Fulvio looked at it and then shook it briefly and walked back to the men, who cheered him all over again.

'Take the cloth and keep dabbing as the blood drips,' Tubruk continued cheerfully. 'You'll need stitches over your eye. We'll have to cut it to get the swelling down as well.'

'Not yet. I'll watch Gaius first.'

'Of course.' Tubruk walked away, still chuckling, and Marcus squinted at him through his one good eye.

Gaius clenched his fists and waited for Tubruk to reach him. His opponent had already taken the floor and was limbering up, stretching his muscular shoulders and legs.

'He's a big brute,' he muttered as Tubruk came alongside.

'True, but he's not a boxer. You have a reasonable chance against this one, as long as you don't get in the way of one of his big punches. He'll put you out like snuffing a candle if he catches you. Stay back and use your feet to move around him.'

Gaius looked at him quizzically. 'Anything else?'

'If you can, punch him in the testicles. He'll watch for it, but it isn't strictly speaking against the rules.'

'Tubruk, you do not have the heart of a decent man.'

'No, I have the heart of a slave and a gladiator. I have two gold pieces on you for this one and I want to win.'

'Did you bet on Marcus?' he asked.

'Of course not. Unlike Marius, I don't throw money away.'

Marius came to the centre and signalled for silence once again.

'After that disappointing loss, the money rides on the next bout. Decidus and Gaius, take your marks. Same rules. When you hear the horn, begin.' He waited until both stood eyeing each other and walked to the wall, folding his great arms over his chest.

As the horn sounded, Gaius stepped in and slammed his fist up into Decidus' throat. The bigger man gave out a choked groan and raised both his hands to his neck, in agony. Gaius threw a scything uppercut that caught Decidus on the chin. He went down onto his knees and then toppled forward, his eyes glassy and blank. Gaius walked slowly back to his stool and sat down. He smiled silently and Renius, watching, remembered the same smile on a younger boy's face as he'd lifted him from the icy waters of a river pool. Renius nodded sharply in approval, his eyes bright, but Gaius did not see it.

The silence roared for a second, then the men released the breath they'd been holding and a rabble of voices broke out – mostly questions and spiced with a few choice swearwords as they realised the bets were all lost.

Marius walked over to the prostrate figure and felt his neck for a second. Silence fell again. Finally, he nodded.

'His heart beats. He'll live. Should have kept his chin down.'

The men gave a half-hearted cheer for the winner, though their spirits weren't really in it.

Marius addressed the crowd, grinning.

'If you have an appetite, there's a feast waiting for you in the dining hall. We'll make a night of it, for tomorrow it's back to planning and work.'

Decidus was revived and taken out, shaking his head groggily. The rest trooped after him, leaving Marcus and Gaius alone with the general. Renius never left his seat and Cabera stayed back as well, his face alive with interest.

'Well, boys, you've made me a lot of money today!' Marius boomed, starting to laugh. He had to lean against a wall for support as the laughter shook his frame.

'Their faces! Two beardless boys and one puts Fulvio on his

backside . . .' The laughter overtook him and he wiped his eyes as they streamed over his red face.

Renius stood up, swaying a little. He walked over to Marcus and Gaius and clapped a hand on each shoulder.

'You've started making your names,' he said quietly.

CHAPTER FIFTEEN

On the night before the Triumph the First-Born camp was anything but peaceful. Gaius sat around one of the campfires and sharpened a dagger that had belonged to his father. All around, the fires and noise of seven thousand soldiers and camp followers made the darkness busy and cheerful. They were camped in open country, less than five miles from the gates of the city. For the last week, armour had been polished, leather waxed, tears in cloth stitched. Horses were groomed until they shone like chestnuts. Marching drills had become tense affairs; mistakes were not tolerated and no one wanted to be left behind when they marched into Rome.

The men were all proud of Marius and themselves. There was no false modesty in the camp; they knew they and he deserved the honour.

Gaius stopped sharpening as Marcus came into the firelight and took a seat on a bench. Gaius looked into the flames and didn't smile.

'What's the word?' he said, angrily, without turning his head.

'I leave at dawn tomorrow,' Marcus replied. He too looked into the fire as he continued speaking. 'This is for the best, you know. Marius has written a letter for me to take to my new century. Would you like to see it?'

Gaius nodded and Marcus passed a scroll over to him. He read:

I recommend this young man to you, Carac. He will make a first-rate soldier in a few years. He has a good mind and excellent reflexes. He was trained by Renius, who will accompany him to your camp. Give him responsibility as soon as he has proved he can handle it. He is a friend of my house.

Marius. Primigenia.

'Fine words. I wish you luck,' Gaius said bitterly as he finished, passing back the scroll.

Marcus snorted. 'More than just fine words! Your uncle has given me my ticket into another legion. You don't understand what this means to me. Of course I would like to stay with you, but you will be learning politics in the Senate, then taking a high post in the army and the temples. I own nothing except my skills and my wits and the equipment Marius has given me. Without his patronage, I would be pushed to get a post as a temple guard! With it, I have a chance to make something of myself. Do you grudge it of me?'

Gaius turned to him, his anger surprising Marcus.

'I know it's what you have to do, I just never saw myself tackling Rome alone. I always expected you to be with me. That is what friendship means.'

Marcus gripped his arm tightly.

'You will always be my greatest friend. If ever you need me to be at your side, then call and I will come to you. You remember the pact before we came to the city? We look out for each other and we can trust each other completely. That is my oath and I have never broken it.'

Gaius did not look at him and Marcus let his hand fall away.

'You can have Alexandria,' Marcus said, attempting a noble expression.

Gaius gasped. 'A parting gift? What a generous friend you are! You are too ugly for her, as she told me only yesterday. She only likes your company for the contrast. You make her look more beautiful when your monkey face is around.'

Marcus nodded cheerfully. 'She does seem to want me only for sex. Perhaps you can read poetry to her while I run her through the positions.'

Gaius took a quick breath of indignation, then smiled slowly at his friend.

'With you gone, I will be the one showing her the positions.' He chuckled to himself at this, hiding his thoughts. What positions? He could only think of two.

'You will be like a bullock after me, with all the practice I have been getting. Marius is a generous man.'

Gaius looked at his friend, trying to judge how much of his boasting was just that. He knew Marcus had proved a favourite with the slave girls of Marius' house and was rarely to be found in his own room after dark. As for himself, he didn't know what he felt. Sometimes he wanted Alexandria so much it hurt him and other times he wanted to be chasing the girls along the corridors as Marcus did. He did know that if he ever tried to force her as a slave, he would lose all that he found precious. A silver coin would buy him that kind of union. The idea that Marcus might have already enjoyed what he wanted made his blood thump in irritation.

Marcus broke in on these thoughts, his voice low. 'You will need friends when you are older, men you can trust. We've both seen what sort of power your uncle has and I think both of us would like a taste of it.'

Gaius nodded.

'Then what good will I be to you as a penniless son of a city whore? I can make my name and fortune in my new legion and *then* we can make real plans for the future.'

'I understand. I remember our oath and I will stick to it.' Gaius was silent for a moment, then shook his head to clear it of thoughts of Alexandria. 'Where will you be stationed?'

'I'm with the Fourth Macedonia, so Renius and I are going to Greece – the home of civilisation, they say. I'm looking forward to seeing alien lands. I have heard that the women run races without clothes on, you know. Makes the mind bulge a bit. Not just the mind, either.' He laughed and Gaius smiled sickly, still thinking of Alexandria. Would she have given herself to him?

'I'm glad Renius is your escort. It'll do him good to take his mind off his troubles for a while.'

Marcus grimaced. 'True, though he won't be the best of company. He's been out of sorts ever since he turned up drunk at your uncle's, but I can understand why.'

'If the slaves had burned my house down, I'd be a bit lost as well. They even took his savings, you know. Had them under the floor, he said, but they must have been found by looters. That was not a glorious chapter in our history, slaves stealing an old man's savings. Mind you, he's not really an old man any more, is he?'

Marcus looked sideways at him. They had never discussed it, but Gaius hadn't seemed to need telling.

'Cabera?' Gaius said, catching his eye.

Marcus nodded.

'I thought so; he did something similar for me, when I was wounded. He is certainly a useful man to have around.'

'I am glad he's staying with you. He has faith in your future. He should be able to keep you alive until I can come back, covered in glory and draped with beautiful women, all of whom will be the winners of foot-races.'

'I might not recognise you underneath all that glory and those women.'

'I'll be the same. I'm sorry I'll miss the Triumph tomorrow. It should really be something special. You know he has had silver coins printed with his face? He's going to throw them to the crowds in the streets.'

Gaius laughed. 'Typical of my uncle. He likes to be recognised.

193

He enjoys fame more than winning battles, I think. He's already paying the men with those coins so the money gets spread around Rome even faster. It should annoy Sulla at least, which is probably what he really wants.'

Cabera and Renius came out of the darkness and took up the spaces on Marcus' bench.

'There you are!' Renius said. 'I was beginning to think I couldn't find you to say goodbye.'

Gaius noted again the fresh strength of the man. He looked no more than forty, or a well-preserved forty-five. His grip was like a trap as he put out his hand and Gaius took it.

'We'll all meet again,' Cabera said.

They looked at him.

He held his palms up and smiled. 'It's not a prophecy, but I feel it. We haven't finished our paths yet.'

'I'm glad you're staying, at least. With Tubruk back at the estate and these two off to Greece, I would be all on my own here,' Gaius said, smiling a little shyly.

'You look after him, you old scoundrel,' Renius said. 'I didn't go to all the trouble of training him to hear he's been kicked by a horse. Keep him away from bad women and too much drink.' He turned to Gaius and held up a finger. 'Train every day. Your father never let himself become soft and neither should you if you are to be of any use to our city.'

'I will. What are you going to do when you have delivered Marcus?'

Renius' face darkened for a second.

'I don't know. I don't have the funds to retire any more, so we'll see . . . It is in the hands of the gods as always.'

For a moment, they all looked a little sad. Nothing ever stayed the same.

'Come on,' he continued, gruffly. 'Time for sleep. Dawn can't be more than a few hours away and we all have a long day ahead of us.'

They shook hands in silence for the last time and returned to their tents.

When Gaius awoke the following morning, Marcus and Renius were gone.

By him, folded carefully, was the *toga virilis,* a man's garment. He looked at it for a long time, trying to recall Tubruk's lessons on the correct way to wear one. A boy's tunic was so much simpler, and the low toga hem would become dirty very quickly. The message was clear in its simplicity: a man did not climb trees and throw himself through muddy rivers. Boyish pursuits were to be put behind him.

In daylight, the large ten-man tents could be seen stretching into the distance, the orderly lines showing the discipline of the men and their general. Marius had spent most of the month mapping out a six-mile route along the streets that ended, as before, at the Senate steps. The filth had been scrubbed from the stones of the roads, but they were still narrow, winding courses and the legion could get only six men or three horses across. There were going to be just under eleven hundred rows of soldiers, horses and equipment. After a lot of argument with his engineers, Marius had agreed to leave his siege weapons at the camp – there was just no way to get them around the tight corners. The estimate was that it would take three hours to complete the march and that was without hold-ups or mistakes of any kind.

By the time Gaius had washed, dressed and eaten, the sun was clear of the horizon and the great shining mass of soldiers was in position and almost ready to march. Gaius had been told to dress in a full toga and sandals and to leave his weapons in the camp. After so long carrying a legionary's tools, he felt a little defenceless without them, but obeyed.

Marius himself would be riding on a throne set atop a flat open carriage, pulled by a team of six horses. He would wear a purple toga, a colour that could only be worn by a general at the head of a Triumph. The dye was incredibly expensive, gathered from rare seashells and distilled. It was a garment to wear only once, and the colour of the ancient kings of Rome.

As he passed under the city gates, a slave would raise a gilded laurel wreath above his head and hold it there for the rest of the journey. Four words had to be whispered throughout the Triumph, cheerfully ignored by Marius: 'Remember thou art mortal.'

The carriage had been put together by the legion engineers, made to fit perfectly between the street stepping stones. The heavy wooden wheels were shod with an iron band and the axles freshly greased. The main body had been gilded and shone in the morning sun as if made of pure gold.

As Gaius approached, the general was inspecting his troops, his expression serious. He spoke to many of the men and they answered him without moving their gaze from the middle distance.

At last, the general seemed satisfied and climbed up onto the carriage.

'The people of our city will not forget this day. The sight of you will inspire the children to join the forces that keep us all safe. Foreign ambassadors will watch us and be cautious in their dealings with Rome, with the vision of our ranks always in their minds. Merchants will watch us and know there is something more in the world than making money. Women will watch us and compare their little husbands to the best of Rome! See your reflections in the eyes as we pass. You will give the people something more than bread and coin today; you will give them glory.'

The men cheered at the last and Gaius found himself cheering as well. He walked to the throned carriage and Marius saw him.

'Where shall I stand, Uncle?' he asked.

'Up here, lad. Stand at my right shoulder, so that they will know you are beloved of my house.'

Gaius grinned and clambered on, taking position. He could see into the far distance from his new height and felt a thrill of anticipation.

Marius dropped his arm and horns sounded, echoing down the line to the far back. The legionaries took their first step on the hard-packed soil.

On each side of the great gold carriage, Gaius recognised faces from the first bloody trip to the Senate. Even on a day of rejoicing, Marius had his hand-picked men with him. Only a fool would risk a thrown knife with the legion in the streets; they would destroy the city in rage – but Marius had warned his men that there were always fools, and there were no smiles in the ranks.

'To be alive on such a day is a precious gift of the gods,' Marius said, his voice carrying.

Gaius nodded and rested his hand on the throne.

'There are six hundred thousand people in the city and not one of them will be tending his business today. They have already begun lining the streets and buying seats at windows to cheer us through. The roads are strewn with fresh rushes, a carpet for us to walk on for each step of the six miles. Only the forum is being kept clear so that we can halt the whole five thousand in one block there. I shall sacrifice a bull to Jupiter and a boar to Minerva and then you and I, Gaius, we will walk into the Senate to attend our first vote.'

'What is the vote about?' Gaius asked.

Marius laughed. 'A simple matter of officially accepting you into the ranks of the nobilitas and adulthood. In truth, it is only a formality. You have the right through your father, or, indeed, my sponsorship would do it. Remember, this city was built and is maintained on talent. There are the old houses, the pure-bloods; Sulla himself is from one such. But other men are there because they have dragged themselves up to power, as I have. We respect strength and cherish what is good for the city, regardless of the parentage.'

197

'Are your supporters from the new men?' Gaius asked.

Marius shook his head. 'Strangely enough, no. They are often too wary of being seen to side with one of their own. Many of them support Sulla, but those who follow me are as often high-born as they are new wolves in the fold. The people's tribunes make a great show of being untouched by politics and take each vote as they find it, although they can always be depended on to vote for cheaper corn or more rights for the slaves. With their veto, they can never be ignored.'

'Could they prevent my acceptance then?'

Marius chuckled. 'Take off the worried look. They do not vote in internal matters, such as new members, only in city policy. Even if they did, it would be a brave man to vote against me with my legion standing thousands deep in the forum outside. Sulla and I are consuls – the supreme commanders of all the military might of Rome. We lead the Senate, not the other way around.' He smiled complacently and called for wine, having the full cup handed to him.

'What happens if you disagree with the Senate, or with Sulla?' Gaius asked.

Marius snorted into his wine cup.

'All too common. The people elect the Senate to make and enforce the laws – and to build the empire. They also elect the other, more senior posts: aediles, praetors and consuls. Sulla and I are here because the people voted for us and the Senate do not forget that. If we disagree, a consul may forbid any piece of legislation and its passage stops immediately. Sulla or I have only to say, "*Veto*" – I forbid it – as the speeches begin and that is the end for that year. We can also block each other in this way, although that does not happen often.'

'But how does the Senate control the consuls?' Gaius pressed, interested.

Marius took a deep draught of the wine and patted his stomach, smiling.

'They could vote against me, even remove me from office in theory. In practice, my supporters and clients would prevent any such vote going through, so for the whole year, a consul is almost untouchable in power.'

'You said a consul was only elected for one year and has to step down,' Gaius said.

'The law bends for strong men, Gaius. Each year, the Senate clamours for an exception to be made and I should be re-elected. I am good for Rome, you see – and they know it.'

Gaius felt pleased at the quiet conversation, or as quiet as the general ever managed, at least. He understood why his father had been wary of the man. Marius was like summer lightning – it was impossible to tell what he would strike next – but he had the city in the palm of his hand for the moment and Gaius had discovered that was where he too wanted to be: at the centre of things.

They could hear the roar of Rome long before they reached the gates. The sound was like the sea, a formless, crashing wave that engulfed them as they halted at the border tower. City guards approached the golden carriage and Marius stood to receive them. They too were polished and perfectly turned out and they had a formal air.

'Give your name and state your business,' one said.

'Marius, general of the First-Born. I am here. I will hold a Triumph on the streets of Rome.'

The man flushed a little and Marius grinned.

'You may enter the city,' the guard said, stepping back and waving the gate open.

Marius leaned close to Gaius as he sat down again.

'Protocol says I have to ask permission, but this is too fine a day to be polite to guards who couldn't cut it in the legions. Take us in.' He signalled and again the horns blew all down the line.

The gates opened and the crowd peered around, roaring in excitement. The noise crashed out at the legion and Marius' driver had to snap the reins sharply to make the horses move on.

The First-Born entered Rome.

'You must get out of bed now if you want to be ready in time to see the Triumph! Everyone says it will be glorious and your father and mother are already dressed and with their attendants while you lie and drowse!'

Cornelia opened her eyes and stretched, careless of the covers falling away from her golden skin. Her nurse, Clodia, busied herself with the window hangings, parting them to air the room and letting sunshine spill in.

'Look, the sun is high and you are not even dressed. It is shameless to find you without clothes. What if I was a male, or your father?'

'He wouldn't dare come in. He knows I don't bother with nightclothes when it's hot.'

Still yawning, Cornelia rose naked from her bed and stretched like a cat, arching her back and pressing her fists into the air. Clodia crossed to the bedroom door and dropped the locking bar in case someone looked in.

'I suppose you'll be wanting a dip in the bath before you dress,' Clodia said, affection spoiling the attempt at a stern tone.

Cornelia nodded and padded through to the bathing room. The water steamed, reminding her that the rest of the house had been up and working since the first moments of dawn. She felt vaguely guilty, but that dissolved in the soothing heat as she swung a leg over the side and climbed in, sighing. It was a luxury she enjoyed, preferring not to wait until the formal bathing session later in the day.

Clodia bustled in after her, carrying an armful of warm linen.

She was never still, a woman of immense energy. To a stranger, there was nothing in her dress or manner to indicate her slavery. Even the jewels she wore were real and she chose her clothes from a sumptuous wardrobe.

'Hurry! Dry yourself with these and put on this *mamillare*.'

Cornelia groaned. 'It binds me too tightly to wear on hot days.'

'It will keep your breasts from hanging like empty bags in a few years.' Clodia snorted. 'You'll be pleased enough to have worn it then. Up! Out of that water, you lazy thing. There's a glass of water on the side to clean your mouth.'

As Cornelia dabbed her body dry, Clodia laid out her robes and opened a series of small silver boxes of paint and oils.

'On with this,' she said, dropping a long white tunic over Cornelia's outstretched arms. The girl shrugged herself into it and sat at the single table, propping up an oval bronze mirror to see herself.

'I would like my hair to be curled,' she said wistfully, holding a lock of it in her fingers. It was a dark gold, but straight for all its thickness.

'Wouldn't suit you, Lia. And there's no time today. I should think your mother is already finished with her *ornatrix* and will be waiting for us. Simple, understated beauty is what we're after today.'

'A little ochre on the lips and cheeks then, unless you want to paint me with that stinking white lead?'

Clodia blew air out of her lips in irritation.

'It will be a few years before you need to conceal your complexion. What are you now, seventeen?'

'You know I am, you were drunk at the feast,' Cornelia replied with a smile, holding still while the colour was applied.

'I was merry, dear, just as everybody else was. There is nothing wrong with a little drink in moderation, I have always said.' Clodia nodded to herself as she rubbed in the colours.

'Now a little powdered antimony around the eyes to make men think they are dark and mysterious and we can start on the hair. Don't touch it! Hands to yourself, remember, in case you smudge.'

Swiftly and dextrously, Clodia parted the dark-gold hair and gathered it into a chignon at the back, revealing the slender length of Cornelia's neck. She looked at the face in the mirror and smiled at the effect.

'Why your father hasn't found a man for you, I will never know. You're certainly attractive enough.'

'He said he'd let me choose and I haven't found anyone to like yet,' Cornelia replied, touching the pins in her hair.

Clodia tutted to herself. 'Your father is a good man, but tradition is important. He should find you a young man with good prospects and you should have a house of your own to run. I think you will enjoy that, somehow.'

'I'll take you with me when that happens. I'd miss you if I didn't, like . . . a dress that is a bit old and out of fashion but still comfortable, you know?'

'How beautifully you put your affection for me, my dear,' Clodia replied, buffeting Cornelia's head with her hand as she turned away to pick up the robe.

It was a great square of gold cloth that hung down to Cornelia's knees. It had to be artfully arranged for the best effect, but Clodia had been doing it for years and knew Cornelia's tastes in the cut and style.

'It is beautiful – but heavy,' Cornelia muttered.

'So are men, dear, as you will find out,' Clodia replied with a sparkle in her eyes. 'Now run to your parents. We must be early enough to have a good place to watch the Triumph. We're going to the house of one of your father's friends.'

*　*　*

'Oh, Father, you should have lived to see this,' Gaius whispered as they passed into the streets. The way ahead was dark green, with every spot of stone covered by rushes. The people too wore their best and brightest clothes, a surging throng of colour and noise. Hands were held out and hot, envious eyes watched them. The shops were all boarded shut, as Marius had said. It seemed the whole city had turned out for a holiday to see the great general. Gaius was astonished at the numbers and the enthusiasm. Did they not remember these same soldiers cutting themselves room on the forum only a month before? Marius had said they respected only strength and the proof was in their cheers, booming and echoing in the narrow streets. Gaius glanced to his right into a window and saw a woman of some beauty throwing flowers at him. He caught one and the crowd roared again in appreciation.

Not a soul pushed onto the road, despite the lack of soldiers or guards along the edge. The lesson of the last time had clearly been learned and it was as if there was an invisible barrier holding them back. Even the hard-faced men of Marius' own guard were grinning as they marched.

Marius sat like a god. He placed his massive hands on the arms of the golden throne and smiled at the crowd. The slave behind him raised the garland of gilded laurel over his head and the shadow fell on his features. Every eye followed his progress. His horses were trained for the battlefield and ignored the yelling people, even when some of the more daring landed flowers around their necks as well.

Gaius stood at the great man's shoulder as the ride went on and the pride he felt lifted his soul. Would his father have appreciated this? The answer was probably not and Gaius felt a pang of sorrow at that. Marius was right: just to be alive on this day was to touch the gods. He knew he would never forget it and could see in the eyes of the people that they too would store away the moments to warm them in the dark winters of years yet to pass.

Halfway along the route, Gaius saw Tubruk standing on a corner. As their eyes met, Gaius could feel all the history between them. Tubruk raised his arm in a salute and Gaius returned it. The men around Tubruk turned to look at him and wonder at his connection. He nodded as they passed and Gaius nodded back, swallowing down the catch in his throat. He was drunk with emotion and gripped the back of the throne to keep from swaying in the tide of cheering.

Marius gave a signal to two of his men and they climbed onto the carriage, holding soft leather bags. Hands were plunged into the dark recesses and came up glinting with fistfuls of silver coins. Marius' image went flying over the crowd and they screamed his name as they scrabbled for the metal in his wake. Marius too reached in and his fingers emerged dripping pieces of silver, spraying the coins high with a gesture and laughing as they fell and the crowd dipped to pick up the gifts. He smiled at their pleasure and they blessed him.

From a low window, Cornelia looked out over the bobbing mass of people, pleased to be clear of the crowds. She felt a thrill as Marius drew close on his throne and cheered with the rest. He was a handsome general and the city loved heroes.

There was a young man next to him, too young to be a legionary. Cornelia strained forward to get a better look. He was smiling and his eyes flashed blue as he laughed at something Marius said.

The procession came abreast of where Cornelia and her family watched. She saw coins go flying and the people rush to grab the pieces of silver. Her father, Cinna, sniffed at this.

'Waste of money. Rome loves a frugal general,' he said waspishly.

Cornelia ignored him, her gaze on Marius' companion. He was attractive and healthy-looking, but there was something else about him, about the way he held himself. There was an inner confidence and, as Clodia often said, there was nothing in the world so attractive as confidence.

'Every mother in Rome will be after that young cockerel for their daughters,' Clodia whispered at her elbow.

Cornelia blushed and Clodia's eyebrows shot up in surprise and pleasure.

The Triumph passed on for another two hours, but for Cornelia it was wasted time.

The colours and faces had blurred together, the men were heavily draped in flowers and the sun had reached noon by the time they began the entry to the forum. Marius signalled to his driver to put the carriage at the front, by the Senate steps. The space echoed as the hooves struck the stone slabs and the noise of the streets was slowly left behind. For the first time, Gaius could see Sulla's soldiers guarding the entrances to the plaza and the boiling mass of the crowds beyond.

It was almost peaceful after the colourful riot of the trip into the centre.

'Stop her here,' Marius said, and stood from the throne to watch his men come in. They were well drilled and formed tidy ranks, layer on layer from the furthest corner to the Senate steps, until the forum was full of the shining rows of his soldiers. No human voice could carry to every man so a horn gave the order to stand to attention and they crashed their feet together and down, making thunder. Marius smiled with pride. He gripped Gaius' shoulder.

'Remember this. This is why we slog through battlefields a thousand miles from home.'

'I could never forget today,' Gaius replied honestly and the grip tightened for a moment before letting go.

Marius walked to where a white bull was held steady by four

205

of his men. A great black-bristled boar was similarly held, but snorted and chafed against the ropes.

Marius accepted a taper and lit the incense in a golden bowl. His men bowed their heads and he stepped forward with his dagger, speaking softly as he cut the two throats.

'Bring us all through war and pestilence, safe home to our city,' he said. He wiped the blade on the skin of the bull as it sank to its knees, bawling its fear and pain. Sheathing the dagger, he put an arm around Gaius' shoulder and together they walked up the wide white steps of the Senate building.

It was the seat of power in all the world. Columns that could not be girdled by three large men holding their arms outstretched supported a sloping roof that was itself mounted with distant statues. Bronze doors that dwarfed even Marius stood closed at the top of the steps. Made of interlocking panels, they looked as if they were designed to stand against an army, but as the pair ascended, the doors opened silently, pulled from within. Marius nodded and Gaius swallowed his awe.

'Come, lad, let us go and meet our masters. It would not do to keep the Senate waiting.'

CHAPTER SIXTEEN

Marcus wondered at the tight expression on Renius' face as they travelled the road to the sea. From dawn until late in the afternoon, they had trotted and walked the stone surface without a word. He was hungry and desperately thirsty, but would not admit it. He had decided at noon that if Renius wanted to do the whole trip to the docks without stopping, then he would not give up first.

Finally, when the smell of dead fish and seaweed soured the clean country air, Renius pulled up and, to his surprise, Marcus noticed the man was pale.

'I want to break off here, to see a friend of mine. You can go on to the docks and get a room there. There's an inn . . .'

'I'm coming with you,' Marcus said, shortly.

Renius' jaw tightened and he muttered, 'As you please,' before turning off the main road onto a lesser track.

Mystified, Marcus followed him as the track wound through woods for miles. He didn't ask where they were going, just kept his sword loose in his scabbard in case there were bandits hidden in the foliage. Not that a sword would be much use against a bow, he noted.

The sun, where it could be seen at all through the canopy, had dropped down towards the horizon when they rode into a small village. There were no more than twenty small houses, but the place had a well-kept air to it. Chickens were penned and goats tethered outside most dwellings and Marcus felt no sense of danger. Renius dismounted.

'Are you coming in?' he said, as he walked to a door.

Marcus nodded, and tied the two horses to a post. Renius was inside by the time he was done and he frowned, resting a hand on his dagger as he went in. It was a little dark inside, lit only by a candle and a small fire in the hearth, but Marcus could see Renius hugging an ancient old man with his one good arm.

'This is my brother, Primus. Primus, this is the lad I mentioned, travelling with me to Greece.'

The man must have been eighty years old, but he had a firm grip.

'My brother has written about your progress and the other one, Gaius. He doesn't like anyone, but I think he dislikes you two less than most people.'

Marcus grunted.

'Take a seat, boy. We have a long night ahead of us.' He went over to his small wood fire and placed a long metal poker in its fiery heart.

'What is happening?' Marcus asked.

Renius sighed. 'My brother was a surgeon. He is going to take my arm off.'

Marcus felt a sick horror come over him as he realised what he was going to see. Guilt too flushed his face. He hoped Renius wouldn't mention how he had been injured. To cover his embarrassment, he spoke quickly. 'Lucius or Cabera could have done it, I'm sure.'

Renius silenced him with a raised hand.

'Many people could do the job, but Primus was . . . is the best.'

Primus cackled, revealing a mouth with very few teeth.

'My little brother used to chop people up and I would stitch them back together,' he said cheerfully. 'Let us have a light for this.' He turned to an oil lamp and lit it from a candle. When he turned back, he squinted at Renius.

'I know my eyes are not what they were, but did you dye your hair?'

Renius flushed. 'I do not want to be told your eyes are failing before you start cutting me, Primus. I am ageing well, that is all.'

'Damned well,' Primus agreed.

He emptied a leather satchel of tools onto a table surface and gestured to his brother to sit down. Looking at the saws and needles, Marcus wished he had taken the advice and gone on to the docks, but it was too late. Renius sat and sweat dripped from his forehead. Primus gave him a bottle of brown liquid and he raised it, taking great swallows.

'You, boy, get that rope and tie him to the chair. I don't want him thrashing around and breaking my furniture.'

Feeling sick, Marcus took the lengths of rope, noting with a quiet horror that they were all stained with ancient blood. He busied himself with the knots and tried not to think about it.

After a few minutes, Renius was immobile and Primus poured the last of the brown liquid into his throat.

'That's all I have, I'm afraid. It will take the edge off, but not much.'

'Just get on with it,' Renius growled through clenched teeth.

Primus raised a thick piece of leather to his mouth and told him to bite it.

'It will save your teeth, at least.'

He turned to Marcus. 'You hold the arm still. It will make the sawing quicker.' He placed Marcus' hands on the corded bicep and checked the ropes held the wrist and elbow securely. He slid a vicious-looking blade from his pack and held it up to the light, squinting at the edge.

'I will cut a circle around the bone, then another below it to give the saws room. We will take out a ring of flesh, saw the bone and cauterise the leaks. It must be fast, or he will bleed to death. I will leave enough skin to fold over the stump, then it must be

209

bound securely. He must not touch it for the first week, then he should rub in an ointment I will give you each morning and night. I have no leather cup for the stump, you will have to make or buy one yourself.'

Marcus swallowed nervously.

Primus plunged his fingers into the muscles and nerves of the useless arm, feeling around. After a minute, he tutted to himself, his face sad.

'It is as you said. There is no feeling at all. The muscles are cut and beginning to waste. Was it a fight?'

Involuntarily, Marcus glanced up at Renius. The eyes above the bared teeth were manic and he looked away. 'A training accident,' he said softly, his voice muffled by the leather strap.

Primus nodded and pressed the blade to the skin. Renius tensed and Marcus gripped the arm.

With deft, sure strokes, Primus cut deep, stopping only to dab at the wound with a piece of cloth to remove obscuring gouts of blood. Marcus felt his stomach heave, but Renius' brother seemed completely relaxed, blowing air between his teeth in something close to a little tune. White bone sheathed in a pink curtain appeared and Primus grunted in satisfaction. After only a few seconds, he had reached the bone all the way around and begun the second cut.

Renius looked down at the gory hands of his brother and his lip curled into a bitter grimace. After that, he stared at the wall, his jaw clenched. A slight tremble of his breathing was the only sign of his fear.

Blood spilled over Marcus' hands, the chair, the floor, everything. There were lakes of it inside Renius and it was all coming out, shining and wet. The second ring was gouged out leaving great flaps of hanging skin. Primus notched and sliced, removing the dark lumps of meat and dropping them carelessly on the floor.

'Don't worry about the mess. I have two dogs that will love this when I let them in.'

Marcus turned his head away and vomited helplessly. Primus tutted and rearranged the hands that held the arm. A white spike of bone was visible a hand's breadth up from the elbow.

Renius had begun to breathe in hard blasts from his nose and Primus pressed a hand against his brother's neck, feeling for the pulse.

'I'll be as quick as I can,' he muttered.

Renius nodded, unblinking.

Primus stood up and wiped his hands on a cloth. He looked his brother in the eyes and grimaced at what he found there.

'This is the hard part. You will feel the pain when I cut the bone and the vibration is very unpleasant. I will be as fast as I can. Hold him very still. For two minutes, you must be like a rock. No more of this puking, understand?'

Marcus took deep breaths, miserably, and Primus brought out a thin-bladed saw, set in a wooden handle like a kitchen knife.

'Ready?'

They both muttered assent and Primus set the blade and began to cut, his elbow moving back and forth almost in a blur.

Renius went rigid and his whole body rose against the ropes holding him. Marcus gripped as if his life depended on it, and winced whenever the blood made his fingers slip and the saw snagged.

Without warning, the arm came free, leaning sideways and away from Renius. Renius looked down at it and grunted in anger. Primus wiped his hands and pressed a wad of cloth into the wound. He gestured to Marcus to hold it in place and fetched the iron bar that had been heating in the fire. The tip glowed and Marcus winced in anticipation.

When the cloth was removed, Primus worked quickly, stabbing the tip into every spot of welling blood. Each contact sizzled and

211

the stench was horrible. Marcus dry-heaved onto the floor, a line of sticky yellow bile connecting him with it.

'Put this back in the fire, quickly. I will hold the cloth while it heats again.'

Marcus staggered upright and took the bar, jamming it back into the flames. Renius' head lolled on his shoulders and the leather strip fell from his slack mouth.

Primus kept holding the cloth, then removing it to watch the blood come. He swore viciously.

'I've missed half the pipes at least. Used to be, I could hit each one with one go, but I haven't done this in a few years. It has to be done right, or the wound will poison itself. Is the iron ready yet?'

Marcus withdrew it, but the point was still black. 'No. Will he be all right?'

'Not if I can't seal the wound, no. Get outside and fetch some wood to build up the fire.'

Marcus was thankful for the excuse and left quickly, taking great gulps of sweet air as he stood outside. It was almost dark – gods, how long had they been in there? He noticed a couple of large hounds tied to a wall around the side, asleep. He shuddered and gathered heavy chunks of wood from the pile near them. They woke at his approach and growled softly, but didn't get up. Without looking at them, he went back inside, dumping two billets onto the flames.

'Bring me the iron as soon as the tip is red,' Primus muttered, pressing the wad of cloth hard against the stump.

Marcus avoided looking at the detached arm. It seemed wrong, away from a body, and his stomach heaved in a series of quick spasms before he had the sense to gaze back at the flames.

Once more the bar had to be reheated before Primus was finally satisfied. Marcus knew he would never be able to forget the *fsss* sound of the burning and repressed a shudder as he helped bind the stump in clean cloth bandages. Together, they lifted Renius onto a pallet bed in another room and Marcus sat on the edge, wiping the sweat out of his eyes and thankful it was over.

'What happens to . . . that?' He gestured towards the arm that was still tied to the chair.

Primus shrugged. 'Doesn't seem right to give the whole thing to my dogs. I'll probably bury it somewhere in the woods. It would only rot and smell if I didn't, but a lot of men ask for them. There are so many memories wrapped up in a hand. I mean, those fingers have held women and patted children. It is a lot to lose; but my brother is strong. I hope strong enough even for this.'

'Our ship leaves in four days, on the best tide,' Marcus said, weakly.

Primus scratched his chin. 'He can sit a horse. He will be weak for a few days, but he's as strong as a bull. The problems will be with balance. He will have to retrain, almost from scratch. How long is the sea trip?'

'A month, with good winds,' Marcus replied.

'Use the time. Practise with him every day. Of all men, my brother will not enjoy being less than capable.'

CHAPTER SEVENTEEN

Marius paused at the inner doors of the Senate chamber.

'You are not allowed to enter until you are officially accepted as a citizen, and then only as my guest for the day. I will propose you and make a short speech on your behalf. It is a formality. Wait until I return and show you where you may sit.'

Gaius nodded calmly and stood back as Marius rapped on the doors and walked through them as they opened. He was left alone in the outer chamber and paced up and down it for a while.

After twenty minutes, he began to fret at the delay and wandered over to the open outer doors, looking down onto the massed soldiers in the forum. They were an impressive sight, standing rigidly to attention despite the heat of the day. From the height of the Senate doors and with the open plaza ahead of him, Gaius had a good view of the bustling city beyond. He was lost in his inspection of this when he heard the creak of hinges from the inner doors and Marius stepped out.

'Welcome to the nobilitas, Gaius. You are a citizen of Rome and your father would be proud. Sit next to me and listen to the matters of the day. You will find them interesting, I suspect.'

Gaius followed and met the eyes of the senators as they watched him enter. One or two nodded to him and he wondered if they had known his father, memorising faces in case he had a chance to speak to them later on. He glanced around the hall, trying not to stare. The world listened to what these few had to say.

The arrangement was very like the circus in miniature, he thought, as he took the seat Marius indicated. Five stepped tiers of seating curled around a central space where one speaker at a time could address the others. Gaius remembered from his tutors that the rostrum was made from the prow of a Carthaginian warship and was fascinated to imagine its history.

The seats were built into the curving rows, with dark wooden arms protruding where they were not obscured by seated men. Everyone wore white togas and sandals and the effect was of a working room, a place that crackled with energy. Most of the men had white hair, but a few were young and physically commanding. Several of the senators were standing and he guessed this was to show they wanted to raise a point or add to the debate at hand. Sulla himself stood at the centre of it all, talking about taxation and corn. He smiled at Gaius when he saw the young man looking over at him and Gaius felt the power of it. Here was another like Marius, he judged on the instant, but was there room in Rome for two of that kind? Sulla looked as he had when Gaius had seen him at the games. He was dressed in a simple white toga, belted with a band of red. His hair was oiled and gleamed in dark-gold curls. He glowed with health and vitality and seemed completely relaxed. As Gaius took his seat next to his uncle, Sulla coughed into his hand, delicately.

'I think, given the more serious business of the day, that this taxation debate can be postponed until next week. Are there any objections?' Those who were standing sat down, looking unperturbed. Sulla smiled again, revealing even, white teeth.

'I welcome the new citizen and offer the hope of the Senate that he will serve the city as well as his father did.' There was a murmur of approval and Gaius dipped his head slightly in acknowledgement.

215

'However, our formal welcome must also be put aside for the moment. I have received grave news of a threat to the city this very morning.' He paused and waited patiently for the senators to stop talking. 'To the east, a Greek general, Mithridates, has overrun a garrison of ours in Asia Minor. He may have as many as eight thousand men in rebellion. They have apparently become aware of the overstretched state of our current fighting forces and are gambling on our being too weak to regain the territory. However, if we do not act to repel him, we risk his army growing in strength and threatening the security of our Greek possessions.'

Several senators rose to their feet and shouted arguments began on the benches. Sulla held his hands up for quiet.

'A decision must be made here. The legions already in Greece are committed to controlling the unstable borders. They do not have the men to break this new threat. We cannot leave the city defenceless, especially after the most recent riots, but it is of equal importance that we send a legion to meet the man in the field. Greece is watching to see how we will respond – it must be with speed and fury.'

Heads nodded in violent agreement. Rome had not been built on caution and compromise. Gaius looked at Marius in sudden thought. The general sat with his hands clenched in front of him and his face was tight and cold.

'Marius and I command a legion each. We are months closer than any other from the north. The decision I put to the vote is which of the two should take ship to meet the enemy army.'

He flashed a look at Marius and, for the first time, Gaius could see the bright malice in his eyes. Marius rose to his feet and the chamber hushed. Those standing sat to allow the first response to the other consul. Marius put his hands behind his back and Gaius could see the whiteness of his knuckles.

'I find no fault with Sulla's proposed course of action. The situation is clear: our forces must be split to defend Rome and our foreign dominions. I must ask him whether he will volunteer to be the one to banish the invader.'

All eyes turned to Sulla.

'I will trust the judgement of the Senate on this. I am a servant of Rome. My personal wishes do not come into it.'

Marius smiled tightly and the tension could be felt in the air between them.

'I concur,' Marius said clearly, and took his seat.

Sulla looked relieved and cast his gaze around the vaulted room. 'Then it is a simple choice. I will say the name of each legion and those who believe that is the one to fight Mithridates will stand up and be counted. The rest will stand when they hear the second name. No man may abstain in such a vote on the security of the city. Are we all agreed?'

The three hundred senators murmured their assent solemnly and Sulla smiled. Gaius felt fear touch him. Sulla paused for a long moment, clearly enjoying the tension. At last he spoke one word into the silence.

'First-Born.'

Marius placed his hand on Gaius' shoulder. 'You may not vote today, lad.'

Gaius remained on his seat, craning around him to see how many would stand. Marius looked levelly at Sulla, as if the matter were of no importance to him. It seemed that all around them men were getting up and Gaius knew his uncle had lost. Then the noises stopped and no more men stood. He looked down at the handsome consul standing at the centre and could see Sulla's face change from relaxed pleasure to disbelief, then fury. He made the count and had it checked by two others until they agreed.

'One hundred and twenty-one in favour of the First-Born dealing with the invader.'

He bit his lip, his expression brutal for a second. His gaze fastened on Marius, who shrugged and looked away. The standing men sat.

'Second Alaudae,' Sulla whispered, his voice carrying on the well-crafted acoustics of the hall. Again, men stood, and Gaius could see it was a majority. Whatever plan Sulla had attempted had failed and Gaius saw him wave the senators to their seats without allowing the count to be properly finished and recorded. Visibly, he gathered himself and when he spoke he was again the charming young man Gaius had seen when he entered.

'The Senate has spoken and I am the servant of the Senate,' he said formally. 'I trust Marius will use the city barracks for his own men in my absence?'

'I will,' said Marius, his face calm and still.

Sulla went on: 'With the support of our forces in Asia Minor, I do not see this as a long campaign. I will return to Rome as soon as I have crushed Mithridates. Then we will decide the future of this city.' He said the last looking straight at Marius and the message was clear.

'I will have my men vacate the barracks this evening. If there is no further business? Good day to you all.' Sulla left the chamber, with a group of his supporters falling in behind him. The pressure disappeared in the room and suddenly everyone was speaking, chuckling or looking thoughtfully at each other.

Marius stood and immediately there was quiet.

'Thank you for your trust, gentlemen. I will guard this city well against all comers.' Gaius noted that Sulla could well be one of those Marius would guard against, when he returned.

Senators crowded around his uncle, a few shaking his hand in open congratulation. Marius pulled Gaius to him with one hand and reached out with the other to take the shoulder of a scrawny man, who smiled at them both.

'Crassus, this is my nephew, Gaius. You would not believe it to look at him, but Crassus here is probably the richest man in Rome.'

The man had a long, thin neck and his head bobbed at the end of it, with warm brown eyes twinkling in a mass of tiny wrinkles.

'I have been blessed by the gods, it is true. I also have two beautiful daughters.'

Marius chuckled. 'One is tolerably attractive, Crassus, but the other takes after her father.'

Internally, Gaius winced at this, but Crassus didn't seem to mind at all. He laughed ruefully.

'That is true, she is a little bony. I will have to give her a large dowry to tempt the young men of Rome.' He faced Gaius and put out his hand. 'It is a pleasure to meet you, young man. Will you be a general like your uncle?'

'I will,' Gaius said seriously.

Crassus smiled. 'Then you will need money. Come to me when you need a backer?'

Gaius took the offered hand, gripping it briefly before Crassus moved away into the crowd.

Marius leaned over to him and muttered in his ear, 'Well done. He has been a loyal friend to me and he has incredible wealth. I will arrange for you to visit his estate, it is astonishing in its opulence. Now, there is one other I want you to meet. Come with me.'

Gaius followed him through the knots of senators as they talked over the events of the day and Sulla's humiliation. Gaius noted that Marius shook hands with every man who met his eye, saying a few words of congratulation, asking after families and absent friends. He left each group smiling.

Across the other side of the Senate hall, a group of three men were talking quietly, stopping as soon as Marius and Gaius approached.

'This is the man, Gaius,' Marius said cheerfully. 'Gnaeus Pompey,

219

who is described by his supporters as the best field general Rome has at present – when I am ill, or out of the country.'

Pompey shook hands with them both, smiling affably. Unlike the spare Crassus, he was a little overweight, but he was as tall as Marius and carried it well, creating an impression of solid bulk. Gaius guessed him to be no more than thirty, which made his military status very impressive.

'There is no possibility about it, Marius,' Pompey replied. 'Truly I am wondrous in the field of battle. Strong men weep at the beauty of my manoeuvres.'

Marius laughed and clapped him on the shoulder.

Pompey looked Gaius up and down. 'A younger version of you, old fox?' he said to Marius.

'What else could he be, with my blood in his veins?'

Pompey clasped his hands behind his back.

'Your uncle has taken a terrible risk today, by pushing Sulla out of Rome. What did you think of it?'

Marius began to reply, but Pompey held up a hand.

'Let him speak, old fox. Let me see if he has anything to him.'

Gaius answered without hesitation, the words coming surprisingly easily.

'It is a dangerous move to offend Sulla, but my uncle enjoys gambles of this kind. Sulla is the servant of the city and will fight well against this foreign king. When he returns, he will have to make an accommodation with my uncle. Perhaps we can extend the barracks so that both legions can protect the city.'

Pompey blinked and turned to Marius. 'Is he a fool?'

Marius chuckled. 'No. He just doesn't know if I trust you or not. I suspect he has already guessed my plans.'

'What will your uncle do when Sulla returns?' Pompey whispered, close to Gaius' ear.

Gaius looked around, but there was no one close enough to overhear, except for the three Marius obviously trusted.

220

'He will close the gates. If Sulla tries to force an entry, the Senate will have to declare him an enemy of Rome. He will have to either begin a siege or retreat. I suspect he will put himself at Marius' command, as any general in the field might do to the consul of Rome.'

Pompey agreed, unblinking. 'A dangerous path, Marius, as I said. I cannot support you openly, but I will do my best for you in private. Congratulations on your triumphal march. You looked splendid.' He gestured to the two with him and they walked away.

Gaius began to speak again, but Marius shook his head.

'Let us go outside, the air is thick with intrigue in here.' They moved towards the doors and, outside, Marius put a finger to his lips to stop Gaius' questions. 'Not here. There are too many listeners.'

Gaius glanced around and saw that some of Sulla's senators were close, staring over with undisguised hostility. He followed Marius out into the forum, taking a seat on the stone steps away from where they could be overheard. Nearby, the First-Born still stood to attention, looking invincible in their shining armour. It was a peculiar feeling to be in the presence of thousands and yet to sit relaxed with his uncle on the very steps of the Senate.

Gaius could not hold it in any longer.

'How did you swing the vote against Sulla?'

Marius began to laugh and wiped his forehead free of sudden perspiration.

'Planning, my lad. I knew of the landing of Mithridates almost as soon as it happened, days before Sulla heard. I used the oldest lever in the world to persuade the waverers in the Senate to vote for me and, even then, it was closer than I would have liked. It cost me a fortune, but from tomorrow morning I have control of Rome.'

'He will be back, though,' Gaius warned.

Marius snorted. 'In six months or longer, perhaps. He could be killed on the battlefield, he could even lose to Mithridates; I have heard he is a canny general. Even if Sulla beats him in double time and finds fair sea winds to Greece and back, I will have months to prepare. He will leave as easily as he likes, but I tell you now, he won't get back in without a fight.'

Gaius shook his head in disbelief at this confirmation of his thoughts.

'What happens now? Do we go back to your house?'

Marius smiled a little sadly in response. 'No. I had to sell it for the bribes – Sulla was already bribing them, you see, and I had to double his offers in most cases. It took everything I own, except my horse, my sword and my armour. I may be the first penniless general Rome has ever had.' He laughed quietly.

'If you had lost the vote, you would have lost everything!' Gaius whispered, shocked by the stakes.

'But I did not lose! I have Rome and my legion stands in front of us.'

'What would you have done if you had lost, though?'

Marius blew air through his lips in disdain. 'I would have left to fight Mithridates, of course. Am I not a servant of the city? Mind you, it would have taken a brave man to accept my bribe and still vote against me with my legion waiting just outside, wouldn't it? We must be thankful that the Senate value gold as much as they do. They think of new horses and slaves, but they have never been poor as I was poor. I value gold only for what it brings me and this is where it has put me down – on these steps, with the greatest city in the world at my back. Cheer up, lad, this is a day for celebration, not regrets.'

'No, it's not that. I was just thinking that Marcus and Renius are heading east to join the Fourth Macedonia. There's a fair chance they will meet this Mithridates coming the other way.'

'I hope not. Those two would have that Greek for breakfast and I want Sulla to have *something* to do when he gets there.'

Gaius laughed and they stood up together. Marius looked at

222

his legion and Gaius could feel the joy and pride burning out of him.

'This has been a good day. You have met the men of power in the city and I have been loved by the people and backed by the Senate. By the way, that slave girl of yours, the pretty one? I'd sell her if I were you. It's one thing to tumble a girl a few times, but you seem to be sweet on her and that will lead to trouble.'

Gaius looked away, biting his lip. Were there no secrets?

Marius continued blithely, unaware of his companion's discomfort.

'Have you even tried her yet? No? Maybe that will get her out of your system. I know a few good houses here if you want to get a little experience in first. Just ask when you're ready.'

Gaius did not reply, his cheeks hot.

Marius stood and looked with obvious pride at the Primigenia legion ranked before them.

'Shall we march the men over to the city barracks, lad? I think they could do with a good meal and a decent night's sleep after all this marching and standing in the sun.'

CHAPTER EIGHTEEN

Marcus looked out onto the Mediterranean Sea and breathed in the warm air, heavy with salt. After a week at sea, boredom had set in. He knew every inch of the small trading vessel and had even helped in the hold, counting amphorae of thick oil and ebony planking transported from Africa. For a while, his interest had been kindled by the hundreds of rats below the decks and he spent two days crawling to their nests in the darkness, armed with a dagger and a marble paperweight stolen from the captain's cabin. After throwing dozens of the little bodies overboard, they had learned to recognise his smell or his careful tread, retreating into crevices deep in the wood of the ship the moment he set foot on the ladder below.

He sighed and watched the sunset, still awed by the colours of the sinking sun out at sea. As a passenger, he could have stayed in his cabin for the whole journey, as Renius seemed determined to do, but the tiny, cramped space offered nothing in terms of amusement and Marcus had quickly come to use it only to sleep.

The captain had allowed him to stand watch and he had even tried his hand at controlling the two great steering oars at the back, or what he had learned to call the stern, but his interest soon paled.

'Another couple of weeks of this will kill me,' he muttered to himself, using his knife to cut his initials into the wooden rail.

A scuffling noise sounded behind him, but he didn't turn, just smiled and kept watching the sunset. There was silence and then another noise, the sort a small body might make if it was shifting for comfort.

Marcus spun and launched his knife underarm, as Renius had once taught him. It thudded into the mast and quivered. There was a squeak of terror and a flash of dirty white feet in the darkness as something scuttled deeper into shadow, trying too hard to be silent.

Marcus strolled over to the knife and freed it with a wrench. Sliding it back into the waist sheath, he squinted into the blackness.

'Come out, Peppis, I know you're in there,' he called. He heard a sniff. 'I wouldn't have hit you with the knife, it was just a joke. Honestly.'

Slowly, a skeletal little boy emerged from behind some sacking. He was filthy almost beyond belief and his eyes were wide with fear.

'I was just watching you,' Peppis said, nervously.

Marcus looked more closely at him, noticing a small crust of dried blood under his nose and a purple bruise over one eye.

'Have the men been beating you again?' he said, trying to make his voice friendly.

'A little, but it was my fault. I tripped on a rope and pulled a knot undone. I didn't mean to but Firstmate said he would teach me to be clumsy. I'm already clumsy, though, so I said I didn't need no teaching and then he knocked me about.' He sniffed again and wiped his nose with the back of his hand, leaving a silvery trail.

'Why don't you run away at a port?' Marcus asked.

Peppis puffed his chest out as far as it would go, revealing his ribs like white sticks under his skin.

'Not me. I'm going to be a sailor when I'm older. I'm learning all the time, just by watching the men. I can tie ever so many knots now. I could have retied that rope today if Firstmate woulda let me, but he didn't know that.'

'Do you want me to have a word with the . . . first mate? Tell him to stop the beatings?'

Peppis turned even paler and shook his head. 'He'd kill me if you do, maybe this trip or maybe on the way back. He's always saying if I can't learn to be a sailor, he'll put me over the side some night when I'm sleeping. That's why I don't sleep in my bunk, but out here on the decks. I move around a lot so he won't know where to find me if he thinks it's time.'

Marcus sighed. He felt sorry for the little boy, but there was no simple answer to his problems. Even if the first mate were quietly put over the side himself, Peppis would be tortured by the others. They all took part and the first time Marcus had mentioned it to Renius, the old gladiator had laughed and said there was one like him on every ship of the sea. Even so, it galled Marcus to have the boy hurt. He had never forgotten what it was like to be at the mercy of bullies like Suetonius and he knew that if he had built the wolf trap, and not Gaius, he would have dropped rocks in and crushed the older boy. He sighed again and stood up, stretching tired muscles.

Where would he have ended up if Gaius' parents hadn't looked after him and brought him up? He could very easily have stowed away on a trade ship and have been in just the sort of horrible position Peppis found himself. He would never have been trained to fight or defend himself and lack of food would have made him weak and sickly.

'Look,' he said, 'if you won't let me help you with the sailors, at least let me share my food with you. I don't eat much anyway and I've been sending some of it back, especially in rough water. All right? You stay there and I'll bring you something.'

Peppis nodded silently and, a little cheered, Marcus went below

226

decks to his cramped cabin to fetch the cheese and bread left for him earlier. In truth, he was hungry, but he could go without and the little boy was practically starved to death.

Leaving Peppis to chew on the food, Marcus wandered back to the steering oars, knowing that the first mate took a turn about midnight. Like Peppis, he'd never heard the man's real name. Everyone called him by his station and he seemed to do his job well enough, keeping the crew in line with a hard hand. The little ship *Lucidae* had a reputation for honest dealing too, with very little of the cargo ever going missing on voyages. Other ships had to write off such small losses to keep their crews happy, but not the owners of the *Lucidae*.

Marcus brightened as he saw the man had already taken his place, holding one of the two great rudders steady against the currents and chatting in a low voice to his partner on the other.

'A fine evening,' he said, as he came close.

Firstmate grunted and nodded. He had to be polite to paying passengers, but bare civility was all he would offer. He was a powerfully built man and held the rudder with only one arm, while his companion threw his weight and both shoulders into the task of holding his steady. The other man said nothing and Marcus recognised him as one of the crew, tall and long-armed with a shaven skull. He gazed steadfastly ahead, engrossed in his task and the feel of the wood in his hands.

'I'd like to buy one of the crew as a slave. Who should I talk to?' Marcus said, keeping his voice amiable.

Firstmate blinked in surprise, and two gazes rested on the young Roman.

'We're free men,' the other said, his voice showing his distaste.

Marcus looked disconcerted. 'Oh, I didn't mean one of you, of course. I meant the boy Peppis. He's not on the crew lists. I checked, so I thought he might be available for sale. I need a boy to carry my sword and . . .'

227

'I've seen you on the decks,' the first mate rumbled from deep in his chest. 'You were making angry faces when we were giving him his lessons. I reckon you're one of those soft city lads who thinks we're too hard on the ship boys. Either that or you want him in your bed. Which is it?'

Marcus smiled slowly, revealing his teeth.

'Oh dear. That sounds like an insult, my friend. You'd better let that rudder go, so I can give you a lesson myself.'

The first mate opened his mouth to retort and Marcus hit it. For a while, the *Lucidae* wandered off course over the dark sea.

Renius woke him by shaking him roughly.

'Wake up! The captain wants to see you.'

Marcus groaned. His face and upper body were a mass of heavy bruises. Renius whistled softly as he stood up and, wincing, began to dress. Using his tongue, he found a loose tooth and pulled out the water pot under his bed to spit bloody phlegm into it.

With the part of his mind that was active, he was pleased to notice that Renius was wearing his iron breastplate and had his sword strapped on. The stump of his arm was bound with clean bandages and the depression that had kept him in his cabin for the first weeks seemed to have disappeared. When Marcus had pulled on his tunic and wrapped a cloak against the cold morning breeze, Renius held the door open.

'Someone beat the first mate into the ground last night, and another man with him,' Renius said, cheerfully.

Marcus put his hand up to his face and felt a ridge of split skin on his cheek.

'Did he say who did it?' he muttered.

'He says he was jumped from behind, in the dark. He has a broken shoulder, you know.' Renius had definitely lost his depression, but Marcus decided that the new, chuckling Renius was not really an improvement.

The captain was a Greek named Epides. He was a short, energetic man with a beard that looked as if it was pasted on, without a troublesome hair out of place on his face. He stood up as Marcus and Renius entered and rested his hands on his desk, which was held to the floor against the rocking of the ship with heavy iron manacles. Each finger had a valuable stone set into gold on it and they glittered with every movement. The rest of the room was simple, as befitted a working trader. There was no luxury and nowhere to look but the man himself, who glared at both of them.

'Let's not try the protestations of innocence,' he said. 'My first mate has a broken shoulder and collarbone and you did it.'

Marcus tried to speak, but the captain interrupted.

'He won't identify you, Zeus himself knows why. If he did, I'd have you flogged raw on the decks. As it is, you will take up his duties for the remainder of this trip and I will be sending a letter to your legion commander about the sort of ill-disciplined lout he is taking on. You are hereby signed on as crew for this voyage, as is my right as captain of *Lucidae*. If I discover you are shirking your duties in any way, I will flog you. Do you understand?'

Marcus again began to answer, but this time Renius stopped him, speaking quietly and reasonably.

'Captain. When the lad accepted his position in the Fourth Macedonia, he became, from that moment, a member of that legion. As you are in a difficult position, he will volunteer to replace the first mate until we make land in Greece. However, it will be I who makes sure he does not shirk his duties. If he is flogged by your order, I will come up here and rip your heart out. Do we understand each other?' His voice remained calm, almost friendly, right to the end.

Epides paled slightly and raised a hand to smooth his beard in a nervous gesture.

'Just make sure he does the job. Now get out and report to the second mate for work.'

Renius looked at him for a long moment and then nodded slowly, turning to the door and allowing Marcus to walk through first before following.

Left alone, Epides sank into his chair and dipped a hand into a bowl of rosewater, dabbing it onto his neck. Then he composed himself and smiled grimly as he gathered his writing materials. For a while, he mused over the clever, sharp retorts he should have made. Threatened by Renius, by all the gods! When he returned home, the story he would tell would include the blistering ripostes, but, at the actual moment, something naked and violent in the man's eyes had stopped his mouth.

The second mate was a dour man from northern Italy called Parus. He said very little as Marcus and Renius reported to him, just outlined the daily tasks for a first mate of a trader, ending with the stint on the rudder at around midnight.

'Won't seem right, calling you first mate, with him still below decks.'

'I'll be doing his job for him. You'll call me by his name while I'm doing it,' Marcus replied.

The man stiffened. 'What are you, sixteen? The men won't like it either,' he said.

'Seventeen,' Marcus lied smoothly. 'The men will get used to it. Maybe we'd better see them now.'

'Have you sailed before?' Parus asked.

'First trip, but you tell me what needs doing and I'll get it done. All right?'

Puffing out his cheeks in obvious disgust, Parus nodded. 'I'll get the men on deck.'

'I'll get the men on deck, *First Mate*,' Marcus said clearly through

230

his swollen lips. His eyes glinted dangerously and Parus wondered how he'd beaten Firstmate in a fight and why the man wouldn't identify him to the captain when any fool could see who it had been.

'First Mate,' he agreed sullenly and left them.

Marcus turned to Renius, who was looking askance at him.

'What are you thinking?' Marcus asked.

'I'm thinking you'd better watch your back, or you won't ever see Greece,' Renius replied seriously.

All the crew who weren't actively working gathered on the small deck. Marcus counted fifteen sailors, with another five on the rudders and sail rigging around.

Parus cleared his throat for their attention.

'Since Firstmate's arm is broken, the captain says the job belongs to this one for the rest of the trip. Get back to work.'

The men turned to go and Marcus took a step forward, furious.

'Stay where you are,' he bellowed, surprising himself with the strength of his voice. He had their attention for a moment and he didn't intend to waste it.

'Now you all know I broke Firstmate's arm, so I'm not going to deny it. We had a difference of opinion and we fought over it, that's the end of the story. I don't know why he hasn't told the captain who it was, but I respect him a bit more for it. I'll do his job as best I'm able, but I'm no sailor and you know that too. You work with me and I won't mind if you tell me when I'm wrong. But *if* you tell me I'm wrong, you'd better be right. Fair enough?'

There was a mutter from the assembled men.

'If you're no sailor, you ain't going to know what you're doing. What use is a farmer on a trade ship?' called a heavily tattooed sailor. He was sneering and Marcus responded quickly, colouring in anger.

'First thing is for me to walk the ship and speak to each one of you. You tell me exactly what your job is and I'll do it. If I can't do it, I'll go back to the captain and tell him I'm not up to the job. Anyone object?'

There was silence. A few of them looked interested at the challenge, but most faces were bluntly hostile. Marcus clenched his jaw and felt the loose tooth grate.

He pulled his dagger from his belt and held it up. It was a well-crafted weapon, given to him by Marius as a parting gift. Not lavishly decorated, it was nonetheless an expensive piece, with a bronze wire handle.

'If any man can do something I can't do, I will give him this, presented to me by General Marius of the Primigenia. Dismissed.'

This time, there was much more interest in the faces, and a number of the sailors looked at the blade he still held as they went back to their tasks.

Marcus turned to Renius and the gladiator shook his head slowly in disbelief.

'Gods, you're green. That's too good a blade to throw away,' he said.

'I won't lose it. If I have to prove myself to the crew, that's what I'll do. I'm fit enough. How hard can these jobs be?'

CHAPTER NINETEEN

Marcus clung to the mast crosspiece with a knuckle-whitening grip. At this, the highest point of the *Lucidae*, it seemed as if he was swinging with the mast from one horizon to the other. The sea below was spattered grey with choppy white waves, no danger to the sturdy little vessel. His stomach heaved and every part of him responded with discomfort. All his bruises had stiffened by noon and now he found it hard to turn his head to the right without pain sending black and white spots into his vision.

Above him, barefoot and standing without support on the spar, was a sailor, the first to try to win the dagger. The man grinned without malice, but the challenge was clear – Marcus had to join him and risk falling into the sea, or, worse, onto the deck far below.

'These masts didn't look so tall from below,' Marcus grunted through clenched teeth.

The sailor walked over to him, perfectly balanced and adjusting his weight all the time to the roll and pitch of the ship.

'Tall enough to kill you. Firstmate could walk the spar though, so I think you'll just have to make your choice.'

He waited patiently, occasionally checking knots and ropes for tautness out of habit. Marcus gritted his teeth and heaved himself over the crosspiece, resting his unruly stomach on it. He could see the other men below and noted that a few of the faces were turned upwards to see him succeed, or perhaps to be sure of getting out of the way if he fell – he didn't know.

The tip of the mast, festooned with ropes, lay within his reach and he grabbed it and used it to pull himself up enough to get one foot on the cross-spar. The other leg hung below and for a few moments he used its swing to steady himself. Another grunt of effort against his tortured muscles and he was crouching on the spar, gripping the mast-tip with both hands, his knees almost higher than his chin. He watched the horizon move and suddenly felt as if the ship was still and the world spun around him. He felt dizzy and closed his eyes, which helped only a little.

'Come on now,' he muttered to himself. 'Good balance you've got.'

His hands shook as he released the mast, using the muscles in his legs to counteract the great swing. Then he uncrouched like an old man, ready to grab at the mast again as soon as he felt his balance fail. He brought himself up from a low bow to a round-shouldered standing position, his eyes fixed on the mast. He flexed his knees a little and began to adjust to the movement through the air.

'There isn't much wind, of course,' the sailor said equably. 'I've been up here in a storm trying to tie down a ripped sail. This is nothing.'

Marcus suppressed a retort. He didn't want to anger a man who could stand so comfortably with his arms folded, sixty feet above the deck. He looked at him, his eyes leaving the mast for the first time since he reached that height.

The sailor nodded. 'You have to walk the length. From your end to mine. Then you can go down. If your nerve goes, just hand me the dagger before you climb down. It won't be too easy to get if you hit the planks.'

This was more like the sort of thing Marcus understood. The man was trying to make him nervous and achieved the opposite. He knew he could trust his reflexes. If he fell there would be time to grab something. He would just ignore the height and the movement and take the risk. He stood up fully and shuffled back to the edge, leaning forward as the mast seemed determined to take him down as far as the sea for a moment before coming upright and over again. Then he found himself looking down a mountain slope, blocked only by the relaxed sailor.

'Right,' he said, holding his arms out for balance. 'Right.'

He began to shuffle, never taking the soles of his bare feet from the wood. He knew the sailor could walk along it with careless ease, but he wasn't going to try to match years of experience in a few breathtaking steps. He inched along and his confidence grew mightily, until he was almost enjoying the swing, leaning into and away from it and chuckling at the movement.

The sailor looked unperturbed as Marcus reached him.

'Is that it?' Marcus asked.

The man shook his head. 'To the end I said. There's a good three feet to go yet.'

Marcus looked at him in annoyance. 'You're in my way, man!' Surely he wasn't expected to get round him on a piece of wood no wider than his thigh?

'I'll see you down there then,' the man said and stepped off the crosspiece.

Marcus gaped as the figure shot past him. In the same moment as he saw the hand gripping the spar and the face grinning up at him, he lost balance and swayed in panic, suddenly knowing he would be smashed onto the deck. More faces below swam into his vision. They all seemed to be looking up, pale blurs and pointing fingers.

Marcus waved his arms frantically and arched back and forth in whip-like spasms as he fought to save himself. Then he steadied and concentrated on the spar, ignoring the drop below and trying to find the rhythm of muscle he had so enjoyed only moments before.

'You nearly went there,' the sailor said, still casually hanging from the spar by one arm, seemingly oblivious to the drop. It had been a clever trick and had nearly worked. Chuckling and shaking his head, the man started to reach out to a rope when Marcus trod on the fingers that were wrapped around the crosspiece.

'Hey!' the man shouted, but Marcus ignored him, putting all his weight on his heel as he shifted with the movement of the *Lucidae*. Suddenly, he was enjoying it again and took a deep, cleansing breath. The fingers squirmed beneath him and there was an edge of panic in the sailor's voice as he found he couldn't quite reach the nearest rope, even bringing his legs up. With his hand free, he would have swung and released without any difficulty, but, held fast, he could only dangle and shout curses.

Without warning, Marcus moved his foot to take the last step to the end of the spar and was cheered by the scrambling sounds below him as the sailor, caught by surprise, slid and gripped furiously to save himself. Marcus looked down and saw the angry stare as the sailor began to climb back up to the crosspiece. There was murder in his expression and Marcus moved quickly to sit down in the centre of the spar, gripping the mast-top firmly between his thighs. Still feeling unsafe, he wrapped his left leg around the mast below to hold himself steady. He took out Marius' dagger and began to whittle his initials into the wood at the very top.

The sailor almost sprang onto the crosspiece and stood at the end, glaring. Marcus ignored him, but he could practically hear the train of thought as the man realised he had no weapons and that his superior balance was cancelled by the firm grip Marcus had on the mast. To get close enough to shove Marcus off, he would have to risk getting the dagger in his throat. The seconds ticked by.

'All right, then. You keep the knife. Time to get down.'

'You first,' Marcus said, without looking up.

He listened to the dwindling sounds of the sailor's descent and finished carving his initials into the hard wood. In all, he was disappointed. If he carried on making enemies at this rate, there really would be a knife in the dark one night.

Diplomacy was, he decided, a lot harder than it looked.

Renius was not around to congratulate him on his safe return from the high rigging, so Marcus continued his round of the ship on his own. After the initial excitement at the thought of winning the dagger, the stares he received were either uninterested or openly malevolent. Marcus clasped his hands behind his back to stop the involuntary shaking that had hit them as his feet touched the safe wood of the deck. He nodded to every glance as if it was a word of greeting and, to his surprise, one or two nodded back, perhaps only from habit, but it reassured him a little.

One sailor, his long hair tied back with a strip of blue cloth, was clearly trying to meet Marcus' eye. He seemed friendly enough, so Marcus stopped.

'What do you do here?' he asked, a little warily.

'Come to the stern . . . First Mate,' said the man and strode off, gesturing him to follow. Marcus walked with him to stand by the two steering oars.

'My name's Crixus. I do a lot of things when they needs doing, but my special job is to free the rudders when they get fouled. It could be weed, but it's usually fishing nets.'

'How do you free them?'

Marcus could guess at the answer, but he asked anyway, trying to sound light and cheerfully interested. He had never been a strong swimmer, but this man's chest expanded to ridiculous proportions when he took a breath.

'You should find it easy after your little walk on the mast. I just dive off the side, swim down to the rudders and use my knife to cut off whatever is fouling them.'

'That sounds like a dangerous job,' Marcus replied, pleased at the easy grin he received in return.

'It is, if there are sharks down there. They follow *Lucidae*, see, in case we throw any scraps off.'

Marcus rubbed his chin, trying to remember what a shark was.

'Big are they, these sharks?'

Crixus nodded with energy. 'Gods, yes. Some of them could swallow a man whole! One washed up near my village once and it had half a man inside. Bit him in two, it must have done.'

Marcus looked at him and thought he had another one trying to scare him off.

'What do you do when you meet these sharks down there then?' he said.

Crixus laughed. 'You punch them on the nose. It puts them off having you for a meal.'

'Right,' Marcus said dubiously, looking into the dark, cold waters. He wondered if he should put this one off until the following day. The climb down from the mast-top had loosened most of his muscles, but every movement still made him wince and the weather wasn't warm enough to make swimming attractive.

He looked at Crixus and could see the man expected him to refuse. Inwardly, he sighed. Nothing was working out the way he'd intended.

'There isn't anything fouling the rudders today, is there?' he said and Crixus' smile widened as he thought Marcus was trying to find excuses not to try it.

'Not in clear sea, no. Just scrape a barnacle off the bottom of one – it's a shell, a little animal that attaches to ships. Bring one back and I'll buy you a drink. Come back empty-handed and that pretty little blade belongs to me, all right?'

Marcus agreed reluctantly and began to remove his tunic and sandals, leaving him standing in just the undercloth that protected his modesty. Under Crixus' amused eye, he began to stretch his legs, using the wooden rail as a brace. He took his time, knowing from Crixus' enthusiasm that the man thought he'd never manage it.

Finally, he was loose and ready. Taking his knife, he stepped up onto the flat wooden section around the stern, readying himself for the dive. It was a good twenty feet, even in such a low-slung vessel as the *Lucidae*, which fairly wallowed in the water. He tensed, trying to remember the few dives he had managed on a trip to a lake with Gaius' parents when he was eight or nine. Hands together.

'You'd better put this on,' Crixus interrupted his thoughts. The man was holding the tar-sealed end of a slim rope. 'It goes around your waist to stop you being left behind by *Lucidae*. She doesn't look fast, but you couldn't catch her by swimming.'

'Thanks,' Marcus said suspiciously, wondering if Crixus had meant to let him dive without it, changing his mind at the last moment. He tied the rope securely and looked at the cold water below, scythed into plough lines by the rudders. A thought struck him.

'Where's the other end?'

Crixus had the grace to look embarrassed and confirmed Marcus' earlier suspicions. Mutely, he pointed to where the rope was made fast and Marcus nodded, returning to his inspection of the waves.

Then he dived, turning slightly in the air to hit the grey water with a hard smacking sound.

Marcus held his breath as he plunged under the surface, jerking as the rope stopped his descent. He could still feel movement as the ship started to tow him. He fought to reach the surface and gasped in relief as he broke through the waves near the rudders.

He could see their dark flanks cutting the waves and tried to find a handhold on the slippery surface above the waterline. It was impossible and he found he had to swim strongly just to stay near them. As soon as he slowed his hands and legs, he drifted out until the rope was taut again.

The cold was cramping his muscles and Marcus realised he had only a short time before he was useless in the water. Gripping his dagger tightly in his right fist, he gulped breath and dived below, using his hands to guide him down the slippery green underside of the nearest rudder.

At the base, his lungs were bursting. He was able to hold himself for a few seconds while his fingers scrabbled around in the slime, but he could feel nothing that felt like the sort of shell Crixus had told him to expect. Cursing, he kicked his legs back to the surface. As he couldn't hold the rudders to rest, he felt his strength slipping away.

He pulled in another breath and disappeared down into the darkness once more.

Crixus felt the presence of the old gladiator before he saw him reach his side and look down at the quivering rope in the water between the rudders. When he met the man's eyes, Crixus could see grey anger and took a step back in reaction.

'What are you doing?' Renius asked quietly.

'He's checking the rudders and cutting off barnacles,' Crixus replied.

Renius' lip twisted with distaste. Even with one arm, he radiated violence, standing utterly still. Crixus noticed the gladius strapped to his belt and wiped his hands on his ragged cloth leggings. Together, they watched Marcus surface and go under three more times. His arms flapped aimlessly in the water below and both men could hear his exhausted coughing.

'Bring him up now. Before he drowns himself,' Renius said.

Crixus nodded quickly and began to haul in the rope, hand over hand. Renius didn't offer to help him, but standing with his hand resting on the gladius hilt seemed enough encouragement.

Crixus was sweating heavily by the time Marcus reached the deck level. He hung almost limp in the rope, his limbs too tired to control.

As if he was loading a bale of cloth, Crixus pulled him over the edge and rolled him face up on the deck, eyes closed and panting. Crixus smiled as he saw the dagger was still in one hand and reached for it. There was a quick sound behind him and he froze as Renius brought his sword into the line of sight.

'What are you doing now?'

'Taking the dagger! He . . . he had to bring a shell back . . .' the man stammered.

'Check his other hand,' Renius said.

Marcus could barely hear him through the water sounds in his ears and the pain in his chest and limbs, but he opened his left fist and in it, surrounded by scratches and cuts, was a round shell with its live occupant glistening wetly inside.

Crixus' jaw dropped and Renius waved him away with his sword.

'Get that second mate to gather the men . . . Parus, his name was. This has gone far enough.'

Crixus looked at the sword and the man's expression and didn't argue.

Renius crouched at Marcus' side and sheathed his sword. Reaching over, he slapped Marcus' white face a few times, bringing a little colour back. Marcus coughed wretchedly.

'I thought you'd stop when you nearly fell off the spar. What you think you are proving, I don't know. Stay here and rest while I deal with the men.'

Marcus tried to say something, but Renius shook his head.

'Don't argue. I've been dealing with men like these all my life.'

Without another word, he stood and walked to where the crew had gathered, taking a position where they could all see him. He spoke through teeth held tightly together, but his voice carried to all of them.

'His mistake was expecting to be treated with honour by scum like you. Now I don't have the inclination to win your trust or your respect. I'll give you a simple choice from this moment.

241

You do your jobs well. You work hard and stand your watches and keep everything tight until we make port. I have killed more men than I can count and I will gut any man who does not obey me in this. Now be men! If anyone wants to make pretty words to argue with me, let him take up a sword and gather his friends and come against me all at once.'

His voice rose to a bellow. 'Don't walk away from me here and plot in corners like old ladies in the sun! Speak now, fight now, for if you don't and I find whispers later, I will crack your heads open for you, I swear it!'

He glared around at them and the men looked at their feet. No one spoke, but Renius said nothing. The silence went on and on, growing painful. No one moved, they stood like statues on the decks. At last, he took a breath and snarled at them.

'Not a single one of you with courage enough to take on an old man with one arm? Then get back to your work and work well, for I'll be watching each one of you and I won't give warnings.'

He walked through them and they parted, standing mutely aside. Crixus looked at Parus and he shrugged slightly, stepping back with the rest. The *Lucidae* sailed on serenely through the cold sea.

Renius sagged against the cabin door as it closed behind him. He could feel his armpits were damp with sweat and cursed under his breath. He was not used to bluffing men into obedience, but his balance was terrible and he knew he was still weak. He wanted to sleep, but could not until he had finished his exercises. Sighing, he drew his gladius and went through the strokes he had been taught half a century before, faster and faster until the blade hit the roof of the small space and wedged. Renius swore in anger and the men near his door heard him and looked at each other with wide eyes.

*   *   *

That night, Marcus was standing at the prow on his own, looking out at the moonlit waves and feeling miserable. His efforts of the day had earned him nothing and having to have Renius clear up his failure felt like a metal weight in his chest.

He heard low voices behind him and swung to see black figures coming around the raised cabins. He recognised Crixus and Parus, and the man from the high rigging, whose name he did not know. He steadied himself for the blows, knowing he couldn't take them all, but Crixus held out a leather cup of some dark liquid. He was smiling slightly, not sure Marcus wouldn't dash it out of his hand.

'Here. I promised you a drink if you picked up a shell and I keep my promises.'

Marcus took the cup and the three men relaxed visibly, coming over to lean against the side and look out over the black water as it passed below them. All three had similar cups and Crixus filled them from a soft leather bag that gurgled when he shifted its weight under his arm.

Marcus could smell the bitter liquid as he raised it to his mouth. He had never tasted anything stronger than wine before and took a deep gulp before he realised that whatever it was stung the cuts on his lips and gums. In reflex, just to clear his mouth, he swallowed and immediately choked as fire burst in his stomach. He fought for breath and Parus reached out an arm and thumped his back, his face expressionless.

'Does you good, that stuff,' Crixus said, chuckling.

'Does you good, *First Mate*,' Marcus replied through his spluttering.

Crixus smiled. 'I like you, lad. I really do,' he said, refilling his own cup. 'Mind you, that friend of yours, Renius, now he is a truly evil bastard.'

They all nodded and peacefully went back to watching the sea and the sky.

CHAPTER TWENTY

Marcus viewed the busy port with mixed feelings as it grew before him. The *Lucidae* manoeuvred nimbly through the ancient stones that marked the edge of the wild sea and the calm lake of the harbour itself. A host of ships accompanied them and they had had to stand off from the harbour for most of the morning until a harassed pilot took a boat out to guide them in.

At first, Marcus had thought nothing of the month at sea, considering it with as much interest as he might consider a walk from one town to another. Only the destination had been important in his mind. Now though, he knew the name of each one of the small crew and had felt their acceptance after that night spent drinking on the prow. Even the return of Firstmate to light duties hadn't spoiled things with the men. Firstmate, it seemed, bore no grudges and even seemed proud of him, as if his acceptance by the crew was in some way his doing.

Peppis had never stopped sleeping in corners on the decks at night, but he had filled out a little with the food Marcus saved for him and the beatings had stopped by some unseen signal amongst the men. The little boy had become a much more cheerful character and might one day be a sailor, as he hoped.

To some extent, Marcus envied the boy; it was freedom of a kind. These men would see all the ports of the known world while he marched over foreign fields under the baking sun, carrying Rome always with him.

He took a deep breath and closed his eyes, trying to sift apart all the strange scents on the sea breeze. Jasmine and olive oil were strong, but there was also the smell of a mass of people again – sweat and excrement. He sighed and jumped as a hand clapped onto his shoulders.

'It will feel good to get land under our heels again,' Renius said, staring with him into the harbour town. 'We'll hire horses to take us east to the legion and find your century to get you sworn in.'

Marcus nodded in silence and Renius caught his mood. 'Only memories stay the same, lad. Everything else changes. When you see Rome again, you'll hardly know it and all the people you loved will be different. There's no stopping it, it's the most natural thing in the world.'

Seeing Marcus wasn't cheered, he went on.

'This civilisation was ancient when Rome was young. It's an alien place to a Roman and you'll have to watch their ideas of soft living don't spoil you. There are savage tribes that raid across the border in Illyria, though, so you'll see your share of action. That got your interest, did it?' He laughed, a short bark. 'I suppose you thought it would be all drill and standing in the sun? Marius is a good judge, lad. He's sent you to one of the hardest posts in the empire. Even the Greeks don't bend the knee without a good deal of thought and Macedonia is where Alexander was born. This is just the place to put a bit of strength into your steel.'

Together they watched as the *Lucidae* eased against the dockside and ropes were thrown and tied down. In a short while, the little trader was tethered securely and Marcus almost felt sorry for her sudden loss of freedom. Epides came out on deck dressed in a chiton, a traditional Greek tunic worn at knee length. He glittered

245

with jewellery and his hair shone with oil in the sun. He saw the two passengers standing at the side waiting to disembark and walked over to them.

'I have grave news, gentlemen. A Greek army has risen in the north and we could not put in at Dyrrhachium as planned. This is Oricum, about a hundred miles to the south.'

Renius tensed. 'What? You were paid to put us down in the north, so that we could join the lad's legion, I . . .'

'It was not a possibility, as I said,' the captain replied, smiling. 'The flag codes were quite clear as we neared Dyrrhachium. That is why we have been following the coast south. I could not risk the *Lucidae* with a rebel army drunk on broken Roman garrisons. The safety of the ship was at stake.'

Renius grabbed Epides by his chiton, lifting him up to his toes.

'Damn you, man. There's a bloody great mountain between here and Macedonia, as you are well aware. That is another month of hard travel for us and great expense, which is your responsibility!'

Epides struggled, his face purpling in rage.

'Take your hands off me! How dare you accost me on my own ship? I'll call the harbour guards and have you hanged, you arrogant –'

Renius shifted his grip to a ruby on a heavy gold chain around Epides' neck. With a savage jerk, he broke the links and tucked it away into his belt pouch. Epides began stuttering with incoherent anger and Renius shoved him away, turning to Marcus as the man fell sprawling onto the deck.

'Right. Let's get off. At least we can afford to buy supplies for the trip when I sell the chain.'

When he saw Marcus' gaze flick behind him, Renius spun and drew his sword in one motion. Epides was lunging with a jewelled dagger, his face contorted.

Renius swayed inside the blow clumsily and ripped his gladius up into the man's smooth-shaven chest. He withdrew the blade

246

and ran it over the chiton in quick wipes as Epides fell to the deck, writhing.

'Drunk on broken garrisons, was it?' he muttered, struggling to sheathe the sword. 'Damn this scabbard – won't stay still . . .'

Marcus stood stunned at the quick death and the nearby members of the crew gaped at the suddenly violent scene. Renius nodded to them as the gladius slid home.

'Get the ramps down. We have a long journey ahead of us.'

A section in the side was opened and plank gangways were put down to allow the cargo to be unloaded. Marcus shook his head in silent disbelief. He checked his belongings for the last time and patted his sides, feeling again the loss of the dagger he'd given to Firstmate the previous evening. He knew it was the right thing to do somehow, and the smiles of the crew as the man showed it around told him he had made the right choice. There were no smiles now and he wished he'd kept it.

He pulled his pack onto his shoulders and helped Renius with his.

'Let's see what Greece has to offer,' he said.

Renius grinned at his sudden change in mood, walking past the twisted body of Epides without looking down. They left the *Lucidae* without a backward glance.

The ground moved alarmingly under his feet and Marcus swayed uncertainly for a few moments before the habit of years re-established itself.

'Wait!' a voice called behind them. They turned to see Peppis coming down the ramp in a flurry of arms and legs. He pulled up breathlessly and they waited for him to calm enough to speak.

'Take me with you, sir,' he said, looking beseechingly at Marcus, who blinked in surprise.

'I thought you wanted to grow up to be a sailor,' he said.

'Not any more. I want to be a fighter, a legionary like you and

247

Renius,' Peppis said, the words rushing out of him. 'I want to defend the empire from savage hordes.'

Marcus looked at Renius. 'Have you been talking to the boy?'

'I told him a few stories, yes. Many boys dream of being in the legions. It is a good life for a man,' Renius replied without embarrassment.

Peppis saw Marcus waver and pressed on. 'You'll need a servant, someone to carry your sword and look after your horse. Please don't send me back.'

Marcus shrugged his pack from his shoulders and handed it to the boy, who beamed at him.

'Right. Carry this. Do you know how to look after a horse?'

Peppis shook his head, still beaming.

'Then you will learn.'

'I will. I will be the best servant you ever had,' the boy replied, his arms wrapped around the pack.

'At least the captain can't object,' Marcus said.

'No. I didn't like the man,' Renius replied gruffly. 'Ask someone where the nearest stables are. We'll move on before dark.'

The stables, the travellers' resting house, the people themselves were a peculiar mixture to Marcus. He could see Rome in a thousand small touches, not least the serious-faced legionaries who marched the streets in pairs, looking out for trouble. Yet at every step he would see something new and alien. A pretty girl walking with her guards would speak to them in a string of soft gibberish that they seemed to understand. A temple near the stables was built of pure white marble as at home, but the statues were odd, close to the ones he knew, but with different faces cut into the stone. Beards were much in evidence, perfumed with sweet oils and curled, but the strangest things he saw were on the walls of a temple devoted to healing the sick.

Half- and full-size limbs, perfectly formed in plaster or stone, hung on the outer walls from hooks. A child's leg, bent at the knee, shared the space with the model of a woman's hand and nearby there was a miniature soldier made from reddish marble, beautiful in its detail.

'What are those?' Marcus had asked Renius as they passed.

'Just a custom,' he said, with a shrug. 'If the goddess heals you, you have a cast of the limb made and presented to her. It helps to bring in more people for the temple, I should think. They don't heal anyone without a little gold first, so the models are like a sign for a shop. This isn't Rome, lad. They are not like us when you get down to it.'

'You don't like them?'

'I respect what they achieved, but they live too much in the glories of the past. They are a proud people, Marcus, but not proud enough to take our foot off their necks. They like to think of us as barbarians and the high-bred ones will pretend you don't exist, but what good is thousands of years of art if you can't defend yourself? The first thing men must learn is to be strong. Without strength, anything else you have or make can be taken from you. Remember that, lad.'

At least the stables were like stables anywhere. The smell brought a sudden pang of homesickness to Marcus and he wondered how Tubruk fared on the estate, and how Gaius was handling the dangers of the capital.

Renius patted the flank of a sturdy-looking stallion. He ran his hands down its legs and checked the mouth carefully. Peppis watched him and mimicked his action, patting legs and checking tendons with a serious frown on his face.

'How much for this one?' Renius asked the owner, who stood with two bodyguards. The man had none of the smell of horses about him. He looked clean and somehow polished, with hair and beard that shone darkly.

'He is strong, yes?' he replied, his Latin accented but clear. 'His father won races in Pontus, but he is a little too heavy for speed, more suited for battle.'

Renius shrugged. 'I just want him to take me north, over the mountains. How much are you asking?'

'His name is Apollo. I bought him when a rich man lost his wealth and was forced to sell. I paid a small fortune, but I know horses, I know what he is worth.'

'I like him,' Peppis said.

Both men ignored the boy.

'I will pay five aurei for him and sell him after the journey is over,' Renius said firmly.

'He is worth twenty and I have paid for his feed all winter,' the trader replied.

'I can buy a small house for twenty!'

The trader shrugged and looked apologetic.

'Not any more. Prices have gone up. It is the war in the north. All the best ones are being taken for Mithridates, an upstart who calls himself a king. Apollo is one of the last of the good stock.'

'Ten is my final offer. We are buying two of yours today, so I want a price for both.'

'Let us not argue. Let me show you another of lesser worth that will carry you north. I have two others I could sell together, brothers they are, and fast enough.'

The man walked on down the row of horses and Marcus eyed Apollo, who watched him with interest as he chewed a mouthful of hay. He patted the soft nose as the continuing argument dwindled with distance. Apollo ignored him and reached back for another mouthful, pulled from a string sack nailed to the stable wall.

After a while, Renius returned, looking a little pale.

'We've got two, for tomorrow: Apollo and another one he called Lancer. I'm sure he makes the names up on the spot. Peppis will ride with you, his small weight won't be any trouble. Gods, the prices these people ask for! If your uncle hadn't provided so generously, we'd be walking tomorrow.'

'He's not my uncle,' Marcus reminded. 'How much did they cost us?'

'Don't ask and don't expect to eat much on the journey. Come on, we'll pick the horses up tomorrow at dawn. Let us hope that the prices for rooms haven't risen as high, or we'll be sneaking back in here when it gets dark.'

Continuing to grumble, Renius strode out of the stables, with Marcus and Peppis following him, trying not to smile.

CHAPTER TWENTY-ONE

Marcus sat easily on his horse, occasionally reaching forward to scratch Lancer's ears as they rode down the mountain path. Peppis was dozing behind him, lulled by the gentle rhythm of the horse's walk. Marcus thought of waking him with an elbow to see the view, but decided to leave him alone.

It seemed as if they could see all of Greece from the heights, spread out below in a rolling green and yellow landscape with groves of olive trees and isolated farms speckling the hills and valleys. The clean air smelled different, carrying the scent of unknown flowers.

Marcus remembered gentle Vepax, the tutor, and wondered if he had walked these hills. Or perhaps Alexander himself had taken armies through to the plains on his way to battle distant Persia. He imagined the grim Cretan archers and the Macedonian phalanx as they followed the boy king, and his back straightened in the saddle.

Renius rode ahead, his eyes swinging from the narrow trail to the surrounding scrub foliage and back in a monotonous pattern of alertness. He had withdrawn into himself more and more over the previous week of travel and whole days had passed without more than a few words spoken between them. Only Peppis broke the long silences with exclamations of wonder at birds or lizards on the rocks. Marcus hadn't pushed for conversation, sensing that the gladiator was happier with silence. He smiled wryly at the man's back as they rode, mulling over how he felt about him.

He had hated him once, at that moment in the courtyard of the estate, with Gaius lying wounded in the dust. Yet a grudging respect had existed even before Marcus had raised his sword against him. Renius had a solidity to him that made other men seem insubstantial in comparison. He could be brutal and had a great capacity for callous violence, oblivious to pain or fear. Others followed his lead without a thought, as if they somehow knew this man would see them through. Marcus had seen it on the estate and on the ship and it was difficult not to feel a touch of awe himself. Even age couldn't hold him. Marcus remembered the moment as Cabera closed the old man's wounds, and his surprise at the way the healing took so quickly. They had both watched in astonishment as life swelled in the broken figure and the skin flushed with suddenly rushing blood.

'He walks a greater path than most,' Cabera had said later, when Renius had been laid out on a cool bed in the house to finish his healing. 'His feet are strong in the earth.'

Marcus had wondered at Cabera's tone as he tried to make the young man understand the importance of what he had seen.

'Never have I seen death take its grip off a man as it did with Renius. The gods were whispering in my mind when I touched him.'

The path twisted and turned and they slowed to let the horses pick their way through the broken surface stones, unwilling to risk a sprain or a fall on the steep slope.

'What does the future hold for you, I wonder?' Marcus thought to himself in the comfortable silence. 'Father.'

The word came to him and he realised the idea had been there for some time. He had never known a man to call father and the word unlocked a door in his mind as he explored his feelings further without pain. Renius was not his blood, but a part of him wished he was travelling these lands with his father, protecting each other from dangers. It was a grand daydream and he pictured men's faces as they heard he was the son of Renius. They would look at him with a little awe of their own perhaps and he would simply smile.

Renius broke wind noisily, shifting his weight to the left without looking back. Marcus laughed suddenly at this interruption to his thoughts and continued chuckling to himself at intervals for some time after. The gladiator rode on, his thoughts on the descent and his future once he had delivered Marcus to his legion.

As they approached a narrow part of the trail, boulders rose on both sides as if the thin path had been cut through them. Renius laid his hand on his sword and loosened the blade.

'We're being watched. Be ready,' he called back in a low voice.

Almost as he finished speaking, a dark figure rose from the undergrowth nearby.

'Stop.'

The word was spoken with casual confidence and in good, clear Latin, but Renius ignored it. Marcus part drew his sword and kept the horse walking with pressure from his knees. From the sudden stiffness in the arms around his waist, he knew Peppis was awake and alert, but for once staying silent.

The man looked like a Greek, with the distinctive curled beard, but, unlike the merchants of the town they'd seen, he had the air of a warrior about him. He smiled and called out again.

'Stop, or you will be killed. Last chance.'

'Renius?' Marcus muttered nervously.

The old man scowled, but kept going, digging his heels into Apollo's flanks to urge him into a trot.

An arrow cut the air, taking the horse high in the shoulder with a dull thumping sound. Apollo screamed and fell, pitching Renius to the ground in a crash of metal and swearing. Peppis cried out in fear and Marcus reined in, scanning the undergrowth for the archer. Was there only one, or were there more out there? These men were obviously brigands; they would be lucky to escape alive if they submitted meekly.

Renius came to his feet awkwardly, yanking out his sword. His eyes glinted. He nodded to Marcus, who dismounted smoothly, using his horse to block the sight of the hidden archer. He drew his gladius, reassured by its familiar weight. Peppis came off the horse in a scramble and tried to hide behind a leg, muttering nervously to himself.

The stranger spoke again, his voice friendly. 'Do not do anything foolish. My companions are very good with their bows. Practice is the only way to fill the hours here in the mountains, that and relieving the occasional traveller of his possessions.'

'There is only one archer, I think,' Renius growled, staying light on the balls of his feet and keeping an eye on the scrub. He knew the man would not have stayed in the same place and could be creeping in to get a clean kill as they spoke.

'You wish to gamble your life on this, yes?'

The two men looked at each other and Peppis gripped Lancer's leg, making the horse snort with displeasure.

The outlaw was clean and simply dressed. He looked much like one of the huntsmen Marcus had known on the estate, burned a deep brown by constant exposure to the sun and wind. He did not look like a man given to empty threats and Marcus groaned inwardly. At best, they would arrive at the legion with no kit or equipment, a beginning he might never live down. At worst, death was a few moments away.

'You look like an intelligent man,' the outlaw continued. 'If I drop my hand, you will be dead on the instant. Put your sword on the ground and you will live a few moments more, perhaps until you grow old, yes?'

'I've been old. It isn't worth it,' Renius replied, already beginning to move.

He threw his gladius at the man, end over end in the air. Before it struck, he was leaping away into the shadow of the rock-side. An arrow cut the air where he had been, but no others accompanied it. Only one archer.

Marcus had used the moment to duck under his horse's belly past Peppis, and came up running, throwing himself at the slope, trusting to his speed to keep him steady. He cleared the main ridge without slowing down and accelerated, guessing where the archer must be hiding. As he approached, a man broke from the cover of a grove of fig trees off to his right and he almost skidded as he turned to follow.

He had him in twenty paces along the loose rock surface, bringing him down from behind in a leap. The impact jarred the gladius from his hand and he found himself locked in a struggle with a man who was bigger and stronger than he was. The archer twisted violently in Marcus' grip and they found each other's throats with grasping hands. Marcus began to panic. The man's face was red, but his neck appeared to be made of wood and he couldn't seem to get a crushing grip on the thick flesh.

He would have called for Renius, but the man couldn't have climbed the ridge with only one arm, and anyway he could not draw breath with the archer's great paws on his throat. Marcus dug his thumbs into the windpipe and heaved all his downward weight onto them. The man grunted in pain, but the hairy hands tightened still further and Marcus saw flashes of white light across his vision as his body began to scream for air. His own hands seemed to weaken and he despaired for a second. His right hand came off the throat, almost without his conscious thought and began to hammer the grunting face. The white lights were streaked with flashes of black and his vision began to narrow into a dark tunnel, but he kept striking over and over. The face below him was a messy red pulp, but the hands on his throat were merciless.

Then they fell away, without drama, lying limp on the ground.

Marcus sobbed in air and rolled off to one side. His heart was beating at an impossible speed and he felt light-headed, almost as if he was floating. He pulled himself onto his knees and his fingers scrabbled without strength for the hilt of his sword in ever-widening circles.

Finally, they closed on the leather grip and he breathed a silent prayer of thanks. He could hear Renius and Peppis calling for him below, but had no breath to answer. Staggering, he took a few steps back to the man and froze as he saw the eyes were open and looking at him, the heavy chest heaving as raggedly as his own.

Rasping words grated past the man's smashed lips, but they were Greek and Marcus couldn't understand them. Still panting, he pressed the sharp tip of the gladius against the man's chest and shoved down hard. Then his grip slipped off the hilt and he collapsed in a sprawl, turning weakly to empty his stomach onto the ground.

By the time Marcus climbed stiffly back to the path, Peppis had recovered Renius' sword and the gladiator was holding a pad of cloth to the wound in Apollo's shoulder. The big horse was shivering visibly with shock, but was on his feet and aware. Peppis had to hold Lancer's reins tightly as the horse stepped and skittered, wide nostrils and eyes showing his fear at the smell of blood.

'Are you all right, lad?' Renius asked.

Marcus nodded, unable to speak. His throat felt crushed and air seemed to whistle with each breath. He pointed at it and Renius beckoned him closer so he could take a look. He made the movement slow, so as not to alarm the horses.

'Nothing permanent,' he judged a moment later. 'Big hands, judging by the prints.'

Marcus could only gasp weakly. He hoped Renius couldn't smell the sour vomit odour that seemed to surround him in a cloud, but guessed he could and chose not to mention it.

'They made a mistake attacking us,' Peppis observed, his little face serious.

'Yes, they did, boy, though we were lucky as well,' Renius replied. He looked at Marcus. 'Don't try to speak, just help the boy strap the equipment to your horse. Apollo will be lame for a week or two. We'll ride in turns unless those bandits have mounts nearby.'

Lancer whinnied and an answering snort came from further down the mountain. Renius grinned.

'Luck is with us again, I see,' he said cheerfully. 'Did you search the body?'

Marcus shook his head and Renius shrugged.

'Not worth climbing up again. They wouldn't have had much and a bow's no use to a man with one arm. Let's get going. We can get off this rock by sunset if we keep a fast pace.'

Marcus began removing Apollo's packs, taking the reins. Renius patted his shoulder as he turned away. The action was worth far more than words.

After a month of long days and cold nights, it was good to see the legion camp from far away across the plain. Even at that distance, thin sounds carried. It seemed like a town on the horizon, with eight thousand men, women and children engaged in the simple day-to-day tasks necessary to keep such a large body of men in the field. Marcus tried to imagine the armouries and smithies, built and taken apart with each camp. There would be food kitchens, building supply dumps, stonemasons, carpenters, leather-workers, slaves, prostitutes and thousands of other civilians who lived and were paid to support the might of Rome in battle. Unlike the tent rows of Marius' legion, this was a permanent camp, with a solid wall and fortifications surrounding the main grounds. In a sense, it was a town, but a town constantly prepared for war.

Renius pulled up and Marcus drew alongside on Lancer, tugging on the reins to halt the third horse they had named Bandit after his last owner. Peppis sat awkwardly on Bandit's riding blanket, his mouth open at the sight of the encamped legion. Renius smiled at the boy's awe.

'That's it, Marcus. That is your new home. Do you still have the papers Marius gave you?'

Marcus patted his chest in response, feeling the folded pack of parchment under the tunic.

'Are you coming in?' he asked. He hoped so. Renius had been a part of his life for so long that the thought of seeing the man riding away while he rode up to the gates alone was too painful to express.

'I'll see you and Peppis to the *Praefectus castrorum* – the quartermaster. He will tell you which century you will join. Learn the history quickly; each has its own record and pride.'

'Any other advice?'

'Obey every order without complaint. At the moment you fight like an individual, like one of the savage tribes. They will teach you to trust your companions and to fight as a unit, but the learning does not come easily to some.'

He turned to Peppis. 'Life will be hard for you. Do as you are told and when you are grown you will be allowed to join the legion. Do nothing that shames you. Do you understand?'

Peppis nodded, his throat dry from fear of this alien life.

'I will learn. So will he,' Marcus said.

Renius nodded and clicked his tongue at his horse to move on. 'That you will.'

Marcus felt an obscure satisfaction at the clean, orderly layout of streets, complete with rows of long, low buildings for the men. He and Renius had been greeted warmly at the gate as soon as he had shown his papers and proceeded on foot to the Prefect's quarters, where he would pledge years of his life in the field service of Rome. He took confidence from Renius as the man strode confidently through the narrow roads, nodding in approval at the polished perfection of the soldiers who marched past in squads of ten. Peppis trotted behind them, carrying a heavy pack of equipment on his back.

The papers had to be shown twice more as they approached the small, white building from which the camp Prefect ran the business of a Roman town in a foreign land. At last they were allowed entry and a slim man dressed in a white toga and sandals came into the outer rooms to meet them as they passed through the door.

'Renius! I heard it was you in the camp. The men are already talking about you losing your arm. Gods, it is good to see you!' He beamed at them, the image of Roman efficiency, suntanned and hard, with a strong grip as he greeted each of them in turn.

Renius smiled back with genuine warmth.

'Marius didn't tell me you were here, Carac. I am glad to see you well.'

'You haven't aged, I swear it! Gods, you don't look a day over forty. How do you do it?'

'Clean living,' Renius grunted, still uncomfortable with the change Cabera had wrought.

The Prefect raised an eyebrow in disbelief, but let the subject drop.

'And the arm?'

'Training accident. The lad here, Marcus, cut me and I had it taken off.'

The Prefect whistled and shook Marcus' hand again.

'I never thought I'd meet a man who could get to Renius. May I see the papers you brought with you?'

Marcus felt nervous all of a sudden. He passed them over and the Prefect motioned them to long benches as he read.

Finally, he passed them back. 'You come very well recommended, Marcus. Who is the boy?'

'He was on the merchant ship we took from the coast. He wants to be my servant and join the legion when he is older.'

The Prefect nodded. 'We have many such in the camp, usually the bastard children of the men and the whores. If he shapes up there may be a place, but the competition will be fierce. I am more interested in you, young man.'

He turned to Renius. 'Tell me about him. I will trust your judgement.'

Renius spoke firmly, as if reporting. 'Marcus is unusually fast, even more so when his blood is fired. As he matures, I expect him to become a name. He is impetuous and brash and likes to fight, which is partly his nature and partly his youth. He will serve the Fourth Macedonia well. I gave him his basic training, but he has gone beyond that and will go further.'

'He reminds me of your son. Have you noticed the resemblance?' the Prefect asked quietly.

'It had not . . . occurred to me,' Renius replied uncomfortably.

'I doubt that. Still, we always have need of men of quality and this is the place for him to find maturity. I will place him with the fifth century, the Bronze Fist.'

Renius took in a sharp breath. 'You honour me.'

The Prefect shook his head. 'You saved my life once. I am sorry I could not save your son's. This is a small part of my debt to you.'

Once again they shook hands. Marcus looked on in some confusion.

'What now for you, old friend? Will you return to Rome to spend your gold?'

'I had hoped there would be a place for me here,' Renius said quietly.

The Prefect smiled. 'I had begun to think you would not ask. The Fist is short of a weapons master to train them. Old Belius died of a fever six months ago and there is no one else as good. Will you take the post?'

Renius grinned suddenly, the old sharp grin. 'I will, Carac. Thank you.'

The Prefect slapped him on the shoulder in obvious pleasure.

'Welcome to the Fourth Macedonia, gentlemen.' He signalled to a legionary standing to attention nearby. 'Take this young man to his new quarters in the Bronze Fist century. Send the boy to the stables until I can assign duties to him with the other camp children. Renius and I have a lot of catching up to do – and a lot of wine to drink while we do it.'

CHAPTER TWENTY-TWO

Alexandria sat in silence, polishing grime from an ancient sword in Marius' little armoury. She was pleased he had been able to get back his town house. She'd heard the owner had rushed to make a gift of it to the new ruler of Rome. Much better than the thought of living with the rough soldiers in the city barracks – well, it would have been difficult at best. Gods knew, she wasn't afraid of men; some of her earliest memories were of them with her mother in the next room. They came in reeking of beer and cheap wine and went out with a swagger. They never seemed to last very long. One of them had tried to touch her once and she remembered seeing her mother properly angry for the first time in her young life. She'd cracked his skull with a poker and together they'd dragged him into an alleyway and left him. For days, her mother had expected the door to burst in and men to take her away to be hanged, but no one had come.

She sighed as she worked at the layers of crusted oil on the bronze blade, relic of some old campaign. At first, Rome had seemed a city with limitless possibilities, but Marius had taken control three months before and here she was still working all day for nothing and every day a little older. Others were changing the world, but her life remained the same. Only at night, when she sat with ancient Bant in his little metalwork room, did she feel she was making any progress in her life. He had shown her the uses of his tools and guided her hands through the first clumsy steps. He didn't speak much, but seemed to enjoy her company and she liked his silences and kind blue eyes. She had seen him first as he was shaping a brooch in the workshop and knew in that moment that it was something she could do. It was a skill worth learning, even for a slave.

She rubbed more vigorously. To be worth no more to a man than a horse, or even a good sword like the one she held! It wasn't fair.

'Alexandria!' Carla's voice, calling. For a moment, she was tempted to remain silent, but the woman had a tongue like a whip and her disapproval was feared by most of the female slaves.

'Here,' she called, putting the sword down and wiping her hands on a rag. There would be another task for her, another few hours of labour before sleep.

'There you are, love. I need someone to run down to the market for me; would you do that?'

'Yes!' Alexandria stood up quickly. She had come to look forward to these rare errands over the previous few months. They were the only occasions when she was allowed to leave Marius' house and on the last few she had been trusted on her own. After all, where could she run?

'I have a list of things for you to buy for the house. You always seem to get the best price,' Carla said as she passed a slate over.

Alexandria nodded. She enjoyed bargaining with the traders. It made her feel like a free woman. The first time she hadn't been alone, but, even with a witness, Carla had been shocked at how much money the girl had saved the house. The traders had been charging over market value for years, knowing Marius had deep pockets. The older woman realised the girl had a talent and sent her out as much as possible, seeing also that she needed the little touches of freedom. Some never got used to the condition of slavery and were slowly broken down into depression and occasionally despair. Carla enjoyed watching Alexandria's face light up at the thought of a trip out.

She guessed the girl was keeping a coin or two from what she was given, but what did that matter? She was saving them silvers, so if she kept the odd bronze, Carla didn't begrudge them to her.

'Go on with you. I want you back in two hours and not a minute later, understand?'

'I do, Carla. Two hours. Thank you.'

The older woman grinned at her, remembering when she had been young and the world was such an exciting place. She knew all about Alexandria's visits to Bant the metalworker. The old man had taken quite a liking to her, it seemed. There was very little in the house that Carla didn't find out about sooner or later and she knew that in Alexandria's room was a small bronze disc that she had decorated with a lion's head using Bant's tools. It was a pretty piece.

As she watched the trim figure vanish around a corner, Carla wondered if it was a present for Gaius. Bant had said the girl had a talent for the work. Aye, perhaps because she was making it for love.

The market was a riot of smells and swirling crowds, but Alexandria didn't dawdle over the items on the list for once. She completed her business quickly, getting good prices, but leaving the discussion before they were pared right to the bone. The shopkeepers seemed to enjoy the arguments with the pretty girl, throwing their hands into the air and calling for witnesses to see what she was demanding. She smiled at them then, and for a few the smile dropped the price further than they could believe after she had left. Certainly more than their wives could believe.

With packages stowed safely in two cloth bags, Alexandria hurried on to her real destination, a tiny jewellery shop at the end of the stalls. She had been inside many times to look at the man's designs. Most of the pieces were bronze or pewter. Silver was rarely worked in jewellery, and gold was too expensive unless particular pieces were commissioned. The metalsmith himself was a short man, dressed in a rough tunic and a heavy leather apron. He watched her as she came into the tiny shop and stopped work on a small gold ring to keep an eye on the girl. Tabbic was not a trusting man and Alexandria could feel his steady gaze on her as she looked over his wares.

Finally, she summoned enough courage to speak to him.

'Do you buy items?' she said.

'Sometimes,' came the reply. 'What do you have?'

She produced the bronze disc from a pocket in her tunic and he took it from her hand, holding it up to the daylight to see the design. He held it for a long time and she didn't dare speak for fear of angering him. Still he said nothing, just turned it over and over in his hands, examining every last mark on the metal.

'Where did you get this?' he asked at last.

'I made it. Do you know Bant?'

The man nodded slowly.

'He has been showing me how.'

'This is crude, but I can sell it on. The execution is clumsy, but the design is very good. The lion's face is very well scribed, it's just that you aren't very skilled with the hammer and awl.' He turned it over again.

'Tell me the truth now, you understand? Where did you get the bronze to make this?'

Alexandria looked at him nervously. He returned her stare without blinking, but his eyes seemed kind. Quickly she told him about her bargaining and how she had saved a few tiny coins from the house money, enough to purchase the bare metal circle from a stall of trinkets.

Tabbic shook his head. 'I can't take it then. It isn't yours to sell.

266

The coins belonged to Marius, so the bronze is his as well. You should give it to him.'

Alexandria felt tears threaten to start. She had spent so long on the little piece and now it had all come to nothing. She watched, almost hypnotised, as he turned it over in his grasp. Then he pressed it back into her hands.

Miserable, she put the disc back in her pocket.

'I'm sorry,' she said.

He turned back to her. 'My name is Tabbic. You don't know me, but I have a reputation for honesty and sometimes for pride.' He held up another metal circle, a grey silver in colour.

'This is pewter. It's softer than bronze and you'll find it easier to work. It polishes up nicely and doesn't discolour as badly, just grows dull. Take it, and return it to me when you have made something of it. I'll attach a pin and sell it on as a cloak fastener for a legionary. If it's as good as the bronze one, I could get a silver coin for it. I'll take back the price of the pewter and the pin and you will be left with six, maybe seven quadrantes. A business transaction, understand?'

'Where is your profit in this?' Alexandria asked, her eyes wide at the change in fortune.

'None for this first one. I am making a small investment in a talent I think you have. Give Bant my regards when you see him next.'

Alexandria pocketed the pewter circle and once again had to fight against tears. She wasn't used to kindness.

'Thank you. I will give the bronze to Marius.'

'Make sure you do, Alexandria.'

'How . . . how do you know my name?'

Tabbic picked up the ring he had been working on as she came in.

'Bant talks of little else when I see him.'

* * *

Alexandria had to run to be back before the two hours were up, but her feet were light and she felt like singing. She would make the pewter disc into a beautiful thing and Tabbic would sell it for more than a silver coin and clamour for more until her work brought in gold pieces, and one day she would gather her profits together and buy herself free. Free. It was a giddy dream.

As she was let into Marius' house, the scent of the gardens filled her lungs and she stood for a moment, just breathing in the evening air. Carla appeared and took her bags and the coins, nodding at the savings as always. If the woman noticed anything different about Alexandria, she didn't say, but she smiled as she took the supplies down to the cool basement stores, where they wouldn't spoil too quickly.

Alone with her thoughts, Alexandria didn't see Gaius at first and wasn't expecting him. He spent most of his days matching his uncle's punishing schedule, returning to the house at odd hours only to eat and sleep. The guards at the gate let him in without comment, well used to his comings and goings. He started as he saw Alexandria in the gardens and stood for a moment, simply enjoying the sight of her. Evening was coming on with late-summer slowness, where the air is soft and the light has a touch of grey for hours before it fades.

She turned as he approached and smiled at him.

'You look happy,' he said, smiling in return.

'Oh, I am,' she replied.

He had not kissed her since the moment in the stables back on the estate, but he sensed the time was right at last. Marcus was gone and the town house seemed deserted.

He bent his neck and his heart thumped painfully with something almost like fear.

He felt her warm breath before their lips touched and then he could taste her and he gathered her up in a natural embrace, as they seemed to fit together without effort or design.

'I can't tell you how often I have thought of this,' he murmured.

She looked into his eyes and knew there was a gift she could give him and found she wanted to.

'Come along to my room,' she whispered, taking his hand.

As if in a dream, he followed her through the gardens to her quarters.

Carla watched them go.

'And about bloody time,' she muttered.

At first, Gaius was worried that he would be clumsy, or worse, quick, but Alexandria guided his movements and her hands felt cool on his skin. She took a little bottle of scented oil from a shelf and he watched as she spilled a few sluggish drops onto her palms. It had a rich scent that filled his lungs as she sat astride him, rubbing it gently into his chest and lower, making him gasp. He took some of it from his own skin and reached upwards to her breasts, remembering the first time he had seen their soft swell in the courtyard of the estate so long ago. He pressed his mouth gently against one then the other, tasting her skin and moving his lips over the oily nipples. She opened her mouth slightly, her eyes closing at his touch. Then she bent to kiss him and her unbound hair covered them both.

As the evening darkened, they joined with urgency and then again with playfulness and a kind of delight. There was little light in her room without the candles, but her eyes shone and her limbs were darkened gold as she moved under him.

He woke before dawn to find her gaze on his face.

'This was my first time,' he said quietly. Something in him told him not to ask the question, but he had to know. 'Was it the first for you?'

She smiled, but it was a sad smile.

'I wish it had been,' she said. 'I really do.'

269

'Did you . . . with Marcus?'

Her eyes widened slightly. Was he truly so innocent that he didn't see the insult?

'Oh, I would have, of course,' she replied tartly, 'but he didn't ask.'

'I'm sorry,' he said, blushing, 'I didn't mean . . .'

'Did he say we did?' Alexandria demanded.

Gaius kept his face straight as he replied: 'Yes, I'm afraid he boasted about it.'

'I'll put a dagger in his eye the next time I see him, gods!' Alexandria raged, gathering her clothes to dress.

Gaius nodded seriously, trying not to smile at the thought of Marcus returning innocently.

They dressed hurriedly, as neither wanted the gossips to see him coming out of her room before the sun was up. She left the slave quarters with him and they sat together in the gardens, brushed by a warm night wind that moved in silence.

'When can I see you again?' he said quietly.

She looked away and he thought she wouldn't answer. Fear rose in him.

'Gaius . . . I loved every moment of last night: the touch and feel and taste of you. But you will marry a daughter of Rome. Did you know I wasn't Roman? My mother was from Carthage, taken as a child and enslaved, then made into a prostitute. I was born late. I should never have been born so late to her. She was never strong after me.'

'I love you,' Gaius said, knowing it was true for at least that moment and hoping that was enough. He wanted to give her something that showed she was more than just a night of pleasure for him.

She shook her head lightly at his words.

'If you love me, let me stay here in Marius' home. I can fashion jewellery and one day I will make enough to buy myself free. I

270

can be happy here as I could never be if I let myself love you. I could, but you would be a soldier and leave for distant parts of the world and I would see your wife and your children and have to nod to them in the street. Don't make me your whore, Gaius. I have seen that life and I don't want it. Don't make me sorry for last night. I don't want to be sorry for something so good.'

'I could free you,' he whispered, in pain. Nothing seemed to make sense.

Her eyes flashed in anger, quickly controlled. 'No, you couldn't. Oh, you could take my pride and sign me free by Roman law, but I would have earned it in your bed. I am free where it matters, Gaius. I realise that now. To be a free citizen in law, I must work honestly to buy myself back. Then I am my own. I met a man today who said he had honesty and pride. I have both, Gaius, and I don't want to lose either. I will not forget you. Come and see me in twenty years and I will give you a pendant of gold, fashioned with love.'

'I will,' he said. He leaned in and kissed her cheek, then rose and left the scented gardens.

He let himself out onto the streets of the city and walked until he was lost and too tired to feel anything except numbness.

271

CHAPTER TWENTY-THREE

As the moon rose, Marius frowned at the centurion.

'My orders were clear. Why have you not obeyed them?'

The man stammered a little as he replied: 'General. I assumed there had been a mistake.' His face paled as he spoke. He knew the consequences. Soldiers did not send messengers to query their orders, they obeyed them, but what he had been asked was madness.

'You were told to consider tactics against a Roman legion. Specifically, to find ways to nullify their greater mobility outside the gates. Which part did you not understand?' Marius' voice was grim and the man paled further as he saw his pension and rank disappearing.

'I . . . No one expects Sulla to attack Rome. No one has ever attacked the city –'

Marius interrupted him. 'You are dismissed to the ranks. Fetch me Octavius, your second-in-command. He will take your place.'

Something crumpled out of the man. More than forty years old, he would never see promotion again.

'Sir, if they do come, I would like to be in the first rows to meet them.'

'To redeem yourself?' Marius asked.

The man nodded, sickly.

'Granted. Yours will be the first face they see. And they will come, and not as lambs, but wolves.'

Marius watched the broken man walk stiffly away and shook his head. So many found it difficult to believe that Sulla would turn against their beloved city. For Marius it was a certainty. The news he received daily was that Sulla had finally broken the back of the rebel armies under Mithridates, burning a good part of Greece to the ground in the process. Barely a year had passed, and he would be returning as a conquering hero. The people would grant him anything. With such a strong position, there was no chance of him leaving the legion in the field or in a neighbouring city while he and his cronies came quietly back to take their seats in the Senate and go on as usual. This was the gamble Marius had taken. Though there was nothing else he could find to admire about the man, Sulla was a fine general and Marius had known all along that he could win and return.

'The city is mine now,' he muttered thickly, looking about him at the soldiers building ramparts onto the heavy gates for arrow fire. He wondered where his nephew had got to and noted absently how little he'd seen of him in the last few weeks. Tiredly, he rubbed the bridge of his nose, knowing he was pushing himself too hard.

He had snatched sleep for a year as he built his supply lines and armed his men and planned the siege to come. Rome had been recreated as a city fortress and there was not a weak point in any of the walls. She would stand, he knew, and Sulla would break himself on the gates.

His centurions were hand-picked and the loss of one that morning was a source of irritation. Each man had been promoted for his flexibility, his ability to react to new situations, ready for this time, when the greatest city in the world would face her own children in battle – and destroy them.

Gaius was drunk. He stood on the edge of a balcony with a full goblet of wine, trying to steady his vision. A fountain splashed in the garden below and blearily he decided to go and put his head into the water. The night was warm enough.

The noise from the party was a crashing mix of music, laughter and drunken shouting as he moved back inside. It was past midnight and no one was left sober. The walls were lined with flickering oil lamps, casting an intimate light over the revellers. The wine slaves filled every cup as soon as it was drained and had been doing so for hours.

A woman brushed against Gaius and draped an arm over his shoulder, giggling, making him spill some red wine onto the cream marble floor. Her breasts were uncovered and she pulled his free hand onto them as she pressed her lips to him.

He broke for air and she took his wine, emptying the cup in one. Throwing it over her shoulder, she reached down into the folds of his toga, fondling him with erotic skill. He kissed her again and staggered back under her drunken weight until his back pressed up against a column near the balcony. He could feel its coolness against his back.

The crowd were oblivious. Many were only partly dressed and the sunken pool in the middle of the floor churned with slippery couples. The host had brought in a number of slave girls, but the debauchery had spread with the drunkenness and by this late hour the last hundred guests were ready to accept almost anything.

Gaius groaned as the stranger opened her mouth on him and he signalled a passing slave for another cup of wine. He spilled a few drops down his bare chest and watched as the liquid dribbled down to her working mouth, absently rubbing the wine into her soft lips with his fingers.

The music and laughter swelled around him. The air was hot and humid with steam from the pool and the light of the lamps. He finished the wine and threw the cup out into the darkness over the balcony, never hearing it strike the gardens below. His fifth party in two weeks and he thought he had been too tired to go out again, but Diracius was known for throwing wild ones. The other four had been exhausting and he realised this could be the end of him. His mind seemed slightly detached, an observer to the writhing clumps around him. In truth, Diracius had been right to say the parties would help him forget, but, even after so many months, each moment with Alexandria was still there to be called into his mind. What he had lost was the sense of wonder and of joy.

He closed his eyes and hoped his legs would hold him upright to the end.

Kneeling, Mithridates spat blood over his beard onto the ground, keeping his head bowed. A bull of a man, he had killed many soldiers in the battle of the morning and even now, with his arms tied and his weapons taken, the Roman legionaries walked warily around him. He chuckled at them, but it was a bitter sound. All around lay hundreds of men who had been his friends and followers, and the smell of blood and open bowels hung on the air. His wife and daughters had been torn from his tent and butchered by cold-eyed soldiers. His generals had been impaled and their bodies sagged loosely, held upright on spikes as long as a man. It was a bleak day to see it all end.

His mind wandered back over the months, tasting again the joys of the rebellion, the pride as strong Greeks came to his banner from all the cities, united again in the face of a common enemy. It had all seemed possible for a while, but now there were only ashes in the mouth. He remembered the first fort to fall and the disbelief and shame in the Roman Prefect's eyes as he was made to watch it burn.

'Look on the flames,' Mithridates had whispered to him. 'This will be Rome.' The Roman had tried to reply, but Mithridates had silenced him with a dagger across his throat, to the cheers of his men.

Now, he was the only one left of the band of friends that had dared to throw off the yoke of Roman rule.

'I have been free,' he muttered through the blood, but the words failed to cheer him as they once could.

Trumpets sounded and horses galloped across a cleared path to where Mithridates waited, resting back on his haunches. He raised his shaggy head, his long hair falling over his eyes. The legionaries nearby stood to attention in silence and he knew who it had to be. One eye was stuck with blood, but through the other he could see a golden figure climb down from a stallion and pass the reins to another. The spotless white toga seemed incongruous in this field of death. How was it possible for anything in the world to be untouched by the misery of such a grey afternoon?

Slaves spread rushes over the mud to make a path to the kneeling king. Mithridates straightened. They would not see him broken and begging, not with his daughters lying so close in peaceful stillness.

Cornelius Sulla strode over to the man and stood watching. As if by arrangement with the gods, the sun chose that moment to come from behind the clouds and his dark-blond hair glowed as he drew a gleaming silver gladius from a simple scabbard.

'You have given me a great deal of trouble, Highness,' Sulla said quietly.

At his words, Mithridates squinted.

'I did my best to,' he replied grimly, holding the man's gaze with his one good eye.

'But now it is over. Your army is broken. The rebellion has ended.'

Mithridates shrugged. What good was it to state the obvious?

Sulla continued: 'I had no part in the killing of your wife and daughters. The soldiers involved have all been executed at my command. I do not make war on women and children and I am sorry they were taken from you.'

Mithridates shook his head as if to clear it of the words and the sudden flashes of memory. He had heard his beloved Livia screaming his name, but there were legionaries all around him armed with clubs to take him alive. He had lost his dagger in a man's throat and his sword when it jammed in another's ribs. Even then, with her screams in his ears, he had broken the neck of a man who rushed in on him, but as he stooped to pick up a fallen sword, the others had beaten him senseless and he had woken to find himself bound and battered.

He gazed up at Sulla, looking for mockery. Instead, he found only sternness and believed him. He looked away. Did this man expect Mithridates the King to laugh and say all was forgiven? The soldiers had been men of Rome and this golden figure was their master. Was a huntsman not responsible for his dogs?

'Here is my sword,' Sulla said, offering the blade. 'Swear by your gods that you will not rise against Rome in my lifetime, and I will leave you alive.'

Mithridates looked at the silver gladius, trying to keep the surprise from his face. He had grown used to the fact that he would die, but to suddenly have the offer of life again was like tearing scabs away from hidden wounds. Time to bury his wife.

'Why?' he grunted through the drying blood.

'Because I believe you to be a man of your word. There has been enough death today.'

Mithridates nodded silently in reply and Sulla reached round him with the unstained blade to cut the bonds. The king felt the soldiers nearby tense as they saw the enemy free once more, but he ignored them, reaching out and taking the blade in his scarred right palm. The metal was cold against his skin.

'I swear it.'

'You have sons, what about them?'

Mithridates looked at the Roman general, wondering how much he knew. His sons were in the east, raising support for their father.

They would return with men and supplies and a new reason for vengeance.

'They are not here. I cannot answer for my sons.'

Sulla held the blade still in the man's grip.

'No, but you can warn them. If they return and raise Greece against Rome while I live, I will visit upon her people a scale of grief they have never known.'

Mithridates nodded and let his hand fall from the blade. Sulla resheathed it and turned away, striding back to his horse without a backward glance.

Every Roman in sight moved off with him, leaving Mithridates alone on his knees, surrounded by the dead. Stiffly, he pulled himself to his feet, wincing at last at the score of pains that plagued him. He watched the Romans break camp and move to the west, back to the sea, and his eyes were cold and puzzled.

Sulla rode silently for the first few leagues. His friends exchanged glances, but for a while no one dared to break the grim silence. Finally, Padacus, a pretty young man from northern Italy, put out his hand to touch Sulla's shoulder and the general reined in, looking at him questioningly.

'Why did you leave him alive? Will he not come against us in the spring?'

Sulla shrugged. 'He might, but if he does, at least he is a man I know I can beat. His successor might not make mistakes so easily. I could have spent another six months rooting out every one of his followers left alive in tiny mountain camps, but what would we have gained except their hatred? No, the real enemy, the real battle –' He paused and looked over to the western horizon, almost as if he could see all the way to the gates of Rome. 'The real battle has yet to be fought and we have spent too much time here already. Ride on. We will assemble the legion at the coast, ready for the crossing home.'

CHAPTER TWENTY-FOUR

Gaius leaned on the stone window ledge and watched the sun come up over the city. He heard Cornelia stir on the long bed behind him and smiled to himself as he glanced back. She was still asleep, her long gold hair spilling over her face and shoulders as she shifted restlessly. In the heat of the night they had needed little to cover them and her long legs were revealed almost to the hip by the light cloth that she had gathered in one small hand and pulled closer to her face.

For a moment, his thoughts turned to Alexandria, but it was without pain. It had been hard for the first months, even with friends like Diracius to distract him. He could look back now and wince at his naivety and clumsiness. Yet there was sadness, too. He could never be that innocent boy again.

He had seen Metella privately and signed a document that passed Alexandria's ownership over to the house of Marius, knowing he could trust his aunt to be kind to her. He had also left a sum of gold pieces, taken from his estate funds, to be handed to her on the day she purchased her freedom. She would find out when she was free. It was a small gift, considering what she had given him.

Gaius grinned as he felt arousal stir once more, knowing he would have to be moving before the household came awake. Cornelia's father Cinna was another of the political heavyweights

Marius was flattering and working to control. Not a man to cross, and discovery in his beloved daughter's bedroom would mean death even for Marius' nephew.

He glanced at her again and sighed as he pulled his clothes to him. She had been worth it though, worth the risk many times over. Three years older than him, she had yet been a virgin, which surprised him. She was his alone and that gave him quiet satisfaction and more than a little of the old joy.

They had met at a formal gathering of Senate families, celebrating the birth of twin sons to one of the nobilitas. In the middle of the day, there was nothing like the free licence of one of Diracius' parties, and at first Gaius had been bored with the endless congratulations and speeches. Then, in a quiet moment, she had come over to him and changed everything. She had been wearing a robe of dark gold, almost a brown, with earrings and a torque at her throat of the same rich metal. He had desired her from the first moments, and liked her as quickly. She was intelligent and confident and she wanted him. It was a heady feeling. He had sneaked in over the roofs to her bedroom window, looking on her as she slept, her hair tousled and wild.

He remembered her rising from the bed and sitting on it with her legs drawn up under her and her back straight. It had been a few seconds before he noticed she was smiling. He sighed as he pulled on his clothes and sandals.

With Sulla gone from the city for a whole year as the Greek rebellion grew in ferocity, it was easy for Gaius to forget that there had to be a reckoning at some point. Marius, though, had worked from the first day for the moment that Sulla's standards became visible on the horizon. The city was still buzzing with excitement and dread, as it had been for months. Most had stayed, but a steady trickle of merchants and families leaving the city showed that not every inhabitant shared Marius' confidence about the outcome. Every street had shops that were boarded closed and the Senate criticised many of the decisions made, pushing Marius to rage when he came back to his home in the early hours of the mornings. It was a tension Gaius could barely share, with the pleasures of the city to distract him.

He looked over at Cornelia again as he tightened his toga and saw her eyes were open. He crossed to her and kissed her on the lips, feeling the rush of longing as he did. He dropped one hand to her breast and felt her start against him as he broke for air.

'Will you come to me again, Gaius?'

'I will,' he replied, smiling, and found to his surprise that he actually meant it.

'A good general is prepared for every eventuality,' Marius said as he handed the documents to Gaius. 'These are money orders. They are as good as gold in your hand, drawn on the city treasury. I do not expect to have them repaid, they are a gift to you.'

Gaius looked at the sums and fought to smile. The amounts were large, but would barely cover the debts he had run up with the moneylenders. Marius hadn't been able to keep a close eye on his nephew as the preparations for Sulla's return continued and Gaius had run lines of credit in those first few months after Alexandria, buying women, wine and sculpture – all to increase his standing in a city that had respect only for gold and power. With borrowed wealth, Gaius had come onto a jaded social scene as a young lion. Even those who distrusted his uncle knew Gaius was a man to be watched and there was never a problem with the ever larger sums he required, as the rich struggled to be next to offer finance to Marius' nephew.

Marius must have caught a hint of Gaius' disappointment and interpreted it as worry for the future.

'I expect to win, but only a fool wouldn't plan for disaster where Sulla was involved. If it doesn't go as I have planned, take the drafts and get out of the city. I have included a reference that should get you a berth on a legion vessel to take you to some far post of the empire. I . . . have also written documents naming you as a son of my house. You will be able to join any regiment and make your name for a couple of years.'

'What if you crush Sulla, as you expect?'

'Then we will continue with your advance in Rome. I will secure a post for you that carries life membership of the Senate. They are jealously guarded, come the elections, but it should not be impossible. It will cost us a fortune, but then you are in, truly one of the chosen. Who knows where the future will take you after that?'

Gaius grinned, caught up in the man's enthusiasm. He would use the drafts to pay off the worst of his debts. Of course, the horse sales were next week and the rumour was that Arabian princes were bringing new breeds of warhorses, huge stallions that could be guided with the gentlest touch. They would cost a fortune, a fortune very like the one he held in his hand. He tucked the papers inside his toga as he left. The moneylenders would wait a little longer, he was sure.

In the cool night outside Marius' town house, Gaius weighed up his options for the hours before dawn. As usual, the dark city was far from quiet and he didn't feel ready for sleep. Traders and cart-drivers swore at each other, smiths hammered, somebody laughed in a nearby house and he could hear crockery being smashed. The city was a place of life in a way the estate could never match. Gaius loved it.

He could go and listen to the orators in the forum by torchlight, perhaps joining in one of the endless debates with other young nobles until the dawn made them all go home. Or he could seek out Diracius' home and satisfy other appetites. Wiser not to venture alone through the dark streets, he thought, remembering Marius' warnings about the various *raptores* who lurked in the dim alleys, ready for theft or murder. The city was not safe at night and it was easy to become lost in the maze of unnamed, twisting streets. One wrong turning could lead a wanderer into an alley filled with piles of human filth and great pools of urine, though the smell was usually enough of a warning.

A month before, he might have gathered companions for a wild night, but the face of one girl had been appearing more and more in his thoughts. Far from dwindling, his longing for her seemed to be fired by contact rather than quenched. Cornelia would be thinking of him in her father's estate rooms. He would go to her and scale the outer wall, slipping past her father's house guards one more time.

He grinned to himself, remembering the sudden fear as he had slipped during the last climb, hanging above the hard stones of the street below. It was getting so he knew every inch of that wall, but one mistake would cost him a pair of broken legs or worse.

'Worth the risks for you, my girl,' he whispered to himself, watching the night air frost his breath as he walked through the unlit city streets to his destination.

CHAPTER TWENTY-FIVE

The Cinna estate began the bustle of the working day as early as any other in Rome, heating water, firing the ovens, sweeping, cleaning and readying the clothes of the family before they awoke. Before the sun had risen fully, a slave entered Cornelia's room, looking round for clothes to be collected for washing. Her thoughts were on the thousand chores to be completed before the mid-morning light meal and at first she noticed nothing. Then her eyes strayed to where a muscled leg sprawled over the side of the bed. She froze as she saw the sleeping couple, still entwined.

After a moment of indecision, her eyes lit up with malice and she took a deep breath, cracking the still scene with wild screams.

Gaius rolled naked off the bed and onto the floor in a crouch. He took in the situation in a second, but didn't waste any time on cursing himself. He grabbed toga and sword and bolted for the window. The slave girl ran to the door, still screaming, and Cornelia spat oaths after her. Thundering footsteps sounded, and the nurse Clodia came into the room, her face full of outrage. She swung her hand and connected with the slave girl's face, cutting off the scream with a dull smack of flesh and spinning her right round.

'Get out quickly, lad,' Clodia snapped at him as the slave girl whimpered on the floor. 'You'd better be worth all the trouble this is going to cause!'

Gaius nodded, but turned from the window and came back into the room to Cornelia.

'If I don't go, they'll kill me for an intruder. Tell them my name and tell them you're mine, that I'll marry you. Tell them, if anyone harms you I'll kill him.'

Cornelia didn't answer, just reached up and kissed him.

He pulled away, laughing. 'Gods, let me go! It is a fine morning for a bit of a chase.'

She watched with amusement as his white buttocks flashed over the windowsill and away, trying to compose herself for the drama to come.

Her father's guards entered the room first, led by the dour captain who nodded to her and crossed to the window, looking down.

'Get going,' he shouted to his companions. 'I'll cross the roofs after him, you men intercept him down below. I'll have his skin on my wall for this. Your pardon, lady,' he said as a farewell to Cornelia as his red face dropped out of sight.

Cornelia fought not to giggle with tension.

Gaius slipped and skittered on the tiles, scraping skin from elbows and knees as he sacrificed safety for breakneck speed. He heard the captain shouting behind him, but didn't look back. The tiles offered precious little grip and all he could really do was control the speed of his fall as he slid towards the edge and the street below. He had time to swear as he realised his sandals were in the room above. How could he make any kind of jump in only his bare feet? He'd break bones for sure and then the chase would be over. He lost his grip on the toga to save the gladius, by far the more valuable of the two items. He managed to cling to the edge of the roof and inched along it, not risking standing up in case archers were waiting for him. It would not be unusual for a man of Cinna's wealth to have a small army on his estate, much as Marius had.

Crouching low, he knew he was out of sight to the swearing, puffing captain behind him and Gaius looked around desperately for a way out of the predicament. He had to get off the roof. If he stayed, they would simply search each part of it until they found him and either pitch him off onto his head or drag him before Cinna for punishment. With the heat of betrayal on him, Cinna would be deaf to pleas and death would quickly follow for the charge of rape. In fact, Gaius realised Cinna would not even have to bring charges, he would simply summon a lictor and have the man execute Gaius on the spot. If Cinna was of a mind to, he could have Cornelia strangled to save the honour of his house, though Gaius knew the old man doted on his only daughter. If he had genuinely believed she would suffer, he would have stayed to fight it out, but he thought she would be safe enough against old Cinna's rage.

Down below, where the roof overhung the street, Gaius could hear shouting as the house guards formed a ring that blocked all the exits. Behind him, the scrabbling of iron-shod sandals on tiles was getting closer and so he took a deep breath to calm himself and ran, hoping his speed and balance would keep him on the treacherous surface long enough to find safety. The guard captain cried out in recognition as he broke cover, but Gaius didn't have time to look back. The nearest roof was too far away to leap onto and the only flat place on the whole complex was a bell tower with a small window.

He made the sill with a desperate jump as his legs finally lost all grip and he heaved himself up and over it, panting in great gulps of the cold morning air. The bell room was tiny, with steps leading down inside it to the main house below. At first, Gaius was tempted to run down them, but then a plan surfaced in his mind and he steadied his breathing and stretched a few muscles as he waited for the captain to reach the window.

Moments after his decision to stay, the man blocked the sunlight and his face lit up at the sight of the young man cornered in the bell house. They looked at each other for a moment and Gaius watched with interest as the thought of being killed as he climbed in crossed the other man's face. Gaius nodded to him and stood well back to allow him entrance.

The captain grinned nastily at him, panting from the run.

'You should have killed me while you had the chance,' he said, drawing his sword.

'You would have fallen off the roof and I need your clothes – especially those sandals,' Gaius replied calmly, unsheathing his own gladius and standing relaxed, apparently unaware of his nakedness.

'Will you tell me your name before I kill you? Just so I have something to tell my master, you know,' the captain said, moving lightly into a fighter's crouch.

'Will you give me your clothes? This is too fine a morning for killing,' Gaius countered, smiling easily.

The captain began to reply and Gaius attacked, only to have his sword batted aside. The man had been expecting such a move and was ready for it. Gaius realised quickly that he was facing a skilled opponent and focused, aware of every move in the dance. The floor was too small a space for ease and the stairwell loomed between them, threatening to send one of them tumbling.

They feinted and struck around the space, looking for weaknesses. The captain was puzzled at the young man's skill. He had bought the position in Cinna's guard after winning a city sword tournament and knew he was the better of most men, but time and again his attacks were driven aside with speed and precision. He wasn't worried, though. At worst, he could simply hang on until help arrived, and as soon as the searchers realised where they fought more would be sent up the stairs to overwhelm the intruder. Some of this confidence must have shown in his face as Gaius went on the offensive at last, having got the measure of his man.

287

Gaius lunged through the captain's guard and pierced his shoulder. The man took the wound with a grunt, but Gaius knocked his riposte aside and opened a gash in the leather chestplate. The captain found himself with his back to the wall of the little bell tower and then a bruising blow on his fingers sent his gladius down the stairwell, clattering and rebounding in its fall. The hand felt useless and he looked into Gaius' eyes, expecting the cut that would finish him.

Gaius barely slowed. He turned his sword at the last second so that the flat of it slammed against the man's temple and dropped him senseless onto the floor.

More shouts sounded below and he began to strip the captain, fingers working feverishly.

'Come on, come on . . .' he muttered to himself. Always have a plan, Renius had advised him once, but apart from stealing the man's clothes, he hadn't had time to think the rest of his escape through.

After an age, he was dressed. The captain was stirring and Gaius hit him again with the hilt, nodding as the twitching movements ceased. He hoped he hadn't killed him; the man had been doing what he was paid to do and without malice. Gaius took a deep breath. Stairs or window? He paused for only a second, put his own gladius into the captain's scabbard, now strapped to him, and strode down the stairs back into the main house.

Marius clenched his fists at the news from the breathless messenger.

'How many days behind you are they?' he said, as calmly as he could.

'If they force-march, it can't be more than three or four. I came as fast as I could, changing horses, but most of Sulla's men had landed by the time I set off. I waited to be sure it was the main force and not just a feint.'

'You did well. Did you see Sulla himself?'

'I did, though it was at a distance. It seemed to be a full landing of his legion returning to Rome.'

Marius tossed a gold coin to the man, who snatched it out of the air. Marius stood up.

'Then we must be ready to greet him. Gather the other scouts together. I will prepare messages of welcome for you to take to Sulla.'

'General?' the messenger asked, surprised.

'Ask no questions. Is he not the conquering hero returned to us? Meet me here in an hour to receive the letters.'

Without another word, the man bowed and left.

The captain was found by the searchers as he stumbled naked from the bell tower, holding his head. There was no sign of the intruder, despite the exhaustive search that went on all morning. One of the soldiers remembered a man dressed like the captain who had gone off to check down a side street, but he couldn't remember enough detail to give a good description. At midday, the search was called off and by then the news of Sulla's return had hit the streets of Rome. An hour later, one of the house guards noticed a small wrapped package leaning against the house gate and opened it, finding the captain's uniform, scabbard and sandals. The captain swore as he was handed it.

Gaius was summoned into Marius' presence that afternoon and had prepared a defence of his actions. However, the general seemed not to have heard the scandal and only motioned Gaius to sit with his centurions.

'No doubt by now you will have heard that Sulla has landed his forces on the coast and is only three or four days from the city.'

The others nodded and only Gaius had to try to hide the shock he felt.

'It is a year and four months to the day since Sulla left for Greece. I have had enough time to prepare a suitable homecoming.'

Some of the men chuckled in response and Marius smiled grimly.

'This is no light undertaking. You are all men I trust and nothing I say here is to leave this room. Do not discuss this with your wives or mistresses or most trusted friends. I have no doubt that Sulla has had spies in the city watching my every move. He must be aware of our preparations and will arrive fully warned of Rome's readiness for civil war.'

The words, said at last in the open, chilled the hearts of all who heard them.

'I cannot reveal all my plans even now, save to say this. If Sulla reaches the city alive, and he may not, we will treat his legion as an attacking enemy, destroying them on the field. We have supplies of grain, meat and salt to last us for many months. We will seal the city against him and destroy him on the walls. Even as we speak, the flow of traffic has ceased in and out of Rome. The city stands alone.'

'What if he leaves his legion in camp and comes to demand his rightful entry?' asked a man Gaius didn't know. 'Will you risk the wrath of the Senate, declare yourself dictator?'

Marius was silent for a long time, then he raised his head and spoke quietly, almost in a whisper.

'If Sulla comes alone, then I will have him cut down. The Senate will not brand me a traitor to the state. I have their support in everything I do.'

This much was true: there was not a man of influence who would dare to put a motion to the Senate condemning the general. The position was clear.

'Now, gentlemen, your orders for tomorrow.'

Cornelia waited patiently until her father had finished, allowing his rage to wash over her, leaving her untouched.

'No, Father. You will not have him tracked down. He will be my husband and you will welcome him into our house when the time comes.'

Cinna purpled in renewed anger. 'I'll see his body rot first! He comes like a thief into my home and you sit there like a block of marble and tell me I will accept it? I will not, until his body lies broken at my feet.'

Cornelia sighed gently, waiting for the tirade to slow down. Shutting her ears against the shouting, she counted the flowers that she could see from the window. Finally, the tone changed and she brought her attention back to her father, who was looking at her doubtfully.

'I love him, Father, and he loves me. I am sorry we brought shame to the house, but the marriage will wash it all away, despite the gossips in the market. You did tell me I could choose a man I wanted, remember?'

'Are you pregnant?'

'Not as far as I know. There will be no sign when we are married, no public show.'

Her father nodded, looking older and deflated.

Cornelia stood and put her hand on his shoulder. 'You won't regret it.'

Cinna grunted dubiously. 'Do I know him, this despoiler of innocence?'

Cornelia smiled, relieved at his change in mood. 'You do, I'm sure. He is the nephew of Marius. Gaius Julius Caesar.'

Her father shrugged. 'I have heard the name.'

CHAPTER TWENTY-SIX

Cornelius Sulla sipped cooled wine in the shadow of his tent, looking over the legion camp. It was the last night he would have to bear away from his beloved Rome. He shivered slightly in the breeze and perhaps in anticipation of the conflict to come. Did he know every aspect of Marius' plans or would the old fox surprise him? Messages of official welcome lay upon the table, ignored for the formality they were.

Padacus rode up, pulling the horse into a flashy stop with the rear legs buckling on the turn. Sulla smiled at him. So very young, and such a very beautiful man, he noted to himself.

'The camp is secure, General,' Padacus called as he dismounted. Every inch of his armour was polished and glowing, the leather soft and dark with oil. A young Hercules, Sulla thought as he received and answered the salute. Loyal unto death, though, like a pampered hound.

'Tomorrow night, we will enter the city. This is the last night for hard ground and living like barbarians,' Sulla told him, preferring the simple image over the reality of soft beds and fine linen in the general's tent at least. His heart was with the men, but the privations of a legionary's life had never appealed to the consul.

'Will you share your plans, Cornelius? The others are all eager to know how you will handle Marius.'

Padacus had pressed a little too closely in his enthusiasm and Sulla held up a palm.

'Tomorrow, my friend. Tomorrow will be soon enough for preparations. I will retire early tonight, after a little more wine.'

'Will you require . . . company?' Padacus asked softly.

'No. Wait. Send a couple of the better-looking whores to me. I might as well see if I have anything new to learn.'

Padacus dropped his head as if he'd been struck. He backed to his horse and trotted away.

Sulla watched his stiff retreat and sighed, splashing the remaining wine in his goblet onto the black ground. It was the third time the young man had offered and Sulla had to face the fact that he was becoming a problem. The line between adoration and spite was fine in young Padacus. Better to send him away to some other legion before he caused trouble that could not be ignored. He sighed again and walked into the tent, flicking the leather sheet closed over the entrance behind him.

The lamps had been lit by his slaves, the floor was covered in rugs and cloth. Sweet-smelling oil burned in a tiny cup, a rare mixture he enjoyed. Sulla took a deep breath and caught a flicker of movement coming at him from the right. He collapsed backwards out of the line of the attack and felt the air move as something slashed above him. Sulla kicked out with powerful legs and his attacker was knocked from his feet. As the assassin flailed round, Sulla caught his knife hand in a crushing grip. He levered himself up so that his weight was on the man's chest and he smiled as he watched the man's expression change from anger and fear to surprise and despair.

Sulla was not a soft man. True, he didn't favour the more extreme Roman tests of courage, where injuries and scars showed prowess, but he trained every day and fought in every battle. His wrists were like metal and he had no difficulty in turning the blade inward until it was pointing towards the man's throat.

'How much did Marius pay you?' Sulla sneered, his voice showing little strain.

'Nothing. I kill you for pleasure.'

'Amateur by word *and* deed!' Sulla continued, pressing the knife closer to the heaving flesh. 'Guards! Attend your consul!' he barked and, within seconds, the man was pinned down and Sulla could stand and brush dust from himself.

The guard captain had entered with the rush of people. He was pale, but managed to snap out a clean salute as he stood to attention.

'It seems that an assassin has made his way through the camp and into the tent of a consul of Rome without being challenged,' Sulla said quietly, dipping his hands into a bowl of scented water on an oak table and holding them out to be dried by a slave.

The guard captain took a deep breath to calm himself. 'Torture will get us the names of his masters. I will supervise the questioning myself. I will resign my commission in the morning, General, with your permission?'

Sulla continued as if the man had not spoken. 'I do not enjoy being accosted in my own tent. It seems such a common, grubby incident to disturb my repose in this way.'

He stooped and picked up the dagger, ignoring the owner's frantic struggles as the grim soldiers bound him with vicious tightness. He held the slim blade out to the nervous captain.

'You have left me unprotected. Take this. Go to your tent and cut your throat with it. I will have your body collected in . . . two hours?'

The man nodded stiffly, taking the dagger. He saluted again and turned on his heel, marching out of the tent space.

Padacus placed a warm palm on Sulla's arm. 'Are you wounded?'

Sulla pulled his arm away in irritation. 'I am fine. Gods, it was only one man. Marius must have a very low opinion of me.'

'We don't know it was only one man. I will set guards around your tent tonight.'

Sulla shook his head. 'No. Let Marius think he has scared me? I'll keep those two whores you were bringing me and make sure one of them is awake through the night. Bring them in and get rid of everyone else. I believe I have worked up an appetite for a little vicious entertainment.'

Padacus saluted smartly, but Sulla saw the full lips pout as he turned and made a note. The man was definitely a risk. He would not make it back to Rome. An accident of some kind – a fall from his glorious gelding. Perfect.

At last he was alone and Sulla sat on a low bed, smoothing a hand over the soft material. There was a quiet, female cough from outside and Sulla smiled with pleasure.

The two girls that entered at his call were clean, lithe and richly dressed. Both were beautiful.

'Wonderful,' Sulla sighed, patting the bed beside him. For all his faults, Padacus had an eye for truly beautiful women, a rather wasted gift in the circumstances.

Marius frowned at his nephew.

'I do not question your decision to be wed! Cinna will be a useful support in your career. It will suit you politically as well as personally to marry his daughter. However, I *do* question your timing. With Sulla's legion likely to arrive at the gates of the city tomorrow evening, you want me to arrange a marriage in such haste?'

A legionary rushed up to the general, attempting to salute around an armful of scrolls and documents. Marius raised a hand to hold him off.

'You discussed certain plans with me, if things didn't work out tomorrow?' Gaius asked, his voice quiet.

Marius nodded and turned to the guard. 'Wait outside. I'll fetch you when I'm finished here.'

The man attempted another salute and trotted out of the general's barracks room. As soon as he was out of earshot, Gaius spoke again.

'If somehow things go wrong for us . . . and I have to flee the city, I won't leave Cornelia behind unmarried.'

'She can't go with you!' Marius snapped.

'No. But I can't leave her without my name for protection. She may be pregnant.' He hated to admit the extent of their relationship. It was a private thing between them, but only Marius could get the sacrifices and priests ready in the short time left to them and he had to be made to understand.

'I see. Does her father know of . . . your intimacy?'

Gaius nodded.

'Then we are lucky he is not at the door with a horsewhip. Fair enough. I will make ready for the briefest of vow ceremonies. Dawn tomorrow?'

Gaius smiled suddenly, released from a tension he had felt pressing on him.

'That's more like it,' Marius laughed in response. 'Gods, Sulla isn't even in sight yet and a long way from taking Rome back from me. You look too hard for the worst outcomes, I fear. Tomorrow evening your haste may seem ridiculous as we put old Sulla's head on a spike, but no matter. Go. Buy a wedding robe and presents. Have all the bills sent to me.' He patted Gaius on the back.

'Oh, and see Catia on the way out – a lady of mature years who makes uniforms for the men. She will think of a few things and where to get them in so short a time. Go!'

Gaius left, chuckling.

As soon as he had gone, Marius summoned his aide with a shout and spread the scrolls out on the table, holding the edges with smooth lead weights.

'Right, lad,' he said to the soldier. 'Summon the centurions for another meeting. I want to hear any fresh ideas, no matter how bizarre. What have I missed? What does Sulla plan?'

'Perhaps you have already thought of everything, General.'

'No man can think of everything; all we can do is to be ready for anything.' Marius waved the man away on his errand.

Gaius found Cabera throwing dice with two of Marius' legionaries. The old man was engrossed in the game and Gaius controlled his impatience as he made another throw and clapped his ancient hands together in pleasure. Coins were passed over and Gaius took his arm before another round could begin.

'I spoke to Marius. He can arrange the ceremony for dawn tomorrow. I need help today to get everything ready.'

Cabera looked carefully at him as he tucked his winnings into his ragged brown robe. He nodded to the soldiers and one of them shook hands a little ruefully before walking away.

'I look forward to meeting this girl who has had such an impact on you. I suppose she is terribly beautiful?'

'Of course! She is a young goddess. Sweet brown eyes and golden hair. You cannot possibly imagine.'

'No. I was never young. I was born a wrinkled old man, to the surprise of my mother,' Cabera answered seriously, making Gaius laugh. He felt drunk with excitement, with the threatening shadow of Sulla's arrival pushed right to the back of his mind.

'Marius has given me the purse strings, but the shops close so early. We have no time to waste. Come on!' Gaius pulled Cabera by the arm and the old man chuckled, enjoying the enthusiasm.

As evening darkened over the city, Marius left the centurions and walked out to make another inspection of the wall defences. He stretched as he walked and felt and heard his back clicking, sore from bending over the plans for so many hours. A warning voice in his mind reminded him of how foolish it was to walk around in this city after dark, even with the curfew still in place. He dismissed it with a shrug. Rome would never hurt him. She loved her son too dearly, he knew.

As if in response to his thoughts, he felt the freshening warm wind on his face, drying the sweat that had seeped from him in the cramped barracks. When Sulla was disposed of, he would see about building a greater palace for the Rome legion. There was a slum area adjoining the barracks that could be flattened by senatorial order. He saw it in his mind and imagined entertaining foreign leaders in the great halls. Dreams, but pleasant as he walked through the silent streets, with only the clack-clack of his sandals breaking the perfect stillness.

He could see the silhouettes of his men against the star-filled night sky long before he reached them. Some were still and some walked their prescribed, overlapping routes at random. At a glance, he could see they were alert. Good men. Who knew what awaited them the next time night fell? He shrugged again to himself and was glad no one could see him in the dim streets. Sulla would come and he would be met with steel. There was no point in worrying and Marius took a deep cleansing breath, putting it all away inside him. He smiled cheerfully as the first of many sentries stopped him.

'Good lad. Hold that spear steady now, a *pilum* is a fearful weapon in a strong grip. That's it. I thought I would take a tour of this section. Can't stand the waiting, you know. Can you?'

The sentry saluted gravely.

'I don't mind it, sir. You may pass.'

Marius clapped his hand against the sentry's shoulder. 'Good man. They won't get past you.'

'No, sir.'

The legionary watched him go and nodded to himself. The old man was still hungry.

Marius climbed the steps to the new wall his legion had constructed over and around the old gates of Rome. It was a solid and massive construction of heavy interlocking blocks with a wide walkway at the top, where a smaller wall would protect his men from archers. Marius rested his hands on the smooth stone and looked out into the night. If he were Sulla, how would he take the city?

Sulla's legions had huge siege engines, heavy crossbows, stone throwers and catapults. Marius had used each type and feared them all. He knew that, as well as large stones to batter the wall, Sulla could load his machines with smaller shot that would rip through defenders too slow to duck. He would use fire, launching barrels of rock oil over the wall to ignite the inner buildings. Enough barrels and the men on the wall would be lit from behind, easy targets for archers. Marius had cleared some wooden buildings away from the wall, his men dismantling homes quickly and efficiently. Those he could not move had a huge supply of water at the ready, with trained teams to deal with it. It was a new idea for Rome and one he would have to look into when the battle was over. Every summer, fires gutted houses in the city, sometimes spreading to others before being stopped by a wide street or a thick stone wall. A small group ready with water could . . .

He knuckled his eyes. Too much time spent thinking and planning. He hadn't slept for more than a few hours for weeks and the drain was beginning to tell on even his vitality.

The wall would have to be scaled with ladders. It was strong, but Roman legions were practised in taking fortresses and castles. The techniques were almost mundane now. Marius muttered to himself, knowing the nearest sentry was too far away to hear his voice.

'They have never fought Romans, especially Romans in defence of their own city. That is our true advantage. I know Sulla, but he knows me. They have the mobility, but we have the stronghold and the morale. *My* men are not attacking beloved Rome, after all.'

Cheered by his thoughts, Marius walked on over the section of wall. He spoke to each man and, recalling names here and there, asked them about their progress and promotions and loved ones. There wasn't a hint of weakness in any he spoke to. They were like hard-eyed hunting dogs, eager to be killing for him.

By the time he had walked the section and descended back into the dark streets below, Marius felt lifted by the men's simple faith in him. He would see them through. They would see him through. He hummed a military tune to himself as he strolled back to the barracks and his heart was light.

CHAPTER TWENTY-SEVEN

Gaius Julius Caesar smiled, despite the feeling of anxious weakness that fluttered in his stomach. With the help of Marius' seamstress, he had sent servants off to buy and organise for most of the night. He'd known the ceremony would have to be simple and was astonished at so many members of the nobilitas in attendance on a cold morning. The senators had come, bringing families and slaves to the temple of Jupiter. Every glance that met his was followed by a smile, and the soft odours of flowers and burning scentwood was strong in the air. Marius and Metella were there at the entrance of the marble temple and Metella was dabbing tears from her eyes. Gaius nodded to them both nervously as he waited for his bride to arrive. He twitched the sleeves of his marriage robe, cut low around his neck to reveal a single amethyst on a slender gold chain.

He wished Marcus was there. It would have helped to have someone who really knew him. Everyone else was part of the world he was growing into: Tubruk, Cabera, Marius, even Cornelia herself. With a pang, he realised that to make it all seem real, he needed someone there who could meet his eye and know the whole journey to that point. Instead, Marcus was away in foreign lands, the wild adventurer he always wanted to be. By the time he returned, the wedding day would just be a memory that he could never share.

It was cool in the temple and for a moment Gaius shivered,

feeling his skin prickle as the hairs stood up. He was in a room full of people who didn't know him.

If his father had lived, he could have turned to him as they all waited for Cornelia. They could have shared a smile, or a wink that said, 'Look what I've done.'

Gaius felt tears come into his eyes and he looked up at the domed ceiling, willing them not to spill onto his face. His father's funeral had been the end of his mother's moments of peace. Tubruk had shaken his head when Gaius asked if she was able to come. The old gladiator loved her as much as anyone, he knew. Perhaps he always had.

Gaius cleared his throat and dragged his thoughts back to the moment. He had to put childhood behind him. There were many friends in the room, he told himself. Tubruk was like an uncle with his gruff affection and Marius and Metella seemed to have accepted him without reserve. Marcus should have been there. He owed him that.

Gaius hoped Cinna would be pleasant. He had not spoken to the man since formally asking for Cornelia's hand to be passed from father to husband. It had not been a happy meeting, though the senator had kept his dignity for her sake. At least he had been generous with the dowry for Cornelia. Cinna had handed him the deeds to a large town house in a prosperous area of Rome. With slaves and guards as part of the gift, Gaius had felt a worry ease from him. She would be safe now, no matter what happened. He frowned. He would have to get used to the new name, casting off the old with the other trappings of youth. Julius. His father's name. It had a good sound to the ear, though he guessed he would always be Gaius to those he had known as a boy. His father had not lived to see him adopt his adult name and that saddened him. He wondered if the old man could see his only son and hoped so, wishing for just that one more moment to share pride and love.

He turned and smiled weakly at Cabera, who regarded him

302

with a sour expression, his thinning hair still tousled from being roused at what he considered an ungodly hour. He too was dressed in a new brown robe to mark the occasion, adorned with a simple pewter brooch, a design of a fat-faced moon standing proud on the metal. Julius recognised it as Alexandria's work and smiled at Cabera, who scratched an armpit vigorously. Julius kept smiling and after a few seconds, the ancient features cracked in cheerful response, despite his worries.

The future was dark to Cabera as it always was when he was a part of a particular destiny. The old man felt afresh the irritation at only being able to sense the paths that had little bearing on his own life, but even the scratch of his misgivings couldn't prevent him taking pleasure in the youthful joy he felt coming from Julius like a warm wave.

There was something wonderful about a wedding, even one as quickly arranged as this one. Everyone was happy and for at least this little while the problems to come could be forgotten, or at least ignored until dark.

Julius heard footsteps sound on the marble behind him and he turned to see Tubruk leaving his seat to approach the altar. The estate manager looked his usual self, strong, brown and healthy, and Julius clasped his arm, feeling it as an anchor in the world.

'You looked a bit lost up here. How are you feeling?' Tubruk asked.

'Nervous. Proud. Amazed so many turned up.'

Tubruk looked with fresh interest at the crowd and turned back with eyebrows raised.

'Most of the power in Rome is in this room. Your father would be proud of you. I'm proud of you.' He paused for a moment, unsure of whether to continue. 'Your mother did want to come, but she was just too weak.'

Julius nodded and Tubruk punched his arm affectionately before going back to his seat a few rows behind.

'In my village, we just take a girl by the hair and pull her into our hut,' Cabera muttered, shocking the priest out of his beatific expression. Seeing this, the old man went on cheerfully: 'If it didn't work, you'd give her father a goat and grab one of her sisters. Much simpler that way – no hard feelings and free goat milk for the father. I had a herd of thirty goats when I was a lad, but I had to give most of them away, leaving me without enough to support myself. Not a wise decision, but difficult to regret, no?'

The priest had flushed at these casual references to barbarian practices, but Julius only chuckled.

'You old fraud. You just like to shock these upright Roman citizens.'

Cabera sniffed loudly.

'Maybe,' he admitted, remembering the trouble he'd caused when he had tried to offer his last goat upfront for a night of pleasure. It had seemed like sense at the time, but the girl's father had taken a spear from his wall and chased the young Cabera up into the hills where he had to hide for three days and nights.

The priest eyed Cabera with distaste. He was nobilitas himself, but in his religious role wore a cream toga with a hood that left only his face bare. He waited patiently for the bride with the others. Julius had explained that the ceremony must be as simple as possible because his uncle would want to leave at the earliest moment. The priest had scratched his chin in obvious annoyance at this, before Julius slipped a small pouch of coins into his robe as an 'offering' to the temple. Even the nobilitas had bills and debts. It would be a short service. After Cornelia was brought in to be given away by her father, there would be prayers to Jupiter, Mars and Quirinus. An augur had been paid gold to predict wealth and happiness for them both. The vows would follow and Julius would put a simple gold ring on her finger. She would be his wife. He would be her husband. He felt sweat dampen his armpits and tried to shrug away the nervousness.

304

He turned again and looked straight into the eyes of Alexandria as she stood in a simple dress, wearing a brooch of silver. There were tears sparkling in her gaze, but she nodded at him and something eased within.

Soft music began at the back, swelling to fill the vaulted ceiling like the incense smoke that spilled from the censers. Julius looked round and caught his breath and everything else was forgotten.

Cornelia was there, standing tall and straight in a cream dress and thin golden veil, her hand on the arm of her father, who was clearly unable to keep a beaming smile from his face. Her hair had been tinted darker, and her eyes seemed of the same warm colour. At her throat was a ruby the size of a bird's egg, held in gold against the lighter tone of her skin. She looked beautiful and fragile. There was a small wreath on the crest of her head, made from verbena and sweet marjoram flowers. He could smell their scent as Cornelia and her father approached. Cinna let go of her arm as they reached Julius, remaining a pace behind.

'I pass Cornelia into your care, Gaius Julius Caesar,' he said formally.

Julius nodded. 'I accept her into my care.' He turned to her and she winked at him.

As they knelt, he caught again the scent of flowers from her and couldn't stop himself glancing over to her bowed head. He wondered if he would have loved her if he hadn't known Alexandria, or if he had met her before he had gone to the houses where women could be bought for a night or even an hour. He hadn't been ready for this, not back then, a year and a lifetime ago. The prayers were a peaceful murmur over their heads and he was content. Her eyes were soft as summer darkness.

The rest of the ceremony went in a blur for him. The simple vows were spoken – 'Where you go, there go I.' He knelt under the priest's hands for what seemed like eternity and then they were out in the sunshine and the crowd was cheering and shouting,

'*Felicitas!*' and Marius was bidding him goodbye with a great clap on his back.

'You're a man now, Julius. Or she will make you one very soon!' he said loudly, with a twinkle in his eye. 'You have your father's name. He would be proud of you.'

Julius returned the grip strongly. 'Do you want me on the walls now?'

'I think we can spare you for a few hours. Report to me at four this afternoon. Metella will have finished crying about then, I think.'

They grinned at each other like boys and Julius was left in a space for a moment, alone with his bride in a crowd of well-wishers. Alexandria walked up to him and he smiled, suddenly nervous. Her dark hair was bound with wire and the sight of her made his throat feel tight. There was so much history in those dark eyes.

'That's a beautiful brooch you are wearing,' he said.

She reached up and tapped it with her hand.

'You'd be surprised at how many people have asked about it this morning. I already have some orders.'

'Business on my wedding day!' he exclaimed and she nodded without embarrassment.

'May the gods bless your house,' she said formally.

She moved away and he turned to find Cornelia looking at him quizzically. He kissed her.

'She is very beautiful. Who is she?' she said, her voice betraying a touch of worry.

'Alexandria. She is a slave at Marius' house.'

'She doesn't act like a slave,' Cornelia replied, dubiously.

Julius laughed. 'Do I hear jealousy?'

Cornelia did not smile and he took her hands gently in his.

'You are all I want. My beautiful wife. Come to our new home and I'll show you.'

306

Cornelia relaxed as he kissed her, deciding to find out everything she could about the slave girl with the jewellery.

The new house was bare of furniture, or slaves. They were the only ones there and their voices echoed. The bed was a present from Metella, made of carved, dark wood. At least there was a mattress over the slats, and soft linen.

For a few minutes, they seemed clumsy, self-conscious with the weight of the new titles.

'I think you might remove my toga, wife,' Julius said, his voice light.

'I shall, husband. You could unbind my hair, perhaps.'

Then their old passion returned and the clumsiness was forgotten through the afternoon, as the heat built outside.

Julius panted, his hair wet with perspiration. 'I will be tired out tonight,' he said between breaths.

A light frown creased Cornelia's forehead. 'You'll be careful?'

'Not at all, I shall throw myself into conflict. I may start a battle myself, just to impress you.'

Her fingers traced a line down his chest, dimpling the smooth skin. 'You could impress me in other ways,'

He groaned. 'Not right now I can't, but give it a little time.'

Her eyes glinted mischievously as she moved her delicate fingers.

'I might be too impatient to wait. I think I can awake your interest.'

After a few moments, he groaned again, crumpling the sheets under his clenching fists.

At four o'clock, Julius was hammering at the barracks door, only to be told the general was back up on the walls, walking section after section. Julius had exchanged his toga for a legionary's simple uniform of cloth and leather. His gladius was held to his belt and he carried a helmet under one arm. He felt slightly light-headed after the hours spent with Cornelia, but he found he was able to leave that longing in a compartment inside himself. He would return to her as the young lover, but at that moment he was a soldier, nephew of Marius, trained by Renius himself.

He found Marius talking to a group of his officers and stood a few paces away, looking over the preparations. Marius had split his legion into small mobile groups of sixteen men, each with assigned tasks, but more flexible than having each century man the wall. All the scouts reported Sulla making a straight line for the city, with no attempt to feint or confuse. It looked as if Sulla was going to risk a direct attack, but Marius still suspected some other plan to make itself evident as the army hove into view. He finished giving his final orders and gripped hands with each of his officers before they went to their posts. The sun had dropped past the zenith point and there were only a few hours until evening began.

He turned to his nephew and grinned at the serious expression. 'I want you to walk the wall with me, as fresh eyes. Tell me anything you could improve. Watch the men, their expressions, the way they hold themselves. Judge their morale.'

Julius still looked grim and Marius sighed in exasperation.

'And smile, lad. Raise their spirits.' He leaned in closer. 'Many of these men will be dead by morning. They are professionals, but they will still know fear. Some won't be happy about facing our own people in war, though I have tried to have the worst of those moved back from the first assault wall. Say a few words to as many as you can, not long conversations, just notice what they are doing and compliment them on it. Ask them their names and then use the name in your reply to them. Ready?'

Julius nodded, straightening his spine. He knew that the way he presented himself to others affected how they saw him. If he strode in with shoulders and spine straight, men would take him seriously. He remembered his father telling the boys how to lead soldiers.

'Keep your head high and don't apologise unless you absolutely have to. Then do it once, loudly and clearly. Never whine, never plead, never gush. Think before you speak to a man and, when you have to, use few words. Men respect the silent; they despise the garrulous.'

Renius had taught him how to kill a man as quickly and efficiently as possible. He was still learning how to win loyalty.

They walked slowly along a section of wall, stopping and speaking to each soldier and spending a few minutes longer with the leader of the section, listening to ideas and suggestions and complimenting the men on their readiness.

Julius caught glances and held them as he nodded. The soldiers acknowledged him, tension evident. He stopped by one barrel-chested little man adjusting a powerful metal crossbow, set into the stone of the wall itself.

'What's the range?'

The soldier saluted smartly.

'With the wind behind you, three hundred paces, sir.'

'Excellent. Can the machine be aimed?'

'A little, nothing precise at the moment. The workshop is working on a moving pedestal.'

'Good. It looks a deadly thing indeed.'

The soldier smiled proudly and wiped a rag over the winch mechanism that would wind the heavy arms back to their locking slot.

'She, sir. Something as dangerous as this has to be female.'

Julius chuckled as he thought of Cornelia and his aching muscles.

'What is your name, soldier?'

'Trad Lepidus, sir.'

'I will look to see how many of the enemy she takes down, Lepidus.'

The man smiled again.

'Oh, it will be a few, sir. No one is coming into my city without the permission of the general, sir.'

'Good man.'

Julius moved on, feeling a touch more confidence. If all the men were as steadfast as Trad Lepidus, there couldn't be an army in the world that could take Rome. He caught up with his uncle, who was accepting a drink from a silver flask and spluttering over the contents.

'Sweet Mars! What's in this, vinegar?'

The officer fought not to smile.

'I dare say you are used to better vintages, sir. The spirit is a little raw.'

'Raw! Mind you, it is warming,' Marius said, tilting the flask up once more. Finally, he wiped his mouth with the back of his hand. 'Excellent. Send a chit to the quartermaster in the morning. I think a small flask for officers would be just the thing against the chill of winter's nights.'

'Certainly, sir,' the man replied, frowning slightly as he tried to calculate the profits he would make as the sole supplier to his own legion. The answer obviously pleased him and he saluted smartly as Julius passed.

Finally, Marius reached the flight of stone steps down to the street that marked the end of the section. Julius had spoken or nodded or listened to every one of a hundred or so soldiers on that part of the wall. His facial muscles felt stiff and yet he felt a touch of his uncle's pride. These were good men and it was a great thing to know they were ready to lay down their lives at your order. Power was a seductive thing and Julius enjoyed the reflected warmth of it from his uncle. He felt a mounting excitement as he waited with his city for Sulla to arrive and darkness to come.

* * *

Narrow wooden towers had been placed at intervals all round the city. As the sun set, a lookout shouted from one and the word was passed at a fierce speed. The enemy were on the horizon, marching towards the city. The gates were closed against them.

'At last! The waiting was chafing on me,' Marius bellowed, charging out of his barracks as the warning horns were sounded across the city, long wailing notes.

The reserves took their positions. Those few Romans still on the streets ran for their homes, bolting and barricading their doors against the invaders. The people cared little for who ruled the city as long as their families were safe.

The Senate meetings had been postponed that day and the senators too were in their palatial houses, dotted around the city. Not one of them had taken the roads to the west, though a few had sent their families away to country estates rather than leave them at risk. A few rose with tight smiles, standing at balconies and watching the horizon as the horns moaned across the darkening city. Others lay in baths or beds and had slaves ease muscles that tightened from fear. Rome had never been attacked in its history. They had always been too strong. Even Hannibal had preferred to meet Roman legions on the field rather than to assault the city itself. It had taken a man like Scipio to take his head and that of his brother. Would Marius have the same ability, or would it be Sulla that held Rome in his bloody hand at the end? One or two of the senators burned incense at their private altars for their household gods. They had supported Marius as he tightened his grip on Rome, forced to take his side in public. Many had staked their lives on his success. Sulla had never been a forgiving man.

CHAPTER TWENTY-EIGHT

Torches were lit all around the city as night fell. Julius wondered what it would look like to the gods as they looked down, a great gleaming eye in the black vastness of the land? We look up as they look down, he thought.

He stood with Cabera on ground level, listening to the news as it was shouted down from the wall lookouts and relayed along and deep into the city, a vein of information for those who could see and hear nothing. Over it, despite the nearby noises, he could make out the distant tramp of thousands of armoured men and horses on the move. It filled the soft night and grew louder as they approached.

There was no doubt now. Sulla was bringing his legion right up the Via Sacra to the gates of the city, with no attempt at subterfuge. The lookouts reported a torchlit snake of men stretching for miles back in the darkness, with the tail disappearing over hills. It was a marching formation for friendly lands, not a careful approach to close with an enemy. The confidence of such a casual march made many raise eyebrows and wonder what on earth Sulla was planning. One thing was for certain: Marius was not the man to be cowed by confidence.

Sulla clenched his fists in excitement as the gates and walls of the fortress city began to glow with the reflected light of his legion.

Thousands of fighting men and half as many again in support marched on through the night. The noise was rhythmic and deafening, the crash of feet on the stone road echoing back and around the city and the night. Sulla's eyes sparkled in the flames of torches and he casually raised his right hand. The signal was relayed, great horns wailing into the darkness, setting off responses all the way down the great snake of soldiers.

Stopping a moving legion required skill and training. Each section had to halt to order, or a pile-up would result, with the precision lost in chaos. Sulla turned and looked back down the hill, nodding with satisfaction as each century became still, their torches held in unwavering hands. It took almost half an hour from the first signal to the end, but at last, they all stood on the Via Sacra and the natural silence of the countryside seemed to flow back over them. His legion waited for orders, gleaming gold.

Sulla swept his gaze over the fortifications, imagining the mixed feelings of the men and citizens inside. They would be wondering at his halt, whispering nervously to each other, passing the news back to those who could not see the great procession. The citizens would hear his echoing horns and be expecting attack at any moment.

He smiled. Marius too would be chafing, waiting for the next move. He had to wait, that was the key weakness of the fortified position – they could only defend and play a passive role.

Sulla bided his time, signalling for cool wine to be brought to him. As he did so, he noticed the rather rigid posture of a torch carrier. Why was the man so tense, he wondered. He leaned forward in his saddle and noticed the thin trickle of boiling hot oil that had escaped the torch and was creeping towards the slave's bare hand. Sulla watched the man's eyes as they flicked forward and back to the burning liquid. Was there a touch of flame in the trickle? Yes, the heat would be terrible; it would stick as it burned the man. Sulla observed with interest, noting the sweat on the

313

man's forehead and having a private bet with himself as to what would happen when the heat touched the skin.

He was a believer in omens and at such a moment, before the gates of Rome herself, he knew the gods would be watching. Was this a message from them, a signal for Sulla to interpret? Certainly he was beloved of the gods, as his exalted position showed. His plans were made, but disaster was always possible with a man like Marius. The flickering flames on the oil touched the slave's skin. Sulla raised an eyebrow, his mouth quirking with surprise. Despite the obvious agony of it, the man stood still as rock, letting the oil run on past his knuckles and continue its course into the dust of the road. Sulla could see the flames light his hand with a gentle yellow glow yet still the fellow did not move!

'Slave!' he called.

The man turned to face his master.

Pleased, Sulla smiled at his steadiness.

'You are relieved. Bathe that hand. Your courage is a good omen for tonight.'

The man nodded gratefully, extinguishing the tiny flames with the grasp of his other palm. He scuttled off, red-faced and panting at the release. Sulla accepted a cool goblet graciously and toasted the walls of the city, his eyes hooded as he tipped it back and tasted the wine. Nothing to do now but wait.

Marius gripped the lip of the heavy wall with irritation.

'What is he doing?' he muttered to himself. He could see the legion of Sulla stretching away into the distance, halted not more than a few hundred paces from the gate that opened onto the Via Sacra. Around him his men waited, as tense as himself.

'They are just outside missile range, General,' a centurion observed.

Marius had to control a flare of temper. 'I know. If they cross

314

inside it, begin firing at once. Hit them with everything. They'll never take the city in that formation.'

It made no sense! Only a broad front stood a chance against a well-prepared enemy. The single-point spearhead march stood no chance of breaching the defences. He clenched his fist in anger. What had he missed?

'Sound the horns the moment anything changes,' he ordered the section leader and strode back through the ranks to the steps leading to the city street below.

Julius, Cabera and Tubruk waited patiently for Marius to come over, watching him as he checked in with his advisers, who had nothing new to offer, judging by the shaking of heads. Tubruk loosened his gladius in his scabbard, feeling the light nerves that always came before bloodshed. It was in the air and he was glad he had stayed on through the hot day. Gaius, no, Julius now, had almost sent him home to the estate, but something in the ex-gladiator's eyes had prevented the order.

Julius wished the band of friends could have been complete. He would have appreciated Renius' advice and Marcus' odd sense of humour. As well as that, if it did come to a fight, there were few better to have at your side. He too loosened his sword, rattling the blade against the metal lip of the scabbard a few times to clear it of any obstructions. It was the fifth time he had done so in as many minutes and Cabera clapped a hand to his shoulder, making him start a little.

'Soldiers always complain about the waiting. I prefer it to the killing, myself.' In truth, he felt the swirling paths of the future pressing heavily on him and was caught between the desire to get Julius away to safety or to climb up onto the wall to meet the first assault. Anything to make the paths resolve into simple events!

Julius scanned the walls, noting the number and positions of men, the smooth guard changes, the test runs of the ballistae and army-killer weapons. The streets were silent as Rome held its breath, but still nothing moved or changed. Marius was stamping around, roaring orders that would have been better left to the trusted men in the chain of command. It seemed the tension was affecting even him.

The endless chains of runners were finally still. There was no more water to be carried and the stockpiles of arrows and shot were all in position. Only the breathless footsteps of a messenger from another part of the wall broke the tension every few minutes. Julius could see the worry on Marius' face, made almost worse by the news of no other attack. Could Sulla really be willing to risk his neck in a legal entry to the city? His courage would win admirers if he walked up to the gates himself, but Julius was sure he would be dead, killed by an 'accidental' arrow as he approached. Marius would not leave such a dangerous snake alive if he came within bow shot.

His thoughts were interrupted as a robed messenger jostled by him. In that moment, the scene changed. Julius watched in dawning horror as the men on the closest section of the wall were suddenly overwhelmed from behind, by their own companions. So intent were they on the legion waiting outside that scores fell in a few seconds. Water carriers dropped the buckets they held and sank daggers into the soldiers nearest them, killing men before they even realised they were under attack.

'Gods!' he whispered. 'They're already inside!'

Even as he bared his gladius and felt rather than saw Tubruk do the same, he saw a flaming arrow lit calmly from a brazier and sent soaring into the night. As it arced upwards, the silence of murder was broken. From outside the walls, Sulla's legion roared as if hell had broken open and came on.

In the darkness of the street below, Marius had had his back to the wall when he noticed the stricken expression of a centurion. He spun in time to see the man clawing at the air, impaled on a long dagger that had been thrust into his back.

'What is it? Blood of the gods . . .' He pulled in a great gasp of air to rally the nearest sections and, as he did, saw a flaming arrow sweep out into the ink blackness of the starless night.

'To me! First-Born to the gate! Hold the gate! Sound full warning! They come!'

His voice cracked out, but the horn blowers were lying in pools of their own blood. One still struggled with his assailants, hanging on to the slim bronze tube despite the vicious stabbing his body was taking. Marius drew the sword that had been in his family for generations. His face was black with rage. The two men died and Marius raised the horn to his own lips, tasting the blood that had spattered onto the metal.

All around him in the darkness, other horns answered. Sulla had won the first few moments, but he vowed it wasn't over yet.

Julius saw the group dressed as messengers were all armed and converging on where Marius stood with a bloody horn and his bright sword already dark with blood. The wall loomed behind him, flickering with torch shadows.

'With me! They're going for the general in the confusion,' he barked to Tubruk and Cabera, charging the back of the group as he shouted.

His first blow took one of the running men in the neck as they slowed to negotiate struggling groups of fighters. Finally, Marius' men seemed to have woken up to the fact that the enemy were disguised, but the fighting was difficult and, in the flashing colours and blows of combat, no man knew which of the groups were friends and which were enemies. It was a devastating ploy and inside the walls everything was chaos.

Julius ripped his blade across a leg muscle, crashing his running feet over the body as it collapsed and feeling satisfaction as he felt the bones shift and break under his sandals. At first he was

317

surprised at the group not standing to fight, but he quickly realised they had orders to assassinate Marius and were careless of any other dangers.

Tubruk brought down another with a leap that had them both sprawling on the hard cobbles. Cabera took one more with a dagger throw that caught Sulla's man in the side and sent him staggering. Julius let his blade scythe out as he clattered past and felt a satisfying shock up his arm as it connected and slid free.

Ahead, Marius stood alone and other, black-clad figures converged on him. He roared defiance as he saw them coming and suddenly Julius knew he was too late. More than fifty men were charging at the general. All his soldiers in the area were dead or dying. One or two still screamed their frustration, but they too could not reach his uncle.

Marius spat blood and phlegm and raised his sword menacingly.

'Come on, boys. Don't keep me waiting,' he growled through clenched teeth, anger keeping despair at bay.

Julius felt a hard fist jerk at his collar and drag him to a stop. He roared in anger and felt his sword arm batted away as he spun to face the threat. He found himself looking into Tubruk's stern face.

'No, boy. It's too late. Get out while you can.'

Julius struggled in the grip, swearing with incoherent rage.

'Let go! Marius is . . .'

'I know. We can't save him.' Tubruk's face was cold and white. 'His men are too far away. We've been overlooked for a moment, but there's too many of them. Live to avenge him, Gaius. Live.'

Julius swivelled in the grip and fifty feet away saw Marius go down under a heaving mass of bodies, some of which were loose and boneless, already dead from his blows. The others held clubs, he saw, and they were striking wildly at the general, beating him to the ground in mindless ferocity.

'I can't run,' Julius said.

Tubruk swore. 'No. But you can retreat. This battle is lost. The city is lost. Look, Sulla's traitors are on the gates themselves. The legion will be on us if we don't move now. Come on.' Without waiting for further argument, Tubruk grabbed the young man under the armpits and began pulling him away, with Cabera taking the other arm.

'We'll get the horses and cross the city to one of the other gates. Then on to the coast and a legion galley. You must get clear. Few who have supported Marius will be alive in the morning,' Tubruk continued grimly.

The young man went almost limp in his grasp and then stiffened in fear as the night came alive with more black shapes surrounding them. Swords were pressed up to their throats and Julius tensed for the pain to come as an order broke the night.

'Not these. I know them. Sulla said to keep them alive. Get the ropes.'

They struggled, but there was nothing they could do.

Marius felt his sword pulled from his grasp and heard the clatter as it was thrown on the stones almost distantly. He felt the thudding blows of clubs not as pain, but simply impacts, knocking his head from side to side in the crush of bodies. He felt a rib snap with an icicle of pain and then his arm twisted and his shoulder dislocated with a rip. He pulled up to consciousness and sank again as someone stamped on his fingers, breaking them. Where were his men? Surely they would be coming to save his life. This was not how it was meant to be, how he had seen his end. This was not the man who entered Rome at the head of a great Triumph and wore purple and threw silver coins to the people that loved him. This was a broken thing that wheezed blood and life out onto the sharp stones and wondered if his men would ever come for him, who loved them all as a father loves his children.

He felt his head pulled back and expected a blade to follow across his exposed throat. It didn't come and, after long seconds of agony, his eyes focused on the forbidding black mass of the Sacra gate. Figures swarmed over it and bodies draped it in obscene costume. He saw the huge bar lifted by teams of men and then the crack of torchlight that shone through it. The great gate swung open and Sulla's legion stood beyond, the man himself at the head, wearing a gold circlet to bind back his hair and a pure white toga and golden sandals. Marius blinked blood out of his eyes and in the distance heard a renewed crash of arms as the First-Born poured in from all over the city to save their general.

They were too late. The enemy was already within and he had lost. They would burn Rome, he knew. Nothing could stop that now. His holding troops would be overwhelmed and there would be bloody slaughter, with the city raped and destroyed. Tomorrow, if Sulla still lived, he would inherit a mantle of ashes.

The grip in Marius' hair tightened to bring his head higher, a distant pain amongst all the others. Marius felt a cold anger for the man who strode so mightily towards him, yet it was mixed with a touch of respect for a worthy enemy. Was not a man judged by his enemies? Then truly Marius was great. His thoughts wandered away and back, fogged by the heavy blows. He lost consciousness, he thought only for a few seconds, coming to as a brutal-faced soldier slapped his cheeks, grimacing at the blood that came off onto his hands. The man began to wipe them on his filthy robe, but a strong clear voice sounded.

'Be careful, soldier. Your hands have the blood of Marius on them. A little respect is due, I believe.'

The man gaped at the conqueror, clearly unable to comprehend. He took a few paces away into the growing crowd of soldiers, holding his hands stiffly away from his body.

'So few understand, do they, Marius? Just what it is to be born to greatness?' Sulla moved so that Marius could look him in the face.

His eyes sparkled with a glittering satisfaction that Marius had hoped never to see. Looking away, he hawked up blood from his throat and allowed it to dribble onto his chin. There was no energy to spit, and he had no desire to exchange dry wit in the moments before his death. He wondered if Sulla would spare Metella and knew he probably wouldn't. Julius – he hoped he had escaped, but he too was probably one of the cooling corpses that surrounded them all.

The sounds of battle swelled in the background and Marius heard his name being chanted as his men fought through to him. He tried not to feel hope; it was too painful. Death was coming in seconds. His men would see only his corpse.

Sulla tapped his teeth with a fingernail, his face thoughtful.

'You know, with any other general I would simply execute him and then negotiate with the legion to cease hostilities. I am, after all, a consul and well within my rights. It should be a simple enough matter to allow the opposing forces to withdraw outside the city and lead my men into the city barracks in their place. I do believe, though, that your men will carry on until the last man stands, costing hundreds more of my own in the process. Are you not the people's general, beloved of the First-Born?' He tapped his teeth again and Marius strove to concentrate and ignore the pain and weariness that threatened to drag him back down to darkness.

'With you, Marius, I must make a special solution. This is my offer. Can he hear me?' he asked one of the men Marius could not see. More slaps woke him from his stupor.

'Still with us? Tell your men to accept my legal authority as consul of Rome. The Primigenia must surrender and my legion be allowed to deploy into the city without incident or attack. They are in anyway, you know. If you can deliver this, I will allow you to leave Rome with your wife, protected by my honour. If you refuse, not one of your men will be left alive. I will destroy them from street to street, from house to house, along with all who have ever shown you favour or support, their wives, children and slaves. In short, I will wipe your name from the annals of the city, so that no man will live who would have called you friend. Do you understand, Marius? Pull him to his feet and support him. Fetch the man water to ease his throat.'

Marius heard the words and tried to hold them in his swirling, leaden thoughts. He didn't trust Sulla's honour further than he could spit, but his legion would be saved. They would be sent far from Rome, of course, given some degrading task of guarding tin mines in the far north against the painted savages, but they would be alive. He had gambled and lost. Grim despair filled him, blunting the sharpness of the pain as broken bones shifted in the rough grip of Sulla's men, men who would not have dared lay a finger on him only a year before. His arm hung slack, feeling numb and detached from him, but that didn't matter any more. A last thought stopped him from speaking at once. Should he delay in the hope that his men could win through and turn the situation to his advantage? He turned his head and saw the mass of Sulla's men fanning out to secure the local streets and realised the chance for a quick retaliation had gone. From now on, it would be the messiest, most vicious kind of fighting, and most of his legion was still on the walls around the city, unable to engage. No.

'I agree. My word on it. Let the nearest of my men see me, so that I may pass the order on to them.'

Sulla nodded, his face twisted with suspicion. 'Thousands will die if you tell untruth. Your wife will be tortured to death. Let there be an end to this. Bring him forward.'

Marius groaned with pain as he was dragged away from the shadow of the wall, to where the clash of arms was intense.

Sulla nodded to his aides. 'Sound the disengage,' he snapped, his voice betraying the first touch of nerves since Marius had seen him. The horns sounded the pattern and at once the first and second rows took two paces back from the enemy, holding position with bloody swords.

Marius' legion had left the walls on the southeast side of the city, swarming through the streets. They massed down every alley and road, eyes bright with rage and bloodlust. Behind them, every second, more gathered as the city walls were stripped of defenders. As Marius was propped up to speak, a great howl went up from the men, an animal noise of vengeance. Sulla stood his ground, but the muscles tightened around his eyes in response. Marius took a deep breath to speak and felt the press of a dagger by his spine.

'First-Born.' Marius' voice was a croak, and he tried again, finding strength. 'First-Born. There is no dishonour. We were not betrayed but attacked by Sulla's own men left behind. Now, if you love me, if you have ever loved me, *kill them all and burn Rome!*'

He ignored the agony of the dagger as it tore into him, standing strong before his men for one long moment as they roared in fierce joy. Then his body collapsed.

'Fires of hell!' Sulla roared as the First-Born surged forward. 'Form fours. Mêlée formation and engage. Sixth company to me. Attack!' He drew his sword as the closest company clustered round to protect him. Already, he could smell blood and smoke on the air and dawn was still hours away.

CHAPTER TWENTY-NINE

Marcus looked over the parapet, straining his eyes at the distant campfires of the enemy. It was a beautiful land, but there was nothing soft in it. The winters killed the old and weak and even the scrub bushes had a wilted, defeated look as they clung to the steep crags of the mountain passes. After more than a year as a hill scout, his skin was a dark brown and his body was corded with wiry muscle. He had begun to develop what the older soldiers called the 'itch', the ability to smell out an ambush, to spot a tracker and move unseen over rocks in the dark. All the experienced trackers had the itch and those who hadn't acquired it after a year never would – and would never be first-rate, they claimed.

Marcus had first been promoted to command eight men after he successfully spotted an ambush by blueskin tribesmen, directing his scouts around and behind the waiting enemy. His men had cut them to pieces and only afterwards did anyone remark that they had followed his lead without argument. It had been the first time he had seen the wild nomads up close and the sight of their blue-dyed faces still slid into his dreams after bad food or cheap wine.

The policy of the legion was to control and pacify the area, which in practice meant a blanket permission to kill as many of the savages as they could. Atrocities were common. Roman guards were lost and found staked out, their entrails exposed to the brutal sun. Mercy and kindness were quickly burned away in the heat, dust and flies.

Most of the actions were minor – there could be none of the set-piece battles so beloved of the Roman legionaries on such broken and hostile terrain. The patrols went out and came back with a couple of heads or a few men short. It seemed to be a stalemate, with neither side having the strength for extermination.

After twelve months of this, the raids on the supply caravans suddenly became more frequent and more brutal. Along with a number of other units, Marcus' men had been added to the supply guards, to make sure the water barrels and salted provisions reached their most isolated outposts.

It had always been clear that these buildings were barbs under the skin of the tribespeople and attacks on the small stone forts in the hills were common. The legion rotated the men stationed there at regular intervals and many came back to the permanent camp with grisly stories of heads thrown over the parapets, or words of blood found on the walls when the sun rose.

At first the duties of caravan guard had not been onerous for Marcus. Five of his eight men were experienced, cool hands and completed their duties without fuss or complaint. Of the other three, Japek complained constantly, seeming not to care that he was disliked by the others, Rupis was close to retirement and had been broken back to the ranks after some failure of command and the third was Peppis. Each presented different problems and Renius had only shaken his head when asked for advice.

'They're your men, you sort it out,' had been his only word on the subject.

Marcus had made Rupis his second, in charge of four of the men, in the hope that this would restore a little of his pride. Instead, he seemed to take some obscure insult from this and practically sneered whenever Marcus gave him an order. After a little thought, Marcus had ordered Japek to write down every one of his complaints as they occurred to him, forming a catalogue that he would allow Japek to present to their centurion back at the permanent camp. The man was famous for not suffering fools and Marcus was glad to note that not a single complaint had gone down on the parchment he had provided from the legion stores. A small triumph, perhaps, but Marcus was struggling to learn the skills of dealing with people or, as Renius put it, making them do what you want without being so annoyed they do it badly. When he thought about it, it made Marcus smile that the only teacher he'd ever had for diplomacy was Renius.

Peppis was the kind of problem that couldn't be resolved with a few words or a blow. He had made a promising start at the permanent barracks, growing quickly in size and bulk with good food and exercise. Unfortunately, he had a tendency to steal from the stores, often bringing the items to Marcus, which had caused him a great deal of embarrassment. Even being forced to return everything he took and a brief but solid lashing had failed to cure Peppis of the habit and eventually the Bronze Fist centurion, Leonides, had sent the boy to Marcus with a note that read: '*Your responsibility. Your back.*'

The guard duty had started well, with the kind of efficiency Marcus had begun to take for granted but which he guessed was not the standard all over the empire. They had set off one hour before dawn, trailing along the paths into the dark granite hills. Four flat ox carts had been loaded with tightly lashed barrels and thirty-two soldiers detailed for guard duty. They were under the command of an old scout named Peritas, who had twenty years of experience under his belt and was no one's fool. Altogether, they were a formidable force to be trundling through the winding hill paths and although Marcus had felt hidden eyes on them almost from the beginning, that was a feeling you quickly became used to. His unit had been given the task of scouting ahead and Marcus was leading two of his men up a steep bank of loose stone and dried moss when they came face to face with about fifty painted, blue-skinned figures, fully armed for war.

For a few seconds, both groups merely gaped at each other and then Marcus had turned and scrambled back down the slope, his two companions only slightly slower. Behind them a great yell went up, making unnecessary the need to call any warning to the caravan. The blueskins poured over the lip of the hidden ledge and fell on the caravan guards with their long swords held high and wild screams rending the mountain air.

The legionaries had not paused to gape. As the blueskins charged, arrows were fitted to bowstrings and a humming wave of death passed over the heads of Marcus and his men, giving them time to reach the path and turn to face the enemy. Marcus remembered having drawn his gladius and killing a warrior who had screamed at him right up to the moment when Marcus chopped his blade into the creature's throat.

For a moment, the legionaries were overwhelmed. Their strength was in units, but on the ragged path it was every man for himself and little chance to link shields with anyone else. Nonetheless, Marcus saw that each of the Romans was standing and cutting, their faces grim and unyielding before the blue horror of the tribe. More men fell on both sides and Marcus found himself with his back to a cart, ducking under a sword cut to bury his shorter blade in a heaving blue stomach and ripping it out to the side. The intestines seemed bright yellow against the blue dye, some part of him noted as he defended against two more. He took one hand off at the wrist and sliced another warrior in the groin as he tried to leap onto the cart. The snarling tribesman fell back into the choking dust and Marcus stamped down on him blindly while slicing the bicep of the next. It seemed to last a long time and, when they finally broke and raced away up the banks into cover, Marcus was surprised to see the sun where it had been when they attacked. Only a few minutes had passed at most. He looked round for his unit and was relieved to see faces he knew well, panting and splashed with blood, but alive.

Many had not been so lucky. Rupis would never sneer again.

He lay with his legs sprawled against one of the carts, a wide red smile opened in his throat. Twelve others had been butchered in the attack and around them lay almost thirty of the still blue bodies, dribbling blood onto their land. It was a grim sight and the flies were already arriving in droves for the feast.

As Marcus had called for Peppis to bring him a flask of water, Peritas had begun setting the guards again and called the commanders to him for a quick report. Marcus had taken the flask from Peppis and trotted to the head of the column.

Peritas looked as if the heat and dust had baked all moisture out of him over the years, leaving only a sort of hard wood and eyes that peered out at the world with amused indifference. Of the whole group, he was the only one who was mounted. He nodded as Marcus saluted.

'We could turn back, but my guess is we've seen the worst they have to offer at the moment. I think if we took the bodies back, that would be a little victory for the savages, so we go on. Strap the dead to the carts and change the guards over. I want the freshest men on lookout, just in case of more trouble. Well done those men who surprised the enemy and made them show themselves early. Probably saved a few Roman lives. It's only thirty miles to the hill fort, so we had better press on. Questions?'

Marcus looked at the horizon. There was nothing to ask. Men died and were cremated and sent back to Rome. That was army life. Those who survived received promotions. He hadn't realised there was as much luck involved as there seemed to be, but Renius had nodded when asked and pointed out that, although the gods may well have heroic favourites, an arrow doesn't care who it kills.

The real trouble started when the depleted company reached the last few miles of the journey. They had begun to see blueskins watching them from the undergrowth, a flash of colour here

328

and there. They hadn't the numbers to send a unit to attack and the blueskins had never used missile weapons, so the legionaries just ignored the tribesmen and kept a good grip on their swords.

The closer they came to the fort, the more of the enemy they could see. At least twenty of them were keeping pace on a higher level than the path, using the trees and undergrowth for cover, but occasionally coming out into the open to hoot and jeer at the grim soldiers of Rome. Peritas frowned as his horse trotted on and kept his hand on his sword hilt.

Marcus kept expecting a spear to be thrown. He imagined one of the blue warriors sighting on him and could practically feel the spot between his shoulder blades where the point would land. They certainly carried spears, but seemed to avoid throwing them, or at least had in the past. It didn't stop the spot itching, though. He began willing the fort to be close and at the same time dreading what they might find. More than one tribe must be gathered; certainly none of the men had ever seen so many blueskins in one place before. If any of them lived to report back to the rest of the legion, someone would have to warn them that the tribes had grown in confidence and numbers.

At last they rounded a turn in the track and saw the last segment of the journey, half a mile of steeply rising path up to a small fortress on a grey hill. Roaming the flat lands around the outcropping were more of the blue men. Some were even camped in sight of the fortress and watched the caravan with slitted eyes. Footfalls on rock could be heard behind them, and rocks dislodged by scrambling bare feet spattered and bounced against the ground. With every man on edge, they had begun the slow climb to the fort, the ox-drivers waving and cracking their whips nervously.

Marcus could see no lookouts and began to feel a sense of dull fear. They wouldn't make it – and what would they find when they did?

The slow march continued until they were close enough to see the details of the fort. Still there was no one on the ramparts and Marcus knew with a sinking heart that no one could be alive inside. He had his sword drawn and was swinging it nervously as he walked.

Suddenly a great howl went up from every blueskin around. Marcus had risked a glance back down the path and saw what must have been a hundred of the warriors charging at them.

Peritas rode down the line of legionaries.

'Abandon the wagons! Make for the fort. Go!' he shouted and suddenly they were running. The howls increased in savage joy behind them as the drivers leapt off and sprinted the last hundred feet. Marcus held his sword away from his body and ran, not daring to look back again. He could hear the slap of hard bare feet and the high screaming of a blueskin attack too close for comfort. He saw the gate come up and was through it with a knot of shoving, heaving soldiers, turning immediately to yell encouragement to the slower men.

Most made it. Only two men, either too tired or too scared to make the sprint, were run down, turning in the last moment like trapped animals and spitted with many blades. Wet red metal was raised in defiance as the survivors shut and barred the gate and Peritas was off his horse and shouting to search and secure the fort. Who could understand the sick reasoning of the savages? Perhaps they had more men waiting inside, just for the pleasure of picking them off when they thought they had reached safety.

The fort was empty, however, except for the bodies. A Fifty manned each fort, with twenty horses. Man and beast lay where they had been killed and then mutilated. Even the horses had their stinking guts spread over the stone floor and clouds of blue-black flies buzzed into the air as they were disturbed. Two men vomited as the smell hit them and Marcus' heart sank even more. They were trapped, with only disease and death in the future. Outside, the blueskins chanted and whooped.

CHAPTER THIRTY

Before night fell, Peritas had the bodies of the legionaries locked in an empty basement store. The dead horses proved a more difficult problem. All weapons had been stripped from the fort and there wasn't an axe to be found anywhere. The slippery carcasses could be lifted by five or six of the men working at once, but not carried up the stone steps to be put over the ramparts. In the end, Peritas had stacked the heavy, limp bodies against the gate to slow down attackers. It was the best they could hope for. No one expected to make it through the night and fear and resignation hung heavily on all of them. Up on the walls, Marcus watched the campfires with narrowed eyes.

'What I don't understand,' he muttered to Peppis, 'is why we were allowed back into the fort. They have taken it once and they must have lost some lives, so why not cut us down on the trail?'

Peppis shrugged. 'They're savages, sir. Perhaps they enjoy a challenge, or humiliating us.' He carried on with his task of sharpening blades on a worn concave whetstone. 'Peritas says we will be missed when we don't get back by morning and they'll send out a strike force by tomorrow evening, perhaps even earlier. We don't have to hold out for long, but I don't think the blueskins will give us that kind of time.' He continued wiping the stone along a silver blade.

'I think we could hold this place for a day or so. They have the

331

numbers, granted, but that's all they have. Mind you, they did take it once.'

Marcus paused as a chant began in the near darkness. If he strained his eyes, he could see dancing figures silhouetted against the flames of the fires.

'Someone is having a good time tonight,' he muttered. His mouth watered. The fort well had been poisoned with rotting flesh and everything else edible had been removed. Truth to tell, if the reinforcements didn't get to them in a day or two, thirst would do the blueskins' job for them. Perhaps they intended the Romans to die with dry throats in the burning sun. That would match the cruel tales he had heard about them, given a fresh airing amongst the nervous soldiers as night fell on the fort.

Peppis peered over the wall into the gloom and snorted.

'There's one of them peeing against the wall down there,' he said, his voice caught between outrage and amusement.

'Watch yourself, don't lean out or put your head up too high,' Marcus replied as he pressed his own head closer to the rough stone, trying to peer over the edge whilst exposing as little of himself as possible.

Astonishingly close and directly below them was a swaying blueskin holding his parts and spraying the fort with dark urine in short sweeping arcs. The grinning figure caught sight of the movement above and jumped, recovering quickly. He waved a hand at the pair who watched him and waggled his privates in their direction.

'He's had a little too much to drink, I'd say,' Marcus murmured, grinning despite himself. He watched the man pull a bloated wineskin around his body and suck on the mouth of it, spilling more than he took in. Blearily, the blueskin shoved in the stopper on his third attempt and gestured up again, calling out something in his slushy tongue.

Tiring of their lack of response, he took two steps and fell flat on his face.

Marcus and Peppis watched him. He was still.

'Not dead, I can see his chest moving. Dead drunk maybe,' Peppis whispered. 'It's bound to be a trap. Devious, the blueskins are, everyone says.'

'Maybe, but I can only see one of them and I can take one. We could do with that wine. I know I could, anyway,' Marcus replied. 'I'm going down there. Fetch me a rope. I can drop over the wall and climb back up before there's any real danger.'

Peppis scurried off on his errand and Marcus focused on the prone figure and the surrounding ground. He weighed the risks and then smiled sardonically. They were all going to die in the night or at dawn, so what did the risks matter? The problem receded and he felt his tension relax. There was something about almost certain death that was quite calming in its way. At least he would have a drink. That wine sack had looked full enough to give nearly all of them a cupful.

Peppis tied up his end of the rope and sent the rest uncoiling silently down the twenty-foot drop. Marcus made sure his gladius was secure and ruffled the hair of the lad.

'See you soon,' he whispered, putting one leg over the parapet and disappearing into the gloom below. The dark was so complete that Peppis could barely make him out as he crept towards the still figure, the gladius drawn and ready in his hand.

Marcus felt the itch again and clenched his jaw. Something was wrong with the scene and it was too late to avoid the trap. He reached out a foot to stir the drunken blueskin and wasn't surprised when the man suddenly sprang up. Marcus took his throat out before the expression of triumph could fully form. Then two more blue men rose out of the dirt. It was their presence he'd sensed, hidden in shallow graves and lying perfectly still for hours with almost inhuman discipline. They had probably dug themselves in to wait before the Roman caravan even appeared, Marcus realised as he attacked. They were not wild savages, but warriors.

There seemed to be just the three of them, young men out for status or a first kill. They had risen with swords in their hands and his first backhand blow was blocked with a loud ring of metal that made Marcus wince. There would be more of them coming. He had to get clear before the whole blueskin army arrived.

Marcus' blade slid along the dust-covered warrior's and clashed against a crude bronze guard. The man leered and Marcus punched him in the stomach with his other fist, ripping the blade back and through him as he doubled over in pained surprise. He collapsed as his neck veins parted and hit the ground wretchedly.

The third was not as skilled as his companion, but Marcus could hear shouts and knew time was running out. His haste made him careless and he ducked late on a wild slash that nicked his ear and scored a line in his scalp.

He slid to his left and punched the blade into the man's heart through the blue-stained ribs from the side. As the warrior fell with a gurgling cry, Marcus could hear the slap of running feet he remembered so vividly from the afternoon scramble into the fort. It was too late to run for the rope, so he turned and detached the wineskin from the first body, pulling out the stopper and taking a deep draught as the night around him filled with swords and blue shadows.

They formed a circle around him, swords ready, eyes bright even in the darkness. Marcus eased the wine bag to his feet and held his gladius high. They made no move and he saw eyes roam over the bodies. Long seconds stretched in silence, then one of them stepped forward, large, bald and blue, and carrying a long, curved blade.

The warrior pointed off into the distance and gestured at Marcus. Marcus shook his head and pointed back at the fort. Someone jeered, but a curt hand signal from the man cut their noise off. The warrior stepped forward fearlessly, his sword pointed at Marcus' throat. With his other arm he pointed again at the campfires and then at the young Roman. The circle tightened silently and Marcus could feel the closeness of the men behind him.

'Tortured to death over the fire it is, then,' he said, pointing to the campfires himself.

The big blue warrior nodded, his eyes never leaving Marcus. He spoke a few words of command and another warrior placed his hand on Marcus' sword blade, gently removing it from his grip.

'Oh, *unarmed* and tortured to death, I didn't understand at first,' Marcus continued, forcing his voice to pleasant tones and knowing they didn't understand. He smiled and they smiled back at him.

They left the fort behind in the darkness and it was probably just his imagination that he caught a glimpse of Peppis' face outlined against the sky for a moment when he looked back.

They walked with strutting confidence into the blueskin camp with their prisoner. Marcus could see they were readying themselves for war. Weapons were stacked in bundles and the warriors danced and howled at the fires, spitting what must have been raw alcohol, judging by the blue flames that burst and flickered as the streams of liquid hit them. They whooped and wrestled and more than one sat slathering a pale mud onto his arms and face – the source, Marcus guessed, of the blue dye.

He barely had time to take all this in before he was shoved to his knees at the side of the bonfire and a crude clay cup of clear spirit was pressed into his hands. His eyes watered as he caught the evaporating fumes, but he swallowed it all and then fought not to choke. It was powerful liquor and he waved away the offer of another cup, wanting to keep a clear head. His guards settled on the ground all around him and seemed to be commenting on his clothes and manners to each other. Certainly it involved much pointing and laughing. Marcus ignored them, wondering if there would be a chance to run. He eyed the swords of the warriors nearest him, noting how they were removed from belts and laid on the scrub grass near to hand. He might be able to grab one . . .

Horns blew and interrupted his concentration. As everyone looked towards the source of the sound, Marcus stole one more look at the closest blade and saw the warrior's hand was resting on it. As his gaze travelled upward, he met the man's eyes and chuckled wryly as the burly warrior shook his head and smiled, revealing brown and rotting teeth.

The horn was held by the first old blueskin Marcus had seen. He must have been fifty and, unlike the hard muscular bodies of the young fighters, he had a heavy belly that bowed out his robe and jiggled as he moved skinny arms. He must have been a leader, as the warriors reacted to his shouted commands with speed. Three handy-looking types unsheathed their long swords and nodded to friends in the circle. Small drums were produced and a fast rhythm sounded. The three men stood relaxed as the rhythm filled the night and then they moved, faster than Marcus would have believed possible. The swords were like bars of dawn light and the moves were fluid, flowing into one another, so unlike the Roman sequences that Marcus had learned.

He could see the fight was staged, more a dance than a contest of violence. The men spun and leapt and their swords hummed as they cut the hot night air.

Marcus watched entranced to the end as the men once again resumed their relaxed positions and the drumming ceased. The warriors whooped and Marcus joined them without embarrassment, tensing as the old man walked over to him.

'Do you like? They are skilful?' the man said in a heavy accent.

Marcus covered his confusion and agreed, his expression carefully blank.

'These men took your little fort. They are the Krajka, the best of us, yes?'

Marcus nodded.

'Your men fought well, but the Krajka train when they stand, yes, as young children? We will take back all your ugly forts this way, yes? Stone from stone and ashes scattered? We will do this.'

'How many . . . Krajka are there?' Marcus asked.

The old man smiled, showing only three teeth in black gums.

'Not enough. We practise on those came with you today. Other warriors need to see how you people fight, yes?'

Marcus looked at him in disbelief. The future was clearly bleak for those left in the fort. They had been allowed to make the safety of the walls just so the young blueskins could blood themselves against reduced defenders. It was chilling. The legion believed the blueskins to be close to animals in intelligence. Any captured prisoners went berserk, biting through ropes and killing themselves on anything sharp if they couldn't escape. This evidence of careful planning – and one who spoke a civilised language – would wake them up to a threat they didn't treat seriously enough.

'Why didn't the men kill me?' Marcus asked. He fought to remain calm as the old man leaned closer to his face and sour breath washed over him.

'They very impressed. Three men you kill with short sword. Kill like man, not with bow or spear throwing. They bring you to show to me, as a strange thing, yes?'

A curiosity, a Roman good at killing. He guessed what had to come next before the old man spoke.

'Not good to have young warriors admire Roman. You fight Krajka, yes? If win, you go back to fort. If Krajka kill you, then all men see and know hope for future days, yes?'

Marcus agreed. There was nothing else to do. He looked into the flames and wondered if they would let him use his gladius.

Blueskins had come over from all the other campfires, leaving them barely defended. Marcus realised the men in the fort could not be aware of the opportunity. They would still see the spots of light in the mountain darkness and not know the bulk of them had trotted over to see the contest.

Marcus was allowed to stand and a circle was marked out with daggers stuck into the soil. The blueskins gathered outside the line, some balancing friends on their shoulders so they could see. Whichever way Marcus turned, he could see a heaving wall of blue flesh and grinning yellow teeth. He noticed how many of the eyes were pink-rimmed and decided it must be something in the dye that irritated the skin. The older, potbellied blueskin stepped into the circle and gravely handed Marcus his gladius, stepping back warily. Marcus ignored him. You didn't need the scout's eye to sense the hostility here. Lose and be cut to pieces to show their superiority, win and be torn apart by the mob. For a fleeting moment, he wondered what Gaius would do and had to smile at the thought. Gaius would have killed the leader as soon as he handed over the sword. It couldn't get any worse, after all.

The leader was still visible, his belly sticking into the circle space, but somehow it didn't seem right to run over and stick the old devil. Perhaps they would let him go. He looked around at the faces again and shrugged. Not very likely.

A low cheer built as one of the Krajka came through the circle, with the warriors parting briefly and then shoving their way back into position to get a good view. Marcus looked him up and down. He was much taller than the average blueskin and had a good three inches on Marcus, even after the growth he'd put on since leaving Rome. He was bare-chested and muscles shifted easily under the painted skin. Marcus guessed they were probably about equal in reach. His own arms were long, with powerful wrists from hours of sword practice. He knew he had a chance, no matter how good the man was. Renius still worked with him every day and Marcus was running out of opponents to give him a challenge in the practices.

338

He watched the way the tall man moved and walked. He looked into his eyes and found no give. The man didn't smile and wouldn't understand insults anyway. He walked around the edge of the circle, always staying out of reach in case Marcus tried a wild attack. Marcus turned on the spot, watching him all the time until he took up his position on the opposite side, twenty feet away. Tactics, tactics. Renius said never to stop thinking. The point was to win, not to be fair. Marcus winced as the man drew a long sword that reached from his hip to the ground, a shining length of polished bronze. There was the edge. He hadn't really noticed before, but the blueskins were using bronze weapons and a hard iron gladius would soon take the edge off it, if he could survive the first few blows. His thoughts raced. Bronze blunted. It was softer than iron.

The man walked closer and loosened his bare shoulders. He was wearing only leggings over bare feet and looked supremely athletic, moving like a great cat.

Marcus called to the leader, 'If I kill him, I walk free, yes?'

A great jeer went up from the crowd, making him wonder how many understood the language. The old blueskin nodded, smiling, and signalled with his hand to begin.

Marcus jumped as drums sounded over the chatter of the crowd. His opponent relaxed visibly as the rhythms were pounded out. Marcus watched him lower into a fighter's stance, the sword held out unwavering. The extra inches on the blade would give him the advantage in reach, Marcus thought, rolling his shoulders. He held up his hand and took a step back to remove his tunic. It was a relief to be free of it in the stifling heat, made worse by the nearby fire and the sweating crowd. The drumming intensified and Marcus focused his gaze on the man's throat. It unnerved some opponents. He became utterly still while the other swayed gently. Two different styles.

The Krajka barely seemed to move, but Marcus felt the attack

339

and shifted aside, making the bronze blade miss him. He didn't engage the gladius with the blade, trying to judge the man's speed.

A second cut, a smooth continuation of the first, came at his face and Marcus brought his gladius up desperately with a ring of metal. The blades slid together and he felt fresh sweat prickle on his hairline. The man was fast and fluid, with killing strikes that seemed only flicks and feints. Marcus blocked another low cut into his stomach and stepped and punched forward into the blue body.

It was not there and he went sprawling on the hard ground. He got up quickly, noting the fact that the Krajka stood well back to let him. This was not to be a quick kill then. Marcus nodded to him, his jaw clenched. Feel no anger, he told himself, nor shame. He remembered Renius' words. It does not matter what happens in battle as long as the enemy lies at your feet at the end of it.

The Krajka skipped lightly forward to meet him. At the last second, the bronze sword flicked out and Marcus was forced to duck under it. This time he didn't follow through with a lunge under the blow and saw the man's readiness to reverse his sword into a downwards slash. *He had fought Romans before!* The thought flashed into Marcus' head. This man knew their style of fighting, perhaps he had even learned it with a few of the legionaries who had disappeared over previous months before killing them.

It was galling. Everything he had been taught came from Renius, a Roman-trained soldier and gladiator. He had no other style to fall back on. The Krajka was clearly a master of his art.

The bronze sword licked out and Marcus blocked it. He focused on the lightly pulsing blue throat and could still see the shifting arms and sinuous moves of the body. He let one blow slide by him and stepped away from another, judging the distance perfectly. In the space, he struck like a snake and scored a thin line of red in the Krajka's side.

The crowd fell suddenly silent, shocked. The Krajka looked

puzzled and took two sliding steps away from Marcus. He frowned and Marcus saw he had not felt the scratch. He pressed his hand to the red line and looked at it, his face blank. Then he shrugged and danced in again, his bronze sword a blur in the light and shadows.

Marcus felt the rhythm of the movements and began working against the flowing style, breaking the smoothness, causing the Krajka to jump back from a sword held out rigidly and again when Marcus' hard sandals cracked against his toes.

Marcus advanced, knowing his opponent's confidence was wavering. Each step was accompanied by a blow that became another, a flowing pattern that mimicked the style the Krajka employed against him. The gladius became an extension of his arm, a thorn in his hand that required just a touch to kill. The Krajka let a throat cut pass a hair's-breadth from his skin, and Marcus could feel the hot gaze above his own. The man was angry that he had not won easily. Another blow was blocked and once again the bare feet were crunched under hard Roman sandals.

The Krajka gave out a strangled groan of pain and spun, leaping into the air like a spirit, as Marcus had seen the others do before. It was a move from the dance and the bronze sword whirled with him, coming out of the spin unseen and slicing Marcus' skin across the chest. The crowd roared and, as the man landed, Marcus reached up and caught the bronze blade with his bare left hand.

The Krajka looked in astonishment into Marcus' eyes and found for the first time in the whole battle that they were looking back at him, cold and black. He froze under that gaze and the hesitation killed him. He felt the iron gladius enter his throat from the front and the pouring wetness of blood that stole his strength. He would have liked to pull his blade back, cutting the fingers away like over-ripe stalks, but there was no strength left and he dropped into a boneless sprawl at Marcus' feet.

Marcus breathed slowly and picked up the bronze sword, noting the twisted and buckled edge where he had caught it. He could feel blood trickle over his knuckles from the cut on his palm, but was able to move the fingers stiffly. He waited then for the crowd to rush in and kill him.

They were silent for some time and in that silence the old blueskin's voice called out harsh-sounding commands. Marcus kept his eyes on the ground and the swords loose in his hands. He was aware of footsteps and turned as the old blueskin took his arm. The man's eyes were dark with astonishment and something else.

'Come. I keep my word. You go back to friends. We come for you all in morning.'

Marcus nodded, scarcely daring to believe it was true. He looked for something to say.

'He was a fine fighter, the Krajka. I have never fought better.'

'Of course. He was my son.' The man seemed older as he spoke, as if years were settling on his shoulders and weighing him down. He led Marcus outside the circle and into the open and pointed into the night.

'Walk home now.'

He stayed silent as Marcus handed him the bronze blade and walked away into the dark.

The fort wall was black in the darkness as Marcus approached. While he was still some distance away, he whistled a tune so that the soldiers would hear him and not put a crossbow bolt into his chest as he drew close.

'I'm alone! Peppis, throw that rope back down,' he called into the silence.

There was scrambling inside as the others moved to peer over the edge.

A head appeared above him in the gloom and Marcus recognised the sour features of Peritas.

'Marcus? Peppis said the 'skins had you.'

'They did, but they let me go. Are you going to throw a rope down to me or not?' Marcus snapped. It was colder away from the fires and he held his damaged hand in his armpit to keep the stiff fingers warm. He could hear whispered conversations above and cursed Peritas for his cautious ways. Why would the tribesmen set a trap when they could just wait for them all to die of thirst?

Finally, a rope came slithering over the wall and he pulled himself up it, his arms burning with tiredness. At the top, there were hands to help pull him onto the inner wall ledge and then he was almost knocked from his feet by Peppis, who threw his arms around him.

'I thought they was going to eat you,' the boy said. His dirty face was streaked where he had been crying and Marcus felt a pang of sorrow that he had brought the boy to this dismal place for his last night.

He reached out a hand and ruffled his hair affectionately. 'No, lad. They said I was too stringy. They like them young and tender.'

Peppis gasped in horror and Peritas chuckled. 'You have all night to tell us what happened. I don't think anyone will sleep. Are there many of them out there?'

Marcus looked at the older man and understood what couldn't be said openly in front of the boy.

'There's enough,' he replied, his voice low.

Peritas looked away and nodded to himself.

As dawn broke, Marcus and the others waited grimly for the assault, bleary-eyed from lack of sleep. Every man of them stood on the walls, swinging their heads nervously at the slightest move-ment of a bird or hare down on the scrubland. The silence was frightening, but when a sword falling over interrupted it more than a few swore at the soldier who'd let it slip.

Then, in the distance, they heard the brassy horns of a Roman legion, echoing in the hills. Peritas jogged along the narrow walkway inside the walls and cheered as they watched three centuries of men come out of the mountain trails at a double-speed march.

It was only a few minutes before a voice sounded, 'Approaching the fort,' and the gates were thrown open.

The legion commanders had not been slow in sending out a strike force when the caravan was late returning. After the recent attacks, they wanted a show of strength and had marched through the dark hours over rough terrain, making twenty miles in the night.

'Did you see any sign of the blueskins?' Peritas asked, frowning. 'There were hundreds around the fort when we arrived. We were expecting an attack.'

A centurion shook his head and pursed his lips. 'We saw signs of them, smouldering campfires and rubbish. It looks like they all moved out in the night. There is no accounting for the way savages think, you know. One of their magic men probably saw an unlucky bird or some kind of omen.'

He looked around at the fort and caught the stench of the bodies.

'Looks like we have work to do here. Orders are to man this place until relieved. I'll send a Fifty back with you to permanent camp. No one moves without a heavy armed force from now on. This is hostile territory, you know.'

Marcus opened his mouth to reply and Peritas turned him deftly around with an arm on his shoulder, sending him off with a gentle push.

'We know,' he said, before turning away to ready his men for the march home.

CHAPTER THIRTY-ONE

The street gang was already draped in expensive bolts of cloth, stolen from a shop or seamstress. They carried clay vessels that sloshed red wine onto the stone street as they wove and staggered along.

Alexandria peered out of the locked gates of Marius' town house, frowning.

'The filth of Rome,' she muttered to herself. With all the soldiers in the city engaged in battle, it had not taken long for those who enjoyed chaos to come out onto the streets. As always, it was the poor who suffered the most. Without guards of any kind, houses were broken into and everything of value carried away by yelling, jeering looters.

Alexandria could see one of the bolts of cloth was splashed with blood and her fingers itched for a bow to send a shaft into the man's drunken mouth.

She ducked back behind the gatepost as they went past, wincing as a burly hand reached out to rattle the gate, testing for weakness. She gripped the hammer she had taken from Bant's workshop. If they tried to climb the gates, she was ready to crack someone's head. Her heart thudded as they paused and she could hear every slurred word between them.

'There's a whorehouse on Via Tantius, lads. We could get a little free trade,' came a rough voice.

'They'll have guards, Brac. I wouldn't leave a post like that, would you? I'd make sure I got paid for my service as well. Those whores would be glad to have a strong man protecting them. What we want is another nice little wife with a couple of young daughters. We'll offer to look after them while the husband's away.'

'I'm first, though. I didn't get much of a turn last time,' the first voice said.

'I was too much for her, that's why. After me, a woman don't want another.'

The laughter was coarse and brutal and Alexandria shuddered as they moved away.

She heard light footsteps behind her and spun, raising the hammer.

'It's all right, it's me,' Metella said, her face pale. She had heard the end of it. Both women had tears in their eyes.

'Are you certain about this, mistress?'

'Quite certain, Alexandria, but you'll have to run. It will be worse if you stay here. Sulla is a vengeful man and there is no reason for you to be caught up in his spite. Go and find this Tabbic. You have the paper I signed?'

'Of course. It is the dearest thing I own.'

'Keep it safe. The next few months will be difficult and dangerous. You will need proof you are a free woman. Invest the money Gaius left for you and stay safe until the city legion has restored order.'

'I just wish I could thank him.'

'I hope you have the chance one day.' Metella stepped up to the bars and unlocked them, looking up and down the street. 'Go quickly now. The road is clear for the moment, but you must hurry down to the market. Don't stop for anything, you understand?'

Alexandria nodded stiffly, not needing to be told after what she had heard. She looked at Metella's pale skin and dark eyes and felt fear touch her.

'I just worry about you in this great house, all alone. Who will look after you, with the house empty?'

Metella held up a hand in a gentle gesture.

'Have no fear for me, Alexandria. I have friends who will spirit me away from the city. I will find a warm foreign land and retire there, away from all the intrigue and pains of a growing city. Somewhere ancient appeals to me, where all the struggle of youth is but a distant memory. Stay to the main street. I can't relax until the last of my family is safely away.'

Alexandria held her gaze for a second, her eyes bright with tears. Then she nodded once and passed through the gates, closing them firmly behind her and hurrying away.

Metella watched her go, feeling every one of her years in comparison to the young girl's light steps. She envied the ability of the young to start anew, without looking back at the old. Metella kept her in sight until she turned a street corner and then looked inwards to her empty, echoing home. The great house and gardens were empty at last.

How could Marius not be here? It was an eerie thought. He had been gone so often on long campaigns, yet always returned, full of life and wit and strength. The idea that he would not return once more for her was an ugly wound that she would not examine. It was too easy to imagine that he was away with his legion, conquering new lands or building huge aqueducts for foreign kings. She would sleep and, when she awoke, the awful sucking pain inside her would be gone and he would be there to hold her.

She could smell smoke on the air. Ever since Sulla's attack on the city three days before, there had been fire, raging untended from house to house and street to street. It had not reached the stone houses of the rich yet, but the fire that roared in Rome would consume them all eventually, piling ashes on ashes until there was nothing left of dreams.

Metella looked out at the city that sloped away from the hill.

She leaned against a marble wall and felt its coolness as a comfort against the thick heat. There were vast black plumes of churning smoke lifting into the air from a dozen points and spreading into a grey layer, the colour of despair. Screams carried on the wind as the marauding soldiers fought without mercy and the raptores on the streets killed or raped anything that crossed their path.

She hoped Alexandria would get through safely. The house guards had deserted her the morning they heard of Marius' death. She supposed she was lucky they had not murdered her in her bed and looted the house, but the betrayal still stung. Had they not been treated fairly and well? What was left to stand on in a world where a man's oath could vanish in the first warm breeze?

She had lied to Alexandria of course. There was no way out of the city for her. If it was dangerous to send a young slave girl on a journey of only a few streets, it was impossible for a well-known lady to transport her wealth past the wolves that roamed the roads of Rome, looking for just such opportunities. Perhaps she could have disguised herself as a slave, even travelled with one of the slaves. With luck, they might have got out alive, though she thought it more than likely that they would have been hurt and abused and left for the dogs somewhere. There had been no law in Rome for three days and to some that was a heady freedom. If she had been younger and braver she might have taken the risk, but Marius had been her courage for too long.

With him, she could stand the sniggers of society ladies as they discussed her childless state behind her back. With him, she could face the world with an empty womb and still smile and not give way to screaming. Without him, she could not dare the streets alone and start again as a penniless refugee.

Metal-studded sandals ran past the gates and Metella felt a shiver start in her shoulders and run through her. It would not be long before the fighting reached this area and the looters and murderers that moved with Sulla would be breaking down the iron gates of Marius' old city home. She had received reports for the first two days until her messengers too had deserted her. Sulla's men had poured into the city, taking and holding street after street, using the advantage that Marius had created for them. With the First-Born spread all around the city walls, they could not bring the bulk of their forces against the invader for most of the first night of fighting and by then Sulla had dug in and was content to continue a creeping battle, dragging his siege engines through the streets to smash barricades and lining the roads behind him with the heads of Marius' men. It was said the great temple of Jupiter had been burned, with flames so hot that the marble slabs cracked and exploded, bringing down the columns and the heavy pillars, spilling them onto the piazza with thunderous reports. The people said it was an omen, that the gods were displeased with Sulla, but still he seemed to be winning.

Then her reports had ended, and at night she knew that the rhythmic victory chants echoing across Rome were not from the throats of the First-Born.

Metella reached up to her shoulder and took hold of the strap there, lifting it away from her skin. She shrugged it off and reached for the other. In a moment, her dress slipped into a puddle of material and she stepped naked from it, her back to the gates as she walked through the arches and doors, deeper into the house. The air felt cooler on her uncovered skin and she shivered again, this time with a touch of pleasure. How strange it was to be naked in these formal rooms!

As she walked, she slipped bangles from her hands and rings from her fingers, placing the handful of precious metal on a table. Marius' wedding ring she kept, as she had promised him that she would never take it off. She loosed her hair from the bands and let it spill down her back in a wave, tossing her head to make the crimps and curls fall out.

She was barefoot and clean as she entered the bathing hall and felt the steam coat her with the tiniest trace of gleaming moisture. She breathed it in and let the warmth fill her lungs.

The pool was deep and the water freshly heated, the last task of the departing slaves and servants. She let out a small sigh as she stepped down into the clear pool, made dark blue by the mosaic base. For a few seconds, she closed her eyes and thought back over the years with Marius. She'd never minded the long periods he spent away from Rome and their home with the First-Born. Had she known how short the time would be, she would have gone with him, but it was not the moment for pointless regrets. Fresh tears slid from under her eyelids without effort or any release of tension.

She remembered when he was first commissioned and his pleasure at each rise in rank and authority. He had been glorious in his youth and the lovemaking had been joyous and wild. She had been an innocent girl when the muscular young soldier had proposed. She hadn't known about the ugly side of life, about the pain as year after year passed without children to bring her joy. Each one of her friends had pressed out screaming child after child and some of them broke her heart just to look at them, just from the sudden emptiness. Those were the years when Marius had spent more and more time away from her, unable to cope with her rages and accusations. For a while she had hoped he would have an affair and she had told him that she would even accept a child from such a union as her own.

He had taken her head tenderly in his hands and kissed her softly. 'There is only you, Metella,' he had said. 'If fate has taken this one pleasure from us, I won't spit in her eye.'

She had thought she would never be able to stop the sobs that pulled at her throat. Finally he had lifted her up and taken her to bed where he was so gentle she cried once more, at the end. He had been a good husband, a good man.

She reached over to the side of the pool without opening her eyes. Her fingers found the thin iron knife she had left there. One of his, given after his century had held a hill fort for a week against a swarming army of savages. She gripped the blade between two fingers and guided it blindly down to her wrist. She took a deep breath and her mind was numb and filled with peace.

The blade cut and the strange thing was it didn't really hurt. The pain was a distant thing, almost unnoticed as her inner eye relived old summers.

'Marius.' She thought she'd said the name aloud, but the room was still and silent and the blue water had turned red.

Cornelia frowned at her father.

'I will *not* leave here. This is my home and it is as safe as anywhere else in the city at the moment.'

Cinna looked about him, noting the heavy gates that blocked off the town house from the street outside. The house he had given as her dowry was a simple one of only eight rooms, all on one floor. It was a beautiful home, but he would have preferred an ugly one, with a high brick wall around it.

'If a mob comes for you, or Sulla's men, looking to rape and destroy . . .' His voice shook with suppressed emotion as he spoke, but Cornelia held firm.

'I have guards to handle a mob and nothing in Rome will stop Sulla if the First-Born cannot,' Cornelia replied. Her voice was calm but, inside, doubts nagged at her. True, her father's home was built like a fortress, but this belonged to her and to Julius. It was where he would look for her, if he survived.

Her father's voice rose almost to a screech. 'You haven't seen what the streets are like! Gangs of animals looking for easy targets. I couldn't go out myself without my guards. Many homes have been set on fire, or looted. It is chaos.' He rubbed his face with his hands and his daughter saw that he hadn't shaved.

'Rome will come through it, Father. Didn't you want to move

out to the country when the riots were going on a year ago? If I had left then, I would not have met Julius and I would not be married.'

'I wish I had left!' Cinna snapped, his voice savage. 'I wish I had taken you away then. You would not be here, in danger, with . . .'

She stepped closer to him and put her hand out to touch his cheek.

'Calm, Father, calm. You will hurt yourself with all your worries. This city has seen upheavals before. It will pass. I will be safe. You should have shaved.'

There were tears in his eyes and she stepped into a crushing hug.

'Gently, old man. I am delicate now.'

Her father straightened his arms, looking at her questioningly.

'Pregnant?' he asked, his voice rough with affection.

Cornelia nodded.

'My beautiful girl,' he said, gathering her in again, but carefully.

'You will be a grandfather,' she whispered into his ear.

'Cornelia,' he said. 'You must come now. My house is safer than this. Why take such a risk? Come home.'

The word was so powerful. She wanted to let him take her to safety, wanted very much to be a little girl again, but could not. She shook her head, smiling tightly to try to take away the sting of rejection.

'Leave more guards if it will make you feel happy, but this is my home now. My child will be born here and when Julius is able to return to the city he will come here first.'

'What if he has been killed?'

She closed her eyes against the sudden stab of pain, feeling tears sting under the lids.

'Father, please . . . Julius *will* come back to me. I . . . I am sure of it.'

'Does he know about the child?'

She kept her eyes closed, willing the weakness to pass. She would not start sobbing, though part of her wanted to bury her head in her father's chest and let him carry her away.

'Not yet.'

Cinna sat on a bench next to a trickling pool in the garden. He remembered the conversations with the architect when he had been readying the house for his daughter. It seemed such a long time ago. He sighed.

'You defeat me, girl. What will I tell your mother?'

Cornelia sat next to him. 'You will tell her that I am well and happy and going to give birth in about seven months. You will tell her that I am preparing my home for the birth and she will understand that. I will send messengers to you when the streets are quiet again and . . . that we have enough food and are in good health. Simple.'

Her father's voice was cracking slightly as he tried to find a note of firmness. 'This Julius had better be a good husband to you – and a good father. I will have him whipped if he isn't. Should have done it when I heard he was running about on my roof after you.'

Cornelia wiped a hand over her eyes, pressing the worry back inside her. She forced herself to smile. 'There's no cruelty in you, Father, so don't try and pretend there is.'

He grimaced, and the silence stretched for long moments.

'I will wait another two days and then I will have my guards take you home.'

Cornelia pressed a hand on her father's arm. 'No. I am not yours any more. Julius is my husband and he will expect me to be here.'

Then the tears could no longer be held back and she began to sob. Cinna pulled her to him and embraced her tightly.

* * *

Sulla frowned as his men raced to secure the main streets, which would give them access to the great forum and the heart of the city. After the first bloody scramble, the battle for Rome had gone well for him, with area after area taken with quick, brutal skirmishes and then held against an enemy in disarray. Before the sun had risen fully, most of the lower east quarter of Rome was under his control, creating a large area in which they could rest and regroup. Then tactical problems had arisen. With his controlled areas expanding in a line, he had fewer and fewer men to hold the border and knew he was always in danger from any sort of attack that massed men against a section where his were spread thinly.

Sulla's advance slowed and orders flowed ever more swiftly from him, moving units around, or making them hold. He knew he had to have a secure base before he asked for any kind of surrender. After Marius' last words to them, Sulla accepted that there was a chance his soldiers would fight to the last man – their loyalty was legendary even in a system where such loyalty was fostered and nurtured. He had to make them lose hope and a slowing advance would not do that.

Now he was standing in an open square at the top of the Caelius hill. All the massed streets behind him back to the Caelimontana gate were his. The fires had been put out and his legion were entrenched from there all the way to Porta Raudusculana at the southern tip of the city walls.

In the small square were nearly a hundred of his men, split into groups of four. Each man had volunteered and he was touched by it. Was this what Marius felt when his men offered their lives for him?

'You have your orders. Keep moving and cause havoc. If you are outnumbered, get away until you can attack again. You are my luck and the luck of the legion. Gods speed you.'

As one, they saluted him and he returned it, his arm stiff.

He expected most to be dead within the hour. If it had been night, they would have been more useful, but in the bright daylight they were little better than a distraction. He watched the last group of four squeeze through the barricade and hare off along a side street.

'Have Marius' body wrapped and placed in cool shadow,' Sulla said to a nearby soldier. 'I cannot say when I will have the leisure to organise a proper funeral for him.'

A sudden flight of arrows was launched from two or three streets away. Sulla watched the arc with interest, noting the most likely site for the archers and hoping a few of his four-man squads were in the area. The black shafts passed overhead and then all around them, shattering on the stone of the courtyard Sulla had adopted as a temporary command post. One of his messengers dropped with a barbed arrow through his chest and another screamed, though he seemed not to have been touched. Sulla frowned.

'Guard. Take that messenger somewhere close and flog him. Romans don't scream or faint at the sight of blood. Make sure I can see a little of his on his back when you return.'

The guard nodded and the messenger was borne away in silence, terrified lest his punishment be increased.

A centurion ran up and saluted.

'General. This area is secure. Shall I sound the slow advance?'

Sulla stared at him.

'I chafe at the pace we are setting. Sound the charge for this section. Let the others catch us up as they may.'

'We will be exposed, sir, to flanking attacks,' the man stammered.

'Question an order of mine again in war and I will have you hanged like a common criminal.'

The man paled and spun to give the order.

Sulla ground his teeth in irritation. Oh, for an enemy who would meet him on an open field. This city fighting was unseen and violent. Men ripping each other with blades out of sight in distant alleyways.

Where were the glorious charges? The singing battle weapons? But he would be patient and he would eventually grind them down to despair. He heard the charge horn sound and saw his men lift their barricades and prepare to carry them forward. He felt his blood quicken with excitement. Let them try to flank him, with so many of his squads mingling out there to attack from behind.

He smelled fresh smoke on the air and could see flames lick from high windows in the streets just ahead. Screams sounded above the eternal clash of arms and desperate figures climbed out onto stone ledges, thirty, forty feet above the sprawling mêlée below. They would die on the great stones of the roadways. Sulla saw one woman lose her grip and fall headfirst onto the heavy kerb. It broke her into a twisted doll. Smoke swirled in his nostrils. One more street and then another.

His men were moving quickly.

'Forward!' he urged, feeling his heart beat faster.

Orso Ferito spread a map of Rome on a heavy wooden table and looked around at the faces of the centurions of the First-Born.

'The line I have marked is how much territory Sulla has under his control. He fights on an expanding line and is vulnerable to a spear-point attack at almost any part of it. I suggest we attack here and here at the same time.' He indicated the two points on the map, looking round at the other men in the room. Like Orso, they were tired and dirty. Few had slept more than an hour or two at a time in the previous three-day battle and, like the men, they were close to complete exhaustion.

Orso himself had been in command of five centuries when he had witnessed Marius' murder at the hands of Sulla. He had heard his general's last shout and he still burned with rage when he thought of smug Sulla shoving a blade into a man Orso loved more dearly than his own father.

The following day had been chaos, with hundreds dying on both sides. Orso had kept control over his own men, launching short and bloody attacks and then withdrawing before reserves could be brought up. Like many of Marius' men, he was not high-born and had grown up on the streets of Rome. He understood how to fight in the roads and alleys he had scrambled along as a boy, and before dawn on the second day he had emerged as the unofficial leader of the First-Born.

His influence was felt immediately as he began to coordinate the attacks and defences. Some streets Orso would let go as strategically unimportant. He ordered the occupants out of houses, set the fires and had his men withdraw under arrow cover. Other streets they fought for again and again, concentrating their available forces on preventing Sulla from breaking through. Many had been lost, but the headlong rush into the city had been slowed and stopped in many areas. It would not be over quickly now and Sulla had a fight on his hands.

Whatever Orso's mother had called him, he had always been Orso, the bear, to his men. His squat body and most of his face was covered in black, wiry hair, right up onto his cheeks. His slab-muscled shoulders were matted with dried blood and, like the others in the room who had been forced to give up their Roman taste for cleanliness, he stank of smoke and old sweat.

The meeting room had been chosen at random, a kitchen in someone's town house. The group of centurions had walked in off the street and spread the map out. The owner was upstairs somewhere. Orso sighed as he looked at the map. Breakthroughs were possible, but they would need the luck of the gods to beat Sulla. He looked around at the faces at the table again and was hard put not to wince at the hope he saw reflected there. He was no Marius, he knew that. If the general had remained alive to be in this room, they would have had a fighting chance. As it was . . .

'They have no more than twenty to fifty men at any given point on the line. If we break through quickly, with two centuries at each position, we should be able to cut them to pieces before reinforcements arrive.'

'What then? Go for Sulla?' one of the centurions asked. Marius would have known his name, Orso acknowledged to himself.

'We can't be sure where that snake has positioned himself. He is quite capable of setting up a command tent as a decoy for assassins. I suggest we pull straight back out, leaving a few men in civilian clothes to watch for an opportunity to take him.'

'The men won't be pleased. It is not a crushing victory and they want one.'

Orso snapped back his ire. 'The men are legionaries of the finest damn legion in Rome. They will do as they're told. This is a game of numbers, if it is a game at all. They have more. We control similar ground with far fewer men. They can reinforce faster than we can and . . . they have a far more experienced commander. The best we can do is to destroy a hundred of their men and pull out, losing as few of ours as possible. Sulla still has the same problem of defending a lengthening line.'

'We have the same problem, to some extent.'

'Not half as badly. If they break through, it is into the vast city, where they can be flanked with ease and cut off. We are still in control of the larger area by far. When we break their line, it will be straight into the heart of their territory.'

'Where they have their men, Orso. I am not convinced your plan will work,' the man continued.

Orso looked at him. 'What is your name?'

'Bar Gallienus, sir.'

'Did you hear what Marius called out before he was killed?'

The man reddened slightly. 'I did, sir.'

'So did I. We are defending our city and her inhabitants from an illegal invader. My commander is dead. I have assumed temporary command until the current crisis is over. Unless you have something useful to add to the discussion, I suggest you wait outside and I'll let you know when we are finished. Is that clear?' Although Orso's voice remained calm and polite throughout the exchange, all the men in the room could feel the anger coming off him like a physical force. It took a little courage not to edge away.

Bar Gallienus spoke quietly.

'I would like to stay.'

Orso clapped a hand on his shoulder and looked away from him.

'Anything we have that can launch a missile, including every man with a bow, will mass at those two points, one hour from now. We will hit them with everything and then two centuries will charge their defences on my signal. I will lead the attack through the old market area as I know it well. Bar Gallienus will lead the other. Any questions?'

There was silence at the table. Gallienus looked Orso in the eye and nodded his agreement.

'Then gather your legionaries, gentlemen. Let's make the old man proud. "Marius" is the shout. The signal will be three short blasts. One hour.'

Sulla stepped back from the bloodied men panting in front of him. Of the hundred he had sent into the fray hours before, only eleven had made it back to report and these were wounded, every one.

'General. The mobile squads were only partially successful,' a soldier said, trying hard to stand erect over the weakness of his heaving lungs. 'We did a lot of damage in the first hour and at a guess took down more than fifty of the enemy in small skirmishes. Where possible, we caught them alone or in pairs and overwhelmed them as you suggested. Then the word must have gone out and we found ourselves being tracked through the streets. Whoever was directing them must know the city very well. Some of us took to the roofs, but there were men waiting up there.' He paused for breath again and Sulla waited impatiently for the man to calm himself.

'I saw several of the men brought down by women or children coming out of the houses with knives. They hesitated to kill civilians and were cut to pieces. My own squad was lost to a similar group of First-Born who had removed their outer armour and carried only short swords. We had been running a long time and they cornered us in an alleyway. I . . .'

'You said you had information to report. It was clear from the beginning that the mobile groups would do only limited damage. I had hoped to spread fear and chaos, but it seems there is a semblance of discipline left in the First-Born. One of Marius' seconds must have taken overall tactical control. He will be looking to strike back quickly. Did your men see any signs of this?'

'Yes, General. They were bringing men up quietly through the streets. I do not know when or where they will attack, but there will be some sort of skirmish soon.'

'Hardly worth eighty of my men, but useful enough to me. Get yourselves to the surgeons. Centurion!' he snapped at a man nearby. 'Get every man up to the barricades. They will try to break through. Triple the men on the line.'

The centurion nodded and signalled to the messengers to carry the news to the outposts of the line.

Suddenly the sky turned black with arrow shafts, a stinging, humming swarm of death. Sulla watched them fall. He clenched his fists and tightened his jaw as they whirred towards his position. Men around him threw themselves down, but he stood straight and unblinking with his eyes glittering.

The shafts rained and shattered around him, but he was

untouched. He turned and laughed at his scrambling advisers and officers. One was on his knees, pulling at an arrow in his chest and spilling blood from his mouth. Two others stared glassily at the sky, unmoving.

'A good omen, don't you think?' he said, still smiling.

Ahead, somewhere in the city, a horn blew three short blasts and a roar rose in response. Sulla heard one name chanted above the noise and for a moment knew doubt.

'Ma-ri-us!' howled the First-Born. And they came on.

CHAPTER THIRTY-TWO

Alexandria hammered at the door of the little jeweller's shop. There had to be someone there! She knew he could have left the city as so many others had done and the thought that she might be just drawing attention to herself made her go pale. Something scraped in the street nearby, like a door opening.

'Tabbic! It's me, Alexandria! Gods, open up, man!' She let her arm fall, panting. Shouts came from nearby and her heart thudded wildly.

'Come on. Come on,' she whispered.

Then the door was wrenched aside and Tabbic stood glaring, a hatchet held tightly in his hand. When he saw her he looked relieved and something of the anger faded.

'Get in, girl. The animals are out tonight,' he said gruffly. He looked up and down the street. It seemed deserted, though he could feel eyes on him.

Inside, she was faint from relief.

'Metella . . . sent me, she . . .' she said.

'It's all right, girl. You can explain later. The wife and kids are upstairs putting a meal together. Go up and join them. You're safe here.'

She paused for a moment and turned to him, unable to hold it in.

'Tabbic. I have papers and everything. I'm free.'

He leaned close and looked her in the eyes, a smile beginning.

'When were you anything else? Get upstairs now. My wife will be wondering what all the fuss is about.'

There was nothing in the battle manuals for assaulting a broken barricade set across a city street. Orso Ferito simply roared his dead general's name and launched himself up the litter of broken carts and doors into the arms of the enemy. Two hundred men came behind him.

Orso buried his gladius in the first throat he saw and only missed being cut by slipping on the shifting barricade and rolling down the other side. He came up swinging and was rewarded with a satisfying crunch of bone. His men were all around him, hacking and cutting onward. Orso couldn't tell how well they were doing or how many had died. He only knew that the enemy was in front of him and he had a sword in his hand. He roared and cut a man's arm from his shoulder as it was raising a shield to block him. He grabbed the shield with the limp arm falling out of the grip and used it to shoulder-charge two men from his path, trampling over them. One of them stabbed upwards and he felt a warmth rush over his legs but paid it no attention. The area was clear, but the end of the street was filling with men. Orso saw their captain sound the charge and met it at full speed across the open space. He knew in that moment how it felt to be a berserker in one of the savage nations they had conquered. It was a strange freedom. There was no pain, only an exhilarating distance from fear or exhaustion.

More men went under his sword and the First-Born carried all before them, cutting and dealing death on bright metal.

'Sir! The side streets. They have more reinforcements!'

Orso almost shook off the hand tugging at his arm, but then his training came to the fore.

'Too many of them. Back, lads! We've cut them enough for now!' He raised his sword in triumph and began to run back the way they had come, panting even as he noted the numbers of Sulla's dead. More than a hundred, if he was any judge.

Here and there were faces he had known. One or two stirred feebly and he was tempted to stop for them, but behind came the crash of sandals on stone and he knew they had to reach the barricades or be routed with their backs to them.

'On, lads. Ma-ri-us!'

The cry was answered from all around and then again they were climbing. At the top, Orso looked back and saw the slowest of his men being brought down and trampled. Most had made it clear and as he turned to run down the other side, the First-Born archers fired again over his men's heads, sending more bodies to die on the stone road, screaming and writhing. Orso chuckled as he ran, his sword drooping from the exhaustion that was threatening to unman him. He ducked inside a building and stood gasping, his hands braced on his knees. The cut in his thigh was bad and blood ran freely. He felt light-headed and could only mumble as hands took him onwards away from the barricade.

'Can't stop here, sir. The archers can only cover us until they run out of arrows. Have to keep going a road or two further. Come on, sir.'

He registered the words, but wasn't sure if he had responded. Where had his energy gone? His leg felt weak. He hoped Bar Gallienus had done as well.

Bar Gallienus lay in his own blood, with Sulla's sword pressing against his throat. He knew he was dying and tried to spit at the general, but could not raise more than a sputter of liquid. His men had found a freshly reinforced century over the barricade and had very nearly been broken on the first assault. After minutes of furious fighting, they had breached the wall of piled stone and wood and thrown themselves into the mass of soldiers beyond. His men had taken many with them, but it was simply too much. The line had not been thin at all.

Bar smiled to himself, revealing bloody teeth. He *knew* Sulla could reinforce quickly. It was a shame he wouldn't have the chance to mention this to Orso. He hoped the hairy man had done better than he had, or the legion would be leaderless again. Foolhardy to risk himself on such a venture, but too many of them had died in that dreadful first day of havoc and execution. He'd *known* Sulla would reinforce.

'I think he's dead, sir,' Bar heard a voice say.

He heard Sulla's voice reply. 'A pity. He has the strangest expression. I wanted to ask him what he was thinking.'

Orso snarled at the centurion who tried to help him stand. His leg ached and he had a crutch under one shoulder, but he was in no mood to be helped.

'No one came back?' he asked.

'We lost both centuries. That section had been reinforced just before we charged it, sir. It doesn't look like that tactic will work again.'

'I was lucky then,' Orso grunted. No one met his eye. He had been, to hit a section of the wall where the strength was low. Bar Gallienus must have laughed to see himself proved right about that. It was a shame he couldn't buy the man a drink.

'Sir? Do you have any other orders?' asked one of the centurions.

Orso shook his head. 'Not yet. But I will have when I know where we stand.'

'Sir.' The younger man hesitated.

Orso swung to face him. 'What is it? Spit it out, lad.'

'Some of the men are talking of surrender. We are down to half-strength and Sulla has the supply routes to the sea. We cannot win and . . .'

'Win? Who said we were going to win? When I saw Marius die, I knew we couldn't win. I realised then that Sulla would break the back of the First-Born before enough could gather to cause him any real difficulty. This isn't about winning, boy, it's about fighting for a just cause, following orders and honouring a great man's life and death.'

He looked at the men around the room. Only a few couldn't meet his eyes and he knew he was among friends. He smiled. How would Marius have put it?

'A man can wait a lifetime for a moment like this and never see one. Some just grow old and wither, never getting their chance. We will die young and strong and I wouldn't have it any other way.'

'But, sir, perhaps we could break out of the city. Head for the mountains . . .'

'Come outside. I am not going to waste a great speech on you buggers.'

Orso grunted and hobbled out of the door. In the street were a hundred or so of the First-Born, weary and dirty, with bandages wrapped around cuts. They looked defeated already and that thought gave him the words.

'I am a soldier of Rome!' His voice, by nature deep and rough, carried across them, stiffening backs.

'All I ever wanted was to serve my time and retire to a nice little plot of land. I didn't want to lose my life on some foreign ground and be forgotten. But then I found myself serving with a man who was more father to me than my own father ever was and I saw his death and I heard his words and I thought, Orso, this may be where you stand, old son. And maybe that's enough, after all.

366

'Anyone here think they will live for ever? Let other men plant cabbages and grow dry in the sun. I will die like a soldier, on the streets of the city I love, in her defence.'

His voice dropped a little as if he was imparting a secret. The men leaned close and more joined the growing crowd.

'I understand this truth. Few things are worth more than dreams or wives, pleasures of the flesh or even children. Some things are, though, and that knowledge is what makes us men. Life is just a warm, short day between long nights. It grows dark for everyone, even those who struggle and pretend they will always be young and strong.'

He pointed to a mature soldier, slowly flexing his leg as he listened.

'Tinasta! I see you testing that old knee of yours. Did you think age would ease the pain of it? Why wait until it buckles from weakness and have younger men shoulder you aside? No, my friends; my brothers. Let us go while the light is still strong and the day is still bright.'

A young soldier raised his head and called out, 'Will we be remembered?'

Orso sighed, but smiled. 'For a while, son, but who remembers the heroes of Carthage or Sparta today? *They* know how they ended their day. And that is *enough*. That is all there ever is.'

The young man asked quietly, 'Is there no chance then that we can win?'

Orso limped over to him, using the crutch for support. 'Son. Why don't you get out of the city? A few of you could break off if you slipped past the patrols. You don't have to stay.'

'I know, sir.' The young man paused. 'But I will.'

'Then there is no need to delay the inevitable. Gather the men. Everyone in position to attack Sulla's barricades. Let anyone go who wants to, with my blessing. Let them find other lives some-where and never tell anyone they once fought for Rome when

367

Marius died. One hour, gentlemen. Gather your weapons one more time.'

Orso looked around him while the men stood and checked their blades and armour as they had been trained to do. More than a few clapped him on the shoulder as they went to their positions and he felt his heart would burst with pride.

'Good men, Marius,' he muttered to himself. 'Good men.'

CHAPTER THIRTY-THREE

Cornelius Sulla sat idly on a throne of gold, resting on a mosaic of a million black and white tiles. Near the centre of Rome, his estate had been untouched by the rioting and it was a pleasure to be back and in power once more.

Marius' legion had fought almost to the last man, as he had predicted they would. Only a few had tried to run at the end and Sulla had hunted them down without mercy. Vast fire trenches lined the outer walls of the city and he had been told that the thousands of bodies would burn for days or even weeks before the ashes were finally cold. The gods would notice such a sacrifice to save their chosen city, he was sure.

Rome would need to be cleaned when the fires were out. There wasn't a wall anywhere that had not been speckled with the oily ash that floated in and stung the eyes of the people.

He had denounced the Primigenia as traitors, with their lands and wealth forfeit to the Senate. Families had been dragged out onto the streets by neighbours jealous of their possessions. Hundreds more had been executed and still the work went on. It would be a bitter mark on the glorious history of the seven hills, but what choice had he had?

Sulla mused to himself as a slave girl approached with a cup of ice-cold fruit juice. It was too early in the day for wine and there were so many still to see and to condemn. Rome would rise again in glory, he knew, but for that to happen the last of the friends and supporters of Marius – the last of Sulla's enemies – had to be ripped from the good, healthy flesh.

He winced as he sipped from the gold cup and ran a finger over his swollen eye and the ridges of a purpling gash along his right cheek. It had been the hardest fight of his life, making the campaign against Mithridates look rather pallid in comparison.

Marius' death came into his mind again, as it had so frequently in recent days. Impressive. The body had been saved from the fires. Sulla considered having a statue of the man standing at the top of one of the hills. It would show his own greatness in being able to honour the dead. Or he could just have it thrown into the pits with the others. It wasn't important.

The room where he sat was almost empty. A domed roof showed a pattern of Aphrodite in the Greek style. She looked down on him with love, a beautiful naked woman, with her hair wrapped around her. He wanted those who met him to know he was loved by the gods. The slave girl and her pitcher stood paces from him, ready to refill his cup at a gesture. The only other presence in the room was his torturer, who stood nearby with a small brazier and the grisly tools of his trade laid out on a table in front of him. His leather apron was already spattered from the morning's work and still there was more to do.

Bronze doors, almost as large as those that opened onto the Senate, boomed as they were struck with a mailed gauntlet. They opened to reveal two of his legionaries dragging in a burly soldier with his wrists and feet tied. They pulled him across the shining mosaic towards Sulla and he could see the man's face was already battered, his nose broken. A scribe walked behind the soldiers and consulted a sheaf of parchment for details.

'This one is Orso Ferito, master,' the scribe intoned. 'He was found under a pile of Marius' men and has been identified by two witnesses. He led some of the traitors in the resistance.'

Sulla stood lithely and walked to the figure, signalling for the guards to let him fall. He was conscious, but a dirty cloth gag prevented anything more than animal grunts from him.

'Cut the gag away. I would question him,' Sulla ordered and the deed was done quickly and brutally, a blade bringing fresh blood and a groan from the prostrate man.

'You led one of the attacks, didn't you? Are you that one? My men were saying you had taken over after Marius. Are you that man?'

Orso Ferito looked up with a sparkle of hatred. His gaze played over the bruise and cut on Sulla's face and he smiled, revealing teeth broken and bloody. The voice seemed dragged from some deep well and it croaked out at him.

'I would do it again,' he said.

'Yes. So would I,' Sulla replied. 'Put out his eyes and then hang him.' He nodded to the torturer, who removed a sliver of hot iron from the brazier, holding the darker end in heavy clamps. Orso struggled as his arms were bound with leather straps, his muscles writhing. The torturer was impassive as he brought the metal close enough to singe the lashes, then pressed it in, rewarded with a soft, grunting, animal sound.

Sulla drained his cup without tasting the juice. He looked on without pleasure, congratulating himself for his lack of emotion. He was not a monster, he knew, but the people expected a strong leader and that is what they would get. As soon as the Senate could reconvene, he would declare himself dictator and assume the power of the old kings. Then Rome would see a new era.

The unconscious Ferito was dragged away to be executed and Sulla had only a few minutes alone before the door boomed again and fresh soldiers entered with the little scribe. This time, he knew the young man who stumbled between them.

'Julius Caesar,' he said. 'Captured at the very height of the excitement, I believe. Let him stand, gentlemen; this is not a common man. Remove his gag – gently.'

371

He looked at the young lad and was pleased to note how he straightened. His face bore some bruising, but Sulla knew his men would have been wary of risking their general's displeasure with too much damage before judgement. He stood tall, a fraction under six feet, and his body was well-muscled and sun-dark. Blue eyes looked coldly out from his face and Sulla could feel the force of the man coming at him, seeming to fill the room till it was just the two of them, soldiers, torturer, scribe and slave all forgotten.

Sulla tilted his head back slightly and his mouth stretched and opened into a pleased expression.

'Metella died, I am sorry to say. She took her own life before my men could break in and save her. I would have let her go, but you . . . you are a different problem. Did you know the old man captured with you escaped? He seems to have slipped his bonds and freed the other. Most unusual companions for a young gentleman.' He saw the spark of interest in the other's face.

'Oh, yes. I have men out looking for the pair, but no luck at present. If my men had tied you with them, I dare say you would be free by now. Fate can be a fickle mistress – your membership of the nobilitas leaves you here while those gutter scum run free.'

Julius said nothing. He did not expect to live an hour longer and suddenly saw that nothing he could say would have meaning or use. Raging at Sulla would only amuse him and pleading would arouse his cruelty. He remained silent and glared.

'What do we have on him, scribe?' Sulla spoke to the man with the parchment.

'Nephew of Marius, son of Julius. Both dead. Mother Aurelia, still alive, but deranged. Owns a small estate a few miles outside the city. Considerable debts to private houses, sums undisclosed. Husband of Cornelia, Cinna's daughter, married on the morning of the battle.'

'Ah,' Sulla said, interrupting. 'The heart of the matter. Cinna is no friend of mine, though he is too wily to have supported Marius openly. He is wealthy; I understand why you would want the support of the old man, but surely your life is worth more.

'I will offer you a simple choice. Put this Cornelia aside and swear loyalty to me and I will let you live. If not, my torturer here is heating his tools once again. Marius would want you to live, young man. Make the right choice.'

Julius glared his anger. What he knew of Sulla didn't help him. It could be a cruel trick to make him deny those he loved before executing him anyway.

As if sensing his thoughts, Sulla spoke again.

'Divorce Cornelia and you will live. Such a simple act will shame Cinna, weakening him. You will go free. These men are all witnesses to my word as ruler of Rome. What is your answer?'

Julius held himself perfectly still. He hated this man. He had killed Marius and crippled the Republic his father had loved. No matter what he lost, the answer was clear and the words had to be said.

'My answer is no. Make an end of it.'

Sulla blinked in surprise and then laughed out loud.

'What a strange family! Do you know how many men have died in this very room over the last few days? Do you know how many have been blinded, castrated and scarred? Yet you scorn my mercy?' He laughed again and the sound was harsh under the echoing dome.

'If I let you go free, will you try to kill me?'

Julius nodded. 'I will devote my remaining years to that end.'

Sulla grinned at him in genuine pleasure. 'I thought so. You are fearless, and the only one of the nobilitas to refuse a bargain of mine.' Sulla paused for a moment, raising his hand to signal to the torturer, who stood ready. Then his hand dropped listlessly.

'You may go free. Leave my city before sunset. If you come back while I live, I will have you killed without trial or audience. Cut his ropes, gentlemen. You have bound a free man.' He chuckled for a moment, then was still as the ropes fell in twisted circles by Julius' feet. The young man rubbed his wrists, but his expression was as still as stone.

Sulla stood from his throne.

'Take him to the gates and let him walk.' He turned to look Julius in the eye. 'If anyone ever asks you why, tell them it was because you remind me of myself and perhaps I have killed enough men today. That's all.'

'What about my wife?' Julius called as his arms were taken again by the guards.

Sulla shrugged. 'I may take her as a mistress, if she learns to please me.'

Julius struggled wildly, but could not break free as he was dragged out.

The scribe lingered by the door.

'General? Is that wise? He is Marius' nephew after all . . .'

Sulla sighed and accepted another cup of cold liquid from the slave girl.

'Gods save us from *little* men. I gave you my reason. I have achieved anything I ever wanted and boredom looms. It is good to leave a few dangers to threaten me.'

His gaze focused far away.

'He is an impressive young man. I think there may be two of Marius inside him.'

The scribe's expression showed he understood none of it.

'Shall I have the next one brought in, Consul?'

'No more today. Are the baths heated? Good, the Senate leaders will be dining with me tonight and I want to be fresh.'

Sulla always had his pool as hot as he could possibly stand it. It relaxed him wonderfully. His only attendants were two of his house slave girls and he rose naked out of the water without self-consciousness in front of them. They too were naked, except for bangles of gold on their wrists and around their necks.

Both had been chosen for their full figures and he was pleased as he allowed them to rub the water from his body. It was good for a man to look on beautiful things. It raised the spirit above the level of the beasts.

'The water has brought my blood to the surface, but I feel sluggish,' he murmured to them, walking a few paces to a long massage bench. It was soft under him and he felt himself relax completely. He closed his eyes, listening to the two young women as they tied the thin, springy wands of the birch tree, gathered fresh that morning and still green.

The two slaves stood over his heat-flushed body. Each held a long bunch of the cut branches, almost like a brush, three feet long. At first they almost caressed him with the birch twigs, leaving faint white marks on his skin.

He groaned slightly and they paused.

'Master, would you like it harder?' one of them asked, timidly. Her mouth was bruised purple from his attentions the night before, and her hands trembled slightly.

He smiled without opening his eyes and stretched out on the bench. It was splendidly invigorating.

'Ah yes,' he replied dreamily. 'Lay on, girls, lay on.'

CHAPTER THIRTY-FOUR

Julius stood with Cabera and Tubruk at the docks, his face grey and cold. In contrast, as if to mock the grim events of his life, the day was hot and perfect, with only a light breeze coming off the sea to bring relief to the dust-stained travellers. It had been a hectic flight from the stinking city. At first he had been alone and on a sway-backed pony that was all he could buy for a gold ring. Grimacing, he had skirted around the firepits filled with flesh and trotted onto the main stone road west to the coast.

Then he heard a familiar hail and saw his friends step out from the trees ahead. It had been a joyous reunion to find each other alive, though the mood darkened as they told their stories.

Even in that first moment, Julius could see Tubruk had lost some of his vitality. He looked gaunt and dirty and told briefly of how they had lived as animals in streets where every sort of horror happened in the day and grew worse at night, where screams and shouts were the only clues. He and Cabera had agreed to wait a week on the road to the coast, hoping Julius could win free.

'After that,' Cabera said, 'we were going to steal some swords and cut you out.'

Tubruk laughed in response and Julius could see they had grown closer in their time together. It failed to lighten his mood. Julius told them of Sulla's whimsical cruelty and his fists clenched in fresh anger as the words spilled from him.

'I will come back to Rome. I will cut off his balls if he touches my wife,' he said quietly at the end.

His companions could not hold his gaze for long and even Cabera's usual humour had vanished for a while.

'He has the pick of women in Rome, Gaius,' Tubruk murmured. 'He's just the sort of man who likes to twist the knife a little. Her father will keep her safe, even get her out of Rome if there's a danger. That old man would set his guards on Sulla himself if there was a threat to her. You know this.'

Julius nodded, his eyes distant, needing to be persuaded. At first, he had wanted to try to get to her under cover of night, but the curfew was back and moving in the streets would mean instant death.

At least Cabera had managed to get hold of a few valuable items in the days he had spent on the streets with Tubruk. A gold armlet he had found in ashes bought them horses and bribes to pass the wall guards. The drafts that Julius still carried against his skin were too large to change outside a city and it was infuriating to have to rely on a few bronze coins when paper wealth was so close, but useless to them. Julius was not even sure that Marius' signature would make them good any more, but guessed the wily general would have thought of that. He had prepared for almost anything.

Julius had spent a couple of their valuable coins sending letters, giving each to legionaries on their way back to the city or outwards to the coast and Greece.

Cornelia would know he was safe, at least, but it would be a long time before he could see her again. Until he could return with strength and support, he was not able to return at all and the bitterness of it twisted and ate at him, leaving him empty and tired. Marcus would hear of the disaster in Rome and not come blindly back to look for him when his term of service ended. That was only a small comfort. As never before, he felt the loss of his friend.

A thousand other regrets taunted him as they came into his mind, too painful to be allowed to take root. The world had changed fundamentally for the young man. Marius could not be dead. The world was empty without him.

Weary after days on the road, the three men trotted their horses into the bustling coastal port west of Rome. Tubruk spoke first, after they had dismounted and tied their horses to a post outside an inn.

'The flags of three legions are here. Your papers will get you a commission in any of them. That one is based in Greece, that one in Egypt and the last is on a trade run up to the north.' Tubruk spoke calmly, showing his knowledge of the empire's movements had not waned in the time he had spent running the estate.

Julius felt uncomfortable and exposed on the docks, yet this was not a decision to be hurried. If Sulla changed his mind, even now there could be armed men on their way to kill them or bring them back to Rome.

Tubruk could not give much advice. True, he had recognised the banners of the legions, but he knew he was fifteen years out of date when it came to the reputations of the officers. He felt frustrated to have to put such a serious decision in the hands of the gods. At least two years of Julius' life would be spent with whichever unit they decided upon and they could end up flipping coins.

'I like the sound of Egypt, myself,' Cabera said, looking wistfully across the sea. 'It is a long time since I shook its dust from my sandals.' He could feel the future bending around the three of them. Few lives had such simple choices, or maybe all did but most could not see them when they came. Egypt, Greece or the north? Each beckoned in different ways. The lad must make a choice on his own, but at least Aegyptus was hot.

Tubruk studied the galleys rocking at their moorings, looking for one to rule out. Each was guarded by alert legionaries, and men swarmed over the wallowing vessels, repairing, scrubbing or refitting after voyages all over the world.

He shrugged. He assumed that after the fuss had died down and Rome was peaceful he would return to the estate. Someone had to keep the place alive.

'Marcus and Renius are in Greece. You could meet up with them there, if you wanted,' Tubruk ventured, turning to watch the road for dust raised by trackers.

'No. I haven't achieved anything, except to be married and run out of Rome by my enemy,' Julius muttered.

'Your uncle's enemy,' Cabera corrected.

Julius turned slowly to the old man, his gaze unwavering.

'No. He is my enemy now. I will see him dead, in time.'

'In time, perhaps,' Tubruk said. 'Today, you need to get away and learn to be a soldier and an officer. You are young. This is not the end of you, or your career.' Tubruk held his gaze for a second, thinking how much like his father Julius was becoming.

Eventually, the younger man nodded briefly before turning away. He examined the ships again.

'Egypt it is. I always wanted to see the land of the pharaohs.'

'A fine choice,' Cabera said. 'You will love the Nile and the women are scented and beautiful.' The old man was pleased to see Julius smile for the first time since they had been captured in the night. It was a good omen, he thought.

Tubruk gave a boy a small coin to hold their horses for an hour and the three men walked towards the galley ship that bore an Egyptian legion's flags. As they approached, the busy action of workers became even more apparent.

'Looks like they're getting ready to ship out,' Tubruk noted, jerking his thumb at barrels of supplies being loaded by slaves. Salted meat, oil and fish swung over the narrow strip of water into the arms of sweating slaves on board, each one noted and crossed off a slate with typical Roman efficiency. Tubruk whistled to one of the guards, who stepped over to them.

'We need to speak to the captain. Is he aboard?' Tubruk asked.

The soldier gave them a quick appraisal and appeared to be satisfied, despite the dust of the road. Tubruk and Julius, at least, looked like soldiers.

'He is. We'll be casting off on the noon tide. I can't guarantee he'll see you.'

'Tell him Marius' nephew is here, fresh from the city. We'll wait here,' Tubruk replied.

The soldier's eyebrows raised a fraction and his gaze slid over to Julius.

'Right you are, sir. I'll let him know immediately.'

The man took a step to the dockside and walked the narrow plank bridge onto the deck of the galley. He disappeared behind the raised wooden structure that dominated the ship and, Julius guessed, must house the captain's quarters. While they waited, Julius noted the features of the huge vessel, the oar-holes in the side that would be used to move them out of harbour and in battle to give them the speed to ram enemy vessels, the huge square sails that were waiting to be raised for the wind.

The deck was clear of loose objects as befitted a Roman war vessel. Everything that might cause injury in rough seas was lashed down securely. Steps led to the lower levels at various places in the planking and each could be secured with a bolted hatch to prevent heavy waves from crashing down after the crew. It looked a well-run ship, but until he met the captain he wouldn't know how things would be for the next two years of his life. He could smell tar and salt and sweat, the scents of an alien world he did not know. He felt strangely nervous and almost laughed at himself.

Out of the deck shadows came a tall man in the full uniform of a centurion. He looked hard and neat, with grey hair cut short to his head and his breastplate shined to a bright bronze glow in the sun. His expression was watchful as he crossed the planks to the dockside and greeted the three waiting men.

'Good day, gentlemen. I am Centurion Gaditicus, nominal captain of this vessel for the Third Partica legion. We cast off on the next tide, so I cannot spare you a great deal of time, but the name of Consul Marius carries a lot of weight, even now. State your business and I'll see what I can do.'

Straight to the point, without fuss. Julius felt himself warming to the man. He reached into his tunic and brought out the packet of papers Marius had given him. Gaditicus took them and broke the seal with his thumb. He read quickly, with a frown, nodding occasionally.

'These were written before Sulla was back in control?' he asked, his eyes still on the parchment.

Julius felt the desire to lie, but guessed he was being tested by this man.

'They were. My uncle did not . . . expect Sulla to be successful.'

Gaditicus' eyes were unwavering as he measured the young man in front of him.

'I was sorry when I heard he was lost. He was a popular man and good for Rome. These papers were signed by a consul – they are perfectly valid. However, I am within my rights to refuse you a berth until your personal position vis-à-vis Cornelius Sulla is made clear to me. I *will* take your word if you are a truthful man.'

'I am, sir,' Julius replied.

'Are you wanted for criminal offences?'

'I am not.'

'Are you avoiding scandal of any sort?'

'No.'

Again, the man held his gaze for a few seconds, but Julius did not look away. Gaditicus folded the papers and placed them inside his own clothing.

'I will allow you to take the oath, on the lowest officer's rank of *tesserarius*. Advancement will come quickly if you show ability; slowly or not at all if you don't. Understood?'

Julius nodded, keeping his face impassive. The days of high life in Roman society were over. This was the steel in the empire that allowed the city to relax in softness and joy. He would have to prove himself, this time, without the benefit of a powerful uncle.

'These two, how do they fit in?' Gaditicus asked, motioning towards Tubruk and Cabera.

'Tubruk is my estate manager. He will be returning. The old man is Cabera, my . . . servant. I would like him to accompany me.'

'He's too old for the oars, but we'll find work for him. No one loafs on any ship I run. Everyone works. Everyone.'

'Understood, sir. He has some skill as a healer.'

Cabera had taken on a slightly glassy-eyed expression, but agreed after a pause.

'That will serve. Will you be signing on for two years, or five?' Gaditicus asked.

'Two, to begin with, sir.' Julius kept his voice firm. Marius had warned him not to devote his life to soldiering under long contracts, but to keep his options open to gain a wider experience.

'Then welcome to the Third Partica, Julius Caesar,' Gaditicus said gruffly. 'Now get on board and see the quartermaster for your bunk and supplies. I'll see you in two hours for the oath-taking.'

Julius turned to Tubruk, who reached across and gripped his hand and wrist.

'Gods favour the brave, Julius,' the old warrior said, smiling. He turned to Cabera. 'And you, keep him away from strong drink, weak women and men who own their own dice. Understand?'

Cabera made a vulgar sound with his mouth. '*I* own my own dice,' he replied.

Gaditicus pretended not to notice the exchange as he once again crossed the planks onto his ship.

The old man felt the future settle as the decision was made and a spot of tension in his skull disappeared almost before he had realised it was there. He could sense the sudden lift in Julius' spirits and felt his own mood perk up. The young never worried about the future or the past, not for long. As they boarded the galley, the dark and bloody events in Rome seemed to belong to a different world.

Julius stepped onto the moving deck and pulled a deep breath into his lungs.

A young soldier, perhaps in his early twenties, stood nearby with a sly look on his face. He was tall and solid with a pocked and pitted face bearing old acne scars.

'I thought it must be you, mudfish,' he said. 'I recognised Tubruk on the dock.'

For a moment, Julius didn't recognise the man. Then it clicked.

'Suetonius?' he exclaimed.

The man stiffened slightly.

'Tesserarius Prandus, to you. I am watch commander for this century. An officer.'

'You're signing on as one of those, aren't you, Julius?' Cabera said clearly.

Julius looked at Suetonius. On this day, he hadn't the patience to mind the man's feelings.

'For now,' he replied to Cabera, then turned to his old neighbour.

'How long have you been in that rank?'

'A few years,' Suetonius replied, stiffening.

Julius nodded. 'I'll have to see if I can do better than that. Will you show me to my quarters?'

Anger at the offhand manner coloured Suetonius' features. Without another word, he turned away from them, striding over the decks.

'An old friend?' Cabera muttered as they followed.

'No, not really.' Julius didn't say any more and Cabera didn't press for details. There would be time enough at sea to hear them all.

Inwardly Julius sighed. Two years of his life would be spent with these men, and it would be hard enough without having Suetonius there to remember him as a smooth-faced urchin. The unit would range right across the Mediterranean, holding Roman territories, guaranteeing safe sea trade, perhaps even taking part in land or sea battles. He shrugged at his thoughts. His experience in the city had shown that there was no point worrying about the future – it would always be a surprise. He would become older and stronger and would rise in rank. Eventually, he would be strong enough to return to Rome and look Sulla in the eye. Then they would see.

With Marcus standing at his side, there would be a reckoning, and a payment taken for Marius' death.

CHAPTER THIRTY-FIVE

Marcus waited patiently in the outer chamber of the camp Prefect's rooms. To pass the time before he was admitted to the meeting to determine his future, he read the letter from Gaius again. It had been travelling for many months and had been carried from hand to hand by legionaries passing closer and closer to Illyria. Finally, it had been included in a bundle of orders for the Fourth Macedonia and passed on to the young officer.

Marius' death had come as a terrible blow. Marcus had wanted to be able to show the general that his faith in him had been well founded. He had wanted to thank him as a man, but that was impossible now. Although he had never met Sulla, he wondered if the consul would be a danger for himself and Gaius – Julius now.

He smiled at the news of the marriage and winced at the brief lines about Alexandria, guessing much more than Julius had revealed. Cornelia sounded like an angel to hear Julius write of her. It was really the only piece of good news in the whole thing.

His thoughts were interrupted by the heavy door to the inner rooms opening. A legionary came out and saluted. Marcus rose and returned the gesture smartly.

'The Prefect will see you now,' the man said.

Marcus nodded and marched into the room, standing to attention the regulation three feet from the Prefect's oak table, bare except for a wine jug, inkpot and some neatly arranged parchment.

Renius was there, standing in the corner with a cup of wine. Leonides too, the centurion of the Bronze Fist. Carac, the camp Prefect, rose as the young man entered and gestured to him to sit. Marcus lowered himself onto a heavy chair and sat rigidly.

'At your ease, legionary. This is not a court martial,' Carac muttered, his gaze wandering over the papers on his desk.

Marcus tried to relax his bearing a little.

'Your two years is up in a week, as you are no doubt aware,' Carac said.

'Yes, sir,' Marcus replied.

'Your record has been excellent to date. Command of a contubernium, successful actions against local tribesmen. Winner of the Bronze Fist sword tourney last month. I hear the men respect you, despite your youth, and regard you as dependable in a crisis – some would say especially in a crisis. One officer's opinion was that you do well enough from day to day, but stand out in battle or difficulty. A valuable trait in a young officer suited to active legion life. It is perhaps to your benefit that the empire is expanding. There will be active work for you anywhere should you so desire it.'

Marcus nodded cautiously and Carac motioned to Leonides.

'Your centurion speaks well of you and the way you have curbed the thefts of that boy . . . Peppis. There was some talk at first of whether you could merge your individuality into a legion, but you have been honest and obviously loyal to the Fourth Macedonia. In short, lad, I would like you to sign on again, with promotion to command a Fifty. More pay and status, with time to train for sword tourneys if necessary. What do you say?'

'May I speak freely, sir?' Marcus asked, his heart thudding in his chest.

Carac frowned. 'Of course,' he replied.

'It is a generous offer. The two years with Macedonia have been happy ones for me. I have friends here. However . . . Sir, I grew up on the estate of a Roman who was not my father. His son and I were like brothers and I swore I would support him, be his sword when we were men.' He could feel Renius' gaze on him as he continued. 'He is with the Third Partica at present, a naval legion, with a little more than a year left to serve. When he returns to Rome, I would like to join him there, sir.'

'Renius has explained some of the history between this . . . Gaius Julius and yourself. I understand loyalty of this nature very well. It is what makes us more than beasts in the field, perhaps.' Carac smiled in a cheerful way and Marcus looked at the other two quickly, surprised not to see the censure he had feared.

Leonides spoke up, his voice calm and low. 'Did you think we would not understand? Son, you are very young. You will serve in many legions before they parcel you off with a farm. Most important of all, though, is that you serve Rome, constantly and without complaint. We three have devoted our lives to that aim – to see her safe and strong, envied by the world.'

Marcus looked round at the three of them and caught Renius smiling as he covered his mouth with the wine cup. Together they were the personification of what he had hoped to be as a young boy, linked by beliefs and loyalty and blood into something unbreakable.

Carac reached over for a document on thick parchment.

'Renius was convinced this would be the only way to keep you in the legion long enough to take part in the Graeca sword competition this winter. It indentures you for a year and a day.' He passed it over and Marcus felt his throat tighten with emotion.

He had expected to have to hand back his officer's equipment and collect his pay before beginning a lonely journey back to Italy. To have this offered to him when the future had seemed so bleak was like a gift from the gods. He wondered how much Renius had had to do with it and decided suddenly that he didn't care. He wanted to stay on with the Macedonia and in truth had felt torn between the loyalty to his childhood friend and the satisfaction he had found with his own family, the legion.

Now he had a year longer to grow and prosper. His eyes widened slightly as he read the complex Latin of the document. Carac noticed it.

'You see we have included the promotion. You will command a Fifty under Leonides, directly responsible to his *optio*, Daritus. I suggest you begin the post with an open mind. Fifty men is not eight – the problems will be new to you and the training for war involves complex skills. It will be a hard and challenging year, but I think you might enjoy it.'

'I will, sir. Thank you. It is an honour.'

'An honour earned, young man. I heard about what happened in the blueskin camp. The information you brought back has helped us to reformulate our policy towards them. Who knows, we may even trade with them after a few years.' Carac was clearly enjoying being the bringer of good news to the young man and Renius looked on approvingly.

'This will be my year,' Marcus vowed to himself as he read the document to the end, noting how many ounces of oil and salt he was allowed to draw from the stores, what his allowance for repairs and damages was and so on. The new post had a hundred things he had to learn and quickly. The pay was a vast improvement as well. He knew Julius' family would support him if asked, but the thought that he might be dependent on charity when he returned to Rome had rankled. Now he would be able to save a little and have a few gold coins for the return.

A thought struck him.

'Will you be staying on with the Macedonia?' he asked Renius. The warrior shrugged and sipped his wine.

'Probably, I like the company here. Mind you, I am way past retirement age as it is. Carac has to fiddle the pay figures every time he sends them in. I'd like to see what Sulla has done to the place.

Oh, I heard he had Rome in the bulletins. I wouldn't mind checking he's looking after the old girl properly and, unlike you, I'm not under contract, as sword master.'

Carac sighed. 'I would like to see Rome again. It's been fourteen years since I was last posted there, but I knew that's how it would be when I joined.' He poured cups of wine for all of them, refilling Renius' as it was held out.

'A toast to Rome, gentlemen, and to the next year.'

They stood and knocked the cups together with easy smiles, each one of them a long way from home.

Marcus put his cup down, took up the quill from the inkpot and signed his full name on the formal document.

'Marcus Brutus,' he wrote.

Carac reached over the desk and took his right arm in a solid grip.

'A good decision, Brutus.'

HISTORICAL NOTE

There is very little historical information on the earliest years of Julius Caesar's life. As far as possible, I have given him the sort of childhood that a young boy from a minor Roman family could have had. Some of his skills can be inferred from later accomplishments, of course. For example, swimming saved his life in Egypt, when he was fifty-two years old. The biographer Suetonius said that he had great skill with swords and horses as well as surprising powers of endurance, preferring to march rather than ride and going bareheaded in all weathers. I am sorry to say that Renius is fictional, though it was customary to employ experts in various fields. We know of one tutor from Alexandria who taught Caesar rhetoric and we can read Cicero's reluctant praise of Caesar's ability to speak skilfully and movingly when needed. His father died when Julius was only fifteen and it is true that Julius married Cinna's daughter Cornelia shortly afterwards, apparently for love.

Although Marius was an uncle on his father's side rather than Aurelia's as I have it, the general was very much the sort of character presented here. In flagrant opposition to law and custom, he was Consul seven times in all. Where previously it was possible to join a legion only if a man owned land and had an income from it, Marius abolished that qualification and enjoyed fanatical loyalty from his soldiers. It was Marius who made the eagle the symbol of all Roman legions.

The civil war between Sulla and Marius forms a major part of this book, but I found it necessary to simplify the action for dramatic purposes. Cornelius Sulla did worship Aphrodite and parts of his lifestyle scandalised even the tolerant Roman society. However, he was an extremely able general who had once served under Marius in an African campaign for which they both claimed credit. The two men disliked each other intensely.

When Mithridates rebelled against Roman occupation in the east, both Marius and Sulla wanted to move against him, seeing the campaign as an easy one and a chance to gain great riches. In part from personal motives, Sulla led his men against Rome and Marius in 88 BC, claiming that he would 'free it from tyrants'. Marius was forced to flee to Africa, returning later with the army he had gathered there. The Senate were simply unable to cope with such powerful leaders and allowed him back, declaring Sulla an enemy of the state while he was away fighting Mithridates. Marius was elected Consul for the last time, but died during his term, leaving the dithering Senate in a difficult situation. They sought peace at first, but Sulla was in a strong position, after a crushing victory in Greece. He did let Mithridates live, but confiscated vast wealth, looting ancient treasures. I compressed these years, having Marius dying in the first attack, which may be an unfairly quick ending for such a charismatic man.

When Sulla returned from the Greek campaign, he led his armies to quick victory against those loyal to the Senate, finally marching on the city again in 82 BC. He demanded the role of Dictator and it was in this role that he met Julius Caesar for the first time, brought before Sulla as one of those who had supported Marius. Despite the fact that Julius flatly refused to divorce Cornelia, Sulla did not have him killed. The Dictator is reported to have said that he saw 'Many Mariuses in this Caesar', which if true is something of an insight into the man's character, as I hope I have explored in this book.

Sulla's time as Dictator was a brutal period for the city. The unique position he held and abused had been designed as an emergency measure for times of war, similar in concept to Martial Law in modern democracies. Before Sulla, the strictest time limits had accompanied the title, but he managed to avoid these restrictions and scored a fatal wound on the Republic by doing so. One of the laws he passed forbade armed forces approaching the city, even for the traditional Triumph parades. He died aged sixty and for a while it looked as if the Republic might flower again into its old strength and authority. In Greece at this time, aged twenty-two, there was a young man called Caesar who would make this impossible. After all, Marius and Sulla had shown the fragility of the Republic when faced with determined ambition. We can only speculate how the young Caesar was affected when he saw Marius say, 'Make room for your general,' and watched the jostling crowd cut down in full view of the senate house.

The histories of these characters, especially those written shortly after the period, by Plutarch and Suetonius, make astonishing reading. In researching the life of Caesar, the question that kept coming up was '*How* did he do that?' How did a young man recover from the disaster of being on the losing side in a civil war to the point where his very surname came to mean king? Both Tsar and Kaiser are derived from that name and were still being used two *thousand* years later.

The histories can be a little bare at times, though I would recommend *Caesar* by Christian Meier to any reader interested in the details I had to omit here. There are so many fascinating incidents in this life that it has been a great pleasure putting flesh to them. The events of the second book are even more astonishing.

Conn Iggulden